And Playing the Role of Herself

K. E. Lane

Yellow Rose Books

Nederland, Texas

ISBN 978-1-932300-72-7

First Printing 2006

9 8 7 6 5 4 3 2 1

Cover design by Valerie Hayken

Published by:

Regal Crest Enterprises, LLC
4700 Hwy 365, Ste A
PMB 210
Port Arthur, Texas 77642

Find us on the World Wide Web at
http://www.regalcrest.biz

Printed in the United States of America

Acknowledgements

I have several people to thank for their encouragement, support, and guidance through the many phases of writing this novel. Maggie Guran, who, years ago, was the first to tell me I should try my hand at writing. My mom and dad, for always encouraging and supporting me, and for being role models in both life and love. Meghan O'Brien, for being a sounding board, cheerleader, and wonderful friend. Reneé Robinson for honest, invaluable feedback, TSM advice, and friendship. The Durango Gang for reading and telling me it didn't suck, but especially for the certainty in knowing you'd love me even if it did. The folks at Regal Crest, especially Cathy LeNoir for taking a chance on me, Sylverre for editing and excellent advice, Valerie Hayken for the perfect cover, and Lori L. Lake for encouragement, and for always having an answer to every question I threw at her. The Internet reading and writing community, who gave my work a home and an audience, and who gave me more support than I could possibly have imagined. And finally Deb, who read this story countless times without complaint, who patiently listened to my scattered thoughts, frustrations, and fears, and who makes every day richer - Thank You.

For Deb, whose love is my rock.

Chapter
One

I STEPPED INTO the interrogation room and closed the door softly behind me, smiling gently at the thin, dark-haired boy who huddled on the far side of a battered metal table in the center of the room. "Hi," I said quietly. "I'm Rita. I'm a police officer. Can I talk to you for a little bit?"

The boy nodded hesitantly, looking fragile and pale against the bleak, gray walls of the room, and the worn black teddy bear clutched tightly to his chest only enhanced the heartbreaking image. His huge brown eyes watched me intently as I crossed the floor and slowly lowered myself into a crouch beside his chair.

"What's your name?" I asked.

"S...Samuel," he whispered.

"Samuel, I'd like to have a look at that cut on your face, okay?" I reached out a hand to touch the small cut on his chin, and he flinched away, burying his face in the fur of the stuffed bear. "It's okay," I said soothingly. "I'm not going to hurt you, I promise. Can you look at me, honey? Please?"

Slowly he lifted his chin and turned to look at me, revealing the swollen, purple-and-black discoloration along the left side of his face.

I stilled my body for a few moments, staring at the bruise, and then gently pushed a stray lock of hair off the boy's forehead. "Who did this to you, Samuel?" I kept my voice calm, allowing only a hint of suppressed anger to color the tone. "Who hurt you?"

"I...I fell," the boy mumbled, and ducked his head, hiding his face again in the stuffed toy.

I reached out and gripped his shoulders tightly, turning his whole body to face me. "Who did this?" I hissed angrily, bringing my face close to his. "Who?"

Something that I recognized as real fear flickered in the boy's eyes and I immediately loosened my grip, swearing at myself in annoyance.

"Cut!" The voice sliced across the silent set like a pistol shot, and I could feel the small shoulders under my hands jump in reaction. I sighed and dropped my hands to my thighs as noise and chatter erupted on the set around me. The camera looming to my right moved back, and I pushed myself to my feet.

"Crap."

The boy giggled and wiped at his runny nose, leaving a shiny trail of mucus across his upper lip.

Lovely.

"Becca?" I called over to one of the hovering assistants. "Can we get a Kleenex or something over here?" I'm all for realism in television, but there's no way I was going to hug this kid with all that snot on him, regardless of what the script called for.

While Becca, a tiny redhead in a tight, lime-green top, hurried over and began fussing over the boy, I turned to the sound of approaching footsteps, schooling my face into polite deference that I did not feel. "What's wrong, Adam? I thought that was going well."

That was a big, fat lie. I'd let a lack of sleep, a very long week, and a vicious headache get the better of me, and as a result, my acting had been much too aggressive and I'd nearly scared the pants off that kid. I knew it, but I wasn't about to admit it to an asshole like Kreizeck.

Adam Kreizeck was short, obnoxious and sweaty. I had disliked him on sight, and it had become obvious over the last week of shooting that the feeling was definitely mutual.

"That's why I'm the director, Miss Harris," he said with an icy smile, "and you are not."

You're the director because you're married to the producer's niece, jackass. I forced a noncommittal smile and kept my thoughts to myself.

I hate guest directors. They throw off everyone's game, screw around with the normal pace of shooting, and are generally a pain in the ass. Kreizeck's stint as director had resulted in sixteen-hour days, multiple scenes having to be re-shot, and the killer headache that I'd had for what seemed like the last seventy-two hours.

"Let's try this again," Sweaty Man continued, "with a little more compassion and a little less Rambo. You're trying to help the boy, Miss Harris, not assault him."

The fact that I agreed with him in this case annoyed me even more than his arrogant smile. I nodded curtly, resisting the urge to slap him.

"Okay, people!" He snapped his fingers impatiently, bringing production assistants scurrying to his side. "I believe Miss Harris and I have an understanding..." He looked at me pointedly and raised a condescending eyebrow.

I smiled tightly, slipping my hands into the pockets of my jeans as the urge to commit violence against Kreizeck's person intensified.

"Good. Now," he glanced at his watch, "we've got a schedule to keep, so let's try to make this the last one, hmm? And would someone please tell Miss Stokley we'll be ready for her soon?"

The last request sent production assistants darting away like startled fish just as a rich, very feminine voice drawled, "Miss Stokley is already here."

The effect of that voice on Kreizeck was instantaneous. He spun in the direction of the voice with more athleticism than I'd given him credit for and practically sprinted off the set stage and over to the row of actor's chairs where Elizabeth Ann Stokley was regally settling herself. "Miss Stokley!"

"Hello, Adam," she murmured. "Sorry if I'm a little late. I got held up in wardrobe."

I looked at her outfit—the same one she had worn for day-player rehearsals two hours before—and thought her tardiness was more likely due to a certain muscle-bound intern named Chad, Liz's flavor of the week, than any type of wardrobe problem. Not that it would have mattered what her excuse was. Hell, she could have told him she was blowing the head of the network in the men's room, and I doubt he would have batted an eye or changed his panting eagerness one bit.

"Oh, not a problem, not a problem. Wonderful. You look great, just great."

I rolled my eyes, torn between annoyance and amusement as Liz worked her magic and Kreizeck was reduced to a pool of drooling, fawning Jell-O.

And who could blame him?

Elizabeth Ann Stokley was certainly easy on the eye. Blond hair, blue eyes, a dazzling smile, a body that curved in all the right places and a southern belle charm that could wrap even the biggest of assholes, male or female, around her perfect little finger.

An attractive package, no doubt. She was also a tempermental, moody perfectionist; one hell of an actor; and, since the very first day I started to work on the set of *9th Precinct*, a good friend.

9th Precinct, or *9P* as the cast and crew called it, was a police drama showcasing the lives of six detectives in a Homicide unit in Los Angeles. Liz played the series' main character, Jen Hastings: a young, optimistic detective with a five-year-old daughter, a mortgage, and extremely bad taste in husbands. I played Rita Stone, her rather caustic, intense, and cynical partner. When they were casting for the part of Rita, they were looking for a woman who was basically the polar opposite of Liz. My dark hair, square jaw, and rangy five-foot, ten-inch frame were lucky enough to be in the right place at the right time. I got the part, and my life since then had been quite the roller coaster ride.

One day I'm a no-name, bit-part actor whose biggest acting success to date was a series of popular beer commercials; the next, I've got a starring role in a prime-time show acting opposite an established television personality like Liz Stokley. From beer commercials to the big time in the blink of an eye. The turnabout amazed me still.

Kreizeck's snapping fingers brought me out of my thoughts; I guess he'd finished his fawning and wanted to get back to work. "Miss Harris, can we try this again?"

I met Liz's amused gaze above the director's head—that's how short the little prick was—and smiled slightly. "Sure, Adam. I'm ready when you are."

"Okay, people!" More snapping. "Places!"

I rolled my shoulders, blew out a long breath, and looked down at my snotty co-star. Despite the Kleenex, he was still oozing mucus.

"Mark...and... Action!"

It was going to be a long, long day.

SOME LAST MINUTE rearranging of the day's shooting schedule had turned my long day into a relatively short one, and by two that afternoon I was done with my scenes and not due back on the set until the following morning at seven-thirty. I hummed tunelessly as I opened the door to my trailer, pleasant thoughts of comfortable clothes, a good book, and spring sunshine from the comfort of my backyard hammock dancing in my head.

I didn't realize I had company until I kicked the door shut behind me and the tall, lean woman on my couch jerked awake at the resulting thump. She blinked at me in confusion for a moment, then rubbed her eyes and smiled sleepily.

"Caidence. Hey." The voice was low, rough and husky— whiskey-soaked, I'd heard someone in the media call it—and I felt it, and that smile, all the way down to my toes.

She stretched luxuriously, like a big, satisfied cat, making a little mewling sound that turned into a long, satisfied groan. With effort, I tore my eyes away from the flash of skin above the waistband of her jeans, and the way her breasts—*Jesus, is she even wearing a bra? Christ, Caid, stop looking at her breasts!*—strained against the fabric of her shirt.

"Robyn." I cleared my throat and sat down heavily in the chair in front of the mirror, managing a weak smile while I scrambled for a half-assed excuse for my dazed expression and suddenly weak legs. "Shit. You scared me."

Oh, good one Caid. Very creative.

You'd think I would be used to it by now.

I'd known Robyn Ward for the last year and a half, and had worked with her several times, either on the set of *9th Precinct*, or on *In Their Defense*, the law firm series that Robyn worked on for the same network. *9P* was actually a spin-off of *In Their Defense*, created after a particularly popular set of guest spots Liz had done during the show's rookie year, and quite often actors from one show did guest appearances on the other, as Robyn had been doing on *9P* for the last three weeks. I couldn't say that we were friends, but we certainly weren't unfriendly, and the woman even shared my trailer when she worked on *9P*, which explained why she was on my couch.

But no matter how many times I saw Robyn Ward, worked with her, or shared her space, her stunning looks and raw sensuality still left me tongue-tied, slightly off-center, and just a little bit breathless.

"Sorry," she said through a yawn, and swung long legs off the couch to sit up. She looked around the room blearily, running a hand through long, slightly tousled dark hair. "I think doing this double duty is finally catching up to me. I nearly fell asleep on the set today between takes."

"I'll bet," I agreed, watching her reflection in the mirror while I went through the motions of removing the makeup that, onscreen, was suppose to make it look as though I didn't wear any. "I'm only working one show this week, and I'm about to drop. If there'd been more space on that couch, I might have joined you."

Remember what I said about the tongue-tied part? Let me rephrase. I either couldn't think of anything to say, or the stuff that did come out of my mouth was really embarrassing and led to uncontrollable blushing, like I did when her eyes focused on me

"Really?" She quirked her eyebrow and shot me an amused grin. "I'll remember that for next time, and make sure to leave you some room."

I watched the arch of her perfectly plucked eyebrow in fascination. Oh, how I adored it when she did that thing with her eyebrow.

In fact, her eyebrows were one of my favorite things about her, sweeping upward across her brow in dark, linear precision, wielded with devastating effect at opportune moments. Indeed, I loved those eyebrows. They ranked right up there with intense, piercing brown eyes; silky, dark hair; a wide, full mouth; angular face; endless legs; beautiful hands; smooth, tan skin; tall, graceful body; the tiny cleft in her chin; and the mole on the side of her neck, just below her ear, that you could see when she casually pushed her hair back...

I blinked, realizing that I was staring.

"Caidence?" She leaned back, draping a long arm across the back of the couch and regarding me with a look she'd begun to favor me with recently—a secretive little smile that was a mixture of amusement, curiosity, and taunting.

I was starting to think that perhaps Ms. Ward was quite aware of the effect she had on me, and enjoyed watching me make an idiot of myself. "Uh, sorry. Spaced out there for a second." I smiled wanly, took a last swipe at my face, and turned around to face her.

"I can relate, believe me," she said with a tired smile, and stretched out her legs to their full length—which took up nearly half of the room—crossing them at the ankle. "So, what's your opinion of Kreizeck? I haven't had to work with him yet, but I have three scenes today. I talked with Liz, and she said he was fine, but Danny said he was an 'effin' looza.' "

She mimicked the actor's New York accent flawlessly and I laughed, startled by a less serious side of the normally very reserved woman; a side that I didn't see very often. The laugh was spontaneous, and seemed to take us both by surprise, probably because my laughter in her presence usually sounded slightly giddy or hysterical, like a twelve-year-old girl hopped up on Pop Tarts and Ho-Hos.

Hey, maybe I could behave like a normal adult around her, after all.

"Well," I said, laughing again and pleased that, again, it seemed very natural. "Liz, in typical Liz-like fashion, has the poor man eating out of her hand. Her only complaint should be that he drools a little too much and could maybe be a tad more liberal with the deodorant. I, on the other hand, would have to agree with Danny. The guy's an arrogant prick."

This was probably one of the longer statements I had managed to string together in front of her without sounding like a deranged chipmunk, and I was quite proud of myself. The nervousness I normally felt around her was gone, replaced by a kind of heady euphoria just be in her presence and have her attention focused on me. Unable to stop myself, I flashed a huge grin.

She blinked and returned the smile tentatively, but her brows were furrowed in what looked like confusion. "You..." she started, but paused.

"Hmm?" I cocked my head to the side, still smiling happily. I didn't think anything could wipe that smile from my face.

"You..." She hesitated again, and smiled slightly. "You have a great laugh, Caidence. I don't think I've really heard it before."

Okay. That worked. Smile now turned into stunned "O" of disbelief.

"Uh, thanks," I stammered, and dropped my gaze, blushing furiously.

My sudden and obvious loss of equilibrium had the opposite effect on Robyn, and when I managed to meet her gaze again, the little secretive smile was firmly back in place.

My nervousness returned, although not at the near-debilitating levels I'd come to expect, and I was pleased and more than a little surprised to realize that I'd be able to continue the conversation without making a further idiot of myself.

"So Kreizeck's a prick, huh? That's just great." She raised one arm off the back of the couch and rubbed at her temple, closing her eyes for a moment. "Shit. I hate guest directors."

I smiled slightly at that, and gave her more bad news: "And I've noticed that he's not particularly fond of tall people."

Robyn topped my five-foot-ten by at least an inch. It was going to drive Kreizeck insane.

She stopped rubbing and opened her eyes to stare at me. "You're kidding."

"Sorry." I shrugged in sympathy. "But if you really want to piss him off, stand close to him so that he has to look up to talk to you. Works like a charm."

The eyebrow went up, and she said dryly, "Sounds like a technique you may have used yourself, a time or two."

"A time or two," I replied with a wink.

Holy crap.

I winked at Robyn Ward.

One might even construe what I had just done as...flirting.

I was flirting with Robyn Ward.

Me — who had just a few years ago come to the cautious conclusion that I was attracted to women, and had yet to act upon that attraction — flirting with Robyn Ward, who was constantly being photographed with her very handsome, very famous, very sweet, tennis-playing boyfriend Josh Riley; together the poster children for blissful, rich-and-famous heterosexual coupling.

Holy fucking crap. What in the hell was I *thinking*?

Robyn seemed as stunned as I was, whether by the fact that I had winked and was quite possibly flirting with her, or the fact that, contrary to what she had believed before, I had shown in the last few minutes that I actually possessed a personality equal to my thirty-four years, and could be somewhat charming when I put my mind to it.

The moment was broken by a loud knock on the trailer door,

and both of us jumped at the sound.

"Caid?" The muffled voice of the Second Assistant Director, Mariel Lacey, came from outside.

"Yeah," I answered, dragging my eyes away from Robyn's. "Come on in, Mari."

The dark-skinned woman poked her head in the door, the beads in her tightly braided hair clacking gently together. "Caid, I'm glad you're still here. Thought I was going to have to call you back in..." She noticed the woman on the couch, and smiled happily, "Oh, hey, Robyn. I'm glad you're both here."

She stepped up into the trailer and handed a stapled set of papers to me, then shuffled through a stack of papers she was carrying and pulled out another set, handing them to Robyn. "Josiah's dad was hospitalized this afternoon with chest pains, and he left as soon as he heard... Adam doesn't want to wait for him to get back, so he had the writers rework some of the remaining scenes, using the people we had. These are your sides. Robyn, yours haven't changed much, you'll just be doing two of the scenes with Danny only, and the one you had with Josiah, you'll be doing with Caid."

I took the papers automatically. "Uh..."

"Great. We'll see you both in the Break Room set in," she glanced down at a minuscule watch on her wrist, "one hour." She looked at Robyn. "You'd better get to wardrobe, and you," she pointed at me, "get to makeup. Now I've gotta go find Danny..."

The woman bustled out of the trailer and I leafed through the sheets with a sigh. The hammock was going to have to wait for another day.

"Well, you heard the woman," Robyn rasped eventually. "We'd better get ourselves going."

"Yeah," I said, sighing heavily as I stood up and stretched. "There go my big plans for the afternoon."

She followed me outside and we walked along the row of trailers toward the back entrance to the soundstage building, side by side. I kept the pace slow, enjoying the unexpected ease of our current exchange and in no hurry to end it. Robyn seemed quite content with both my pace and my company, details which pleased me enormously.

"You had something special planned for the rest of the day?" she asked after a few moments of silence.

"Probably not what most people would call special...just a good book and the hammock in my yard, and maybe a nap." I shrugged, and glanced over to find her watching me with a relaxed, interested expression that was quite different from the reserved look I was used to. It made her, if possible, even more attractive, and shot straight to the top of my list of things I adored about Robyn Ward.

"Mmm," she sighed, and then gave me warm smile that nearly made me trip, "that sounds heavenly. Sign me up."

"Done." I nodded and grinned back, thinking I'd sign her up for whatever the heck she wanted, whenever and however she wanted it, as long as I got a glimpse of that smile again.

We parted company in the hallway in front of wardrobe and I made my way to hair and makeup, feeling almost high from our encounter.

Jules spared me a curious look as I plopped down in a chair in one of the four makeup stations in the long, narrow room. "Back again?"

"Can't seem to stay away."

She shook her head and set about reapplying my non-makeup as Drew the hairstylist finished with a day-player in a different station and came by to *tsk* at my hair with pursed lips.

"Hon, what did you do to yourself?"

I looked at my reflection in the mirror. My hair looked the same as it had for the past few months: short and dark with highlighted streaks sticking out wildly in every direction. I just smiled at him as he started teasing and spraying, he and Jules moving around me in a comfortable, silent synchrony that spoke of hundreds of hours working together.

The first year on the show, I'd had slightly longer, wavy dark hair, but for this season, they'd asked for a change, wanting me "edgier." The porcupine on my head was the result of my acquiescence, and I was actually starting to like it quite a bit. I found it extremely easy to take care of, but Drew always fussed over it, working hard to make it look like it already looked when I rolled out of bed. I told him once that I could just save him the trouble by not washing it in the morning before I came in, and the horrified look I received from him had made me laugh so hard that Jules nearly poked my eye out with the eyeliner pencil.

I heard someone enter the room, and moments later Liz dropped herself heavily in the chair beside me.

Drew and Jules both looked at her expectantly until Liz waved a vague hand. "No, no, I'm just here to talk to Caid."

"What are you still doing here?" I asked after the two went back to work on my hair and face. "I thought you'd be long gone."

She snorted; a decidedly un-southern-belle-like sound. "Fuck. That man won't leave me alone."

I didn't have to ask who "that man" was. Every time I had left the set that week, Kreizeck had been hovering all over her like a bad smell. "If you'd let Bitchy Liz show up, instead of Charming

Liz, you wouldn't be having this problem." I pointed out reasonably.

She frowned at my lack of sympathy. "There are certain people who respond better to charming, and Adam is definitely one of those." She sniffed. "You should work on charming. It's amazing what it can get you sometimes."

I thought of my earlier conversation with Robyn and smiled to myself.

Liz was running a hand through her hair and stopped when she saw the smile. "What?" she demanded, narrowing her eyes.

"What, what?" I tried for innocence. I was an actor, goddammit, I should be able to manage a little innocence.

"What's that satisfied little smirk for?" She leaned forward, peering at me intently. "Caidence Harris, what aren't you telling me?"

I laughed lightly. "There are lots of things I don't tell you, Liz, because you can't keep a secret to save your life. This is just one more of those things."

"*Ohhh*, so it's a secret?"

Shit. Walked right into that one.

"It's nothing."

"It's something."

"No, it's not."

"Yes, it is, and I'm going to find out what it is."

I rolled my eyes and shrugged. "Suit yourself, but there's nothing to find out."

She smiled sweetly, and turned her attention onto Drew. "Drew?"

He shrugged, not taking his attention from my hair. Liz frowned, and looked at Jules. "Jules?"

The makeup artist paused in her task and shrugged. "I don't know, she seems the same to me."

Liz pouted, and I smiled at her smugly.

"...although she was whistling when she came in," Jules finished.

Traitor.

I shot her a wounded look, while Liz's eyes lit up in glee.

"Caid was whistling?" she cooed, and reached out to pinch me on the arm. "Our own little Grumpy Gus?"

"Ow." I jerked my arm away. "I was not whistling. I do not whistle."

Jules just raised her eyebrows in disbelief. I scowled.

"Come on, Caid, fess up. Who is it?" Liz turned her chair and propped her elbows on her knees, like she was getting ready for me to read her a bedtime story. "Is it that sexy little extra that played the barrista? I *knew* he was hitting on you. Yum-yum! He had a great ass. Good choice, Caid. God knows you need to get laid."

Shit. I nearly groaned out loud.

If there were two people on the set who were bigger gossips than Liz, they were Jules and Drew. By tomorrow morning it would be all over the set that I'd been caught spanking some extra's ass in the prop room. There would probably be a monkey involved, and a steaming cup of cappuccino. Half-caff, double-tall.

Double shit.

"Liz," I said sharply, and risked Jules's ire by turning my head to meet Liz's blue gaze. "I told you it's nothing, okay? Now, did you come in here for a reason?"

She pouted prettily, but dropped the subject with a nod, knowing from experience that I could be less than forthcoming when I was pissed off. "Actually, there was. You know that Q & A session I'm doing tomorrow at the Four Seasons?"

I nodded.

"Well, I was supposed to go with Josiah... I assume you heard Josiah's gone?"

I nodded again and asked, "Has anyone heard how his father is?"

She blinked, and frowned as though the question had never occurred to her, though she knew it should have.

For Liz, one of the residual effects of being in the spotlight since the age of seven was that unless she forced herself to, she rarely thought of others. It wasn't selfishness, really, just a lack of ever having to hear about, or deal with, other people's problems. She really was a genuinely nice person; she just hadn't been trained to show it.

"George said that Josiah called from the plane, but he hadn't heard anything else," Drew broke in, saving Liz any embarrassment.

She smiled at him, and turned her attention back to me. "Yes, so anyway, they asked Danny to do it with me, but he has a pretty heavy schedule tomorrow, and so does Henry, and you know how Micah is..."

I smiled slightly, picturing Micah—who hated the press and wasn't at all shy about saying so—at a Q & A session with a bunch of reporters firing questions at him. "So that leaves me." At her nod, I continued, "I've got a seven-thirty call-time tomorrow..."

"Already taken care of. They're rearranging the schedules, and we don't need to be in until late afternoon."

Which meant a nice, long evening of work for me, after what promised to be a nerve-wracking morning with the press. Wonderful.

"So, basically," I said as Jules turned my face back to the front impatiently, "you're not here to ask me, you're here to tell me that I'm doing this."

"Well, basically, yes. They thought you'd be nicer to me if I told you...you know, Charming Liz."

I sighed. "What time?"

Liz smiled — the brilliant smile that had graced countless magazine covers and helped make her famous. "Meet me here at eight; they'll have a car for us."

I nodded, resigned to my fate, and after a few more minutes of chatting, Liz left me to my primping. Two fluffs of my hair and a critical look from Jules later, I was deemed presentable, and I headed for the sets to find a quiet spot to look over the scene and my lines before my call-time.

Pushing through a small side door to the soundstage where the three permanent 9P sets were housed, I was immediately hit by a rush of warm, stale air, and grimaced at the reminder of how unpleasant the cavernous, impossible-to-cool space would be in the coming summer months. Smells of sawdust, metal, and coffee that had been sitting on a burner for far too long filled the air, along with the faint scent of leather and machine oil, lingering evidence of the building's former life as an industrial warehouse for a luggage manufacturing company.

From behind the heavy tarps that separated the set construction and prep area from the rest of the soundstage came the whine of a circular saw and the staccato raps of a hammer, and from somewhere above me came cursing and raised voices as the lighting crew clambered around on the lighting grid suspended above the sets, making some kind of adjustment. I glanced up and shook my head, amazed at their monkey-like, scampering-around abilities.

The 9P sets were positioned in a row along the south side of the soundstage, and from the far end I could hear the murmur of voices and laughter. I followed the noise, passing the empty Squad Room and the smaller Interrogation Room sets that wouldn't be used that afternoon, and finally reached the Break Room set, which was already bustling with activity, despite the fact that no actual shooting would be going on for a least an hour.

I waved in response to a few called greetings and continued past the action on to the lounge area, a scattering of old couches and plastic lawn furniture taking up a small, semi-lit corner in the back of the soundstage next to the water cooler. The area was deserted, although strewn sections of newspaper, several articles of discarded clothing, numerous mugs, cups and soda cans, and two empty bakery boxes were testament to the area's recent use. After moving a stack of newspapers off one of the couches and onto the floor, I settled into the resulting empty space with a sigh and thumbed through the sides Mariel had given me.

I looked through the sheets once, then again, and didn't know whether to be elated or terrified. The scene was between my character, Rita, and Robyn's character, Judith Torrington—a slightly smarmy but hot-enough-to-get-away-with-it defense attorney from a prestigious law firm. In this episode, Judith was defending the pedophile son of a state senator accused of raping and murdering a young boy. My character, although gruff and cynical, had a big soft spot for kids, and the scene called for me to lose my temper and push Robyn/Judith physically up against a wall.

The thought of pushing Robyn up against a wall sent shivers up my spine.

A very, very good kind of shiver.

I closed my eyes and steadied my suddenly ragged breathing.

Whoa. That was new. Apparently in the last few hours I'd moved from adolescent crush to full-on adult lust, complete with NC-17 rated video.

"I saw you over here all alone," came a raspy voice above me, "and thought I'd come keep you company, but now I'm not sure if I should interrupt."

I snapped my eyes open in panic to find Robyn standing in front of me, gazing down with a thoughtful look.

"I don't know whether to feel sorry for whoever you're thinking about, or to be insanely jealous," she mused, putting her hands on her hips and tilting her head a little to the side.

The video played again, and I looked away. "What do you mean?" I mumbled.

"You looked..." She paused for a long moment, and I risked a glance at her face. She was staring at me intently. "...hungry."

I coughed. "Must have been because I missed lunch." I smiled sickly and scrambled to my feet before my brain could add the picture of her length towering above me to the new video collection.

She looked at me for a second longer, and then glanced down at the couch. "You actually sit on that thing?"

The couch in question was covered with worn, red-and-white-speckled faux cowhide upholstery, and the stuffing was coming out of an armrest and one of the cushions.

"Pretty comfortable, actually." I gestured at the busy set. "I wanted to get away from the noise a little."

"Mm-hmm." She looked at me, and then down at the couch again, and crossed her arms, nodding. "Yes, I've heard very nice things about that couch. In fact, I heard that Chad and Liz *reaaaallly* like that couch."

"Oh, God," I groaned, and began wiping desperately at my pants. "Ew-ew-ew, gross-gross-gross..."

Robyn's loud, delighted laugh stopped my movements, as well as the movements of every one else within hearing range.

Robyn had a fantastic laugh.

"Gotcha," she said, winking as she walked past me and headed for the set, a definite swagger to her step.

Oh, honey. You have no idea.

I grinned and followed her.

"CUT!" KREIZECK YELLED again, and I gritted my teeth, stepping back from Robyn and turning to face the director.

I didn't know how much more of this I could take. This was the sixth take of the scene between Robyn and me; six times of pushing her up against a wall, feeling her shoulders under my hands, looking into her eyes from a distance of less than a foot. I felt like I was going to explode.

Explode or kiss her—both of which were probably career-ending moves.

"Adam," Robyn began, but he cut her off with an imperious wave from the safety of his directing chair, where he had decided to stay after both Robyn and I had gotten into his space one too many times. Not on purpose, of course.

"No, Miss Ward, you're doing fine. Although a little more smugness, perhaps. You're a slimy defense lawyer defending a rapist and murderer of children. The audience doesn't want to sympathize with you, no matter how good you look."

I looked at her quickly, startled that Adam was once again right. From the look on her face, and the grudging nod, I could tell that she was, too.

"But you, Miss Harris. I saw more emotion from you this morning when you asked for tissues than I've seen in all six takes. You're supposed to be angry! Seething! This is a slimy defense attorney defending a rapist and murderer of children! You are a female police detective, disgusted that anyone—especially another woman—could defend such a scumbag! Let's see some fury, some emotion, some chemistry! And stop being so timid. You're touching her like a china doll. You're angry, damn it, act like it!"

Damn.

I knew he was right. I'd been so conscious of being near Robyn that I'd forgotten what the scene was about; just saying my lines and praying it would be over soon.

Shit.

And if Adam didn't watch it, I might even come to the conclusion that he was a halfway-decent director. Still an asshole, but an asshole that could direct.

"Let's take it from 'if you hadn't mishandled evidence,' " he yelled, and snapped several times. "Okay, people! Places, and quiet on the set."

I glanced at Robyn, who shrugged and moved back to her mark. I did the same, closing my eyes for a moment, trying to come up with a way to act around what I was feeling. Then it dawned on me that I shouldn't. I shouldn't act around it, I should use it. And if all went well, I'd only have to do it once.

"Roll it..."

"Rolling!"

"And... Action!"

A look of smug conceit fell across Robyn's face as though someone had flipped a switch. She crossed her arms and sneered at me, the tone of her voice mocking. "If you hadn't mishandled evidence, *Detective*, my client wouldn't be walking around free. I guess I should thank you."

Okay. I took a deep breath. *Here goes nothing.* I looked at Robyn, letting every lustful thought, every fantasy, every desperate wish come to the surface, and then, hoping people would mistake lust for anger, I lunged at her. I used my entire body this time, not just my hands, and pinned her against the wall with my arm across her chest and my stomach pressed up against hers.

"You defended a man who brutally raped and killed an eight-year-old boy, and now he's out walking around, looking for his next victim," I whispered harshly, ignoring the close-up camera that was moving in. "The evidence was clean—you brought up the doubt, and most likely destroyed a good detective's career in the process. That is *your* fault."

At this point in the scene, Robyn was supposed to struggle and break away, yelling that I had made my point.

She didn't move.

She stood there, staring at me with wide eyes, her breath coming in quick gasps, her body molded to mine. I could feel her breath on my lips, and feel the hard muscles of her abdomen tense and stretch against me.

After what seemed like an endless stretch of time, she finally whispered softly, her voice barely audible. "Take your hands off me, Detective. You've made your point."

Going on instinct, I stayed where I was, not releasing her. More endless moments went by as we stood locked in that embrace, breathing in each other's air, staring unblinkingly at each other.

Someone yell cut, goddammit! I felt like screaming. *Jesus, yell cut before I kiss her...*

"And... Cut! Nice job, ladies. Print that."

The normal set noise was slow in starting, mostly consisting of low whispers.

Kreizeck's annoyed voice cut across the murmur of conversation. "Let's go, people! We've got a print, time to move on. You can stand around and chat later, let's get set up for seven-D..."

Voices swelled around us, but Robyn and I still stood chest to chest. I blinked and stepped back.

"Robyn, I'm sorry..." I started.

"Shhh." She placed two thin, elegant fingers against my lips. "Caidence, it was great. *You* were great."

I nodded dumbly, feeling slightly disoriented and just wanting to get away from people, but enjoying the pressure of her fingers.

She smiled at me, not the cool, taunting smile, but another of her genuine, honest smiles, this one laced with friendliness and respect. "Now, I need to get to wardrobe before the next take. I'll see you later."

She took her fingers from my lips, trailed them down my arm and squeeze my hand before turning and walking off the set.

Chapter
Two

AT SEVEN FIFTY-FIVE the next morning, I tapped on the door to Liz's trailer with the toe of my shoe, sipping from a large paper coffee cup in one hand and dangling a cardboard carrier containing two more steaming cups from the other.

The door opened and Liz's assistant, Paula, motioned me in. I grunted in greeting and entered the trailer, holding up the carrier and gesturing with my chin at the one closest to Paula.

"White mocha something-or-other. With soy."

She took the indicated cup out of the carrier, murmuring, "You're a doll. Thank you." As I moved past her, she touched my arm. "And I don't believe a word of it."

I frowned. "A word of what?"

"What they're saying. About you and that extra and the goat."

Goat, monkey...not much difference when you're supposedly fucking them.

I smiled politely. "Thank you, Paula, I'm flattered you think so highly of me." She frowned, not quite believing the sincerity of my words. Before she could say anything more about my rumored love of goats, I continued on. "How's Liz this morning?"

Liz was sometimes not at her best in the mornings, and it was always good to know where her mood was before conversing with her.

"Well, she's..."

The door to the trailer's tiny bathroom swung open and Liz stomped out, glaring at Paula and me. "Liz is an adult who doesn't like it when people talk about her as though she's not present." She flopped down on the couch, still glaring. "And for God's sake, Paula, I told you that thing about the goat was just a stupid rumor. Honestly, I don't know how those crazy things get started."

"Amazing, isn't it?" I commented dryly, and held the carrier up as a peace offering. "The most caffeinated, sugary thing they had."

Her eyes softened a little and she reached out her hands.

"*Ohhh*. Gimme."

I set the carrier down and handed her the cup. She sniffed at it and took a sip, closing her eyes and groaning in a way that should have made me blush, considering my recently acknowledged sexual orientation, but didn't. Liz, despite her undeniable attractiveness, had never affected me in a sexual way. That put me in a very minuscule percentage of people on this planet, and was most likely the reason why Liz liked me.

Someone pounded on the trailer door. "Car here for Stokley and Harris!"

I reached out a hand and hauled Liz to her feet. "Let's get this over with," I said, with trepidation.

"It's not that bad, Caid," Liz cooed, and patted my cheek. "You need to work on your people skills, anyway."

I scowled and she laughed, leading us out of the trailer and stopping on the top step with a little squeak of dismay when the bright sunshine hit her face. She turned to Paula, who was already reaching out to hand her a pair of sunglasses that were designed with more thought to style than function. She took them without a word.

I shook my head, pulling my own sunglasses down from where they rested on top of my head and sliding them into place before following Liz and Paula down the stairs and into the gray limo where two people from the network's PR department were already waiting.

Liz absolutely hated sharing limos with people she didn't know and sat in sullen silence during the ride to the hotel, shooting daggers at the car's two extra passengers. The two looked uncomfortable, but I didn't have enough sympathy to start a conversation that might have eased the tension. Liz's preference for riding by herself was well known, as was her unfriendly behavior when she wasn't happy, and these two should have known better. Instead, I sat back and sipped my cooling coffee, letting the caffeine do its work while Paula typed furiously on a thin laptop and occasionally talked on her cell phone.

At the hotel, we were escorted to a large meeting room and offered croissants, muffins and more coffee. A few minutes later, forty-plus reporters from various national and international media outlets streamed in, took their seats, and started a barrage of questions.

I was nervous at first, still not used to the growing celebrity that *9th Precinct* had brought me, and unsure of myself with the press. The majority of questions, though, were aimed at Liz, and soon I relaxed, enjoying the show that was Elizabeth Ann Stokley. The woman was truly a master at handling the press, deflecting questions with a charm that left the reporters smiling, serious one moment and flirting the next, controlling the room without letting them know they were being controlled.

Finally, after an hour and a half, the moderator called for last questions.

"This question is for both Ms. Stokley and Ms. Harris," a short, stocky woman in the back said. "Are you aware that over the past two years there has been an explosion of on-line stories depicting the two of you in homosexual relationships, with each other and various other *9th Precinct* cast members? Has this affected your working relationship at all, and what do you think of the chances of such a relationship storyline ever making it into primetime?"

I heard Liz's shocked intake of breath beside me, but kept my eyes on the reporter with what I hoped was a casual smile on my face, even though my heart was pounding so loudly it was a wonder the mics didn't pick it up.

Taking a calming breath, I glanced over at Liz, noting that she was as rattled as I'd ever seen her. I felt a flash of annoyance. Was the thought of being a lesbian, or being thought of as a lesbian, so appalling? I immediately pushed the annoyance aside; my own initial reaction to the question hadn't been much better, and I *was* a lesbian. At least in theory.

Amazing how society has trained us.

"I guess I'll take that one, if you don't mind, Liz?" I said, giving her a reassuring smile.

She seemed to regain some of her composure, and even managed to smile back. "Go right ahead."

I directed my attention back to the reporter, noticing that the other reporters were awfully damn quiet.

I thought for a moment.

Okay, Caid, let's go easy with this. I had barely come out to myself, and certainly wasn't ready to come out to the world. "Yes, I'm aware that there are websites that contain stories about our characters on *9th Precinct*, and that some of the stories are lesbian in nature."

I was surprised at how natural it sounded to use the word.

Lesbian.

I was a lesbian.

I hadn't actually said it to myself yet; it was much easier than I expected.

I paused at my internal revelation, and the reporter who asked the question opened her mouth to speak. I cut her off before she could expand on her question. "How do these stories affect my relationship, working or personal, with Liz?" I shrugged. "They don't. Liz and I are good friends, and have a very comfortable working relationship, contrary to what the occasional newspaper or magazine might report. None of you, of course." I smiled my most charming smile, taking a lesson from Liz, and was gratified to hear several chuckles. "I don't see either of those relationships changing because people are writing stories about the characters we play on a TV show.

"As to whether I think a homosexual storyline will ever make it into primetime, I thought it already had. There have been several gay characters in primetime television. Granted, maybe we've got a ways to go before it's an established, popular character on a drama like *9th Precinct*, and their sexuality is handled with the same casualness as it is for heterosexual characters, but we're getting there." I smiled at the woman. "So, to answer your question, I'd say the chances of that kind of storyline showing up on primetime are good, but I'm not going to guess at a timeline."

Several reporters raised their hands after I was done, but one of the PR people—Nick, I think his name was—announced that we had engagements elsewhere, and the session politely, if reluctantly, broke up.

We signed some autographs for a group of people waiting in the lobby and then climbed back into the limo, the two men from PR wisely electing to take a cab.

As soon as the car door had closed, Liz turned to me and gripped my arm. "What the fuck was all of that about? People think I'm a lesbian, and they're writing about it on the Internet? That's illegal! Can I sue them or something? Shit, I need to call Woody and see if I can sue. Paula, get me Woody."

I sighed. "Liz. Calm down. Jesus." I pulled my arm away and sat back, running a hand through my hair. "They're not stories about you, for fuck's sake; they're stories about Jen Hastings. A fictional character."

This seemed to calm her a little, but she still took the phone when Paula handed it to her. "Woody? Of course it's Liz. I'm having a crappy day, thank you very much. Did you know about these Internet people who think I'm a lesbian?"

I rolled my eyes. "Liz..."

"Here, Woody, let me give you to Caid. She knows all about it."

The phone was thrust into my hand, and I resignedly put it to my ear. "Woody? It's Caid."

"Caid, what the hell is she talking about?" Woody Stein's harried, nasal voice came over the line.

I put my fingers to the bridge of my nose and closed my eyes. "Listen, let me call you back, okay?"

"Caid..."

"I'll call you back." I snapped the phone shut, knowing that would piss Woody off, but also knowing that Liz would smooth it over for me.

"What are you doing?" Liz asked angrily, "You need to..."

"Liz."

" — tell Woody about this — "

"Liz."

"I'll sue them — "

"Liz, shut up!"

Liz blinked, and Paula looked at me in shock, but the car was finally quiet.

"Thank you. Now just listen to me for a second, okay? These stories — they're called fan fiction. People write stories about the characters on TV shows, and then put them out on these Internet sites for other people to read. They aren't about you. You can't sue anyone, because they aren't about you. They're about the characters in the show."

"I can't?"

"No, you can't."

She was quiet for a moment, then frowned. "How did you know about this stuff? And why didn't you tell me?"

I scratched absently at my neck. "I was doing some...ah, research on the Internet one night, and I came across a site that had some stuff about the show. I was curious, so I read some of it." I didn't think she needed to know exactly what my "research" was about. "I didn't tell you because I didn't think it was important. They're just stories, Liz. It's not about you. No one is accusing you of being a lesbian."

She was still frowning, her brows furrowed in thought. "I want to see some," she said abruptly.

I shrugged. "Fine, I'll send you some URLs."

"Some what?" Liz was hopeless with computers.

I looked over at Paula, who nodded. "Paula knows what I mean, and she'll show you."

"Show me now. Use Paula's computer. It's a half-hour trip back to the studio at least."

Sometimes her attitude really ticked me off. "Say please."

Liz blinked. "What?"

"Say please. I'm not your goddamn assistant, Liz. No offense, Paula." I glanced over at the assistant apologetically. She smiled slightly and shook her head. "I'm your friend and coworker. Say please."

We stared at each other for a long moment, and finally she sighed. "I'm sorry, Caid." Her voice was subdued. "Please."

I let out my own sigh, and turned to Paula. "Paula, can we

borrow your laptop for a bit, please? This car has wireless, doesn't it?"

"Of course, Caid." The woman nodded, clicking a few times to get out of what she was doing, and handed the laptop over to me.

I opened up a browser window, Googled a few keywords I knew would get me what I was looking for, and browsed through the results. Finally selecting one, I glanced at it quickly and placed the computer in Liz's lap. "Here's one. Press this button when you want to go down more."

"Thank you," she murmured politely, and started reading.

I divided my attention between watching the cars around us that were also caught in lunch-time traffic, and watching Liz's expression go from curious and slightly bored to intent and involved. I smiled slightly at her absorbed expression. I actually hadn't read a lot of *9P* fan fiction—it seemed slightly egomaniacal—but I had enjoyed this one very much.

Liz was still reading when the limo pulled up in front of the network administration offices, a squatty structure next to the soundstage building and one of four structures on the five-acre production complex in Pasadena that the network had recently purchased and converted for their use.

"Liz, we're here," Paula announced, and Liz looked up from the screen reluctantly.

"But I'm not done. Can I save it somehow, or print it out or something?" she asked sheepishly.

Paula assured her they could and took the laptop from her, bookmarking the site and looking over at me with a wink.

I smiled back and we both followed Liz out of the limo and along the sidewalk between the buildings to the back parking lot where the actor's trailers were parked. Liz had a thoughtful look on her face that had me curious, and when we reached her trailer, I stopped her before she followed Paula inside.

"Penny for 'em."

She shrugged casually. "Just thinking about this morning."

"Uh-huh."

She acknowledged the skepticism in my voice with a purse of her lips and faintly annoyed look, but didn't respond.

"Come on, Liz, you're not still thinking about trying to sue anyone, are you? I told you—"

"Are there are a lot of these stories?" she asked abruptly, cutting me off in mid-cajole. She was staring out over the back lot, her thoughtful expression now turned slightly calculating. The fingernails of the thumb and ring finger on her right hand tapped together rapidly, a sure sign something big was going on in that blond head. When I didn't answer immediately, she glanced at me impatiently. "Well? Are there?"

"Yes." I nodded slowly. "Hundreds...thousands, even, I suppose."

That surprised her. "All about Jen and Rita?"

"Oh...no, no. They put all sorts of characters together." That seemed to disappoint her, and I frowned. "Why?"

She ignored my question and asked her own. "How many are lesbian stories? A lot?"

"A lot." I nodded again.

That satisfied her, and she climbed the stairs to her trailer, throwing a vague, "See you later," over her shoulder.

I stared at the closed door to her trailer for a few seconds, wondering what was going through her head, and thinking that whatever it was, I probably wasn't going to like it. Finally, I shrugged and headed for my own trailer, hoping Robyn was on the set today, and thinking about what I could do to maybe see another one of those smiles.

Chapter
Three

KREIZECK'S EPISODE, TITLED "Snap," wrapped shooting early the following week, and despite my original misgivings and intense dislike of the man, when post-production was finished, it turned out to be one of the better episodes we'd done. Still, we were all glad to have some of our regular directors back in the director's chair, and the next few weeks went by quickly as we settled back into our normal routine.

9th Precinct worked on a sixteen-day cycle for each episode, with the first eight days dedicated to pre-production activities such as casting, researching, and confirming locations, while the next eight days consisted of actual shooting. By rotating direction and production teams, they were able to overlap the pre-production of an upcoming episode with the actual shooting of the current episode, so the actors were always shooting, the casting department was always casting, and one of the production teams was always working on setting up our next week.

It was a punishing schedule that ran from early August until mid-May, and I knew I wasn't the only one looking forward to the summer hiatus. Like many of the other cast members, I had a few projects going on during the break, so I wouldn't be completely off, but a change of pace would be very welcome.

Liz hadn't mentioned the dreaded Internet-authors-who-thought-she-was-a-lesbian again after the day of the Q & A, but Paula told me she had asked for more sites and spent a lot of time on Paula's laptop, much to the assistant's annoyance.

I ordered a new laptop online that evening and gave it to Paula when it arrived a few days later, telling her she could keep it and give the other one to Liz. She seemed stunned by my generosity, but, Christ, I made more money than I'd ever be able to spend. I might as well spend it on people I liked.

The plot arc that Robyn was involved in on *9P* stretched out over another two episodes and I saw her fairly regularly over the next few weeks. I had expected our physical scene together during

"Snap" to add another layer of tension to our already peculiar interaction, but instead, we became increasingly comfortable with each other. I was still often tongue-tied around her, and she still watched my embarrassed floundering with open amusement, but there was a new ease to our conversations when we were in the trailer together, and we'd even begun to joke lightly with each other on the set. The conversations stayed fairly superficial, and I didn't feel as though I knew her much better than I had the first day we'd met, but she could make me laugh and I enjoyed being around her. When her plot arc on *9P* concluded and she was no longer on the set regularly, I felt her absence much more than I'd expected.

When she was done on *9P*, she took a week off and caused a stir in Brazil during Davis Cup play, watching from reserved seats as Josh Riley served and backhand-volleyed his way to two match wins, helping the US gain a victory over a strong Brazilian team. Her sunglass-shaded face and bronze skin were shown and commented on so many times during Josh's matches that it was amazing anyone watching actually remembered there was a tennis match going on. I watched what matches I could, not even making the effort to lie to myself and say I was watching for the tennis, although the tennis was pretty damn good. I just wanted to see her face, as pathetic as that sounds.

I'd seen her rarely and only in passing since she left for Brazil, so I was surprised one morning, more than a month after the wrapping of "Snap," when she showed up for the preliminary table read for the season finale that would start shooting at the end of our current eight-day shoot.

A table read is a sit-down reading of a script for an upcoming episode with the writers, producers, director and the regular cast members present to give feedback and discuss any location or casting issues. It's one of the only roles that the *9P* cast members had in the pre-production process, and I liked the chance to get a peek at what we would be doing the following week, as well as having the opportunity to give feedback.

I arrived about ten minutes early and poured myself a glass of water, chatting idly with Josiah Rollins, a short, slightly rotund man with thinning red hair; and Micah Saams, a beautiful giant of a man with rich, deep-brown skin and startling green eyes. Both were regular cast members, playing two of the other four detectives on the series besides Liz and me.

The rest of the regulars sat across from us: Danny DeLorenzo, a loud but undeniably likable Italian ladies' man; Henry Stoddard, stocky and strong with a bald head and bushy mustache; and finally, Arturo Garza, a former Latin soap opera star with a dazzling smile, a charming accent, and an ego the size of California.

I glanced at my watch. None of the writers had arrived yet, which was odd. They were usually there before anyone else, eager to pass out script drafts and get first thoughts before the producer or producers showed up. The producers were absent as well, but that was normal, and Liz, of course, would be one of the last people to walk through the door. She always arrived when the dramatic impact of her entrance would be the greatest, and none of us expected her for another fifteen minutes at least.

I smiled slightly as Danny and Henry debated the physical improbability of the latest story making the rounds of the gossip circuit, which involved two crewmembers, several pulleys, and a power tool. Finally, my goat-loving days appeared to be over. Maybe people would stop bleating behind my back and joking about goat cheese sandwiches during lunch.

One could only hope.

The door swung open and Robyn walked in, pausing in the doorway to survey the room. "Hey, all," she rasped.

Good God, she's an attractive woman.

I probably wasn't the only person thinking along those lines, as Danny stopped in mid-sentence, and Josiah and Micah fell silent.

Her dark hair was held back in a loose braid that highlighted the clean angles of her face, and a snug, black spaghetti-strap top showed off toned arms and miles of gloriously tan skin. Her endlessly long legs were tightly sheathed in white jeans, and flat, simple sandals showed burgundy-painted toenails and two gold toe rings.

I stared at the toe rings for a moment.

Christ. Even her feet are beautiful.

Arturo was the first to recover. "Ah, Robyn. You are a vision, as always. Please, come sit with me." He stood and pulled out the chair next to him, bowing gallantly.

I rolled my eyes, and when I looked back at Robyn, she was watching me, a tiny smile twitching at the corners of her mouth.

I felt a return smile curve my lips. Damn, it was good to see her. Very, very good.

And not just because she made my hormones sit up and beg—it was much more than that. I had genuinely missed her presence in my life; missed her smile, missed her voice, missed her teasing—missed *her*. And what the hell. Why not tell her? It was the friendly thing to do, wasn't it? It didn't mean I wanted to strip her naked and eat caramel sundaes off of her stomach. Of course it didn't.

"Hey, Robyn, long time." I smiled shyly. "It's good to see you."

She nodded at me, her mouth curling into a genuine smile. "Caidence."

I blushed.

Goddammit.

"Yeah, Robyn, we haven't seen you in a while," Micah's deep voice rumbled, drawing the room's attention away from me. "What brings you here today? We don't normally see you for these prelim things. They gotcha doing something big for the finale?"

Robyn walked around the table, ignoring the chair Arturo had pulled out, and slid into the chair next to me. It was normally Liz's chair, but I sure as hell wasn't going to say anything. "All I know is that I got a message last night to show up here this morning, nine o'clock sharp." She shrugged. "And here I am."

You certainly are, I thought, taking a sip of water from the glass in front of me, eyeing her surreptitiously while her attention was on Micah.

"Yes, you certainly are," Arturo said with smooth, perfectly accented charm.

Oh, God. I was a female Arturo.

I choked as I swallowed, coughing until my eyes watered. Josiah pounded heavily on my back in concern.

"Take it easy, Joe, you're gonna kill her," Robyn drawled, laying a hand on my arm. Josiah stopped thumping on me, and Robyn bent her worried face near my own. "You okay, Caid?"

"Yeah," I squeaked after a moment and nodded, too busy trying to breathe to react to her nearness, or the fact that this was the first time in memory that she'd used the shortened version of my name.

"Yo, Caid, y'all right there?"

I raised my head, giving Danny a watery smile. "Yeah, Danny, I'm good." I gave one final cough, and blinked rapidly. Crap. My throat felt raw, my head hurt, and I was extremely embarrassed.

But on the bright side, Robyn had her hand on my arm and was looking at me with concern...life could be worse.

"Water?" She took her hand off me and reached for my glass, still half full on the table.

"Yeah, thanks."

Conversation around us started up again as I sipped and swallowed cautiously.

"Hey." Her voice was soft.

I looked over questioningly.

"It's good to see you, too." She gave me a crooked smile, and bumped into my shoulder with her own. "I missed ya."

It was such a guy thing to do, I couldn't help laughing. Even as the words made my heart beat double-time. "Yeah?" I said with a stupid grin.

"Yeah."

We sat smiling at each other, and I felt sad and elated at the same time. Robyn was beautiful, smart, funny...

And very, very straight.

I might never eat caramel sundaes off her stomach, but maybe I'd ask her to go for coffee sometime, or dinner, or a hike, just as friends. Because I realized that I sincerely liked Robyn as a friend. On impulse, I asked, "You have plans after this? For lunch?"

"I have to be back at *ITD* by one thirty," she answered with a raised eyebrow, but no hesitation.

"Care to join me on a little trip?"

"Well, I certainly can't turn that down."

"Great, I'll..."

The room fell silent as the show's creator, Grant Hardy, walked in, along with the two other executive producers, two co-execs, and four writers, including the head-writer, or showrunner, Dorn Talren.

What the fuck was going on? Dorn rarely showed for these things, and Grant? Never. And how many executive producers did it take to do a preliminary read of a script?

I glanced over at Robyn, who looked as perplexed as I was.

"Good morning, everyone!" Grant boomed.

A chorus of muted hellos welcomed the group as they settled into places around the long table, and Grant surveyed his cast members.

"Where's Liz?"

"Right here, Grant," came the reply from the door as Liz entered the room, frowning slightly when she noticed Robyn in the spot next to me. She walked by me, giving my shoulder a squeeze of greeting, and took the vacant seat on the other side of Robyn.

"Oh, good. I wouldn't want you to miss this. It was, after all, partially your idea." He waved at one of the writers, who began distributing copies of the script around the table.

Liz looked confused for a moment, and then smiled brilliantly. "You liked it?"

"We sure did. The premise, anyway. We made a few changes that we think will work better."

Her smile faltered, but she took the offered script with a nod.

"Now," he boomed. "You're all probably wondering what's going on."

There were cautious nods around the table, and Grant smiled. "You all know how well the show is doing. We've been in the top five in our time slot all this season, and the numbers just keep getting better. The suits see that as a sign to keep doing things like we're doing them, but I didn't get here by sitting back and being cautious. I see this as an opportunity to take risks, to push the envelope, to see just what we can get away with. This season finale is going to set us up for some big things next year."

He stood and began pacing. "Our numbers in eighteen to forty-nine are the strongest, and that works perfectly for what we have in mind, since that's a demographic slightly more open-minded than the older or younger dems." He stopped pacing and leaned his hands on the table, catching each cast member's eye. "We're going to take advantage of that, and make television history while we do it."

He sat down and opened his copy of the script. "Let's get started, shall we?"

There was an expectant pause, and finally Micah cleared his throat and spoke. "Grant? Are you going to tell us..."

The creator waved his hand. "No, I want you to look at this fresh, with no preconceptions. Just like the audience will."

Micah shrugged and opened his script, and the rest of us did the same.

Scripts are broken up into four acts, each act accounting for approximately twelve minutes of the show and containing three to five scenes. The script was a good one, revisiting some of the threads from previous shows involving Robyn, and playing up the tension between her character and mine from the infamous wall-slamming scene in "Snap."

The bombshell didn't come until halfway through the fourth act, in the next-to-final scene which had our characters, Rita and Judith, trading barbs during a run-in at Judith's office.

I read my lines, then skipped ahead a bit as Robyn read hers, noting that this time, it was Robyn's character that got physical, grabbing Rita and...

I skipped forward another page.

...kissing her.

I re-read the last few lines, blinking in shock. Beside me, Robyn's voice stuttered to a halt.

"*What?*" Liz screeched, jolting me out of my dazed state.

I looked swiftly over at Robyn. She was staring at the pages, her eyes wide and her face very pale.

"Grant, this was supposed to be me!" Liz fumed. "This storyline was for me! Remember our conversation? Me wanting to take a few risks, and branch out a little?"

"Liz, honey, calm down," the man said soothingly, "we really liked the idea, but when we ran it by our test groups, people just didn't want to see you kissing another woman."

"But they wanted *her*?" The words and the look she cast my way were venomous, disbelieving.

I drew in a sharp breath. It had been a while since I'd been on the receiving end of one of Liz's tirades. I'd forgotten what a bitch she could be.

"Well, actually, yes. Her character, at least," Grant said, nodding at one of the exec-producers. "Raj?"

Raj Matis shuffled through some papers in front of him, pulling out a pale blue sheet. "We polled a group of eighteen to thirty-five, and only thirteen percent of the group believed that Jen would kiss a woman, and only two percent thought she would work as a lesbian. For Rita," he glanced at me, "seventy-one percent believed she would kiss a woman, and forty percent thought she worked as a lesbian, with several commenting that they already assumed she was."

Jesus. Forty percent of the public knew before I did.

"Numbers for Judith are higher than Jen's, but not nearly as high as Rita's, except when asked specifically about the Judith/Rita pairing — most say the scene in 'Snap' left them wondering."

"No fuckin' way!" Danny said, finally cluing into what all the commotion was about. "You're gonna make Caid a lesbian? And *Robyn?*" His voice was incredulous.

There were other murmurs around the table.

"I'm fairly certain he means our characters, Danny," Robyn said drolly, having regained her cool. "Caid and I won't suddenly be morphing into lesbians...sorry to disappoint."

Danny looked crestfallen.

I felt his pain. I wouldn't mind Robyn morphing into a lesbian, either.

Liz's anger had faded into a slightly shell-shocked expression. I doubted she'd ever polled that low in anything in her career. She stared at the script, and then gently, deliberately, closed it.

Uh-oh.

It was never good when Liz did anything with that kind of careful, deliberate calm.

She stood, and looked at me for a long moment. The look on her face was wounded, as though I'd betrayed her somehow.

It killed me. "Liz..." I didn't know what I would say, but I wanted to say something, anything, to stop that look.

"I don't want to talk to you right now, Caid," she said, holding up a hand. "I can't believe you'd..." She shook her head, picked up the script, and left the room.

"Goddammit!" I spit out after the door had closed behind her. I tossed my script down in aggravation and shook my head. "I didn't do anything!" I rounded on Grant. "Thanks for the heads-up there, big guy. This may just fuck up our friendship beyond repair, not to mention our working relationship — a little notice would have been nice."

The room went deathly silent.

No one talked to Grant that way. Especially not some ex-beer commercial actress. A very expendable ex-beer commercial actress who had just picked an extremely stupid time to lose her temper.

Under the table, Robyn grabbed my thigh and squeezed hard, telling me without words to shut the hell up.

I took several deep breaths, trying to regain control. Grant watched me through narrowed eyes.

"Grant," Robyn said, in a tone I'd never heard before. It was soaked in promise, hinted at fantasies come true, and had every man in the room shifting uncomfortably in their seats. It was sex and heat and forbidden things, meant to get attention, then to get Robyn whatever she wanted.

Damn. I needed a trick like that.

"Grant, do you think that Caid and I could talk with you privately after we finish the read? I think there are some things we need to discuss." Her smile promised everything that her voice had, and more.

Goddamn. And I thought Liz was good at this.

I pried her hand off my thigh and gently placed it back in her lap. Even though I was aware of its manipulative intent, I was far from immune to Robyn's sudden come-and-get-it aura. Her hand on that area of my anatomy...I could do without it.

She glanced at me quickly and I gave her a tight smile, assuring her that I was back in control of my suicidal, producer-insulting urges.

"Of course, Robyn," Grant agreed obediently, forgetting my transgressions for the moment. He looked around the table. "In fact, why don't we wrap this up? Read through the rest on your own, let Kenny or Bren know if you've got any comments or suggestions before the writer's meeting, tomorrow at two. Okay?"

From the pitying looks thrown my way as the others left the room, I knew that I needed to administer a major dose of damage control.

Pucker lips and apply to insulted ass, *stat.*

As the last writer filed from the room, I rose from my chair, ignoring Robyn's warning look. I hadn't needed them much over the last few years, but I used to work in the service industry, and my ass-kissing skills were alive and functioning. This was a perfect time to take them out for a little exercise.

Now, I don't have the classic beauty of Robyn or Liz, but I do have big, expressive, green eyes and a full, wide mouth that had recently been deemed one of television's twenty most kissable, and was probably on other lists that I didn't really want to contemplate. I turned those big eyes on Grant and arranged my face in a properly sorrowful expression as I knelt down beside him.

"Grant, I am so sorry I snapped at you. I was upset at Liz's reaction, but that's absolutely no reason to speak to you that way." I laid a hand on his arm. "I hope you can accept my apology. I promise it will never, ever happen again."

After several moments of me kneeling beside him, in essence begging for forgiveness, Grant nodded. "See that it doesn't, Caidence. See that it doesn't."

"It won't." I squeezed his arm in thanks and straightened, smiling slightly at Robyn's surprised expression. I couldn't fault her for her surprise; until recently, she'd been under the impression that I had the intellect and maturity level of a twelve-year-old.

My job re-secured, I walked back to my chair and dropped into it heavily, the problem with Liz filling my thoughts. I forgot all about that kissing-Robyn-in-front-of-a-bunch-of-cameras thing.

Not for long.

"Grant," Robyn said, "about this script. I really wish you had run it by us before okaying it. This is something I'll need to talk over with Mark." Mark Goodhead was her agent, and Robyn would want to talk to him about how this might affect her future prospects, career-wise.

"Do you need to talk to someone, too?" Grant asked me, dragging me back in conversation. The look on his face was predatory—the wrong answer and my groveling would be for nothing.

Robyn had been in the business much longer than I had been, modeling for the first few years before moving into acting, and over her last three seasons on *In Their Defense*, she had surprised a lot of people by taking a minor, supposedly unlikable character and transforming her into one of the show's driving plot forces. Robyn Ward had enough of a name, enough of a foothold, to decline this script and withstand any backlash. Caidence Harris did not. Despite the popularity of *9th Precinct*, I was still a newbie in the business, and couldn't afford to turn this down. Especially after being a colossal ass to a man who could break my career with a few casual words.

He knew it, and I knew it.

"No, I'm fine with it," I answered, as he knew I would.

In eight days' time, when we started shooting for this script, I'd be kissing a woman on camera. It was up to Robyn who that woman would be.

WE WALKED BACK to the trailer in silence after our meeting with Grant, my mind back on Liz, and how to fix the sudden rift between us. I'd think about having to kiss Robyn, or some other woman, later.

When I could freak out in private.

Robyn was busy on her cell phone, setting up a meeting with her agent. She told him they needed to talk about "an interesting opportunity."

An interesting way to put it.

We walked across the lot, and my steps slowed to a stop as we passed Liz's trailer. I felt a gentle pressure on my arm.

"I don't think talking to her right now is such a good idea, Caid." Robyn said softly. I hesitated, and she wrapped a long-fingered hand around my wrist, stopping me from moving toward the trailer. "Trust me, Caid. Just let her be for a while. Try tomorrow."

She tugged lightly in the direction of our trailer and after a moment, I started walking again. We entered the trailer without speaking; I walked around, absentmindedly picking up the few things I'd left out that morning before the table read.

"Caid..."

I swung around, blinking at her. "Hmm?"

She looked as though she was going to say something, but then changed her mind. "So, what about this little trip you were talking about? I've got..." she looked at the bulky silver watch on her wrist, "two and a half hours, give or take."

"Oh." I stood staring at her stupidly.

"We're still on, right? You promised me lunch, Harris. Don't let me down."

My lips curled into a smile. "Well, I do hate to disappoint."

"Good. I hate to be disappointed." She held her arms out and looked down at herself. "Am I dressed appropriately for this trip?"

I cocked my head to the side, taking the offered opportunity to study her from head to toe. "You're perfect," I said, and meant it. I looked at her feet. "Those look pretty comfy. Can you walk in those sandals?"

She raised both eyebrows. "Will I need to?"

"It's a good possibility," I replied vaguely.

"I can."

"Well then. Like I said—perfect." I grinned, and grabbed a small duffel bag off the table. "Let's get out of here."

I led the way to my baby, a metallic blue Audi S4 Cabriolet convertible. It had been my first big purchase after landing my four-year deal on *9P*; completely frivolous, impractical, and I loved it. The top was already down—I'd left it down that morning when I drove in—and I tossed my bag in the back seat, pulling the driver's side door open and sliding in behind the wheel.

Robyn moved around the car slowly, giving it the once-over. "Oh, Caid, I didn't know this was yours. I've wondered. This car is great." Robyn trailed a finger along the hood as she walked to the other side, pulled open the door, and slipped in beside me. "I've always wanted a convertible, but I'm depressingly practical about things like that." She ran a hand over the dashboard with a delighted smile. "This is so cool."

Lucky damn dashboard.

I patted the steering wheel. "Twila, this is Robyn. Robyn, Twila."

Yes, I name my cars. I know, I'm a dork, and I was definitely clueing Robyn in to my dorkiness, but I didn't really care. I was glad to be leaving the complex for a while, and happy to have her along as company.

She patted the dashboard, her face completely serious. "Nice to meet ya, Twila."

The woman is perfect.

I shook my head and checked my pockets for the keys, grunting when I remembered that I'd left them in my bag. I reached back through the space between our seats and pulled the bag into my lap, grabbing the keys from where they were clipped in the outside pocket, and rummaging around a bit more before pulling out a faded baseball cap from a charity event I'd done a few years back.

"Might get a little breezy," I said, and handed the cap to her before zipping the bag up and tossing it in back.

"Thanks." She was already pulling her long braid through the hole in back and settling it on her head. "So, where are we going?"

She looked adorable. How can someone look so goddamn sexy and adorable at the same time? I shook my head again and started the car. "To lunch."

She leaned back in soft leather and smiled. "To lunch."

The network's production complex was on the western edge of Pasadena, and I hopped on 210 for a bit before exiting north on Lake Avenue. Having the top down made conversation difficult, so by unspoken agreement we just enjoyed the sunshine and cool breeze with minimal conversation. At a deli along the way, I ran in and picked up a bag of goodies, and then we continued on through Altadena and on to Chaney Trail.

I caught Robyn's smile out of the corner of my eye when we passed the sign telling us we were entering Angeles National Forest, and let out a relieved sigh, not realizing that I had been worried she would be less than thrilled with our destination. I pulled the car into a parking spot, noting with satisfaction that there were only a few other cars in the lot.

Robyn turned to me, still smiling. "So, this is lunch?"

"Nope." I grabbed the deli bag, pushed the button to put the convertible top back up, and rolled up the windows, not wanting to tempt anyone with a wide-open car. "You're going to have to work just a little for your lunch."

I opened the door and got out, and she did the same.

"Hey," she said as she slammed the door. "No one said anything about working for my lunch."

I just smiled and started walking, confident she would follow. We walked through a small campground, following the signs to Millard Canyon Falls. The trail wound along a stream through a small, shaded canyon, and we reached the falls in less than fifteen minutes. The area around the falls was empty; the owners of the cars in the lot must have hiked on further behind the falls to the mine.

I led us off the trail, over a few boulders, and under a tall oak tree near the canyon wall before plopping myself down on a flat rock. Robyn folded herself gracefully beside me, staring at the fifty-foot cascade of water not twenty yards from us. The stream was high from recent rains, and the falls were impressive. We hadn't spoken once during the short walk, but the silence had seemed comfortable, and not at all strained.

I opened the deli bag, and the crinkling of paper attracted Robyn's attention. She looked at me expectantly. "So this is lunch?" she asked hopefully.

I pulled two sandwiches, two bottles of water, a slightly greasy bag of kettle chips, an apple, an orange, and a brownie out of the bag, along with some napkins. "This is lunch." I handed her a sandwich and a bottle of water. "Apple or orange?"

"Orange, please."

I handed her the orange, and took a swig of water as she unwrapped her sandwich.

She peeled back the bread, frowning slightly. "Roast beef?"

"I've got turkey and avocado, if you'd rather. I'll take that one."

She was still looking at the sandwich. "What if I'm vegetarian?"

I had taken another drink of water and stopped mid-swig. I lowered the bottle. "Are you?" Shit. I should have asked, instead of just assuming...

"Hell, no." She took a huge bite of the sandwich, chewing happily for a while and finally swallowing. "I just wondered how you knew I liked roast beef."

I sighed in relief. "You just seemed like a roast beef kind of gal."

She stopped eating for a moment, contemplating that. "I don't know if I should be offended by that or not."

"I didn't mean..."

"Caid," she laughed, and took another bite, talking around it. "I'm kidding."

"Oh."

We sat in silence for a while, eating our lunches and listening to the splash of the water against the rocks. When I was finished, I balled up the wax paper my sandwich had been wrapped in and put it back in the bag. Popping a chip into my mouth, I leaned back on my elbows and closed my eyes, crunching slowly.

"How was Brazil?" I asked eventually, opening my eyes and sliding them over to her. "You know they showed you almost as much as Josh?"

She laughed, and leaned back next to me. "Caid, you wouldn't believe it. It was insane. I'd look across the court during this intense point, and the camera that was supposed to be pointed at the players was pointing at me. And, God, every time we'd go anywhere, this huge cadre of photographers would follow..."

"That seems to happen to the two of you here in the States, as well."

"To some extent, yes, but nothing like that. Josh loves the attention, though." She shuddered. "Ugh. I can't stand it."

That surprised me. She seemed very comfortable in the spotlight, as though she liked it.

"Josh played well," I said, after a few more minutes of silence.

"He did, didn't he?" She tipped her head back and closed her eyes, catching a stray bit of sunshine through the leaves and giving me an excellent view along the smooth, kissable line of her throat and down to the hint of cleavage where the edge of her shirt dipped lowest.

I looked away and cleared my throat. "That match against Gruspania...that was a close one."

She smiled, her eyes still closed. "I was afraid he'd be so upset after that one. He's usually such a baby when he thinks he didn't play as well as he could have. He wasn't, though."

We both sat quietly for a few minutes, and then Robyn chuckled. "He wants to meet you, actually."

I looked over at her, perplexed. "He does?"

"Oh, he won't admit it, but I remember when I first started getting time on *9th Precinct*, and Josh was all excited that I'd get to work with Caidence Harris, the hottest Ballentine Babe ever."

"Oh, God," I groaned, and closed my eyes. In my beer commercial days, I hawked Ballentine Pilsner, a German-style beer, brewed in America, with an Irish name. It was surprisingly popular, especially with the college crowd, and several commercial spots of me in a bikini top and obscenely tight jeans certainly hadn't hurt sales any. "You're kidding."

"Nope, his exact words." She was quiet for a few seconds. "I'd like you to."

I opened my eyes and looked over at her. She'd been watching me, but looked away.

"You'd like me to what?"

She looked back. "Meet him. Maybe we could all have dinner sometime. You could bring...a date, if you want...I mean, if you're seeing anyone..." Her voice was rushed, and then trailed off. She looked back at the falls.

Wonderful. Girl-talk about my love life with the object of my unrequited affection.

"I'm not," I said with a wry smile. "Frankly, I don't know how you have time for it. I usually fall into bed as soon as I get home. I can hardly get up the energy to brush my teeth, much less date. And that would be nice, by the way."

She had been listening intently, and frowned at the last bit. "Pardon?"

"Dinner," I clarified. "Or something, with you and Josh. If it's okay that it's just me, *sans* date."

"Just you will do just fine. Tomorrow night?" she asked hopefully.

"Um..." She'd caught me off-guard. I ran through my schedule for the next day. "We're shooting in the city tomorrow, so I probably won't be done until eight or so..."

"Come to the house. Josh will grill. He can't boil an egg, but the boy can grill." She touched my arm briefly. "Unless that's too late?" Her head was cocked slightly to the side, watching me with those impossibly dark eyes. She'd left the hat in the car, and wisps of dark hair had come loose from the braid and blown across her face.

I struggled to breathe, overwhelmed by a sudden flood of emotion. Sometimes just looking at her did that to me. She was so damn beautiful it made me ache.

"No, it's not too late. I'd love to," I managed.

She smiled brilliantly, our eyes met, and the ache intensified.

I jumped to my feet, brushed the dirt off my jeans, and gathered the remains of our lunch. "We'd better head back."

"Oh. Yeah." She sounded disappointed, but slowly climbed to her feet. "I guess so." Her hand brushed down my back, leaving a trail of delicious tingles in its wake. "Thanks, Caid. This was really nice. Is this a regular thing for you?"

I looked around for a moment, regaining my equilibrium, and

shrugged. "Depends, I guess. I like to get away from the set when I can, and there are lots of spots in Angeles within a half-hour or forty-five minute drive. I picked this one because it was close, and I didn't know how far you wanted to walk in sandals. I usually like to hike a little further."

"I'll leave a pair of hikers in the trailer, then, so next time, I'll be prepared." She was stretching her arms over her head, leaning one way and then the other to loosen her back, and didn't notice the huge grin on my face.

Next time.

Hot damn. I liked the sound of that.

I packed away our trash and unwrapped the brownie, breaking it in half and handing one part to Robyn. "Energy," I said, "for the long, brutal hike back."

She eyed the treat before taking it with a sigh of resignation. "If I keep hanging out with you, I'm going to have to add another mile to my morning run."

I grinned, and took a bite, chewing happily. "You run?"

She nodded, nibbling on her portion daintily. "Yeah, I started in college...just kind of a habit now. I swim, too, a couple times a week. It was either that or stop eating, and I love to eat."

That explained the lithe, sinewy arms and well-muscled shoulders. Not that I was looking or anything. "How far do you usually run?"

"Around five miles, I guess."

I nodded. That was about what I did most mornings, too. Casually, I said, "We should go together sometime."

She smiled. "Sounds like a good idea. It'd be nice to run with someone again...I used to run with Josh, but he's got this whole 'I am a professional athlete and must crush you' thing going on." She said the last with an Arnold Schwarzenegger accent. "I finally told him to go try to crush someone else. Now he pays someone to get crushed."

I laughed, and stuffed the last bit of brownie into my mouth before leading the way back to the trail; it was wide enough, so we started back walking side by side.

"I promise not to crush you. In fact, with those endless legs of yours, I imagine you'll be the one doing the crushing."

Jesus. Did I just say that?

Robyn shot me a curious look, but didn't comment. "It's a deal."

We walked quietly for a few more minutes, Robyn dropping back behind me when we came up on a group of three chatty, middle-aged women heading to the falls. The woman at the head of the group blinked at me in hazy recognition.

"Hi," I said, and smiled when her eyes widened in surprise.

"Hello, ladies." Robyn's throaty voice drew the woman's attention away from me, and her eyes widened further, to near saucer-size. She slowed as we passed, watching us open-mouthed. The two women behind her, absorbed in conversation, bumped into her back with squawks of surprise. Robyn and I walked on, both smiling at the furious whispering behind us.

Robyn took two long strides and was beside me again, looking around at the canyon walls with a contented smile. She looked at ease, comfortable in this kind of activity.

"I don't suppose you mountain bike, do you?" I asked suddenly.

"I haven't before." She looked over at me and smiled. "But I've been wanting to try."

Hot damn.

I PULLED TWILA into her parking space thirty minutes later, laughing when Robyn patted her gently on the dash and whispered, "Thank you."

"Maybe you should get your own, Robyn." I got out, grabbed my duffel from the back and slung it over my shoulder.

She fell into step beside me. "Don't need to now — I'll just have you chauffeur me around."

I think she expected a comeback, but I had absolutely no problem with it, so I just smiled.

We walked to the trailer and I entered first, stopping abruptly when I saw a haggard-looking Liz on my couch.

"Caid..." She made as if to rise, then sank back down when she spotted Robyn behind me. She looked from me to Robyn, frowning.

Robyn stepped slightly in front of me, her stance relaxed but perceptively aggressive. I looked over at her in surprise. Robyn, defending me? The thought made me ridiculously happy, regardless of whether it was true or not.

I put my hand on her arm gently and stepped back in front of her. "Liz, I'm glad you're here..."

Liz's eyes darted to each of our faces, then down to where my hand was still on Robyn's arm. Her frown deepened. She stared for a moment, then shook her head slightly and stood. "Hi, Robyn." She flicked a glance at the dark-haired woman by my side, and then settled her eyes back on me. "Do you mind if I talk to Caid a minute?"

Robyn gave me a searching look, and I smiled, assuring her that it was okay. She looked back at Liz. "Sure, Liz. I need to get back to *ITD* anyway." She placed a light hand on my shoulder and squeezed gently. "Thanks for today, Caid. It was the nicest lunch I've had in quite a while. I'll call you about tomorrow?"

I nodded, smiling. Robyn threw one final glance at Liz, then left.

Liz frowned after her as the door closed. "What's up with her?"

I shrugged and watched her, trying to gauge her mood. I was hoping she was here to talk things out, but it was just as likely that she was here to yell at me—maybe I shouldn't have sent Robyn off, after all.

She turned abruptly and pulled me into a brief but forceful hug. Liz wasn't normally very touchy, and I was surprised into stillness. Before I could respond, she stepped back, looking embarrassed.

"Liz..."

"Here." She thrust something at me, and I automatically opened my hand to receive it. "I'm sorry I was such a bitch, Caid. I never wanted to be that way with you."

I looked at the objects in my hand. Three miniature Cookies 'N' Cream candy bars.

"Paula said that maybe I should get you flowers or something, but I know you hate crap like that, since they just die and stink up your trailer, and, hell, everyone always sends flowers to suck up, and I know you're a freak for these stupid chocolate things..." Liz rattled on, and I just watched her, smiling slightly.

I *am* a freak for these stupid little candy bars. Maybe four people in the world knew that about me. Liz had remembered, and without Paula's help.

I love it when people surprise me in a good way.

"...I was just so goddamned mad at Grant for blindsiding me like that..."

"Liz, it's okay."

She paused. "Really?"

I nodded. "Really."

Her whole body slumped in relief, and she sank down on the couch. "Thank God."

"But, for the record," I added, "Charming Liz is still my favorite."

She bit her lip. "I'm really sorry, Caid."

"I know you are, hon." I unwrapped one of the candy bars and offered it to her. "Want one?"

She grimaced. "God, no. Those things are disgusting. I don't know how you eat them. They look like squares of lard with ants in them."

The candy paused on its way to my mouth. I looked at it—

really looked at it—and saw that she was right. "When in your entire life have you seen a square of lard, woman?" I popped the candy into my mouth, trying not to think of lard and ants.

She sniffed. "I know what lard looks like."

"Because you cook with it so often."

"Hey, I watch *Iron Chef*. Those guys are big on lard." Her eyes widened. "Hell, the other night I saw them do this thing with some fucked-up kind of melon and a part of a shark that should never be shown on television..."

My loud laugh echoed off the walls of the trailer. I love this woman, and it was nice to be reminded why.

She stopped mid-sentence and frowned. "What?"

"Liz, don't ever change."

She smiled beautifully. "Well of course not, sugar. Why mess with perfection?"

Why, indeed. I laughed again and sat down on the couch next to her.

"So we're okay?" she asked again.

"We're fine."

She turned to me, suddenly very serious. "You're one of the only real friends I have around here, Caid. I couldn't stand it if something messed that up."

"I'd be pretty damn upset about it too, Liz," I said, and patted her on the thigh. "And I think you have a lot more friends around than you think."

I leaned back in the cushions with a deep sigh. So far today, my character's direction on the show had taken an "interesting" new turn, I'd nearly lost a good friend, I almost sank my career, and I moved into a new phase of a promising friendship with a woman I wanted far more than friendship from. It had been one hell of a day, and it was barely half over.

"Speaking of friends, you and Robyn seemed pretty chummy. I didn't know you two hung out."

"We hadn't, really, before today. I needed to get away from the set for a while, and Robyn came along."

"Oh, Caid...you didn't take her on one of your nature hikes, did you?" She wrinkled her nose in distaste. I'd asked Liz along on one of my trips once, after which we both agreed I would never ask again. Nature was not Liz's thing.

"She liked it," I said, somewhat defensively.

"I knew there was something off about that woman..."

"There is not!" The vehemence in my voice startled both of us.

"Whoa, Caid, I was joking. I actually kind of like Robyn. Anyone who can shut Arturo up with a look is okay in my book."

I rubbed my face and sighed. "Sorry, I'm a little on edge today,

I guess."

We sat in silence for a few minutes. I looked at my watch, noting I needed to be in makeup soon.

"Caid?" Liz was staring into space, a puzzled expression on her face.

"Hmm?"

"Why do you think no one thinks I'd kiss a woman?"

Oh, boy. I knew those stupid numbers would worry her. "I don't know, Liz, but I wouldn't worry about it too much. It's just a test group."

She nodded, and fell silent for a while. "Have you?"

I'd been idly studying the ceiling, and turned my head toward her. "Have I what?"

"Kissed a woman?"

"No," I answered honestly, after a moment of hesitation.

But I've wanted to. God, how I've wanted to. During the scene with Robyn, today at the table read, at the falls, and every damn time Robyn walks in the room...

"Have you ever wanted to?"

I drew in a surprised breath, and Liz looked over at me curiously. I sat for a moment, then cleared my throat and said quietly, "Yes."

She nodded thoughtfully. "That must be it. I never have. Wanted to kiss a woman, I mean."

I stared. I wasn't sure what reaction I was expecting, but it certainly wasn't calm logic.

She pushed herself off the couch using the armrest and one of my knees. "Well, I've got a two o'clock call-time. Paula's going to be over here pounding on the door any moment. Might as well save her the trip." She stopped at the door. "I'm glad we're okay, Caid."

I found my voice. "Me, too."

She opened the door, and looked over her shoulder. "And you're not off the hook about this kissing a woman thing. We'll talk about *that* later."

The door closed with a loud *snick*.

I groaned, and put my face in my hands.

Great. Just great.

Chapter
Four

NIGHT WAS MOVING quickly from the orange flair of sunset into the deep gray of dusk when I turned onto a quiet cul-de-sac and spotted the high, white stucco wall Robyn had mentioned in her directions. Behind the wall, through an abundance of unidentifiable greenery, I could see glimpses of red-tiled roofs, arched windows, and more white stucco. Muted lamp-light glowed weakly from within two miniature campaniles set atop the wall, marking the entrance to a walled cobblestone drive, and following Robyn's instructions, I pulled in and parked Twila in front of one of the heavy wooden doors of a three-car garage. I checked that my hair wasn't too wild-looking after a full day of shooting in the city, grabbed the bottle of wine I'd stopped for on my way over, and let myself through a wrought-iron gate just to the left of the garage. On the other side of the gate, I followed a curved, red sandstone path that sloped gently up through established, well-kept landscaping, and finally climbed the two steps up onto a wide front porch.

An arched, wooden door carved with intricate Mexican designs greeted me, and after pausing for a moment to calm my nerves, I pushed the lit doorbell and stepped back, shifting nervously from foot to foot and gripping the bottle of wine tightly. I took another step back to get a better look at the house, noting that it was smaller than I'd expected, at least at first glance, though I knew how deceiving that could be in hilly areas like Silver Lake. The rounded lines, white walls, and low red roof blended nicely with the surrounding greenery and landscape, giving it a warm, welcoming feel despite the obvious privacy measures that Robyn had taken. It was private without being a fortress, and that was something hard to come by and even harder to afford in this town.

The door rattled, interrupting my architectural musings, and I drew a deep breath, plastering what I hoped was a pleasant smile on my face. The heavy wood swung inward to reveal a tall, blond-haired man with light blue eyes and a mega-watt smile, currently aimed at me.

"Ms. Harris," he held out a large hand, "it's great to meet you. Josh Riley."

Like I didn't know who he was.

In photographs, Josh Riley was an attractive man, but in the flesh, he was quite a bit more than that. I felt an instant, visceral reaction, and had to squelch an urge to touch him to see if he was real.

Good God. No wonder people followed these two around, wanting pictures.

Slightly dazed, I took his hand. "Caidence Harris. Please, call me Caid."

His grip was strong without being overbearing. "Caid," he said, as though trying it out. He grinned. "And you should call me Josh." Before releasing my hand, he tugged me lightly through the door and closed it behind us.

I held up the wine. "Robyn said not to bring anything, but my mother would kill me if I showed up empty-handed."

"Ah. Fully house-trained. No wonder Robyn likes you." He took my hand again. "I'll let you deliver that yourself. Robby's just in the kitchen, I think."

I let him pull me further into the house, slightly disconcerted by his complete disregard of the physical boundaries that normally existed between virtual strangers. He led me past a curving, stone stairway going up to our left, and down a wide hallway, our footsteps muffled by expensive-looking woven rugs that covered smooth tile floors.

A railed landing at the end of the hall overlooked a huge, open living room with a two-story wall of glass offering a breathtaking view of Los Angeles at night.

I stopped, pulling Josh to a halt as well. "Wow."

"Nice, isn't it?" He tugged me toward a gently curving wrought-metal staircase with tiled steps that led down to the main level. "You should see the view of the mountains in the daytime. That's really why she paid out the ass for this place."

"I bet," I murmured, following Josh down the stairs, still gazing at the view.

The staircase widened at the bottom and spilled out into the living room where more woven rugs and several pieces of sage-gray furniture covered tiled floors. As we hit the bottom of the steps, Josh paused, glancing around. "Robby? Your guest is here."

"Caid." The husky voice affected me like a jolt of electricity and I dropped Josh's hand hastily, afraid my feelings could somehow be transferred by the contact. Robyn emerged from a wide arched opening that led into a large kitchen, wiping her hands on a towel. "I'm so glad you could make it. Welcome."

"Thanks," I said, unable to stop the large smile that spread across my face at the sight of her. Her long hair fell loose down her back and she wore a faded green T-shirt tucked into worn jeans and no shoes.

This was by far my favorite view in the house.

She answered my smile with one of her own, and we stood like that for several moments, until Josh tried to move past her into the kitchen.

"Where's my meat, woman? I'm starving."

Robyn threw the towel over her shoulder and stopped him with a hand to his chest. "Uh-uh. Stay out of my kitchen, grill-boy." She turned him around and motioned to a sliding glass door leading out onto a wide deck. "Go light the grill and I'll bring it out to you."

He pouted a little, but did as she asked, flashing me a quick grin as he walked by. Robyn watched him go with a fond smile and motioned for me to follow her into the kitchen.

"You have a beautiful home, Robyn. That view is incredible," I told her as we walked under the arched entrance.

She glanced over her shoulder at me with a slight smile. "Isn't it great? Yeah, that pretty much sold me on the place." She turned when she reached the counter and gestured at a foil-covered pan. "I'd give you a tour, but I need to get this out to Josh—he's a pest when he's hungry. How about later?"

"Please. I'd love to see the rest."

She nodded, and glanced at the wine in my hand. "Want me to open that?"

"Oh. Not necessarily, unless you want to." I held it out to her and she took it, glancing at the label and treating me to a raised eyebrow.

It was a nice wine. At least it better be, for what I paid for it.

"I'll let you get away with it this time, but next time you really don't need to bring anything." She glanced at the label again. "I think we'll save this one for later. I've got a merlot open that I've been working on," she motioned to an opened bottle and half-full glass on the counter, "or there's beer, or pop...I think I've got some iced tea made. Or a cocktail of some sort, if you'd rather."

I nodded at the open bottle. "Some of that would be great, thanks."

She picked up the foil-covered pan and handed it to me. "If you take this out to Josh, I'll bring you out a glass."

"Hey!" I took the pan with a mock-pout. "No one told me I'd have to work for my dinner."

"At least you've got the right shoes," she said with a smile.

"Now shoo. I'll be out in a second."

I wandered through the living room and out onto the deck, spotting Josh in a corner where the deck wrapped around the other side of the house, scrubbing vigorously at a monstrous grill with a wire brush.

"Delivery for you." I walked over and set the pan down on a nearby table.

"Oh, great!" He set down the brush and rubbed his hands together in anticipation before peeling the foil back to reveal three large steaks, a pile of chopped peppers, onions and zucchini, and a dish filled with marinade. "You are in for a treat. I don't know what magic sauce stuff Robyn puts on these steaks, but it's damn tasty."

"It looks wonderful," I said, meaning it. My stomach grumbled in agreement.

Josh and I chatted about the art of grilling until Robyn brought out our drinks, then the two of them proceeded to charm the hell out of me with their comfortable banter and obvious affection for each other. Josh told some hilarious stories about his life on tour and some of the other players, and Robyn countered with tales of her days as a model and a recent encounter with a very enthusiastic fan.

By the time we sat down to dinner at the heavy wooden table in a dining nook on the far side of the spacious kitchen, my sides ached from laughing, and the three of us were giggling like teenagers. By the time dinner was through, I felt as comfortable with the two of them as I had with anyone in a long, long time.

We all chipped in clearing the table and stacking the dishes next to the sink, and then Josh announced that he needed to head home. That surprised me—I'd just assumed that this *was* home.

"Amazing how you always mange to leave just when it's time to do dishes," Robyn said dryly, slapping him lightly on the stomach.

"My timing is impeccable, isn't it?" He smiled charmingly and wrapped an arm around her shoulders, pulling her close. She leaned into him, resting her chin on his shoulder and threading her arms around his waist. They stood like that for several long seconds, and I wanted to look away but couldn't. They were beautiful together.

Finally, he kissed her dark hair, murmuring, "Love you."

"Love you too," she answered.

They untangled themselves from each other with a final, private smile, and Josh turned to me, grinning hugely. "Caid." He took my hand and held it within both of his. "It's been a true pleasure to meet you. I hope I get to see a lot more of you."

"Me, too," I said, and meant it. I stepped forward to kiss him on the cheek.

He was surprised but pleased, and bent his head in an endearing display of bashfulness.

Well, if Robyn wasn't going to fall madly in love with *me*, I supposed she could do a lot worse.

"I'll walk you out," Robyn said, and glanced over at me. "Be right back."

I nodded and turned to the sink, secretly relieved to miss their final good-byes, which would no doubt be steamier than the chaste, almost sisterly one I had witnessed.

I could hear the low murmur of voices, and Josh's laughter, followed by Robyn's. Then the door closed and Robyn's bare feet padded back down the stairs.

I started rinsing off plates, stacking them by the side of the sink. Robyn came in and pulled out what I had assumed was a cupboard, but turned out to be a dishwasher.

"Clever," I said, and started setting the plates inside while Robyn moved next to me at the sink and took over my rinsing job, handing me dishes as she finished. We were through within five minutes and I wiped my hands on a towel, chewing on the inside of my cheek. Robyn had been silent since she came back into the kitchen. That was probably my cue to leave.

"Well," I said, smiling brightly, "I guess I'd better head out, too. Thanks so much for dinner...it was delicious. And Josh is a sweetheart. You're very lucky."

And he's the luckiest person on this planet.

She picked up her wine glass and swirled what was left, smiling the affectionate smile that I'd begun to associate with Josh. "Yes, I'm very lucky to have Josh in my life. He's the best friend I could ever ask for." She looked over at me, hesitated, and continued, "Do you need to go home? Or can you stay for a while? I still owe you the grand tour, remember?"

I corralled my giddiness, fighting down the urge to grin like a maniac. "I can stay."

"Great." Her happy smile, showing even, white teeth and crinkling the corners of her eyes just a little, brought on another one of those breathless moments that I'd labeled "Robyn Rush." I looked down at the towel in my hands and took a few steadying breaths.

She poured us both another glass of wine, handed me mine, and grabbed my hand. "*Venido.* Right this way for the tour."

I wondered if this habit of dragging people around by the hand was one she'd picked up from Josh, or if he'd picked it up from her. Either way, I wasn't complaining, enjoying the casual contact as she led me enthusiastically around her home, showing me two spare rooms, a shared full bath, an exercise room, a laundry room, and a recreation room with a fancy home theater system on the carpeted lower floor, plus two more spare rooms, both with their own half-baths, on the entry floor. We took the curving stairway near the front door that I'd noticed when I first came in, and at the top of the stairs was a huge room with a gigantic bed on a simple log frame, the headboard filled with books.

Robyn dropped my hand, muttering, "One sec," before crossing the room to disappear into an arched doorway that led to a large walk-in closet.

I stood stock-still. I was standing in Robyn Ward's bedroom.

I glanced around nervously, shifting uncomfortably and trying not to stare at the bed. I felt like a voyeur and it was not a pleasant feeling.

Robyn emerged from the closet with a sweatshirt in one hand and another shirt draped over her shoulder. She gestured vaguely around the room. "So, this is the master bedroom..." she pointed with the sweatshirt to a small doorway, "Master bath in there," she pointed with her wine glass, "closet there, bed there, the usual stuff."

I nodded and looked that way politely, trying not to *really* look at the bed where Robyn slept, every night, wearing God knows what, or what not.

"But what I really want to show you is out here," she went on, and gestured to a set of French doors as she tossed the sweatshirt at me. "Here, it's getting a little chilly."

I snagged it out of the air on pure reflex, my mind still busy with the fact that I was standing in her bedroom, and mutely followed her through the doors out onto another deck. This one was smaller and cozier, offering an even better view of the city, with a low table and a large Adirondack chair taking up a good portion of the space. Robyn set her wine and the shirt down on the table and ducked back inside, emerging moments later carrying a high-backed chair that I'd noticed tucked under a desk in the corner of the bedroom.

"I don't get much company up here," she said in explanation, setting the chair on the other side of the table. She picked up her shirt and threaded long arms through the sleeves, buttoning up a few of the buttons as she sat down in the chair she'd just set down, and motioned me to take the Adirondack. "Have a seat."

I set my wine glass next to hers on the table and quickly pulled the sweatshirt over my head, settling it down around my torso. The cloth was soft and warm against the skin of my arms, and it smelled like her. I had to stop myself from burying my face in the folds and just breathing the scent of her in.

Difficult to explain that kind of behavior.

I settled into the chair, and we sat looking over the city, not speaking. Or rather, Robyn sat looking over the city—I spent more of my time watching Robyn's profile in the dim light, wanting to trace every curve, every line, every hollow.

"This is a great place, Robyn," I said eventually, dragging my eyes back to the cityscape.

"Yeah," she sighed contentedly. "I love it here."

"I can see why."

She picked up her glass and held it balanced on her thigh, tracing the rim absently with a thin, elegant finger. "I'm going to miss it. I'll be gone most of the summer filming on another project. Lynne Wesson's latest. We'll be on location in the Florida Keys for about half of it, and then in New York for soundstage work."

I loved her hands. The fingers were long and slender, strong and graceful...she used her hands often when she spoke, and I'd caught myself several times that evening mesmerized by the movements of those hands.

Her words finally registered and I dragged my eyes away from her hands and leaned forward. Lynne Wesson was a hot independent director, and landing a role in one of her movies was quite a coup. "Lynne Wesson? Robyn, that's great! Hell, that's fantastic!" I touched her on the arm. "Congratulations."

She looked over at me with a pleased, slightly embarrassed smile. "Thanks. I'm a little freaked out about it, to be completely honest. I don't even know how in the hell I got the part." She laughed and shook her head. "I didn't even see the script first—I just got this call out of the blue from one of Lynne's assistants, wondering if I wanted to read for a part in her new film. Auditions were in New York and, damn, I couldn't get on the plane fast enough. I met her, and after we'd talked about five minutes—she kind of weirded me out because she kept staring at me—she told me I had the part, handed me the script, and left. I didn't even have to read for it. It was pretty damn strange, but I'm not complaining."

"I bet you're not. Have you done films before?"

"No...well, a made-for-TV thing a few years back where I had about five lines total, but nothing like this. And the part is a good one, too. The movie's about a thirty-something family man from the Midwest who just walks out on his life one day and goes to the Florida Keys to try to get some perspective but ends up getting caught up in a lot of nastiness. She's cast Lonnie Colchev as the lead, and I get to play his strung-out, ex-stripper girlfriend. The working title of the script is *Lost Key*." The excitement and pleasure in her voice was evident.

"Lynne Wesson and Lonnie Colchev? Damn, woman, that

sounds great," I said, impressed and a little awed that she was going to be in a Lynne Wesson movie. Made my summer seem pretty pathetic.

As if in answer to my thought, she asked, "Got any projects lined up this summer?"

I laughed. "Well, none as exciting as yours. Let's see...a golf tournament right after we break for the summer—and I suck at golf—a week of remodeling a house in New Mexico on the celebrity version of *Fix This House*, a couple charity 5Ks...Connie is still working on some stuff." I shrugged. "If it pans out, that's great; if not, I won't be too upset. I kinda like having the free time."

She took a sip of wine, and glanced at me curiously. "Why are you doing a golf tournament if you suck at golf?"

"Because Liz doesn't play golf, and Danny is really persuasive," I replied dryly. She raised an eyebrow, and I elaborated. "Danny is a golf freak. It's a little scary, actually, how much that game means to him. Anyway, he got asked to do this celebrity co-ed tournament, and he agreed to do it, thinking he'd get Liz to play. The two of them talk golf all the time, so Danny just assumed she played, but it turns out she doesn't. She's just an avid watcher, and so Danny asked me. But I don't think he realizes how truly awful I am at golf. He might as well just play with Liz."

She chuckled and sighed, settling back into her seat and stretching her legs out. We were quiet for several minutes, just enjoying the night and the view.

"Thanks for coming over tonight, Caid," she said finally, and looked over at me. "It's nice to get to know you better."

I thought of how much I enjoyed her company, how I liked her intelligence, her humor—and then I remembered how good she and Josh had looked together in the kitchen. My smile was bittersweet. "Yes, it is."

She took a sip of wine and looked away. "Especially since I'm going to be kissing you in a week or so."

Goddamn. The woman had all sorts of ways to leave me breathless.

"You are?" My voice cracked. Like a freaking fourteen-year-old boy.

"Mm-hmm." She went back to tracing the rim of her glass, staring at it intently. "That is, if you're sure you're okay with it. I know Grant was being kind of a dickhead yesterday and didn't give you much choice, so if you're not okay with it, I can probably talk to someone..."

"No, really. I'm okay with it." It was nice she was willing to do that, but I really was fine with it, especially now that I knew it was going to be her. *Although it would probably be better for me if it wasn't.*

"You're sure?"

"Absolutely." I frowned, and asked cautiously, "Are you?"

"Absolutely."

"Good."

"Good."

I gulped at my wine. "Uh...how does Josh feel about all this?"

She was quiet for a moment, staring at her glass. "We're not together, you know. Not a couple, I mean." She delivered the information matter-of-factly, as though she hadn't just said something that completely stunned me. Then she laughed. "Actually, Josh thinks I'm very lucky."

"Ex-excuse me?" I stammered.

"Josh thinks I'm lucky. To get a chance to kiss you —"

"No, no... I mean the 'not together' part." I sat up in my chair and put my wineglass down. "Robyn, the last time I was at the store, I saw the two of you on no less than five magazine or newspaper covers. Most of them speculating on the date of your impending nuptials, except for the one that said Josh was wildly jealous because you were pregnant with George Clooney's baby."

"Caid," she said lightly, amusement coloring her tone, "you should know as well as anyone not to believe a word of that garbage. Don't tell me you actually read those things."

"I was bored," I mumbled defensively, my head spinning with the realization that Robyn had suddenly gone from completely, unattainably safe, to something else. I didn't know what that "else" was yet, but it scared the crap out of me. "I don't..."

"Besides," she waved her hand dismissively, "I've never even met George Clooney."

The look on my face must have been priceless, because when she looked at me, she burst out laughing. "Oh, God, Caid. You are so damn cute."

She thinks I'm cute. I shook my head. I'd think about that later. Right now, I wanted her to stay on the subject. "I just spent the evening with the two of you, and you seemed pretty damned together to me. This isn't just me believing what I read in the tabloids, Robyn, this is what the entire world has been led to believe for the past few years."

She shrugged and took a sip of wine. "We're good friends and enjoy being with each other, but we're not together romantically. If the tabloids misconstrue that, that's their problem."

She seemed so nonchalant about it, and I tried to match her attitude. Honestly, I should be leaping for joy. Praising the heavens. She was — technically — single. But instead I was angry. I'm like any other human being and I don't like to be duped. Robyn presented herself to the world as one thing, while the truth was something very different. I didn't like contemplating whether there were other things about her that might not be genuine.

Conversation after that was forced; she tried to draw me out, but I was distracted by her announcement and I'm sure my answers seemed curt, verging on outright rude. When I told her I needed to head home, she didn't argue, only nodded resignedly and walked me to the door.

The mixture of sadness and confusion on her face as we said painfully polite goodbyes made me feel like an ass, and I berated myself the entire way home, trying to figure out why I'd reacted the way I had. So Robyn wasn't with Josh. So what? So they let the public think they were. So what?

What really had set me off, I realized, was my fear at her sudden change in status from forbidden to not-so-forbidden, and that was ridiculous. She was still just as straight, just as unattainable, as ever.

Wasn't she?

That was the question. All my dealings with Robyn up to now — the smiles, the slightly flirtatious banter, the touches — all that time I'd been under the impression that she was with Josh. I'd assumed she was flirtatious by nature, and touchy.

But what if...

What if.

I sighed, frustrated. With guys, it was easy. But I'd never done this before with a woman. Were the signs the same? How did you know? How could you tell what was friendship and what was more?

I let myself into my small, cottage-style house in the hills outside of La Canada, still puzzling over these questions and no closer to an answer, although I had come to the conclusion that I needed to call Robyn first thing in the morning and apologize.

She beat me to it.

The voice on my machine was hesitant and subdued. "Caid, it's Robyn. I don't know what happened, but I feel like somehow I upset you. Whatever I did, I'm sorry." There was a sigh and I could picture her running a hand through her hair. "I'd like to talk to you, please call me."

She left a number, which I automatically wrote down and then stared at.

I picked up the phone and tapped it against my forehead a few times.

Okay. You can do this. Just tell her you're sorry, that you had a nice evening — something like that.

I took a breath and punched in the numbers.

Her breathless voice answered on the fourth ring, and I basked for just a moment in the warmth that flowed through my body at the sound.

"Robyn? It's..."

"Caid." The relief in her voice was obvious and I kicked myself again for being such an ass. "Caid, I'm sorry. Whatever I did—"

"No," I stopped her. "It's me that should apologize. I'm sorry, Robyn, you just...you just surprised me, and I felt like I'd been lied to, and I overreacted."

Ohhh. Good thinking on your feet, Harris. Maybe you should go into acting.

"Oh." That stopped her, and it was several seconds before she spoke again. "I'm sorry, Caid, I never thought about it that way. Josh and I...we've never actually lied about it, but I guess lies of omission are just as bad. It's been good for both of our careers to be seen as a couple..."

"You don't owe me any explanation, Robyn. It's your business and I had no right to act the way I did."

She sighed. "Caid, I like you. Very much. I haven't felt...I haven't had a new...friend...in a long time. That's why I told you tonight." She paused, and continued quietly, "I'm sorry if you felt as though I'd lied to you. I didn't do it purposely. Josh and I, we've just been doing this so long..."

"Are you running in the morning?" I asked abruptly. I didn't want to hear her apologize any more for my stupid behavior.

A beat.

"Yes," came the hesitant answer.

"When?"

"Usually at six-thirty or so." No hesitation this time.

"Where?"

"Silver Lake trail. I start out from here, there's an entrance about five blocks down the hill."

"I'll see you at six-thirty, then."

Another pause, then she laughed. "Deal."

WHEN I PULLED into Robyn's drive the next morning, she was already out front, pushing against the garage door and stretching out her calves. She wore mid-calf black running tights and a gray and black zip-up top against the morning chill, both items hugging the flat planes and subtle curves of her body, accentuating her athletic build and long limbs. I'd been hoping she wouldn't run in shorts, not knowing if I could function with a view of her bare legs, but I wasn't so sure this was any better.

I took a deep, calming breath, got out of the car and walked over.

She smiled a greeting, pulling her hair back into a tight ponytail as I approached. "Morning."

"Morning."

"Gonna be warm enough?" she asked with a teasing grin. I had chosen loose navy blue running pants, a gray hooded sweatshirt with the sleeves cut out, and a lightweight white skull hat. It was a cold morning, and I hated running cold, especially my ears. Compared to Robyn, though, I looked like a thug.

I smiled back at the jab, wondering if I should bring up the night before or wait for her to do it.

"Ready to go?" she asked, bouncing on her toes a few times.

Or maybe we wouldn't talk about it at all. That was okay by me.

"Sure."

She nodded and set off down the drive at a good clip. I chased after her and settled into step on her left. I'd been right about those endless legs of hers; she had a long, easy stride and I could tell immediately I was going to have my work cut out for me this morning.

I felt a competitive spark flare inside me and did my best to squelch it. I didn't know how far Robyn planned to run, and already her pace was faster than my usual speed. I'd end up killing myself if I tried to outrun her.

Robyn told me during one of our few spurts of conversation that the trail around Silver Lake was just over two and a half miles long, and she usually ran it twice. I was welcome to go further if I wanted.

"Twice is fine," I assured her hastily, trying to keep from showing that I was already breathing heavily.

I did myself proud for four miles, keeping up with her stride for stride. Then she glanced over at me with a wicked grin.

Damn.

I was about to get crushed.

She lengthened her stride and I managed to keep up for another hundred yards before my lack of breakfast and lack of sleep the night before caught up with me. At least that's what I told myself.

Soon Robyn was just a speck in the distance, and I shook my head with a wry grin, slowing down and finishing the last mile at a more comfortable pace.

She was sitting against a tree on the grass, pretending to take a nap, when I jogged up and collapsed beside her, breathing heavily. She opened one eye and looked over at me with a lazy grin. "I was wondering when you'd show up."

"Bite me, Ward," I growled through heavy breaths, shedding

my sweatshirt and wiping the sweat from my arms and face with it before tossing it to the side. I groaned and leaned back on my elbows, closing my eyes and listening to my breathing and heart rate slow. Underneath the sweatshirt, I'd worn a gray and white bra top that ended a few inches above my navel, and the early morning sun felt good on the damp, exposed skin of my stomach and shoulders. I sighed in pleasure and turned to Robyn to comment on how quickly it had warmed up. The words stuck in my throat when I saw the look on her face as she watched the rise and fall of my stomach. She seemed...enthralled would be a good word for it, I guess.

I tensed in reaction, and she flicked a glance at my face before looking away quickly "Nice morning," she said, and picked at the grass under her hand.

"Sure is," I replied when I was able. "Warmed up quick."

"Supposed to rain this weekend, though." She held up several blades of grass and let them go, watching as they floated away in the breeze.

"Well, we could use the moisture." I watched the grass fall to the ground between us.

"Yeah, they're predicting a pretty bad fire season this year."

Jesus.

Add a line or two about crop yield and the "damn city-folks who keep building their mansions in the middle of farmland" and this was the exact conversation I'd had with my grandfather about a million times. I never expected to be having it with Robyn.

I rolled on my side and propped my head on my hand. "Robyn..." I was silent until she met my gaze. "I'm sorry about last night. I was having a really nice time, and I feel like I ruined it. I haven't had a new friend in a while either...I hope we can try again some time."

She looked down at the grass again, then back at me. "How about Friday?"

I felt the smile spread across my face. "Really?"

She smiled back. "Eight o'clock again?"

"That's fine, but I can probably get off a little earlier. Unless they change the shooting schedule, we're on the sets all day. I should be finished by seven at the latest."

"Why don't you just come over whenever you can, then?" She paused, thinking. "I might be a little later than that, myself. Josh will be here, though. Uh...oh." She bit her lip. "If that's okay?"

"That Josh is at your house?"

She nodded.

"Robyn." Again, I waited until she met my gaze. "I wasn't just being nice when I said Josh was a sweetheart. I like him, very much. Of course I wouldn't mind. Why do you think I would?"

She brushed her hands off on her pants and pushed herself to her feet. "Come on, let's walk back." She reached down, and after a brief hesitation, I grabbed her hand and let her pull me up. I scooped up my sweatshirt and tossed it over my shoulder.

We started walking and she looked over at me. "Caid, when I talked about me and Josh before...you kinda wigged out."

"I didn't...it wasn't..." I sighed. "It wasn't about Josh. It was never about Josh, really." I glanced over at her. "Tell me about the two of you? I didn't stay around last night long enough to hear the whole story."

She was quiet for a while and then started speaking as we left the trail and started up the street. "Josh and I met at school. UCLA," she said. "I was two years ahead of him, but we both played sports. He was on the tennis team, obviously, and I played some volleyball — we met at an athletic awards banquet and hit if off immediately. Like you said, he's a sweetheart. We dated through most of college, even lived together for a while.

"And then I graduated and went off to Europe to model, and Josh joined the circuit. We decided not to do the long-distance thing, but kept in touch for the next few years, on and off. I moved back to the US, to New York, and we'd see each other occasionally, but then when I came back to LA, we started seeing each other a lot, just as friends. We'd always made better friends than lovers, and we'd both...changed a lot in that time apart."

She glanced at me, and I nodded encouragement but stayed quiet. "Josh had just broken the top fifty at that point and was trying to find some sponsors, and I was only managing to pick up some minor acting gigs, but together," she shrugged, "we got noticed."

"The year I moved back to LA, I flew out to New York to watch him play in the US Open. I watched a few of his practices, we went out a few times before the matches started and then the morning after the first match, my agent called. He'd gotten over fifty inquiries about me. And Josh was getting some interest suddenly from sponsors..." She shook her head. "It was surreal for both of us. We were both nothing, then suddenly, the press was all over us.

"Anyway," she said as we got to the top of the hill, "needless to say, both our agents pushed us to do things together, and, hell...I love Josh. He's my best friend. I don't want to sleep with him anymore, but I love him like family. It's no hardship for me to do things with him, and it's certainly good for my career." She shrugged. "So that's the story."

"So..." I didn't know if I really wanted to know this, but I asked anyway. "What if one of you..."

"Wants to date? Finds someone they're really interested in?" She paused, and made quoting motions with her fingers. "Falls in love?"

"Uh, yeah." I said, wondering at the mocking tone in her voice.

She shrugged again. "It's never been an issue before. When we started doing things together again, we were both just out of bad relationships and neither of us was looking to get serious with someone. We didn't have any fantasies about getting back together; we were just spending time with each other and being seen. We—both of us—have always pursued things on the side..."

"Things?" I repeated. I didn't like how she'd said that.

"People, affairs, trysts, whatever you want to call them. I know Josh sees other women sometimes, and he knows that I...have lovers, too." She looked slightly embarrassed. "Neither of us are saints, Caid, far from it. But we're both aware of the fact that what we do affects the other, and we're discreet...and so far, it's worked out."

"Uh, wow. Okay..." I wasn't quite sure what to say. Congratulations, nice ruse?

We walked for a block in silence, until we turned onto Robyn's street.

"So," she asked hesitantly, "do you still want to have dinner on Friday?"

"Of course," I said, silencing any internal objections.

"Great," she replied, smiling hugely.

We turned into her drive. "Wanna come in for a bit? Have some coffee?"

I checked my watch, thought for a second, then shook my head. "I need to go home before I go to the set," I said regretfully.

"Next time, bring your clothes and you can change here."

I fought back a grin. "Okay."

As we walked up to my car, I unlocked the doors with the key fob clipped inside the pocket of my pants and pulled the door open.

Robyn stopped beside me and gently patted the car's roof. "Heya, Twila."

She talked to my car.

If I wasn't careful, I'd fall head over heels for this woman.

There was a good chance I already had.

I slid into the driver's seat and put the key in the ignition, turning it partway, enough to roll down the window but not start the engine.

Robyn leaned in, smiling. "Thanks for the run."

I snorted. "Thanks for the whompin'."

She laughed, and I grinned up at her. "That wasn't really fair, you know."

"What?" she asked innocently.

"You said when you used to run with Josh, he crushed you." I allowed myself a glance up her long frame. "I imagine you kept up with him just fine."

"I said he *tried* to crush me," she corrected, placing her hands on the windowsill and gently closing the door. She leaned against the frame for a moment. "I never said he succeeded." She winked and walked away, whistling.

I laughed and started the car.

Yep, a very good chance I already had.

Chapter
Five

"NICE JOB, LIZ, Caid...you too, Danny." Nate Wiley rapped on his bound script and pointed at the three of us on the set. "That one will work fine; let's print it and move on. You three are off for now—check with Addy for when we need you back." He turned and raised his voice further. "Micah, Henry, Joe, Arturo, Irene...you're up. Extras for twelve, check in with Brent. Brent, where are you?"

There was a whistle from across the stage. "Over here!"

The director pointed. "Check in with Brent over there. Regulars, let's get this blocked out, and do a run-through..."

"Thank God," Liz sighed, blowing a stray piece of hair out of her eyes and rolling the tension from her neck. "I thought he was going to make us go again."

I just grunted, arching my back until it popped.

"I thought we nailed it the first time," Danny grumbled. "Picky damn bastard."

There was no venom in his words—we all liked Nate, and trusted his direction.

The three of us moved off the Squad Room set where we'd done the last scene, dodging members of the crew who darted around purposefully in the organized, tightly controlled synchrony that always accompanied the shoots that Nate directed.

"Danny, back here in forty-five," yelled Addison Couch, a small, curly-haired man who was several yards away, conferring with the lighting tech. "Liz, we need you here at one, and Caid..." he consulted the clipboard in his hands, "two thirty, Interrogation."

We all nodded, and headed for the back exit the warehouse.

"Caid, hang on a sec," Addy called, and I paused expectantly, noting that Liz had stopped at the door and was waiting for me. He finished his conversation with the lighting tech and walked over to me, flipping through the papers on his clipboard. Eventually he pulled out a small envelope and handed it to me. "This came with a script delivery from *ITD*..."

I frowned, but took the envelope. I'd only done one guest spot on *In Their Defense*, and to my knowledge, I wasn't up for another any time in the near future, so I wondered what this was for. "Thanks, Addy," I said distractedly, looking at the envelope. It was small, invitation or note card size, with my name written in bold, very precise capital letters on the front. There were no other markings on it.

I felt Liz move over beside me. "What's that for?"

I shrugged. "I don't know. As far as I know, I don't have anything going on over there."

I slipped a finger under the flap and drew out a small card.

Caid,

> I'll give you a chance to redeem yourself. Tomorrow, same time and place.
> Loser buys coffee, winner gets taunting rights.

Robyn

The grin that split my face was huge and I laughed out loud. Several crewmembers stopped what they were doing to stare. Okay, more than several. In fact, just about all of them. I'm not known for my spontaneous laughter.

"Caid?" Liz was frowning, and she looked genuinely concerned. "Are you okay?"

Jeez, can't a woman laugh like an idiot anymore?

"I'm fine," I answered, dimming the wattage of my smile but still thinking of Robyn. "Just fine."

Liz shrugged and started walking toward the door. "Paula's picking up from that Thai place you like so much. Come by in ten."

It was not optional.

I'd managed to avoid talking with Liz since the "have you ever wanted to kiss a woman?" incident, but it didn't look like I was going to be able to avoid it any longer. I sighed internally and nodded. "See you in a bit." At least she made the effort to get something I liked.

In my trailer, I gratefully pulled off the black, lightweight jacket I'd worn for the last scene and hung it neatly on the back of the door. I unclipped the leather holster and rubber prop gun from my hip and clipped it on the hanger with the jacket so I wouldn't forget it, and then looked down at the wine colored V-neck shirt I wore. After a moment of debate, I stripped it off too, hung it on a different hanger, and pulled on the tank top I'd worn to the set that morning. Zoe in wardrobe would kill me if I dribbled *pad thai* all over the V-neck and they had to find something similar to finish up with today.

I checked my cell for messages: one from my agent, Connie, who wanted to know my thoughts about shampoo commercials, and one from my brother, Perry. He and a friend were hiking a two-week section of the Pacific Crest Trail in June, ending up in Big Bear. I'd agreed to send them a resupply package in Idyllwild and, when they were through, pick the two up in Big Bear, let them stay with me a few days, and put them on a plane back to Madison, where they were both in school at UW. Perry was calling to confirm dates and try to taunt me into joining him on the trip, clucking like a chicken and spouting insults about my advanced age in some kind of weird Slavic accent that made me chuckle.

I made a mental note to call him later when I had more time, then phoned Connie back and left her a reminder that I'd just gotten out of doing commercials and I didn't want to get back into them any time soon. Finally, after some hesitation, I called Tricia at the admin office's main switchboard and talked her out of Robyn's cell number. I only felt slightly guilty about lying to get the number—I didn't think Robyn would mind.

I dialed the number, expecting, and hoping, to get voicemail, but that raspy voice answered on the third ring. "Yeah?" She sounded annoyed at the interruption and I winced. Maybe I shouldn't have called her on the set.

Too late now.

"I got your message, Ward, and you got a deal," I told her, "but let's make it Ledos Canyon at six...we'll see how those pencil-legs do in some real terrain. Six o'clock, woman—be there." I heard her laughter as I hung up and smiled like a Cheshire cat.

After puttering around for a while longer, my ten minutes were up, and I strolled over to Liz's trailer, hopefully ready for whatever she wanted to discuss. I knocked on the trailer door and let myself in; Paula was sitting at a desk at the far end of the trailer, talking rapidly into her headset while working away on her laptop. Liz looked up guiltily from a bowl of noodles, slurping them up hurriedly.

"Sorry, I was starving. Couldn't wait," she said when the noodles were chewed enough that she could talk.

I shrugged and started poking around in the other containers, my mouth watering at the smell.

"This one's yours," she tapped a container with her chopsticks, "extra sauce, and spicy."

"Oh, yum. Thanks."

We both dug in hungrily, eating for several minutes without

talking, the only sound in the room Paula's voice and her furious typing.

Liz eventually sighed and sat back, stabbing at the noodles. "You took off fast after shooting wrapped last night. Hot date?" Another few stabs at the defenseless noodles, then a sly look up at me. "Was it a woman?"

I concentrated very hard on swallowing and not choking, finally managing after a few swigs from a bottle of water Liz calmly handed me. "Jesus, Liz." I coughed, and took another sip. "At least wait until I'm not eating to throw shit like that at me."

"Shit like what? It's just a simple question, or rather two simple questions." Seeing that I wasn't going to give her water back any time soon, she leaned over and grabbed another out of the mini-fridge. "One: was it a hot date?"

I shook my head. "No, it was not a hot date. I went to dinner—"

She pounced on that. "With a woman?"

"Well, one of them was—"

"Oh, Caid, a threesome?" She looked at me speculatively. "I never pegged you for the type."

I rolled my eyes. "Liz, do you want to know what I did last night or not? Do I even need to be present for this conversation?"

"So you didn't have a threesome?"

"No, I did not."

This seemed to disappoint her greatly and she stared at me intently. "Did you want to? Because in those online story thingies, lots of the women seemed to want to have threesomes."

"Jesus." I put my food down with a sigh.

"Is that a lesbian thing?" She looked at me expectantly.

"I wouldn't know, Liz." *Maybe I will someday, but I sure don't now.*

"But you've wanted to kiss a woman, though, right?"

I suddenly noticed the silence in the trailer. Paula had stopped typing and was looking at me, her mouth an astonished little "O."

Shit.

"Liz..."

"Because, you know, that makes you an almost lesbian, right?" She nodded, as though it were obvious. "So, who *did* you go out with last night? Oh...was it the same person who sent you that note today? I don't think I've ever seen you smile like that, Caid, without food being involved. It must have been..."

"I had dinner with Robyn, and Josh Riley," I cut in before she could get rolling about why I might be getting notes that made me smile.

That stopped her. "Really?"

"Really."

"What's Josh Riley like? Is he as attractive in person? *Ohhh,* those blue eyes and those cute, sexy little buns..."

Well, at least we were off the subject of me kissing women.

"...but I've heard that he cheats on her when he's on tour. Marty said that Ken said that Anthony said that he met this girl at a club in Rio who swears she spent the night with Josh Riley..."

"What?"

Maybe Josh needed to work on his discretion.

"Oh, who knows if it's true or not, you know how Anthony is with the girls..."

Indeed I did know how Anthony was with the girls, having made the mistake of letting Liz set me up with him once, and the even greater mistake of dating him for a few weeks. A very pretty man with a serious coke problem and a desperate need to be liked, Anthony would say anything to anyone if he thought it would make him more popular.

"...so, what did you think of him?"

"Josh? I thought he was very nice..." I could tell she expected more. "And he's gorgeous. Much better in person."

That seemed to satisfy her and she sat back with a tiny smile on her face. Then she leaned forward. "Did you ever want to kiss me?"

Jesus. Sometimes, conversations with Liz had more unexpected bounces than a ping-pong match. I cleared my throat and looked over at Paula who was typing again, or at least pretending to. "No, Liz, I never wanted to kiss you."

"Why not! What's wrong with me?"

I sighed. "There's nothing wrong with you..."

"Don't you think I'm attractive? For God's sake, I'm one of *People's* 100 Most Beautiful People!"

"Of course you're attractive, Liz," I said in exasperation, "I just don't want to kiss you, okay?"

"You don't?"

"No, I don't."

She crossed her arms and pouted. "Why?"

"Because you're my friend, Liz." A horrible thought struck me. "You don't want to kiss me, do you?" I asked fearfully.

"God, no." She looked shocked. "Oh, Caid, *ewww!*"

"Hey..." I started to protest, but thought better of it.

"So, do you want to kiss Paula?"

There was a squeak from the other end of the room and the pace of typing increased.

"No, I don't want to kiss Paula," I said with a slight smile.

Liz looked at me intently. "So, who have you wanted to kiss?"

I felt like I was in Junior High playing a game of Truth or Dare, and shook my head.

"*Caaaaiiiidd...*" she whined. I smiled, but kept my mouth shut.

"I'll get it out of you," she promised, and I was certain she was right.

But not today.

Chapter
Six

THE MUSCLES IN my legs were screaming and my lungs burned, but I forced myself to keep going, dodging a hiker and nearly tripping over his dog before spinning and continuing on.

Almost there, almost there, almost there...

I was going to beat her this time, goddammit. I gritted my teeth and pushed harder. Sweat dripped in my eyes and I didn't have the energy to wipe it away, not wanting to break the rhythm of my swinging arms, expecting any second that Robyn would cruise by me, not even breathing hard.

I could see the rim, only fifty yards away.

I pushed harder. Twenty-five yards. Twenty.

I could see the sign for the trailhead, see people milling around it, someone sitting on a bench...

Robyn.

Sitting on the bench, looking like she just stepped out of a Nike commercial, not like she just ran three miles up hill.

Sonofabitch.

I slowed to an abrupt stop, gasping for air. My legs felt shaky and I put my hands on my knees, closing my eyes and fighting off a spell of lightheadedness. Footsteps approached along the path and I opened my eyes, still struggling for breath. A pair of running shoes came into my line of vision, attached to two black-clad legs.

I coughed and straightened slowly, still slightly dizzy.

"Don't...*gasp*...say it...*gasp*...Ward," I warned, and coughed again, looking over at her.

As I watched, the slightly cocky, taunting grin she'd been wearing was chased off her face by wide-eyed concern. "Christ, Caid." She stepped forward and placed a steadying hand on my back. "Are you all right?"

I just nodded and coughed, bending over again until my breathing finally eased a little. Robyn didn't say anything, but she didn't move away, her hand on my back making slow, gentle circles.

I straightened finally and stifled a disappointed sigh as she dropped her hand. I pulled my cap from my head and ran a hand through wet hair.

Lovely.

She wordlessly handed me a water bottle and I gulped greedily. "Thanks."

I handed it back and pulled at the front of my sweatshirt to create a slight breeze to cool the rest of my body, glancing at Robyn, who was still looking at me worriedly. After a moment's hesitation, I pulled the sweatshirt over my head and mopped my face with it.

Yeah, I'm looking real attractive now. I shook my head ruefully. "How in the heck did you get up here so fast?" I finally asked when I had enough oxygen left over for talking. "And how'd you get past me?"

"I, ah, went a different way," she said evasively, a glimmer of humor in her eyes.

I put my hands on my hips and frowned. "I didn't know there was another way. Just the maintenance road..."

She started laughing, backing slowly away from me.

"...and they only allow maintenance vehicles on that path," I puzzled before it finally clicked. "You got a *ride*?"

She held out her hands. "I'm sorry, Caid, I didn't know you'd try to kill yourself..."

I stalked toward her and she backpedaled faster, laughing outright. When I lunged, she yelped and sprinted away, still laughing over her shoulder.

I started after her, my own laughter welling up helplessly. I felt happy and giddy chasing Robyn across the parking lot like we were a couple of kids, with no thought of what I'd do if I actually caught her.

Until I did.

She headed for a forest green Range Rover that I recognized as hers, slowing to pull something — probably the remote entry — out of her pocket. I pressed my advantage and caught her just as she was reaching for the car door, wrapping my arms around her from behind and holding tightly.

"Not so fast, young lady," I growled in her ear, still laughing and delighting in her return laughter. Until the scent of her hair in my face and the heat from her skin, just inches from my lips, registered.

Until I noticed the press of my breasts against her back and the feel of my arms across her stomach and the sudden, absolute stillness of her body.

Neither of us was laughing any more.

"Caid." Her voice was soft, with a slight tremor.

My arms tightened involuntarily, then loosened, falling to my sides as I slowly stepped back.

She turned around slowly and in that moment—that moment before the mask dropped back into place—I knew. Saw the flash of it, felt the heat...

Robyn wanted me.

I'd had that look directed at me enough to know, and I knew.

Robyn Ward wanted me.

Then the mask fell back in place and we stared at each other for long moments. I wanted to push her against the car and kiss her senseless. I wanted to bury my face in her neck, to wrap my arms around her and not let go.

Instead, I smiled shakily and took another tiny step back. "You cheated."

And you're a chickenshit, Harris.

She looked as though she was going to take a step forward and close the distance between us, but then she leaned back against the car and smiled slightly. "Guess that means I owe you coffee."

"Hey, lady!" The yell behind me startled us both. I turned to find a young boy, probably no older than eleven, jogging in our direction, holding out a gray wad of cloth in one hand and a smaller white bundle in the other. "This your stuff? My mom said you dropped it back there."

I stepped forward to meet him and sheepishly took my sweatshirt and hat, thanking him and getting an absent "uh-huh" in response before he jogged away, back to his parents. I turned to find Robyn inside her car, staring at her steering wheel with intense concentration.

I stepped over. "You trying to start the car through the power of your mind? I bet the key would work better."

That only got a tiny smile. "Caid, I'm sorry, but I'm going to have to get you back on the coffee, okay? I just remembered a thing I need to do."

I blinked. "Uh...okay, sure." I stepped back hastily as she started the car and put it in gear. "Robyn?"

But she just waved briefly and pulled away.

I walked to my car slowly, pulling on my sweatshirt.

What the hell just happened?

FRIDAY MORNING ROBYN left a message canceling dinner that evening, saying she was going out of town.

Saturday morning her picture was in the paper. With Josh. The two had been photographed coming out of The Mondrian, a new

LA hotspot, the night before. When she was supposedly out of town. I stared at the picture for a long time, surprised at the intensity of the betrayal I felt.

Sunday morning I went mountain biking, pushing myself hard and taking risks, hoping to push thoughts of Robyn out of my head with adrenaline.

Sunday afternoon after a two-hour stop at the emergency room, I limped into my house with a swollen jaw, bruised ribs, several nasty scratches and a two-thousand-dollar bike in the back of my truck that was probably totaled.

And Robyn was still in my head.

The phone rang as I was loading the blender with ice for an icepack. I let the blender run and took the phone out of the kitchen as I answered.

It was Liz. "Caid, where are you? We expected you hours ago."

I could hear voices in the background and could tell instantly that she was at least one drink on the wrong side of one drink too many. I heard someone in the background—it sounded like Danny—asking very loudly where the fuck I was.

Crap. I'd totally forgotten. Danny's house-warming at his new place in West Hollywood.

"Ah, shit, Liz, I forgot about it. I went biking this morning..."

"You *forgot*?"

I winced, pulling the phone back slightly from my ear. My head throbbed, my jaw ached, and my ribs—my ribs felt like someone had taken a baseball bat to them repeatedly. "Yeah, I'm sorry. Listen, tell Danny..."

"Now that you've been reminded, get your butt over here!" She giggled wildly.

Make that two or three drinks.

"I can't, Liz." I walked back into the kitchen and turned off the blender. Holding the phone to my ear with my shoulder, I poured the crushed ice into a large Ziploc baggie, refilled the blender, and started it up again.

"Of course you can. Just get in that shiny little car of yours and start driving. It'll take you thirty minutes, tops." She paused. "What in the world is that noise? Where are you?"

"I'm at home. You just called me on my home phone, remember?"

"No one likes a smart-ass, Caid." I didn't answer, biting back a groan as I pulled up my shirt and placed the ice on my battered ribs. I pulled the stretchy material down over the bag to hold it in place, then turned off the blender and filled another, smaller bag. "Caid, what are you doing? Why can't you come?"

I thought about making up an excuse, but Liz, along with

everyone else, would see the damage in the morning anyway. "I crashed my bike this morning, and right now I'm putting ice on various parts of my body that didn't fare so well when I went flying over the handlebars at twenty miles an hour and rolled down a hill."

It took her a while to decipher it—I could hear people talking to her in the background, and her trying to shush them and concentrate on what I'd just said. "You crashed? Caid, are you all right?"

I smiled. She really could be very sweet. "Yes, I'm okay. The hospital people said..."

"The *hospital*?" she gasped. "You're at the *hospital*?"

Okay. Maybe the entire truth hadn't been necessary.

I sighed and held the smaller bag to my jaw. "No, Liz, remember, I'm at home? Where you called me?"

"But, Caid, you said the hospital people—"

"Liz," I interrupted firmly, sensing a mini Liz freak-out coming and forestalling it. "I was at the hospital to get checked out. Now, I'm home. I'm fine. Well, I'm not completely fine, but I will be. But I don't feel up to coming to Danny's party, all right?"

"But, Caid..."

"I'm fine," I said again, even more firmly. "Go have fun, Liz, and I'll see you tomorrow. Tell Danny I'm sorry, okay?"

"Caid..."

"Bye." I hung up the phone and limped into the bedroom, removing the ice under my shirt and struggling out of my biking outfit into a pair of cutoff sweats and a baggy T-shirt. Finally, I lowered myself onto the couch, put the icepacks back in place on my ribs and jaw, and closed my eyes.

The icepacks had become lukewarm bags of water and it was near dusk when the doorbell roused me from sleep. I automatically moved to get off the couch, but fell back with a groan as the various aches and bruises I'd gathered earlier in the day made themselves known.

"Hang on!" I croaked and cautiously tried to sit up again. It was painful but bearable as long as I moved slowly, and eventually I shuffled my way to the front entryway. The form on my doorstep, even distorted by four inches of glass block window, was unmistakable.

Robyn.

The jumble of anger and gladness, longing and hurt that washed through me at the sight of her confused the hell out of me and only intensified when I pulled the door open and saw the magnitude of her relief when she saw me.

"Caid," she said breathlessly in that damned smoky, bedroom, honey-soaked voice of hers.

I gripped the door tightly, waiting for the now-familiar emotional havoc that Robyn created inside me to subside. "Robyn," I managed neutrally when it passed. "What are you doing here?"

She ignored the question, cataloging my scraped face and arms, bruised jaw, and pain-stiffened posture with the intensity of a medical resident. "Oh, baby, are you okay?" She stepped forward, and before I could move away, I was pulled tightly against her, engulfed in long, strong arms. I fought it for all of five milliseconds and then relaxed into the embrace, resting my cheek against her neck and soaking up her warmth.

It felt...amazing.

She smelled slightly of cigarette smoke and cooking spices; party smells that told me how she knew I'd been hurt. Underneath was the faint floral scent she wore, the one that clung to the sweatshirt of hers that I still had, the one that lingered in our trailer even when she wasn't there.

I breathed it in — breathed her in — and felt her arms tighten in response.

I gasped as a knife of pain from my ribs sliced through my haze of hug-induced euphoria. "Ow. Shit..."

Robyn released me immediately and stepped back as though stung.

"My ribs." I blew out a steadying breath as the pain eased.

She stood with her hands partially outstretched, looking uncertain, wanting to help but not knowing what to do. At this distance I remembered what had immediately flown from my head the moment Robyn had touched me. She had lied to me, and I was supposed to be angry with her.

"Robyn, why are you here?" I repeated my earlier question and the look of concern she had been giving my ribs turned to a tiny frown at my tone.

"I dropped by Danny's party. Liz told me that you'd been in an accident, a crash of some sort. I couldn't get any more information out of her, so I volunteered to come see how you were." She paused, and asked tentatively, "That bike in the truck?" She glanced behind her in the drive to where a beat-up pickup was parked next to Twila. In the bed lay a red mountain bike, its front rim bent almost in half, the fork twisted, and the handlebars skewed at an odd angle. "Was that..."

I nodded, not looking at the bike. Every time I looked at it, I realized that it could have been much, much worse. If I hadn't been wearing a helmet... I shivered and yawned, suddenly realizing I was very, very tired. "Thank you for coming by, Robyn. You can tell everyone I'm fine. I need to go sit down." I stepped back and started to close the door.

Her frown deepened. "Caid..."

I stopped with the door half-closed, waiting.

"Can I come in for a while?"

I didn't have enough energy to say no, so I just turned and walked into the kitchen, leaving the door open for her to either come in or not. While I slept, the ice machine in my freezer had made enough ice for another couple of icepacks; I filled the blender up and started it crunching. I limped into the living room to retrieve the bags I'd used before, noticing as I crossed the hall that Robyn had stepped inside and was watching me, her dark eyes following my every jerky, painful move.

I dumped the water out of the larger bag, refilled it with ice, and started the blender, motioning to the refrigerator as Robyn stepped into the kitchen. "Forgive me if I'm not up to being hostess today. Help yourself to whatever—there's beer or juice, and some white wine in the fridge, red in the cabinet...whiskey, and some scotch too."

She didn't say anything, but her eyes never left me.

I stopped the blender and filled up the smaller bag, then took them both into the living room, flipped on the television, found a baseball game, and gingerly lowered myself on the couch. I pulled up my shirt to check the swelling and heard her startled intake of breath.

She crossed the room in two long strides and sank onto the couch beside me, reaching out to run gentle fingers across the swollen, blue-black scrape along my ribs.

I swallowed my own startled intake of breath as pinpoints of sensation from the gentle touch skittered along my nerves, straight to my nipples and groin.

Jesus.

I gently but quickly moved her hand away, placed an icepack on the swelling, and pulled my shirt down over it.

She was watching me when I looked up from my task. "Looks like it hurts some."

I smiled slightly and shifted around on the couch, trying to find a more comfortable position. "Some," I replied.

She stood and propped two loose pillows against the end of the couch. "Come on, lie down." She patted the pillows. I hesitated and she patted the pillows again. "Caid, lie down for God's sake. You'll be more comfortable and you won't have to hold the ice on your ribs." She grasped my shoulders and gently lowered me onto the pillows, then carefully swung my feet up onto the couch. "There, that wasn't so bad, was it?"

She busied herself arranging the pillows behind my head, and I just watched her, warmed by the concern in her eyes. She stopped and looked down at me, gently moving aside the smaller icepack that I was holding to my jaw and tracing the swelling with a feather-light touch. "You're a mess," she said quietly and smiled, brushing a stray hair off my forehead. As always, the rush took my breath away and it was a few seconds before I could speak.

"I'm mad at you, you know." I grabbed the hand that had brushed my forehead and held it captive. "Why did you lie to me, Robyn? About Friday night? And why did you take off the other morning?"

Her whole body stilled and she withdrew her hand from mine, straightening slowly.

"FYI," I said with a hint of sarcasm, "if you're going lie to people about being out of town, it's best not to run around in public as one-half of the most photographed couple on the planet."

"Caid..."

I struggled to a sitting position, ignoring the pain, not willing to have this conversation lying on my back with her looming over me. "Damn it, Robyn, if you don't want me around, then just fucking tell me. Don't lie to me about it. I'm not a stalker—you don't need to trick me to get me to leave you alone."

"Oh, no, Caid...no." She sat down next to me and grabbed my hand, holding it between both of hers. "No, no, no. Caid, you are so wrong." She waited until I met her gaze. "So wrong. I...Caid, believe me, I want you around and I certainly don't want you to leave me alone."

"Then why..." My voice trailed off as she closed her eyes.

"I wanted to see you on Friday, I just..." She opened her eyes again and stared at me intently. I blinked, fighting to keep my eyes open, but my eyelids felt heavy, my ribs were throbbing, and my jaw ached painfully.

She smiled gently and pushed me back on the pillows, then stood and lifted my feet back onto the couch. She brushed a hand through my hair and said, "You need to rest. We'll talk about this later, okay? Just know that I don't want you to leave me alone, and I'm very sorry about Friday. It was a stupid, thoughtless thing to do."

"Robyn..."

"Shhh." She put her fingers against my lips and leaned forward to kiss my forehead. "Sleep now."

I had a million questions, but fatigue won out. I sighed and closed my eyes. "Will you stay? For a while?" I mumbled, cringing at how needy I sounded, but too tired to really care.

"I'll be right here, baby."

Baby.

That was the second time she'd called me baby.

I smiled, feeling light fingers running through my hair, and drifted off to sleep.

SOMETIME DURING THE night Robyn shook me awake, led me into the bedroom, and tucked me into bed. I vaguely remembered grumbling in annoyance at being woken, light laughter, and a fleeting touch of lips on my forehead.

It was still dark the next morning when I was yanked from sleep by a stab of pain in my ribs when I attempted to roll over. I lay for several minutes, trying to fall back to sleep, but eventually gave up and painfully eased myself out of bed and shuffled out of my bedroom on a quest for caffeine. I flipped on the hallway and living room lights, and nearly jumped out of my skin when I saw a body sprawled on my couch.

Robyn.

Every sleeping, tousled, glorious inch of her.

Holy shit.

I must have said it out loud because her eyes snapped open in alarm and her body jerked halfway off the couch before she saw me and relaxed, favoring me with a look of warm, sleepy affection that made me smile involuntarily in response.

"Morning." She propped herself up on one elbow and ran a hand through her long hair, glancing around groggily before her eyes settled on me again. "How are you feeling?"

Oh, what that voice did to me. It moved through my body from the inside out, twisting my stomach and tingling in my toes and fingers.

She was looking at me curiously, and I realized I should probably answer her and not just gape like a lust-struck teenager. "Ah..." I started roughly, and cleared my throat. "Good morning. I didn't expect anyone to be here—you startled me."

"Sorry." She pushed the quilt aside and sat up, rubbing her neck. "I didn't want you to be alone in case you needed something during the night. You looked pretty beat up last night."

"And I feel pretty beat up this morning," I said wryly. "Thanks. That was very nice of you."

"You're quite welcome." She smiled, then yawned and stretched her long arms over her head.

It was adorable and sexy all at the same time and I turned away before I got caught staring again. "Want some coffee? I was just about to make some."

"Please."

I grinned at the eagerness in her voice. "It'll just take a minute."

I put water on to boil, ground some beans, and filled the bottom of the French press, hoping Robyn liked her coffee strong. While the water heated, I looked in the refrigerator and found some eggs, peppers, mushrooms, and a small block of cheddar cheese.

I stuck my head around the corner. "Hey." She was folding the quilt and draping it over the back of the couch, and looked at me questioningly. "I've got peppers, mushrooms, and cheese. I was going to make myself an omelet. Would you like one?"

She shook her head. "Thanks, Caid, but you don't have to do that."

I shrugged. "I'm making myself one—it wouldn't be any trouble and it's the least I could do for you staying last night."

She hesitated and then smiled in thanks. "That sounds good, thank you."

"No problem." I moved back into the kitchen where the kettle was just starting to boil. I pulled it off the burner and filled the press with the steaming liquid, very conscious that Robyn had followed me and was leaning in the doorway, watching.

When I'd put the kettle back on the stove and turned to face her, she was somehow standing right in front of me. "Now that we've got some better light, let's take a look at the damage, hmm?"

She laid her hand along my neck, her thumb against my chin, and turned my head to one side to survey my jaw, pursing her lips. She used her other hand to hold my hair off my forehead while she looked at the scrapes along my forehead and cheek. She was so close I could feel the heat coming off her skin, still warm from sleep. I tried to suppress a shiver at the touch, the heat, but failed. Robyn's eyes flicked to mine and held me, barely breathing, for several long moments before finally looking back at my damaged jaw.

"Jaw doesn't look near as bad as I expected," she murmured, dropping her hands. "And Jules shouldn't have a problem covering those scrapes up."

I sagged against the counter weakly, my body still singing from her nearness. Before I could react, she'd pulled my shirt up just below my breasts and was running a light finger across the bruise on my ribs.

"Jesus," I hissed as the touch had the exact same effect that it had had the night before and body parts that I didn't need tingling at the moment started to tingle.

Robyn misread my reaction as pain and jerked her hand back quickly, looking up at me apologetically. "Sorry." She pulled my shirt down and smoothed the fabric over my stomach absently a few times before stepping back.

"S'all right," I replied after a couple of deep breaths. "Just a little tender."

I turned back to the counter and busied myself with finishing the coffee, pouring out two mugs, and getting a carton of half and half out of the refrigerator. "Cream or sugar?" I asked, not turning around.

"Just cream, please."

I poured a healthy slug into each mug, stirred them a few times, and turned around to hand a mug to Robyn, catching her staring at my legs in appreciation. I nearly spilled both mugs when I realized what she was doing.

She looked up guiltily and hastily took one of the mugs from me, muttering a quiet, "Thanks."

"Sure," I answered, leaning my back against the counter with a bemused expression on my face. "No problem."

So. I think I could call it official now: Robyn found me attractive. Or certain parts of me, at least. Twice I'd caught her staring, and the look I had seen that morning at Ledos Canyon...that had been quite a bit more than friendly.

But mutual attraction never guaranteed a corresponding willingness to act on that attraction, and Robyn had given no indication that she wanted anything more than the friendship we had. Hell, I wasn't at all certain what I wanted, either. Oh, I knew I wanted Robyn physically — *God, did I ever* — and I had a suspicion that my feelings went far deeper. Even if Robyn did want something physical, what if the physical was all it was for her? Did I want to set myself up to be another of her "things"? Did I want her badly enough to risk almost certain hurt just for a chance to touch her?

My body, willing to do just about anything to be with Robyn, chimed into the debate with a resounding "Yes!" while my mind, ever the staunch defender of my heart, responded with a firm "No!"

I shook my head, not realizing what I was doing until Robyn gave me a questioning look and asked, "What?"

"Ah." I scrambled for an answer. "Just...thinking about what the shooting schedule might be like this week. I know we shoot in the city today and tomorrow, but I haven't called in to check past that. Actually," I carefully twisted my torso and winced, "I'm wondering how much I'm going to be able to do today. Hopefully it'll just be a bunch of standing around."

Robyn's expression immediately turned worried. "Maybe you should stay home for a day? If you can't..."

I stopped her with a shake of my head. "No, I'll give it a try and do as much as I can. I know they want to wrap this episode on Wednesday and start up the next on Thursday."

"Tough gal, huh?" She smiled slightly and blew on her coffee.

"Yeah, that's me," I said dryly and shook my head. "It's more a matter of self-preservation. I'm pretty sure Grant is still deciding if he wants to can my ass for mouthing off last week, so I'd like to stay off his radar for a while. Holding up the shoot isn't a good way to go about that."

"Well, mouthing off to Grant Hardy wasn't the smartest thing you've ever done, I agree..." I shot her a mock scowl and her smile widened. "I think, though, that your job is relatively safe, especially considering what they've got lined up for us." She sipped at her coffee and added with studied casualness, "Speaking of what they've got lined up for us, I got a call last night. They've scheduled our big, groundbreaking, world-changing kiss for Thursday afternoon."

I blinked and nearly dropped my coffee cup. "They have?" A wave of panic mixed with exhilaration hit me, panic winning out easily.

Robyn watched my anxiety with amusement. "Well, hell, Caid. I don't expect you to be jumping up and down or anything, but I gotta tell you, usually people don't react this way to the prospect of kissing me."

I managed a weak smile. "Sorry. I just...I'm..." I blew out a breath. "I'm pretty nervous about it. I always get a little weird about scenes like this — I just haven't gotten comfortable with them. And this scene," I looked at my coffee, "you have to admit this one is a little different. I've never... I've never kissed a woman before, and I know that shouldn't matter — we're actors, right? But..." I shrugged and looked at her quickly, then hastily back at my coffee. "I'm just nervous, I guess."

"You've never kissed a woman?" I could hear the surprise in her voice and looked up to find her staring at me with an odd expression. "You mean for a scene," she said slowly, "or never ever?"

I shifted uncomfortably under her scrutiny. "Uh...never, ever."

She nodded slowly, dropping her gaze and frowning into her coffee. The silence dragged on until it bordered on awkward. Finally, she murmured, "I thought..."

When she didn't say anything further, I prompted her, "You thought what?"

When she looked back at me something in her expression had changed. It was still friendly, but much of the warmth I'd come to expect was missing. She shrugged and gave me a smile to match the look. Lots of nice, white teeth, but her eyes stayed wary and cool. "Doesn't matter, I guess." She nodded at the coffee carafe. "Mind if I have a little more?"

I shook my head and silently filled her cup, trying to read her expression and maybe get some clue as to what I'd just done wrong. No clues were forthcoming, so I decided to just ask. "Robyn," I asked hesitantly, "did I say something wrong? You seem..." I couldn't finish, unable to put into words what I was seeing.

Her cup paused on its way to her lips. She smiled behind the cup, a little sadly, I thought, and took a sip of coffee before speaking. "No, Caid, you haven't done anything wrong. I just...misunderstood some things."

The tones of a cell phone coming from the living room stopped my reply and Robyn excused herself to answer it, seeming eager to escape the conversation. I poured myself a little more coffee, holding off on the omelet preparation. I was betting that a phone call this early in the morning meant I wouldn't have a guest for breakfast.

She came back into the kitchen, holding up her phone apologetically. "That was Rick Price. They moved the schedule up an hour," she glanced at her watch, "so I really need to get home to shower and change. Thanks for the coffee, and the breakfast offer. Can I take a rain check?"

"Any time," I replied.

She handed me her mug and we looked at each other for several moments in awkward silence. "Thanks," I said finally. "Thanks for being here last night, and for staying. I...it was nice to have you here."

She smiled softly. "You're welcome." The smile faded momentarily and she looked down at her hands. "When Liz told me, and then when I saw the bike..." She looked back up again, her dark eyes swirling with emotion. "It really scared me, Caid. To think of something happening to you. I..."

Her cell rang again and she swore softly, looking at the display. She hesitated, looking at me, and then answered. "Hello... No, Rick, I'm not at home. I'll be there shortly... Have him drop it through the gate, then. It'll be fine—there aren't people creeping around my house at six in the morning looking to steal scripts." She sighed, and pinched the bridge of her nose in annoyance. "Fine. Tell him to wait, then. I'll be there as soon as I can." She straightened, her voice now tinged with anger. "It's none of your damn business where I am, Rick. Tell him I'll get there when I get there."

She closed the phone with a snap, scowling at it for a moment before looking up at me. "Caid..."

I pushed off the counter with a wry smile. "You have to go, I know." I turned her around and pushed her gently toward the living room.

She crossed to the couch and picked up an oversized black leather bag, slipping the phone into it and pulling out a set of keys before sliding it onto her shoulder. She walked to the door slowly and then turned to me abruptly. "Have dinner with me tonight. I'd like..."

"Yes," I said immediately.

Her smile was like sunshine, warming me through and through. "I'll call you later." She looked at me for a moment more, and reached up a hand to brush my injured cheek. "Take it easy today, huh?"

"Yes, ma'am." I smiled, somehow managing to stop myself from turning my head and brushing her hand with my lips.

She gave me another crooked grin and was gone.

AFTER ROBYN LEFT I ate, showered, and dressed before driving to the site of the shoot in the Financial District downtown. Once there, I struggled into my wardrobe, patiently endured Jules's annoyed attempts to make my face appear as though it hadn't recently had an encounter with a pine tree, and tried to appear perky when I presented myself to the crew.

Unfortunately, attitude did not translate to ability and it became apparent within fifteen minutes that although Jules was able to hide the damage to my face, the injury to my ribs was going to keep me from doing any kind of physical scene. Arrest scenes, chase scenes – basically all the kinds of shots scheduled for the day were out for me until my ribs healed. By eleven o'clock, Nate had sent me home with ill-concealed annoyance, grumbling about "stupid macho nature freaks" under his breath.

At home, I took a few painkillers, grabbed a book, and settled into my backyard hammock, managing to read a few chapters before the pills kicked in and I nodded off. I woke at three, made myself a sandwich, took a few more painkillers, and lay down on the couch where I dozed until the phone rang at six-thirty.

" 'Lo," I answered groggily after stumbling into the kitchen to answer it.

"You should have seen it today, Caid. We had this huge crowd of people watching us shoot, and two women practically got into a fist fight when Arturo was signing autographs..."

"Liz?" I croaked, blinking blearily at the clock.

She paused. "Well, of course, it's me." Her tone conveyed her disbelief that I would consider it was someone else.

"Sorry. Just woke up..."

"Well, I'm glad you're awake now. Listen, Paula and I are on our way over to bring you some dinner, okay?"

"Liz, that's nice of you, really, but I'm..."

"Caid, you need to eat." Her tone was final. "We'll be there in about twenty minutes."

"Liz..." I tried again, but she had already hung up.

"Shit." My attempts to call her back went unanswered and finally I sighed and headed for the shower.

Twenty-five minutes later, I had showered and changed into a tank top and pair of khaki shorts. I ran a hand through semi-damp hair as I opened the front door to reveal the grinning faces of Liz, Paula, Danny, Micah, and two of the lighting crew, Doug and Buzz. I blinked in surprise. "Hey, guys."

I received a chorus of greetings in return, and Danny hefted two large pizza boxes. "We thought you'd be hungry."

"I..."

Liz breezed past me, heading straight for the kitchen. "I wanted to pick up something from that rib place you like, but Danny insisted on pizza. Do you have any wine?"

I sighed. "There's white in the fridge," I said, and resignedly stepped back to let the group in.

Micah was the last to enter. He stopped and looked down at me. "We don't need to stay, if you don't want us to. Liz said you knew we were coming, but it's pretty obvious you weren't expecting us."

I shook my head and smiled, threading my arm around his waist to give him a brief hug, which he returned carefully. "It was a surprise, yes, but a nice one. Don't worry about it."

"We won't stay long—you look beat." He nodded and moved past me into the house.

I started to push the door closed, then caught sight of a tall, familiar form walking up my drive, curiously eyeing the three extra cars parked there.

Good God.

I pulled the door open and leaned against the doorframe, not even bothering to hide my appreciative gaze as I watched Robyn approach. She was dressed to be appreciated, after all, and walked with a confidence that said she knew it. Her hair was loose and wild down her back and she wore a tight black leather skirt that stopped mid-thigh, and stiletto heels held on by two skinny black straps. The real attention-getter, though, was a silvery, gauzy top consisting of two swaths of cloth that covered her breasts and not much else, casually displaying miles of smooth, tanned skin and toned muscle.

I was mesmerized by the play of muscles beneath that skin as she walked and the slight hollows just above the low waistband of the skirt. I wanted to put my lips there, in those tiny indentations; wanted to feel that skin against my cheek and run my tongue...

"Caid? Hello?"

I didn't know how long she'd been standing in front of me, watching with a hint of a smile curling her lips as I stood gawking. I dragged my eyes up, blinking slowly as though waking from a dream.

I didn't think about what I said next, I just blurted out what I was thinking. "Jesus, Robyn, you look amazing."

Real smooth, Caid, I berated myself, but changed my mind when I saw the startled but undeniably pleased expression on Robyn's face.

"I...." Her lips curled up even more, into a full smile. "Thank you, Caid."

I shrugged and cleared my throat, giving her a shaky smile. "Just stating the obvious."

One dark eyebrow crept into sight over the rim of the dark glasses she wore. "Why, Caidence Harris. If I didn't know any better, I'd say you were flirting with me."

Her tone was light, teasing, and I replied in kind. "Why, maybe, Ms. Ward, you don't."

She frowned; I could see the slight furrow in her brow behind her glasses. "Maybe I don't what?"

"Know any better," I said lightly, wondering at my sudden spurt of boldness.

I saw a flicker of movement behind dark lenses and her smile faded. "What..."

"Caid," Danny bellowed from inside, causing us both to jump. "What the fuck are you doing..." He came careening into the entryway and stopped short. "Robyn."

Damn. Bad timing, Dano.

"Danny." Robyn shot me a surprised look.

"Whoa. You look fucking incredible," he said after eyeing her up and down. I smiled at that, agreeing whole-heartedly. "Got a hot date with the tennis bum?"

Oh. I'd been so overwhelmed by her appearance that I hadn't stopped to wonder why she was dressed to annihilate. I doubted dinner with me called for an outfit like this.

"Thanks, Danny. And, yes, we're going to a party one of his sponsors is hosting." She turned to me with an apologetic look. "That's why I stopped by, to tell you I'd have to cancel tonight."

Josh wins again. The unkind thought came unbidden and I pushed it to the back of my mind. "I understand." I gestured at Danny, then behind me. "Turns out I've got some company for the evening, anyway."

Without meaning it to, my tone had become cool and Robyn pulled off her glasses and looked at me searchingly. "I really am sorry, Caid. I'd forgotten about this and Josh only reminded me this afternoon. I would have called..."

Someone yelled for Danny, and Robyn looked past us into the house as he excused himself. "Just how many people have you got in there?"

"Danny, Micah, Doug, Buzz, Paula...and, of course, Liz."

She raised an eyebrow. "You're a popular gal, aren't you?"

I shrugged. "I left the set early today — they decided to come by and check up on me."

Concern flashed across her face. "I heard about that. I wanted to call earlier, but I didn't want to disturb you. Are you okay? How are you feeling?"

"I couldn't do much today. They had me set up to chase some guy down a set of stairs, and I made it about three steps and nearly passed out. Nate wasn't too happy with me."

"Nate's an ass sometimes," she said bluntly, "but he'll get over it."

"Yeah, I know, he always does. I slept most of the day, took some pain pills...feel a lot better, doesn't hurt quite as much."

"Good." She nodded and looked at me intently. "You look better than you did this morning, anyway."

Uncomfortable under her gaze, I looked past her and noticed for the first time the gray limousine idling at the end of my drive. The back door was open and Josh, in tailored black slacks, a metallic blue shirt, and a black, small-collared suit coat stepped out and waved.

I waved back, unable to keep myself from smiling at him. I couldn't help it, I liked the guy. "Looks like your date is getting impatient," I commented.

She glanced over her shoulder. "Yeah, he wanted to go early." She folded and unfolded her glasses, fidgeting in a way uncommon for her. "Caid..."

"Go on," I said softly and gestured at the car. "He's waiting."

"I'm sorry."

"I know." I nodded. "We'll have dinner some other time." I hesitated, and then stepped forward to brush my lips across her smooth, fragrant cheek. "Tell Josh hello," I whispered in her ear, resting my hand briefly on the warm skin above her hip and stroking gently with my thumb.

I felt her whole body tremble in reaction and hid a wild grin of triumph as I stepped back.

There is something there, damn it, and I'm going to find out what it is.

"Talk to you later?" I asked.

"Uh, yeah, sure," she said faintly and slipped her sunglasses back on before raising her eyes. "Later."

I watched as she walked away, glad for the support of the doorframe when I saw that her silver ensemble was held in place by one miniscule silver strap across her back. The expanse of skin my eyes were treated to was breathtaking.

"Sometimes, I hate that woman. I could never get away with wearing something like that. I don't have the height for it. Or the back. I think I need to talk to my trainer about working on my back... *Ohhh*, and is that Josh? God, he's yummy."

I jumped at least three inches off the ground at the voice behind me and spun around, hitting my hand against the doorframe with a solid *thwack*! "Shit! Jesus, Liz," I complained, rubbing my hand. "Don't sneak up on me like that."

She rolled her eyes. "I didn't sneak, I just walked up, and you were too busy ogling Robyn's boyfriend to notice."

Yeah, you just keep thinking that, Liz.

I stared a moment longer after the limo, and finally Liz tugged my arm. "Come on. If you want any food, you'd better get your ass in there quick. You know what pigs those guys are."

I nodded distractedly and followed her into the kitchen, still feeling the tingle of Robyn's cheek under my lips and the heat of her skin under my palm.

"Caid, are you all right?" Paula's worried voice snapped my out of my preoccupation. I looked up to see her holding a plate out to me with two slices of pizza on it.

"Fine, just a little spacey from painkillers." I took the plate from her and breathed in garlic and oregano. "Oh, this looks great." I looked around at the group filling my kitchen and breakfast nook, smiling hugely. "Thanks, guys. This was really nice of you."

"Thank Lizzie," Danny said with a grin as he walked by me with a plate piled with slices. "It was her idea to bring you something. We all just came along for the free food."

I looked over at Liz expectantly, waiting for her to take offense to being called "Lizzie," but she continued to nibble serenely, not batting an eye.

"Well then. Thank you, Liz." I nodded at her with a smile and took a bite of pizza, mumbling around cheese and sausage, "The rest of you get to clean up. And Buzz-man, if you drink all my beer again, you owe me a case."

Chapter
Seven

"ARE YOU NERVOUS?" Liz's voice was casual, but I sensed a keen underlying curiosity and smiled at her feigned indifference.

Today was the day. In less than two hours, I'd be kissing Robyn.

"Of course I am," I replied honestly, seeing no reason to lie. I was nervous any time I was required to kiss someone on camera. So was Liz, we had talked about it before. She didn't need to know exactly *how* nervous, or why.

"Well," she said thoughtfully, "I guess if you're going to kiss a woman, Robyn isn't a bad place to start."

We were in Liz's trailer, finishing off a lunch of vegetarian lasagna I'd picked up from the catering truck. I was thankful to have finished swallowing because that comment would have surely made me choke otherwise.

She waved her fork vaguely in the air. "She's got that whole animal, sexy, dark-goddess thing going on, you know?"

Dark-goddess? God lord, what had Liz been reading?

"I bet she's a handful," she said knowingly, nodding to herself.

I put my fork down and pushed the plate away. There was no way I was going to eat through this conversation. I raised a bottle of water to my lips, pausing just in time to avoid serious spewage when Liz looked over at me and asked, "Don't you think so? I bet she's a screamer."

"Jesus, Liz..." I choked, but then bunched up my napkin and threw it at her when I saw that she was grinning. "Asshole," I grumbled.

"Just trying to take your mind off it, sugar," she laughed. "That face was priceless." She turned serious and reached out a hand to squeeze my arm. "It's just another scene, Caid. Stop worrying about it so much. And it's just Robyn. Y'all are friends, right?"

I nodded, although at this point I wasn't sure what was going on between Robyn and me. I'd called a few times to try and reschedule dinner, but she hadn't returned my calls, and I'd only seen her once since Monday night, at a cast meeting on Wednesday morning. We exchanged pleasantries like virtual strangers and afterward she hurried off without saying goodbye. I didn't know what in the hell was going on, but whatever it was, it was pissing me off.

"Well, then," Liz said, as though that made everything better.

"Yeah," I muttered, unable to keep the sarcasm from my voice.

Liz looked at me sharply, but I stood up and tossed my plate into the trash. "I'd better head over."

The scene was written to take place in Judith Torrington's office, one of the permanent sets for *In Their Defense*. The *ITD* sets had been built before the network bought the Pasadena complex, and were still housed on a rented soundstage in Burbank, a twenty-minute drive away. The crew and various members of the cast were also using the *ITD* sets to shoot courtroom footage for an upcoming episode, so almost the entire cast and crew would be present for the scene.

Oh, goody.

"Do you want to ride over with me and Paula?" Liz employed a full-time car and driver and it would be easier for me to just ride over with her, but the thought of having my own transportation was comforting. At this point, I needed all the comfort I could get.

"No, thanks. I'll just see you over there."

She nodded and gave my leg a pat as I walked by. "Okay, we'll see you in a little while."

I drove myself over to the *ITD* complex and checked in with the crew, getting an updated shooting schedule and instructions to meet with the director sometime before the shooting started. I'd be doing two scenes: one with Robyn, and another with Liz on the courtroom set. The one with Robyn was scheduled first, and I couldn't decide if I was happy to get it over with or if I'd rather postpone it as long as possible.

Using one of the dressing room trailers, I changed into the outfit I'd brought over from wardrobe at *9P*: dark brown pants, low-heeled boots, and a tight, sleeveless, hunter green blouse. I draped the lightweight, dark brown leather jacket that completed the outfit over my arm, knowing it would be stifling on the set and not wanting to start sweating any sooner than absolutely necessary. After a final stop at makeup and hair, I headed to the soundstages, greeting arriving members of the cast and crew as I crossed the lot.

Once in the soundstage building I made my way to the set we'd be shooting at and dropped my script in a chair with my name stenciled across it in white block lettering. I hung my jacket across the back of it and looked around the bustling set, searching for the small, redheaded form of the episode's director, Susan Yazi. I finally found her conversing animatedly with someone behind a rack of lights near the rear exit of the building and I started toward them, weaving my way through crewmembers and equipment.

As I moved across the room, the person Susan was conversing with came into view and my footsteps faltered momentarily.

Robyn.

Long and lean in a severe, black Prada suit that she wore extremely well, the sight of her sent a rush of familiar emotion through me, followed by an unfamiliar flash of anger.

Robyn was the first to notice me as I approached, flicking her eyes over my shirt briefly and curling her mouth into a welcoming smile. For some reason, it annoyed the hell out of me.

She blows me off all week and now she's here, staring at my chest and smiling at me?

I ignored the smile and nodded curtly to her before turning my attention to the director. "Susan," I greeted her with a neutral smile. "Nice to see you."

Susan Yazi barely topped five feet and had a slight, wiry frame and auburn hair just beginning to gray. She exuded an aura of barely controlled chaos, seeming to constantly be in motion even when standing still, and being around her always made me slightly uneasy. She also had a habit of emphasizing random — or at least what seemed like random to me — words in a sentence.

"*Hello,* Caid. Robyn was just *telling* me about your bicycle mishap. Are you *all right*?"

"Was she?" I asked flatly, flicking my eyes over to Robyn, who was watching me with a puzzled expression. "How nice. I'm doing fine, thank you, Susan. Good as new."

"Good. *Good.* I wanted to talk to you and Robyn about the *scene.* I was telling her I really wanted to give you free *rein* on this, *play* with it, do what feels *right* in the *moment,* okay? I realize you might be *uncomfortable* with it, so I want you to have *fun.*"

Have fun, she says. I'm probably hemorrhaging from the brain because my stress level is so high and she says have fun.

Fantastic.

Robyn started to say something, but I cut her off. "Sure, Susan, no problem," I said with a quick nod, hiding my anger and growing anxiety. "Anything else?"

"No, no, that's all," Susan said vaguely as she looked across the set, not noticing or not caring about my abruptness. "Why don't you two *discuss* it? We'll start in five. Kyle! Don't leave that there!" She moved away from us.

"Caid..." Robyn started.

Without glancing at her, I crossed the floor to my chair and pulled on my jacket with jerky, uncoordinated movements. The collar turned under and I yanked at it ineffectually, stiffening when I felt a pair of hands on my shoulders, smoothing the leather and straightening the collar.

"Caid, you need to relax."

The flare of anger at her words pushed my anxiety aside for the moment, and I grabbed at it with both hands. "Excuse me?" I said, turning slowly.

"I know you're nervous, but this is supposed to be fun, remember?" She smiled, and busied herself straightening the collar of my jacket. "You need to relax."

"You think I'm *nervous*?" I asked, my voice rising.

"Well...yes." Her hands stilled and dropped away as she looked at me searchingly. "Aren't you? Isn't that why..."

"This isn't nervous, Robyn, this is pissed off!" I nearly yelled, drawing the curiosity of some of the nearby crew. I took a breath and lowered my voice. "This is pissed off because someone I thought was a friend isn't acting like one."

She pulled back, startled by the vehemence in my tone. "Caid, I..."

I was on a roll now, anger firmly in control, the rest of me watching in sick fascination. I made a chopping motion with my hand. "Save it. You've made yourself quite clear."

Robyn's face hardened and her eyes narrowed. "Fine."

Susan's voice cut through the din. "Let's get this blocked *out*, shall we? Caid, Robyn, can you *join* us, please?"

I looked over to see where Susan was and when I turned back, Robyn was already stalking toward the set, her normal grace replaced with rigid stiffness.

"Fine," I muttered and stalked after her.

The anger fueled me through the thirty minutes it took for Susan to block and plan the scene how she wanted it, and helped me ignore the fact that more and more people were trickling into the building and standing around the set, waiting and watching. Grant was there, standing behind Susan and occasionally leaning forward to give an opinion, along with nearly all of the rest of the executive producers and co-producers, writers, cast and crew.

Don't think about it. Just...focus. Focus on what needs to be done.

Susan wanted the scene shot in two sections: our entrance to her office while we argued, then the kiss. I started to relax as we worked through the first section, the familiar actions and sounds of shooting calming some of my anxiety. The anger was still there, though, on both sides, and it sparked between us during the scene's verbal exchanges, coloring both our performances and making Susan a very happy director.

"Great *job*, you two," she called after stopping the action. "I like the *interaction*. Try to keep that *up* in this next part, okay? Robyn, *you* set the pace, you're the aggressor. Caid, *follow* her lead. All right, let's get the *cameras* set up and get this one *done*."

And suddenly, it was time.

I went to my mark and took several deep breaths. *Easy, Caid, easy. It's just a scene.*

And then we were rolling. Susan yelled "Action!" and Robyn was rounding the desk, prowling toward me like a predator stalking her prey, her eyes blazing with cool fury and looking so achingly beautiful that I was transfixed.

"You assaulted me, Detective." Her voice was low and dangerous and she kept moving toward me, stopping when our bodies were only a foot apart. "I could have you thrown in jail for that."

"Why didn't you?" I amazed myself by not only remembering my lines, despite Robyn's closeness, but also by dredging up some believable attitude to go with them. "You could have..."

She grabbed me by the shoulders, yanked me forward, and kissed me.

The kiss took me by surprise, even though I'd been expecting it. It was hard and bruising, over in an instant, leaving me trembling and gasping for air.

And wanting more.

Much, much more.

And thinking that this could be the last time I'd have the chance to get it.

My hands were inside her suit jacket gripping her hips where they'd gone for support the moment she'd kissed me. Now, a quick tug pulled her closer and I brought our mouths together again, sensing a momentary resistance before a hand trailed up my neck to cup my cheek and the other hand slipped into my hair, increasing the pressure of the contact. My arms wrapped immediately around her waist, pulling our bodies together completely from hip to chest, and she deepened the kiss with a soft, almost inaudible sigh of satisfaction. I could feel the heat in our response to each other, simmering just below the surface, but the kiss remained gentle and unhurried, the two of us exploring with a reverence and tenderness that made me ache. I marveled at it; marveled at the softness and warmth, and the emotions a simple kiss could invoke.

"Cut!"

Robyn's body stiffened at Susan's voice and she pulled back abruptly, giving me a wide-eyed stare before taking two quick steps away from me.

I blinked, realized my mouth was hanging open, closed it, and blinked again.

Holy shit.

"Well, *hell*. Nice *work*, ladies. I think *that's* all we *need*—it's not going to get much *better* than *that*. Very, *very* nice. *Print* that!"

Gradually the movement and noise of the set around me came into focus, and several people who'd been watching surged onto the set to congratulate us, teasing and laughing. I smiled weakly and mumbled polite thanks, but my eyes were on Robyn, watching as she left the set with a crowd of well-wishers in her wake.

"I knew we'd picked the right girls." Grant's smooth voice and beefy arm across my shoulder pulled my attention away from Robyn's retreating form and I turned to face him, ridding myself of his arm without appearing to do so on purpose.

"I'm thirty-four, Grant. Hardly a girl anymore, but I'm glad that you're pleased with how it went." Job-preservation skills kicked in and I smiled to take any sting out of the words.

He guffawed and pulled me into another one-armed hug, which I endured until someone else caught his attention and he left me alone. The fervor had died down quickly after a few pointed words from Susan and the crew was starting to move the lights and cameras as I left the set, still dazed and wishing I could just go somewhere and think instead of dealing with another few hours of shooting.

Liz was waiting for me at my chair, smiling at me like a proud parent. "You see, sugar, it wasn't so bad, was it?"

I smiled slightly. "No, it wasn't so bad at all."

In fact, it was so completely the opposite of bad that my head was still spinning.

She handed me the script that had been lying in the chair. "It was really good, Caid. That second kiss—I didn't expect that. Neither did anyone else, I'd say, from the reaction. Was that something you and Robyn worked out beforehand?"

"Well, uh, Susan told us to have fun with it and go with what we thought was best..." It was the truth, right?

"Well," she said and started walking to the exit, obviously expecting me to follow. "If Grant's hard-on was anything to go by, I think it was just what they wanted. I could see that thing from forty feet away."

"Jesus, Liz." I grimaced, remembering Grant's arm across my shoulders. "Ick. Shut up! I don't want to know about Grant's—"

"I mean, you couldn't miss it. Everyone knows the man is hung like an elephant, but to actually see it...I thought Susan was going to whack it with her clipboard."

I laughed my first genuine laugh in hours and followed Liz out into the sunshine.

I CLOSED TWILA'S door gently and stood in the gathering darkness, biting my lip and eyeing the five cars parked in Robyn's drive with consternation.

Well, shit.

I had a vague plan that involved coming to Robyn's house and saying...*something*...but Robyn obviously had company, and company was not part of my vague plan. Not part of the plan at all. An inherent problem with vague plans is that they rarely come with a Plan B.

I looked at the cars again, beginning to doubt the wisdom of being here at all.

A sharp shriek of metal pulled my attention toward the gate next to the garage, just as a tall, dark-haired man in khaki shorts and a navy polo slipped through and headed for a white Volvo SUV. His steps slowed as he noticed me, and he waved tentatively, peering into the semi-darkness.

"Hi. Can I help you?" His voice was cautious and he looked back to the gate quickly as though gauging the distance in case he had to make a run for it.

I felt rather foolish, standing in Robyn Ward's driveway and being addressed by a man who probably thought I was a fan looking to rummage through Robyn's garbage. My embarrassment spurred me into action and I pushed off Twila and started toward him. "Hi," I said brightly, giving him a friendly, non-garbage-stealer smile. "I actually stopped by to talk to Robyn, but it looks like she's got some company."

He slowed to a stop as I approached, watching me suspiciously before his eyes suddenly went round. "Oh, my God. You're...you're Caidence Harris."

I smiled slightly and nodded. "That's me." When he was close enough, I stuck out a hand for him to shake. "And you must be a friend of Robyn's?"

He took my hand absently, still staring at my face. I raised an eyebrow at him questioningly and he smiled sheepishly. "Uh...oh. Sorry, I'm Cal. Cal Paskins. My wife went to college with Robyn." He dropped my hand and snapped his fingers. "Damn, that's right. Josh told me that you and Robyn were friends."

I hope, I thought fervently. *I hope we're still friends.*

"Listen, Cal," I said, deciding that my plan could use some tuning and that I could do this another day. "I don't want to interrupt your party. I'll just come by another time."

"Oh, no, don't leave! Shoot, it's not like it's a big to-do or anything, we see each other all the time. Please don't go on our account. I'm sure Robyn would love to see you, and so would Josh, from the way he talked about you..."

I tilted my head. "So Josh is here, too?" *Of course Josh is here.*

"Uh-huh," he answered and turned back to the Volvo. "Hang on a sec and I'll walk in with you." He unlocked the SUV and grabbed a gray sweater from the front passenger seat, holding it out to me triumphantly. "Lisa sent me out to the car to get her sweater. She gets cold when the temperature goes below seventy-five. Amazing to think that woman grew up in Minnesota."

I smiled. "Are you from Minnesota, too?"

We went through the gate and started up the path to the house. "Oh, no, I'm a California boy. Grew up in San Jose. I'm not too fond of the cold either, but this," he waved one arm at the evening around us as we stepped up on the porch, "this is not cold." He opened the door with a flourish and motioned me inside.

I laughed and crossed the threshold into the entryway just as Robyn appeared around the corner of the stairs leading up to her bedroom.

"Cal, are you talking to yourself out there? I told Lisa you were craz—" She stopped short when she saw me, emotions flickering across her face. The one that lingered was anger.

Crap. She was still angry with me. That wasn't really part of my plan, either. I was starting to think my plan sucked.

"Hey, Robyn!" Cal said enthusiastically, oblivious to Robyn's anger and my growing unease. "Look who I found outside. I told her I was sure you wouldn't mind her crashing the party, hope that's okay." He winked at me, confident in his belief that Robyn wouldn't mind me being here. I wasn't going to tell him he'd been dead wrong.

I smiled gamely. "Hi. I was wondering if I could talk to you for a minute?" I still wasn't sure what I was going to say to her, I only knew an apology for behaving like an ass figured prominently in it.

I saw the muscle in her jaw twitch, but she nodded politely. "One second." She looked over at Cal. "Lisa's been bitching about not having that sweater. I'd get down there if I were you." The smile she gave him was much friendlier than the look she turned on me once Cal had excused himself and headed down the hallway.

She walked down the last few steps to the entryway, coming to a stop several feet from me and crossing her arms. "Why are you here, Caid? I have guests."

"I know, and I'm sorry. I just...I needed to talk to you."

"Okay. I'm here, so talk." There was no softening of her stance and I shifted nervously.

"I...crap." I shook my head. "I'm not sure what I want to say."

She looked at me in disbelief and stepped toward the door. "Come on, Caid..."

"No! Wait..."

She stopped and slowly settled back into her defensive stance.

I gnawed on the inside of my cheek, trying to gather my thoughts. "Okay, first, I want to say I'm sorry for being such a bitch this afternoon. You were right, I was nervous and I took it out on you. I'm sorry."

She started to say something, but I continued on. "But to be honest, I really was upset about how you blew me off this week. One day you're talking about making new friends and the next, you don't even talk to me, and I have no idea why. It..." I paused before finishing quietly, "It hurt, Robyn."

I looked over at her, but she hadn't moved and her expression was stony.

This isn't working.

"Is that it?" she asked coolly, uncrossing her arms to walk to the door. "I need to get back to my guests."

I ran a frustrated hand through my hair. "Why are you doing this? Pretending like there's nothing between us?"

"I don't know what you're talking about," she said stiffly and pulled the door open. "I think you should go, Caid."

Angry now, I stepped forward and pushed the door shut, leaving my hand on it so she wouldn't open it again. "We're not finished."

The move brought us close together and she stood her ground. We stood, toe to toe, glaring at each other. The cool remoteness had vanished and her eyes were black pools in the dim light, dark and full of emotion.

Beautiful, I thought. *So beautiful.*

"Damn it, Caid." Her voice was low and rough, her breath whispering across my cheek. "What do you want from me?"

"Whatever you can give me," I whispered, my eyes dropping to her mouth.

We reached for each other at the same time, coming together in a fierce clash of lips and tongues, my hands in her hair and hers splayed across my back, pulling my body against hers roughly. The tenderness of our earlier kiss on the set was gone, replaced by raw need as we swayed and stumbled against the door. She turned and pushed me against the hard surface, her lips seeking mine with an urgency that was devouring, insistent, and overwhelming.

It was like nothing I'd ever felt before; the heat that pulsed through me at her touch, the intense craving for more, and under it all a sense of safety and trust. I wanted to give myself over to it—to her—and let myself fall.

Without thought my hand traced across her cheek, down her neck and over the swell of her breast, pausing briefly at the sharp intake of breath before continuing down the long length of her torso to the hem of her shirt, slipping beneath it and brushing hesitant fingers over warm, soft skin.

Robyn stilled in my arms and then attacked my mouth with renewed ferocity, slipping her hands into the low waistband of my jeans and pulling our hips together, sending a dizzying wave of desire through me that forced a groan from deep in my throat.

"Oh, God," I breathed, tearing my mouth away from hers. She took the opportunity to trail her lips along my chin and suck gently on my neck just below my ear. I trembled, overloaded with sensation. "God," I repeated. "Please," I whispered, not even knowing what I was asking for.

Her whole body stilled and she swore softly in my ear before her hands gripped my hips, and she pushed away from me. "Caid, I can't. This...I can't do this."

I sagged against the door, blinking at her stupidly. "Wha..."

She shook her head violently, avoiding my gaze. "I'm not going to be an experiment, Caid. I can't be that. Not with you."

I stared at her in confusion. "Experiment? What..." I stepped toward her and she took a step back. I frowned. "What are you talking about?"

"This," she said, waving her hand between the two of us. "I'm not going to be your experiment in the wonders of lesbianism. I've been there before and it always ends the same."

That stopped me. "You've done this before?"

"Yes," she admitted quietly.

"But..."

She sighed. "I'm gay, Caid. I haven't been with a man in years."

I processed that for a moment. "Then why are you backing off? There's obviously an attraction...and more. Hell, Robyn, I can't get you out of my head. I think about you constantly, want to see you, to be with you, to make you smile...I'm crazy about you."

She smiled sadly. "And I'm crazy about you, too, Caid, and that's why I can't do this. We're friends and I want to keep it that way. You're straight. I'm not. This can only end badly if we let it start."

I snorted. "Let it start? Don't you think it's a little too late for that? Do I need to remind you what we were just doing?" I held out a hand to show that I was still trembling. "I'm still shaking from what you do to me."

"I'm sorry, I shouldn't have..."

"Don't you dare say you're sorry!" I said sharply. "Don't you dare. I *know* you're not sorry. You want this as much as I do. This isn't an experiment for me, Robyn. Just because I haven't been with a woman, that doesn't make what I'm feeling any less valid. I've known I was attracted to women for a while now, but this is the first time it's gone deeper than just attraction, the first time it's been worth the risk. *You* are worth the risk, Robyn. *This,*" I gestured between us, as she had done, "is worth the risk."

I tried to reach for her hand, but she stepped around me and opened the door, her body ramrod straight. "I'm sorry, Caid. We'd both end up getting hurt."

"And I'm willing to take that chance! Damn it, Robyn, what are you so afraid of? You're the one who pursues her 'things' and lets the media think you're in a relationship with Josh for publicity's sake. If anyone has a reason to be afraid here, it's me. And you're going to let this go because I've never been with a woman? I'm not a teenager with my first crush—I'm in my damn thirties, for Christ's sakes! An adult with very adult emotions. About you." I touched her arm. "Please..."

"Robby?" There were light footsteps on stairs and Josh came into view, smiling in pleasure when he saw me. "Caid! Cal told me he ran into you outside. What are you two doing up here? Come on down and join us."

I opened my mouth to say something to him, but nothing came out. I couldn't even manage a smile. I just looked at him dumbly for a moment before turning back to Robyn. "Robyn..."

"Caid was just leaving," Robyn said in an emotionless voice.

"Robyn, don't do this. *Please* don't do this."

She shook her head, looking at the wall behind me. "I can't. I won't. Please, just...go."

"Rob, what's going on?" Josh's voice was full of concern. "Are you crying?"

My eyes flew to her face and I could see the telltale shine of moisture.

"I won't let you do this," I whispered, leaning in and kissing her hard and quick on the mouth. I drew back and stroked her cheek with the back of my hand. "I won't."

"It's not up to you, Caid," she said quietly before motioning me through the door and softly closing it behind me.

Chapter
Eight

"YOU LOOK LIKE a hooker," I muttered as I eyed my reflection in the full-length mirror critically.

Black had been my mood when I began dressing, and black had been the result. Black, three-inch heeled boots, black leather pants that laced up the front, and a short, black, silk camisole that stopped nowhere near the almost indecently low waistband of the pants. I'd used product to slick my hair back and a touch of black eyeliner to bring out the color and unusual shape of my eyes. The overall effect was...

"Badass, slutty ho," I muttered to myself and shrugged.

Well, I wanted to get noticed tonight. Wanted a mainline of self-confidence right to the jugular after a week of cool, mechanical civility from Robyn that had battered my emotions—and self-esteem—into near submission.

This would definitely get me noticed.

Hell, maybe after the party, I'd go out, find myself a woman, and get this whole first-time thing taken care of. Maybe if I did that enough times, Robyn would see that this wasn't a damn experiment for me and she'd let me back in her life.

I snorted at my reflection. "Yeah, right, Caid, that's so you."

Okay, so I wasn't looking to get laid—at least not by a stranger—no matter what the outfit said to the contrary. There was something, though, about dressing this way, about knowing you looked good and that people were staring at you, wanting you—

I grabbed my keys and grinned ferally at my reflection, feeling my self-confidence come back in a rush.

Let's go, ho.

"LAGAVULIN, ROCKS," I said briefly to the short, thin man standing behind one of the five bars set up on different floors of the enormous concrete-and-glass structure that was Scott Ziem's house. Scott was one of *9P*'s executive producers and he was throwing this bash in celebration of the end of our second season, which we'd wrapped that afternoon.

The bartender nodded and went about filling a heavy glass tumbler with ice and splashing a generous portion of scotch over the top. He handed me the drink and a napkin with a polite "Ma'am."

I smiled my thanks and stepped aside, nodding at a couple I didn't recognize as they took my place at the bar. I sipped my drink, enjoying the cool, earthy flavor on my tongue, and glanced around. Like the main level below, the walls and furnishings were blindingly white, and I had to stop myself from squinting. To my left, a thick white half-wall overlooked the main floor. I walked over to lean against it, watching the flow of guests below and the silent, white-shirted staff that wove through the crowd with practiced ease.

A loud, undistinguishable techno beat poured from hidden speakers, thankfully not as loud on this level as it had been on the main floor. I'd been mingling for an hour and a half with that heavy thudding in my ears and I'd finally come up here to escape it; to escape the press of people, the small talk, the fake smiles, and just breathe.

I idly contemplated going home. I'd caused a stir, raised some eyebrows, and received the appreciative looks I'd been hoping for. Now I was tired, my head hurt, and the person I really wanted to see was probably a no-show.

And my pants were starting to chafe.

"Goddamn, Harris, I heard you were prowling around, looking like a cross between Joan Jett and a Playboy Bunny, but I guess I had to see it to believe it. Shit, girl, you've been holding out on us."

I smiled and turned toward the voice, propping my hip against the wall and regarding the small woman standing at the bar with amusement.

A former LAPD detective, Magda Chu was one of the three police procedure consultants that *9P* employed. Of mixed Chinese and Mexican descent, she had dark, hooded eyes, a small, dainty nose, and a wide mouth—a face that was intriguing rather than beautiful, and I had to admit it had always intrigued me. We weren't close, but we got on well, and the smile I gave her was genuine.

"Magda," I greeted her, watching as she accepted her drink from the bartender and made her way across the room to me with the careful attention of the slightly drunk. "Been here long?"

"Long enough." She grinned and leaned against the wall next to me, blatantly eyeballing me from head to toe. "Da-yum," she said after a moment, and shook her head.

"I'm going to assume that's a compliment and say thank you," I told her and sipped my scotch. "Where did you come from, anyway? I didn't see you downstairs."

She nodded at a set of glass doors and the balcony beyond. "Out with the other outcasts, smoking my filthy cancer sticks. And yes, it was definitely a compliment."

I smiled and tilted my head. "Can I bum one?"

She raised her eyebrows in surprise, but immediately reached into her jacket and pulled out a pack of Marlboro Lights. "I didn't know you smoked."

"I don't, usually. Once or twice a year, I guess. Sounded good just now." I nodded toward the balcony. "Join me?"

"Sure."

I pushed off the wall and straightened to my full height that with the boots was nearly a foot taller than she was. She looked up at me and blinked. "Da-yum," she said again, before leading the way out onto the balcony.

There were other small groups of people on the balcony and I nodded to those I knew, not surprised at the pungent smell of marijuana in the air. Magda walked over to the railing and leaned against it, shaking out two cigarettes and handing me one. We smoked and chatted for a while, until Magda excused herself to find the bathroom. She left her cigarettes and lighter behind and I tapped another one out and lit it, hoping she wouldn't mind.

"So this is where you're hiding! Shit, Caid, I've been looking all over for you."

The low murmur of conversation from the various groups of people around me paused momentarily, and I turned my head to watch Liz sweep across the balcony with a pretty, dark-haired man that I assumed was her date trailing behind her.

"Hey, Liz," I said and turned to face her, leaning my back against the railing. Her hair was parted on the side and fell in a shiny blond curtain over one eye, her pants were dark green and tight, and her blouse a scoop-necked, short-sleeved white leotard that hugged her generous curves and had her companion's undivided attention. "Looks like you found me." I looked pointedly at her date and she waved at him vaguely.

"Caid, this is Bruce. Bruce, Caid."

I nodded at him, got a glassy, vacant smile in return, and wondered for the thousandth time at Liz's taste in men. Liz plucked the cigarette from my fingers and I frowned. "Hey!"

"Disgusting habit," she said, bringing the cigarette to her mouth and taking a deep drag before returning it to me, a smudge of bright red lipstick joining the deeper maroon of my own. "I thought we were quitting."

"We are." I tapped the ash off, took another drag, and handed it back.

She took it and nodded at the pack on the railing. "This is us quitting?"

"They're Magda's."

Liz grimaced with distaste. Liz and Magda were like oil and water. Liz was high maintenance, Magda was low patience, and their mutual contempt for one another was common knowledge. "You're out here with *Magda?*"

"Liz," I said warningly, having had this conversation before.

"I know, I know, you like her, you two are friends, blah, blah, blah." She sucked more smoke into her lungs and blew it out slowly, squinting at me through the smoke. "Shit, Caid," she handed the cigarette back to me, eyeing my clothes, "those are great pants."

"Thanks." I smiled slightly and took a pull on the smoke. At the mention of my pants, Bruce transferred his attention from Liz's chest to my crotch, but the glassy expression did not change. I wondered idly if Bruce could speak. "Elona found them for me. Never thought I'd actually wear them in public, but it seemed like the night for it." I shrugged.

She looked me up and down again and pouted. "Elona never found anything like that for me." Elona Herst was Liz's personal shopper and stylist. After hearing me complain one too many times about how I hated shopping, Liz had hooked the two of us up and Elona had been shopping for me ever since. "You might even be showing more skin than Robyn tonight, and that's saying something."

I coughed out a large cloud of smoke, breathed some of it back in, and coughed some more. Liz handed me my drink, which I drained quickly. "Robyn's here?" I finally managed to croak out.

I felt ill. Suddenly my impulse to dress to get noticed seemed childish, silly, and slightly desperate. I'd been waiting for her arrival all night, but now I wanted nothing more than to get out of here without her seeing me.

Liz looked at me speculatively. "She and that beautiful, beautiful man came in about twenty minutes ago." She took the glass from my hand and handed it to Bruce. "Bruce, honey, could you be a peach and get me and Caid another drink?"

"Uh...yeah, sure, baby." He took the glass automatically and smiled at her adoringly.

She patted him on the cheek. "You're so sweet. I'll have a Pinot Grigio, and Caid's drinking some kind of scotch, I'm sure..." She looked over at me. "What were you drinking?"

"Lagavulin," I told him.

Bruce's smooth, pretty forehead wrinkled in confusion and he nodded hesitantly.

Liz patted him on the arm. "Just ask the bartender for the scotch that starts with an 'L,' okay?" He nodded again and she gave him a gentle shove in the direction of the balcony doors.

I shook my head as he walked away. "I don't get it, Liz. What do you see in these guys? Don't you miss being able to converse with your date?"

"I'm not dating him for his conversation skills, Caid," she said in amusement. "He has other skills I value just as highly." She picked up the cigarette, still smoldering where I had laid it during my coughing fit, and dropped it in an abandoned glass along the railing. "Now," she continued, turning to me and crossing her arms. "Tell me what in the hell is going on between you and Robyn."

Her question took me by surprise and I paused tellingly before answering. "What do you mean?" I finally answered, trying to keep the defensiveness out of my voice. "There's nothing going on between me and Robyn."

She made a dismissing motion with her hand and glared at me. "That's complete hooey, Caid. Two weeks ago, you two were laughing, talking... You were *friends*. Shit, the woman was insane with worry when you crashed your bike. She ran out of the party before I even finished telling her what happened. And now, you treat each other like strangers and I don't think I've heard either of you laugh in a week. Something happened, and I want to know what it is."

"Nothing happened," I snapped. As always, when she used that imperious, *you-will-do-as-I-say* tone of voice, it pissed me off.

"Bullshit," she snapped back. We glared at each other until finally, her gaze softened a little. "Caid, talk to me. I know sometimes I'm a flake, and I'm not the most observant person in the world, but I can tell you're upset and I don't like to see you upset."

"Liz..." I sighed and my anger drained away in the face of her concern. "It's between Robyn and me, something we need to work out. I'm sorry, that's all you're going to get."

She nodded, obviously still curious but willing to let it drop.

Bruce came back with our drinks, Magda came back for her cigarettes, and the four of us stood around uncomfortably while Liz and Magda glared at each other, Bruce stared at my pants, and I resisted the urge to chain-smoke the rest of Magda's smokes in an effort to distract myself from the fact that Robyn was roaming around somewhere close by.

Liz and Bruce eventually left to mingle downstairs, and after smoking one last cigarette with Magda, I decided that it was time to brave downstairs and make my getaway. I thanked Magda for the cigarettes and conversation, and left her talking with a group of crewmembers that had recently joined us on the balcony.

Stepping into the house, I froze when I saw Robyn leaning casually against the bar, holding a small glass and watching me with a predatory gleam in her eyes that immediately made me wary. Her eyes inspected my body — from my face down to my boots and back again. When she met my gaze, she downed the contents of the glass and smiled. It was not a nice smile.

I swallowed and forced myself to nod politely. "Robyn."

She looked, as she always did, amazing. I took in the off-white, wide-legged pants and a black corset-like blouse that ended just below her ribcage, wondering if there was ever a time when she didn't look amazing. Probably not, I decided, and realized she was talking to me.

"Well you didn't waste any time, did you?" Her voice was loud and slightly slurred. "Looks like Magda is happy to help you out in your little 'exploration,' hmm?" She pushed off the bar and walked toward me, wavering a little before catching herself and continuing on.

I hid my surprise. Robyn was drunk. Very drunk.

And about to babble my personal shit to twenty or so people who were watching us eagerly, just hoping this would turn into something worth retelling.

Fantastic.

I forced a pleasant smile and stepped forward. "Can I talk to you for a minute?" I grabbed her arm lightly, attempting to pull her away from the crowd around the bar. "In private," I added quietly but firmly when she resisted.

I ignored her knowing smirk and pulled her across the room, heading down a darkened hallway to look for someplace away from prying eyes to ask her what in the fuck she thought she was doing. I tried a few doors before I found one that was open — I flicked on the light, saw it was a small bathroom, and pushed Robyn into it none too gently.

I followed behind and closed the door, turning to face her with crossed arms. "What the fuck are you doing, Robyn?" I asked angrily. "If you want to cause a scene in front of half the crew, go right ahead. But leave me out of it. And fucking leave Magda out of it, too. She's got nothing to do with this."

She ignored what I'd said, running her eyes over my body appreciatively. Everywhere her eyes touched I felt heat and I cursed my body's betrayal.

"I guess I really can't blame her," she murmured, finally meeting my gaze with a mocking smile. "Hell, Caid, you might as

well hang a flashing sign around your neck that says 'fuck me.'"
She tilted her head to the side. "Is that all you wanted? Hmm? Just
a quick fuck to see what it's like? Because if that's all you want..."

She stepped forward quickly and pushed me against the door,
slipping a leg between mine. Strong hands grabbed my hips and
rocked me slowly against her thigh, and then one of the hands
moved up to cup my breast and squeeze gently. I was too stunned
to move at first and then too overwhelmed with sensation to do
anything but let my head fall back against the door with a groan. I
felt feather-light kisses along my neck, the whisper of her breath on
the skin of my chest, and she laid her forehead on my shoulder, still
rocking our bodies together gently.

"God, you smell so good...feel so good," she mumbled into the
skin of my neck as her thumb brushed over my breast. I closed my
eyes and took a shallow breath at the sensation. "You make me so
crazy," she sighed softly, and I felt her head shake against my
shoulder. "Why do you make me so crazy, Caid?"

The strong smell of alcohol on her breath, along with the
rambling quality of her question, finally brought my mind back
into focus. With tremendous effort, I pushed her away from me.

She stumbled back a few steps, blinking at me blearily.
"What's wrong?"

"Well for one thing, you're fucking plastered," I snapped
angrily. I couldn't believe she was willing to do this, that she
thought so little of me, of us, that this would be enough.

And I'd almost let it happen.

"Baby..." She reached out for me and I slapped her hands
away.

"I guess I know exactly where I stand now." I motioned at the
room around us. "We can't have a romantic relationship, and you
just want to be friends, but apparently it's okay to fuck me in a
bathroom." I nodded curtly. "Fine, Robyn, I get it. You win. I'm out
of your hair. Consider this done. I won't let you treat me like this."

Robyn swayed a little, her forehead furrowed in concentration,
trying to decipher what I'd said.

"Oh for fuck's sake," I said in annoyance. "Sit down before you
fall down."

She immediately dropped onto the toilet seat, her face pale.

I shook my head and got a grip on my anger. It wouldn't do me
a damn bit of good when Robyn was this messed up. Hell, she
probably wouldn't even remember this tomorrow. "I'm going to go
find Josh and get him to take you home. Stay here." She nodded
like a child getting scolded. I shook my head again and went in
search of Josh.

I found him almost immediately, downstairs in the main room, surrounded by a large group of partygoers who were all trying to get close to the famous Josh Riley. Still angry from my encounter with Robyn, I pushed my way through the group roughly and tapped him on the arm. "Josh, can I have a minute?"

He looked over at me and did a double-take. "Caid? Wow. Hey!" He grinned, grabbing my hand. Normally his hand-grabbing was endearing, but now, it kind of annoyed me. Probably because Robyn did the same thing and she was on the top of my shit list right now.

I forced a smile and tugged him toward the stairs. "Sorry, folks, I need Mr. Riley for a few minutes." The crowd reluctantly parted for us and I continued to pull Josh along.

"Where are we going?" When I looked back at him, the grin was gone and he looked slightly wary. He pulled me to a stop. "Listen, Caid, I like you, but this is Robyn's decision and if you're trying to get me to talk to her..."

Stopping him with a glare, I looked around and said with quiet intensity, "I don't want you to talk to her for me. As far as I'm concerned, there is nothing to talk to her about. I don't want anything from her. Nothing. Nada. Zip. She's made it very clear what I can and cannot have, and I choose nothing."

He pulled back in surprise. "Caid, what..."

I cut him off and pointed up the stairs, dropping my voice even further. "Robyn is drunk off her ass in a bathroom upstairs and you need to get her the hell out of here."

His eyes widened and he glanced up the stairs as though he expected to see an inebriated Robyn dancing down them. I looked at my watch, realizing I'd been gone almost five minutes. Maybe he would.

I gestured with my head and jogged up the stairs, Josh's light footsteps right behind me. At the top of the stairs, I slowed and tried to act as casual as possible, meandering my way along the wall and turning down the hallway. I stopped at the third door on the right and knocked softly, then opened the door and poked my head in.

Robyn was still sitting on the toilet, her head pillowed in her arms on top of the counter. I opened the door wider and Josh crowded into the small space and stopped short, staring at Robyn in surprise.

"What happened?"

I rolled my eyes. "She drank too much. That's how people normally get drunk."

At the sound of voices, Robyn raised her head and looked up blearily, smiling when she saw Josh. "Joshie! Heya, Joshie."

She held out her hand and he took it, giving her a look of fond exasperation. "Robby, honey, I think we should get you out of here, okay?"

"Okay," she agreed happily, then frowned. "I think maybe I drank too much." She put her head back on the counter.

"Ya think?" I muttered under my breath.

Josh studied Robyn for a moment, then looked over at me. "I guess I could carry her."

I shook my head. "Only if we can't get her to walk out of here. She already caused a minor scene; I don't think she'd want people to see you carrying her out of here." No matter how annoyed, angry, or hurt I was, I wasn't about to throw Robyn to the gossip wolves. I was pissed off, not spiteful.

He frowned. "A scene? Robyn?"

"Yes, Robyn. And she can tell you all about it when she sobers up. If she remembers."

Robyn's head came up again and she looked at me. "Caid?"

I figured this was as good a time as any to try to coax her up, so I leaned over and gently grabbed her hands. "Yep, it's me. We need to get you home, okay? Can you stand up?"

She just stared at me for a moment and then pulled one of her hands from mine and placed it with incredible tenderness on my cheek. A smile slowly spread across her face as she brushed her thumb across my lips. "My beautiful Caid." After a moment, the smile faded and she frowned. "But you're mad at me, aren't you?"

Her words, and the look in her eyes as she said them, battered at my resolve and I was unable to resist the impulse to kiss her thumb and then press my lips to the palm cupping my cheek. We stayed that way for several seconds, staring at each other, until I heard Josh shifting impatiently behind me.

I sighed and shook my head resignedly. "God, we could have been good," I told her softly, doubting she heard me, and then resolutely pulled her hand away from my face and straightened. "Come on, Robyn, up you get."

She groaned and rose slowly to her feet with Josh's help, swaying slightly but more stable than I'd expected. She glanced around the room with interest, focusing on a small painting of butterflies that hung on the wall. "Ohhh...pretty." She reached out to touch it but I stopped her hand.

"Robyn." I tried to get her attention. She frowned at her hand in mine. "Robyn!" I repeated sharply.

"What?" She jerked her head toward me with a wince, sounding annoyed. Annoyed was good.

"We need to get to the car, but we're going to have to walk through the party. Can you make it on your own?" I asked, sounding as skeptical as I could.

She frowned at me. "Of course I can." She turned to the mirror and straightened her hair and clothes with slightly clumsy but still effective motions. Josh grinned at me, and I smiled despite my annoyance.

He put an arm around her and she sagged against him slightly. "Okay, party girl, let's go. We'll just go straight down the stairs and out the front. You'll have to call Scott and Andi with apologies tomorrow."

She nodded and I pulled the door open, preceding them out into the hall. At the end of the hall I looked back and saw the two walking slowly but steadily down the hall, Robyn with a look of intense concentration and Josh smiling indulgently at her.

I waited and fell into step on the other side of Robyn, talking with Josh about the up-coming French Open and the Brazilian matches I'd watched. We took the stairs slowly — Robyn leaned heavily on Josh but it just looked as though they were being affectionate and no one got close enough to realize Robyn's less-than-sober state. A few people attempted to stop us but I ran a little interference when that would happen and finally we were out the door, walking down the drive to the valet station.

The fresh air seemed to help Robyn and she pulled away from Josh to walk on her own for a while, but when the valet brought Josh's car around and Josh helped her into the seat, she closed her eyes and leaned her head back against the headrest immediately.

I closed the door while Josh walked around the car and slipped in behind the wheel. He rolled Robyn's window down and looked at me for a few seconds. "Thanks for helping out."

I nodded and started to back away.

"I'll have her call you in the morning. I'm sure she'll want to thank you as well."

I glanced at Robyn's profile and shook my head. "Don't bother. I don't think we have anything else to say." I turned away and walked back up the path before he could say anything further.

I wondered if Magda was still around, because a smoke sounded really good.

And another drink.

Chapter
Nine

SCOTTY ZIEM'S PARTY was, for the most part, not something I'd look back on fondly, but something good did happen. Danny tracked me down and told me that he'd found another woman celebrity who could actually *play* golf and my services wouldn't be needed at the Highland Hills Celebrity Golf Tournament. He seemed reluctant to tell me, but when I exuberantly kissed him on the cheek in thanks, I think he realized I was okay with it.

With the commitment for the golf tournament out of the way, I was left with more than a month of free time and a serious need to get out of town to clear my head. I loaded up my backpacking gear and a week's worth of food, made a few calls, and climbed in my truck, pointing the battered vehicle south toward Idyllwild. I found a small gas station just outside of town that would let me leave the truck in their back lot for a week, then I shouldered my pack and the extra box of food I'd brought and walked the half-mile to the post office.

I was leaning up against the building reading a book, my face shaded by a wide-brimmed nylon hat and sunglasses, when two scruffy, dirty hikers walked up and eased their packs to the ground, arguing good-naturedly about college football and the University of Wisconsin's chances this year.

Without looking up from my book I said, "Eh, the Badgers are going to suck this year. Michigan looks good, though."

Both men stopped what they were doing and stared at me in surprise. One of them — a taller, younger, male version of me with brown hair, green eyes and stubbly growth over a strong, square jaw — stepped forward with a smile spreading across his face. "Michigan blows chunks. Bunch of pansy-assed mama's boys."

I put my book down and pulled off my sunglasses, letting them hang from the leash around my neck. "All Wisconsin's got is a bunch of dairy cow-lovin' cheese freaks." I climbed to my feet, brushing off my shorts and smiled into eyes so much like my own. "And Badgers? What the hell kind of mascot is that? A badger is just an overgrown ferret. The University of Wisconsin Overgrown Ferrets."

I grinned at my brother, who whooped in delight and smothered me in a tight, smelly bear hug. He lifted me off the ground and staggered around while I yelled at him to put me down. Finally, as a last resort, I poked him in the ribs and he yelped like a girl, dropping me immediately and taking up a defensive stance to protect his ribs.

"No fair," he said, grinning at me.

I grinned back. "Hey, Per. It's good to see you." I wrinkled my nose. "But, boy, you smell. I hope you're planning on taking a shower in this town, 'cause I don't want to share my campsite with the stench that's wafting off of you."

He looked quickly at my backpack leaned up against the wall, then back at me, taking in my hiking attire. "You're coming with?" he asked hopefully, looking again at the pack.

I smiled. "Through to Big Bear if it's okay with you two..." I looked pointedly his friend, who was staring at the two of us in consternation. "Wanna introduce me?"

"Dude, of course it's cool," he said, still smiling at me in happy amazement.

I looked at his friend again and then back at him with a raised eyebrow. "Dude, introductions?"

"Oh, yeah, right. Sorry." He turned to his friend. "James, this is my sister Caid. Caid, James."

James was a few inches shorter than me, strong and stocky with pale blond hair, blue eyes, and ruddy, sunburned skin. He stared at me, then seemed to shake himself. He stepped forward to grasp my hand awkwardly, as though I'd break. "Hi," he said shyly, sneaking glances at my face as he stepped back.

"Nice to meet you, James." I looked at him questioningly. "Would you mind if I tagged along with you and Perry?"

"Uh, sure...I mean, no, I wouldn't mind at all." He stuffed his hands in his pockets and smiled hesitantly.

"Great." I gave him a friendly smile and glanced over at Perry. "And now, seriously, dude, we need to find you two someplace to shower."

I ADJUSTED THE flame on the stove, set a pot of water on to heat, and settled onto a thin pad I'd laid near the stove, stretching my legs out with a groan.

"How ya feeling, Grandma?" Perry teased me from where he was stretched out on his back a few feet away, his baseball cap tilted over his eyes.

"Shut it, Periwinkle. You're supposed to respect your elders," I replied as I pulled off my boots and wiggled my toes with a sigh. "God, that feels good."

Perry pushed the cap back and propped himself up on his elbows, grinning at me. "I'm sure that James would be happy to rub any part of you that aches."

I stuck my tongue out at him, well aware of doting looks that James was starting to cast my way. "Where is he, anyway?"

Perry waved his hand at the ridge behind us. "He wanted to try to catch a shot of the sunset from higher up."

I'd learned over the past few days that James was quite the shutterbug and nodded, not surprised at Perry's explanation of his whereabouts. I leaned back on my elbows, mimicking Perry's position. We were both quiet for several minutes.

"Caid?" Perry said eventually.

"Hmm?"

"Is..." He paused, and I looked over at him questioningly. "Is everything okay with you? You seem, I don't know, kinda down, and really quiet."

"Ah." I sighed and pulled myself up into a sitting position, wrapping my hands around my knees. "Noticed that, did you?" Perry was a perceptive kid, and we'd always been close despite the twelve-year age difference. Our other brother, Sebastian, was two years older than me and we rarely spoke. Sebastian did not approve of my choice of careers, but then Sebastian did not approve of much.

"Mmm." He nodded in affirmation.

I stared at my feet, wondering how to explain what was bothering me. It never occurred to me not to tell him. "Well," I rocked back and forth a few times, "I think I may have gone and fallen in love."

I heard him sit up and I glanced over. He was watching me with interest. "No shit?"

I smiled slightly. "Mm-hmm, I'm pretty sure."

"You *think*, and you're *pretty sure*? What does that mean? I mean, you've been in love before, right? You and the nerd were together for, what, a year or two?"

He was referring to my year-and-a-half-long relationship with Toby, a software developer with an abundance of brains and a few minor social-skill issues. "He wasn't a nerd," I scolded mildly, feeling obligated to defend my longest relationship to date. "And yes, I loved Toby, but I don't know if I was ever *in* love with him. This is...different."

"Different," he repeated, and thought about that for a bit. "*Okaaayyyy*. So it's different. How, exactly, is this not a good thing?"

"Hmmm, well...that's where it gets a bit complicated." I hugged my knees tighter. "My, ah, affections, are not particularly welcome."

"*What?*" He sounded genuinely shocked and I smiled. "What kind of idiot wouldn't want you? Who is this guy?"

"Ah. Hmm. Yeah. Um. That's part of the complicated bit." I paused, rocking back and forth before glancing over at him again. "It's not a he. It's a she."

His eyes widened, searching my expression to see if I was joking. "No shit?"

"No shit."

"Whoa," he said, nodding slowly. "So, is this..." he hesitated. "Uh, are you..."

"Gay?" I finished for him.

He nodded.

"It's a distinct possibility." We were quiet for a few minutes, and I finally asked, "Would it bother you?"

"Hmm?" Perry blinked and looked over at me. "Oh, shit, Caid, of course not. I guess it doesn't even surprise me all that much." He grinned at me. "But James is going to be devastated."

I let go of my knees and leaned back on my hands, rolling my eyes. "He'll get over it."

Perry looked at me for a moment and then shook his head. "Chick or dude, I still don't get how someone wouldn't want you."

I laughed quietly. "Well, thanks for the vote of confidence." I paused, thinking of Robyn and the heat I'd seen in her eyes on more than one occasion. "And honestly, I don't think it's an issue of want..." I sighed in exasperation. "That's the other complicated bit, and, hell, I don't even understand it. If I ever figure it out, I'll let you know."

Perry rolled onto his hands and knees, and crawled over to scoot in beside me and put a comforting arm around my shoulders. "I'm sorry, Caid. Whoever she is, I still think she's an idiot."

I smiled sadly. "Me, too."

Chapter
Ten

"OH, BABY, YEAH," I moaned in ecstasy when the first needles of hot water touched my skin. I ducked my head under the spray, humming in pleasure as the water sluiced six days of dirt and sweat away.

From Idyllwild and the still snow-covered San Jacinto mountains, down an 8,000-foot plunge into the ninety-plus degree heat of the desert west of Palm Springs, then back up into the San Bernardinos — we'd hiked nearly one hundred miles in six days and my body was feeling it.

We had made it to Big Bear Lake late that afternoon and after doing a small load of laundry to give us clean clothes for the evening and the following day, I had checked us into an upscale inn, insisting it was my treat without much real opposition from Perry or James. We each had a room of our own, and so had split up to shower and rest with the agreement to meet up for dinner at seven. Tomorrow we would pick up the rental car that I had reserved, drive back to Idyllwild to pick up my truck, and head back to LA.

After soaping my body twice, washing my hair three times, and just standing under the hot spray for several minutes, I finally stepped out of the shower with a satisfied sigh. As I padded around my room, naked, there was a quiet knock on the door, and I hurried to pull on the complimentary robe hanging in the bathroom.

The worried faces of Perry and James looked back at me when I squinted through the peephole. I pulled the door open immediately, frowning. "Hey, guys, I thought we said seven?"

Perry pushed the door open further and walked by me. James followed, his eyes widening slightly when he saw my state of undress. He stopped in the doorway, uncertain, and I waved him in.

"It's okay, come on in, James," I assured him, pulling the belt around my waist a little tighter and closing the door after he walked through.

"Caid, did you tell anyone where you were going?" Perry said abruptly.

I raised my eyebrows at his tone, crossing my arms over my chest. "I didn't actually talk to anyone directly, but I left messages with Connie and Liz and I mentioned to a few more people that I'd be out of town. Why?"

"Because apparently, you're missing."

I blinked. "What?"

He looked around my room, found the remote, and turned on the TV, flipping through the channels. "We went down to the bar just now and saw it on the local news..." He continued to flip.

"Saw what?   Perry, what are you talking about," I asked, starting to get annoyed.

"There." He pointed at the TV. A woman stood next to a road in the desert, talking earnestly to the camera, above a line of text on the screen that read "Actress Missing." The picture panned out and swung to the right, showing a battered, burnt-out pickup truck.

My pickup truck.

"What the fuck?" I said and grabbed the remote from Perry to turn the volume up.

"...blood found on the front seat and steering wheel has now been confirmed to be that of the actress, and local police are looking into the possibility of foul play. Samantha Dwyer, Channel Five News, off of I-10 west of Palm Springs."

"What the *fuck*?" I said louder, looking around frantically for the cell phone that I'd carried with me on the hike but never turned on. I found it, flipped it open and turned it on, waiting impatiently for it to power up.

Perry picked up the remote where I'd dropped it on the bed and continued to change channels, stopping at another station just as another "Actress Missing" headline showed up on the anchor's left. I sank down on the bed, cell phone forgotten, watching with morbid curiosity.

"The search for actress Caidence Harris continues today in the desert west of Palm Springs. An abandoned vehicle belonging to the actresses was found by two hikers early Thursday morning, stripped and badly burnt, in a ravine just off of I-10 west of Palm Springs. Blood found on the steering wheel and seat of the truck has now been confirmed as Harris's, and law enforcement officials are expected to expand the investigation to include the possibility of foul play."

The picture changed to a publicity still of me, then a few quick *9th Precinct* clips in the background as the anchor continued. "Harris reportedly left LA on Monday morning for a several-day camping trip. She was last seen at a gas station in the Riverside area.

"Members of Harris's family could not be reached for comment, but friends of the actress say they are optimistic, despite the disturbing new blood evidence, and several have joined together to offer a $500,000 reward to anyone who has information about the actress's whereabouts."

The picture changed again to show Liz, Micah, Danny, and Robyn sitting at a table at some type of press conference. They looked solemn and drawn, and the effect on me was like a punch in the stomach.

"Oh, fuck," I whispered. "Shit, shit, shit...what did I do?" I jumped up and looked around frantically, my brain going in a thousand directions at once. "I need to...I need to..."

"Hey, Caid, whoa. Slow down." Perry's hand on my arm finally calmed me down. He handed me back my cell phone, which I had dropped when I lunged off the bed.

I took a calming breath, then another. *Think, Caid, think. What do you need to do?*

Perry was thinking the same thing. "Okay, we need to tell them that obviously you're not missing, and that you're healthy and alive."

I looked at my cell, and then up at Perry.

"Caid?" he asked cautiously, worry clear in his face.

I shook myself. "I'm fine, just thinking. I need to make some calls..."

"Hey!" James had taken the remote from Perry, and was flipping through stations, pausing at one where a number for a hotline was being displayed. He pointed at the screen. "If I call that number and tell 'em I know where you are, do I get the half mil?" He smirked, amused at his own joke.

Liz and Robyn's drawn, worried faces were still fresh in my mind, and James turned into a handy outlet for my guilt and frustration.

"Jesus, James," I snapped, and yanked the remote out of his hand. "Those people are my *friends*, who've been worried for days that something happened to me."

His face fell, and he looked like he might cry. "I was just joking..."

"This isn't fucking funny." I turned off the TV and tossed the remote onto the bed, turning to Perry, my tone still angry. "Perry, I need you to find out where the police station is up here—it's probably better to show up in person, instead of just calling..." I flicked a glance at James. "And take him with you."

I didn't need the wounded, confused looks that James was giving me as he wondered what had happened to Perry's nice, friendly older sister, and who was this bitch who'd replaced her.

Later, I might apologize for snapping at him, but right now I needed to get dressed, get to the police station, and start making some phone calls. "Go." I waved at the door, giving them both an annoyed glare when I realized they weren't moving.

"Caid..." Perry said hesitantly, looking at me with concern.

I blew out a slow breath. *Don't take it out on him, it's not his fault, or James's, either....* "Just go, Per," I said quietly, managing a slight smile. "I'll meet you at the front desk in a few minutes, okay?"

He nodded, seeming reassured by my returned calm, and he and James filed out of room, leaving me alone.

When they were gone, I sighed and shook my head. "What a mess."

"JESUS, WHAT A mess." I stopped my pacing and dropped into one of the chairs in my room, running a hand through my hair. It was past eleven, and James had long since gone off to bed. Perry was watching TV, sprawled across one of the beds with two pillows propping his head up.

As I'd been doing constantly over the past six hours, I thought back over the strange sequence of events that had caused this whole convoluted misunderstanding. My truck being stolen by several joy-riding teenagers who had been too scared to 'fess up. Traces of blood still present in the cab from my mountain-biking incident. Not specifying where I'd be hiking, or who I was hiking with, in the messages I'd left for Connie and Liz. And finally, reserving the rental car and paying for the hotel rooms with a credit card listing my middle name, Renee, which I often used when traveling.

"It's not really your fault, Caid," Perry said, flipping idly through stations. "Although you should have left an itinerary with someone," he added mildly.

All evening, I'd been battling guilt over all the trouble caused, and frustrated anger at feeling blamed for something that hadn't been my fault. Instead of the comfort I'm sure he was trying to provide, Perry's words sent the pendulum of my emotions swinging back to guilt. Much of what had happened had been out of my control, but that was something that hadn't been. I'd been careless, and no excuses to myself about needing to get out of town and away from memories of Robyn were going to change that. I sighed, knowing the rebuke was well deserved. "I know."

We watched TV for a few minutes and Perry stopped on a station with an "Actress Found" tagline.

The anchor looked happy as he reported, "Actress Caidence

Harris, thought to be missing after her truck was found abandoned along I-10 earlier this week, has surfaced in the Big Bear area, unharmed. The search, which had been concentrated in the desert west of Palm Springs where the vehicle was found, has been called off. John Isaac is live at the Mountain Inn in Big Bear where Miss Harris's party is reported to be staying. John?"

The picture cut to a tall, well-groomed blond man standing on the steps of the inn. "Thanks, Chris." The man glanced at a notepad in his hand and then looked back up at the camera. "Well, it's been a tense, emotional few days for friends of actress Caidence Harris, but it all ends on a happy note tonight." The man was replaced with pictures of Perry, James, and me getting into a police cruiser outside the Big Bear Lake Police Department. "The actress walked into the Big Bear Lake Police Department earlier this evening safe and thankfully unharmed. After talking with San Bernardino County officials, it appears that an unfortunate and rather bizarre series of events are to blame for her feared disappearance..."

I tuned the man out, thinking of the three hours we spent in the Big Bear Lake Police Department, first patiently, and then not so patiently convincing the young deputy on duty that the tired, sunburned, cutoff-clad woman sitting at his desk was indeed a missing celebrity, then answering questions and talking via phone with agencies in Palm Springs who were heading up the investigation of my "disappearance." During lulls in activity I had begun to make some necessary phone calls, one of them being to my agent and publicist, Connie Reynolds. The less-than-scathing, almost positive press the story was getting was all due to her agency's expert handling.

The news program moved on to another story, and Perry changed the channel again, settling finally on ESPN. I pushed myself out of the chair and resumed pacing, stopping at the window and pulling the curtain aside slightly to look out at the parking lot. There were only three news trucks there now where earlier there had been more than ten, and I guiltily thanked a seventeen-car pileup on I-5 and a Midwestern politician's unfortunate choice in sex partners for pushing the story of my reappearance out of the limelight.

The phone rang, startling us both. We looked at each other, then at the phone. Perry reached for it hesitantly. "Should I get it?"

I shrugged. "I guess."

He frowned at my lack of clear direction and reached for the phone. "Hello?"

I wondered if a reporter had finally bribed someone into giving out my room number, but Perry looked up at me, listening, and didn't hang up immediately. I walked over to sit beside him on the bed, watching him curiously.

"Um, I think that's fine, but let me check and make sure," he said and covered the mouthpiece with his hand. "Elizabeth Stokley is downstairs, asking to see you. Demanding to see you, actually. The guy at the front desk is asking if he can have someone show her up. He said they can get up here without anyone seeing."

I raised my eyebrows. "Liz is here?" He nodded and I waved my hand. "Yeah, yeah, of course. Send her up."

"So, I finally get to meet Elizabeth Ann Stokley?" Perry asked when he'd hung up the phone.

"Looks like it," I replied distractedly, still mulling over the fact that Liz was here. When I had called her earlier from the police station, her emotional and tearful response to hearing I was okay had overwhelmed me. Her presence reminded me, again, how much worry I'd caused people I care about, which in turn brought another round of guilt.

There was a gentle knock, and both Perry and I rose from the bed. I crossed the room and pulled open the door, and Liz flew at me, catching me in a tight embrace and whispering fiercely in my ear, "Don't you ever do this to me again. Do you hear me? Never again..." She let out a choked sob and held on tighter.

"Hey, shhh." I held her tightly with one hand and stroked her hair with the other, fighting back tears of my own. "I'm so sorry, Liz. God, I'm sorry."

Eventually, she sniffed and pulled away slowly, running her eyes over me worriedly. "You're really okay?"

"I'm fine." She didn't look convinced. "Honest, Liz, I'm fine. It was all one big...misunderstanding."

She snorted and smacked me hard in the arm.

"Ow!" I rubbed my arm. Liz was a lot stronger than she looked. I was going to have a bruise in the morning.

"Goddammit, Caid," she fumed and hit me again. "If you ever scare me like that again, I'm going to kill you."

Perry's laughter drew both of our attention and we looked over to where he was watching our interaction. "It's nice to see someone beat up on Caid for a change," he said with a charming smile at Liz. I rolled my eyes.

"Liz, this is my brother Perry," I told her. "Perry, Elizabeth Stokley."

Perry stepped forward and shook her hand. "A pleasure, Miss Stokley."

Liz released his hand slowly and cocked her head to the side, eyeing him speculatively. "Well aren't you a handsome one. And those eyes...just like Caid's," she mused.

I watched in open amusement as the Liz-effect took hold and

turned cocky, cool Perry into babbling, bashful Perry. He mumbled a thank you, blushing to the roots of his hair.

"Liz," I admonished mildly. "Play nice."

She turned to me with a cocked eyebrow and an innocent smile. "I always play nice, sugar." She looked back at Perry and smiled. "Call me Liz."

"Uh...sure...Liz," he managed, still blushing but regaining some of his usual confidence. "Caid talks about you all the time. Thank you for being such a good friend to her."

"*Ohhh*," Liz laughed melodically. "And charming, too." She glanced over at me. "Caid, you could take lessons from this one."

"I'll keep that in mind," I said dryly.

She smiled and looked back at Perry. "And, Perry, despite her many flaws, your sister is a very good friend to have."

She really could be very sweet.

"Now." Liz looked at her watch with a graceful flick of her wrist. "It's late, and Paula is waiting for me in the lobby, hopefully getting us a place to sleep." Her gaze ran over me from head to toe. "The police in Palm Springs told me you were fine, but I had to see for myself."

"I'm fine, Liz," I assured her, and after a pause, "thanks for caring."

She nodded briskly, obviously done with emotional outbursts. "How are you getting back to LA?"

"I rented a car..."

"You'll drive back with us," she said firmly. "Let's have breakfast downstairs at eight and all those poor reporters prowling around can take pictures of you happy and alive and eating pancakes, then they can go off and report on something more interesting."

"There are three of us. Perry's friend James is with us too," I warned her.

She shrugged. "Plenty of room for six, it'll be fine."

I nodded and frowned. "Six?"

"Ah." Liz said, frowning a little. "That's the other thing. Robyn is with us. She didn't come up here with me because she is under the impression that you are angry with her and don't want to see her, but she's come all this way to make sure that you're alive and in one piece, so maybe you two could call a time-out in this stupid little feud and talk for a few minutes, hmm?"

"Robyn is here?" I managed as calmly as I could. The narrowing of Liz's eyes told me she'd noticed the slight waver in my voice.

"Yes, she is, and I'm going to send her up." Her tone was final.

"Okay," I said faintly.

Liz looked at me with suspicion for a moment before walking to the door. "Perry, would you mind walking me down to the lobby? I hate walking around by myself in hotels."

"Of course." He literally jumped to the door to open it for her. Then he stopped, and turned to me. "I'll probably just head to my room...you'll be okay?"

I smiled slightly, and stepped forward to hold the door open. "Yeah, I'll be fine, thanks. See you in the morning."

" 'Kay."

Liz stared at me for a moment, and then reached out and brushed her fingers down my arm. "It's good to see you, Caid. I'm glad you're okay."

I caught her hand in mine and squeezed gently, trying to convey my gratitude. "Thanks."

I watched the door close behind them and just stood for a moment, taking a few deep breaths to try and still the fluttering in my stomach. *Robyn is here. In this building. Now.* I wondered what that meant and forced myself not to read too much into it.

I busied myself with straightening out the pillows where Perry had been and calling the front desk to request a wakeup call for seven. At the knock on the door, the fluttering in my stomach came back full force, and I paused to take a few more deep breaths before walking to the door and pulling it open.

Her hair was pulled back from her face in a messy, loose ponytail, and she wore faded jeans, loafers, and a black, short-sleeved mock-turtleneck blouse. Her face was drawn, and she looked at me guardedly, fidgeting with the large black purse slung over her shoulder. "Hi," she said eventually, her voice a near whisper.

"Hey." She looked so good I nearly cried. "Um...would... Do you want to come in?"

She hiked the strap of the purse higher onto her shoulder and nodded. "Please. If it's okay..."

I stepped back, opening the door wider, and she hesitated a moment before stepping past me into the room, taking a quick look around before sliding the bag from her shoulder and depositing it near the door. I closed the door softly behind her and we looked at each other for several long moments, not speaking. Finally, she stepped forward and raised a hand to brush my cheek with her knuckles, then stroked lightly with her thumb. I stood still as she ran her other hand through my hair and down my arm, tilting her chin up to kiss my forehead.

I closed my eyes at the contact, not moving, but when she tugged me forward into her body and wrapped her arms around me, I let my arms drift up around her waist and held on tightly. We both sighed at the same time, and she kissed my hair. "God, I'm so glad you're safe," she whispered in my ear. "I was so scared..."

I tightened my arms briefly, then pulled back, missing her warmth instantly. "I'm sorry I worried everyone."

She smiled slightly, brushing my cheek again and kissing my forehead before taking a small step back. "It was quite a bit more than worry, Caid." The smile faded and her face took on a haunted look. "We thought you..." She dropped her hand abruptly and turned away, walking a few paces to the window before turning around.

"Do you remember the first time we met? When they told you I'd be sharing your trailer?"

I remembered it well. The first time I'd looked into those eyes and lost my breath, the first time that voice had flowed through me like honey, the first time another person's presence had left me completely and utterly befuddled. I nodded slowly, confused at the turn the conversation had taken.

"I wanted you from the first second I saw you." She smiled in remembrance. "I'd seen you in pictures and in commercials, of course, and knew you were attractive, but, God, there was something about meeting you in person. I think it was the eyes," she mused, tilting her head, "or maybe that mouth..." Her eyes dropped to my mouth and then looked back up to meet my startled gaze.

"I remember thinking it would be fun to try and get you into bed." She smiled wryly, adding honestly, "I'm something of a pig when it comes to sex...or at least I have been in the past."

"Robyn," I said, "I don't..."

She shook her head and held up a hand. "No, please. Just...let me talk, okay? And then you can kick me out, or tell me I'm a bitch, or whatever." When I stayed quiet, she continued. "After a few months, I decided that maybe getting you into my bed wasn't such a good idea after all. We work together, for one thing—that in itself made it a bad idea—and from what I could tell, you only dated men..." She grimaced slightly in self-deprecation and rubbed the back of her neck. "To be quite honest, Caid, I usually prefer things a bit less...complicated, so I decided not to pursue anything with you. Hell, I could barely get you to talk to me anyway. You just kind of...giggled a lot and occasionally said really bizarre things."

I stuck my hands in my pockets defensively, embarrassed to know that I had appeared just as stupid as I always felt around her.

"Then one day you started talking to me." She smiled softly. "You were funny and smart and sweet...I started to really like you, and I was still crazy attracted to you. It scared me, I guess. I have friends and I have lovers. I haven't wanted both of those things from one person in a long time." She paused, and pushed a stray piece of hair behind her ear. "I lied to you about going out of town that weekend because I was scared. When you told me you hadn't been with a woman, I used it as an excuse to push you away because I was scared. What I did last weekend at the party, treating you that way," she looked at me sadly, "was because I was scared. It was easier to be an asshole than to admit how much I care about you."

She stopped and took a deep breath before continuing. "But being scared of how I felt about you was nothing — *nothing*," she repeated intensely, "compared to how fucking scared I've been for the past three days. The thought of losing you..." She shook her head. "It terrified me. *Petrified* me. It still does. But it made me realize that what you said the other night, at my house, was true. It's worth the risk. This," she gestured between us, moving toward me, "this is worth the risk. You..." She came to a stop in front of me and laid a hand on my chest. "You are worth the risk. I don't want to lose you again, and I'll do whatever you want, take whatever you're willing to give. I know I've probably fucked things up royally, but I hope that we can at least be friends, and maybe, someday, something more."

I stared at her stupidly. She'd taken my breath away again — this time with words.

When I didn't respond right away, she sighed. "Ah, well." She cupped my cheek. "Now you know, anyway. Would you at least think about what I said? I'd like to be friends at least, if nothing else." She trailed her hand down my arm and squeezed my hand. "I miss you."

I still hadn't said anything, and she gave me a pained smile. Finally, when she moved to the door, I managed to say something. "Stay," I whispered. I held tightly to her hand, not letting her move any closer to the door. "That's what I want."

"What?"

"You said you'd do anything I want," I said, louder now. "I want you to stay. I want to hold you, I want to fall asleep with you. When I wake up tomorrow morning, I want you to be the first thing I see." I pulled gently at her hand, bringing our bodies back together. "That's what I want." I looked into her eyes. "For starters."

The tension in her face slowly faded and she raised an eyebrow, a smile twitching at her lips. "For starters?" Her thumb absently stroked across the back of my hand, raising goose bumps on my arm.

"For starters," I agreed. "Tomorrow, we'll see what happens." I took her hand and placed it on my hip. "Deal?"

She smiled, warm and content. "Deal."

THE STRIDENT RINGING near my head tore me out of deep sleep and I slapped at the noise, thinking it was my alarm clock, puzzled when the noise didn't stop. I blinked a few times before noticing a flashing red light attached to a phone.

Ah. Phone. Ringing. Right.

Pleased to have solved the first puzzle of the day, I frowned when the noise continued and finally realized I needed to *answer* the phone. I grabbed at the receiver, snagging it with clumsy fingers on my third try, and brought it to my ear as I rolled onto my back.

Or at least tried to roll onto my back.

"This is a Mountain Inn courtesy wakeup call," a pre-recorded voice said in my ear, but I was too busy remembering why there was a warm, soft body at my back and a hand under my shirt, stroking my stomach gently, to pay much attention. *"Thank you for staying with us at the Mountain Inn, and have a great day."*

"Uh-huh," I mumbled automatically and replaced the receiver, torn between staying where I was and allowing the soft caresses to continue, and rolling over to verify that Robyn was actually here.

"Good morning," a low voice murmured in my ear and I closed my eyes at the rough, husky sound. I'd wondered for ages what that voice would sound like in the morning. It was much, much better than I'd ever imagined. She dropped a kiss on a very sensitive place behind my ear, sending shivers through my body, and tightened her arm around me.

I stroked the skin of her arm, lacing our fingers together and squeezing her hand tightly to my body before releasing it and slowly rolling over. She shifted a little to allow me some room and I finally settled with my head on her bicep with our faces just inches apart.

"Good morning," I said softly, lifting a hand to trace the features of her face in wonder—her eyebrows, her cheeks, her jaw, her lips. "I can't believe you're here," I whispered, rubbing the pad of my thumb along her lower lip.

She kissed my thumb and leaned in to brush her lips across mine gently, lingering for just a moment before pulling back with a smile that crinkled the corners of her eyes. "Thank you for letting me stay."

I leaned in and brought our lips together softly as she had done, sucking gently on her lower lip, swiping lightly with my tongue. "You're welcome," I answered after I'd pulled back, pleased at the quick intake of breath I had caused and warmed by the lazy desire I saw on her face.

She closed her eyes and gathered me closer, slipping a hand under my shirt and tracing languid patterns on the skin of my back with her fingernails.

"Mmm...that feels good," I murmured, snuggling into her neck and breathing in her scent. We had fallen asleep fully clothed, and I found myself wishing she had worn a different shirt. The mock turtleneck she wore covered far too much of her long, delectable neck. A delectable neck I wanted to explore.

My arms were pinned between our bodies, but I wiggled one hand free and hooked the collar of her shirt with a finger, tugging it down to trail soft kisses along her neck. I lingered at the hollow of her throat before moving back up along the underside of her jaw and up to her ear.

She took a shuddering breath and the fingernails on my back stopped. "Caid..."

"Mm-hmm?" I answered vaguely, intent on my exploration.

Her arms tightened and we rolled until Robyn was lying on top of me, our mouths close together. "You're killing me," she said softly, leaning in to flick her tongue along my lower lip and then my upper lip. I parted my lips in response and she took advantage, kissing me slowly and thoroughly until my head swam.

She pulled back with a groan and one final nip on my lip, and I looked up at her, dazed. She smiled in sympathy.

"We don't have time to do this properly." She dipped down to nuzzle my ear, her voice sending tremors through my already aroused body. "...I really, really want to do this properly." She pulled back a little and kissed the tip of my nose. "So I'm going to roll back over and just hold you a little longer and you're going to behave yourself, okay?"

I nodded mutely, panting, with my head still swimming in a Robyn-induced haze. Good God. It was insane what one kiss from this woman could do to me.

She rolled onto her back and patted her shoulder invitingly. "Com'ere."

I moved over, then paused and looked up at her hesitantly. "Could I...could I hold you?"

She smiled slowly and nodded. "I'd like that."

She scooted down a bit and tucked her body against my side, laying her head on my shoulder and her arm across my stomach. I let her settle in and then put my arms around her and kissed her hair, sighing. "This is nice."

"Mm-hmm," she mumbled, wiggling a little to get closer.

I kissed her hair again and stroked the bare skin of her arm. "Whenever I've been with..." I paused, wondering if this was proper snuggling conversation, "...guys, they always did the holding."

"Ah." She gave a low laugh. "One of the many perks of being

with a woman." She put her hand on my stomach and rubbed lightly. "And it's okay to talk about, you know," she added, reading my pause correctly. "I know you haven't been with a woman, but I'm assuming you're not a virgin..." She stopped and lifted her head quickly to look at me. "You're not, are you?"

I laughed at the trace of panic in her voice. "No, I'm not." I stole a quick kiss while her lips were so close. "It's been a while, but I think it's safe to say I've got the mechanics down fairly well."

She relaxed back onto my shoulder with a chuckle and we were quiet for several moments before she spoke again. "How long..." she paused and I could feel the slight shake of her head. "I'm sorry—it's none of my business."

"How long has it been? Since I was with someone?"

I felt her nod. "Do you mind me asking? You don't need to tell me..."

"Well, I suppose, if we're going to do this properly," I said, using her phrase from earlier, "then it sort of is your business, isn't it?" I thought for a bit, remembering the two-week fling that had been a last-ditch effort to convince myself that I wasn't gay. "I guess around Christmas, year before last."

She raised her head again, staring at me in surprise. "But that's..." she frowned as she calculated, "...that's over a year and a half ago. Surely it can't have been that long?"

I raised my eyebrows at her incredulous tone. "I'm afraid so." She shook her head in disbelief. "I gather it hasn't been quite that long for you?" I asked hesitantly, not sure I wanted to know the answer.

She dropped her gaze from mine and lowered her head back on to my shoulder. "No," she said quietly, making circles on my T-shirt with her finger. "Last month." She paused. "The weekend I told you I was going out of town."

"Ah," was all I could think of to say.

Ouch. That one stung more than I expected. And brought a bit of reality into my idyllic morning. I kissed her hair one last time, and gently moved my arm from under her head before I sat up.

"Caid?" she asked worriedly, placing a hand on my back.

I swung my legs over the side of the bed and ran a hand through my hair, looking over my shoulder at her. "I'm fine...you just brought to mind some realities that I didn't think about last night."

"Realities?" she repeated, sitting up slowly. She looked tousled and beautiful, and all I wanted to do was to lie back down with her and feel her against me again. Instead, I was going to ask for something that might keep me from ever doing that again.

"I've learned lots of things about myself over the years,

Robyn," I said quietly, turning on the bed to face her. "And one of those things is that I'm not very good at sharing. I know that maybe you're used to something...different, something more open, but I know from experience that I don't work that way." I took a breath. "So, if that's not something you want as well, then maybe we should just...stop." I looked down at my hands, afraid of what she would say.

She raised my face to hers with gentle fingers under my chin and smiled softly. "I may have been a pig, Caid, but in the few relationships I've had, I've always been a monogamous pig. I'm glad you said something, because I want—and expect—the same thing."

"You do?" I asked, the smile growing on my face.

She leaned forward and kissed me gently. "I do."

"Sweet," I said without thinking.

"Sweet?" She looked at me with a quizzical smile.

I laughed and shook my head wryly. "God, too much time with my brother and his friend this week. Smack me if I say 'dude' or 'awesome.' Or 'check it.' Really smack me if I say 'check it.' "

She laughed and leaned back on her hands, smiling at me, her eyes warm with laughter and affection. The "Robyn Rush" took me by surprise and I acted on impulse, pushing her back on the bed and sprawling on top of her, kissing her intensely.

She let out a muffled huff of surprise but responded immediately, opening her mouth to deepen the kiss and pushing my shirt up roughly to run her hands up and down my back. Her fingernails scratched up my spine, not lightly, and I arched against her with a gasp.

"God..." I pulled my mouth away from hers to breathe just as a knock sounded at the door. Both of us froze for several moments, staring at each other. I rolled to the side, flopping heavily on my back and staring at the ceiling. "Goddamn." Whether I meant it as a curse for the person at the door, or an expression of amazement at how Robyn affected me, I wasn't sure.

"Jesus Christ, Caid. Where did that come from?" Robyn asked shakily, laying an arm over her eyes.

I rolled my head to the side to look at her and answered honestly, "I have no idea."

She smiled and grasped my hand, squeezing gently. "Well, feel free to do that again, anytime."

"Anytime?" I grinned.

"Within reason, Miss Harris," she answered dryly. "For instance, now is not a good time, so you should stop looking at me that way."

There was another knock and Perry's muffled voice came

through the door. "Yo, Caid. Wake up!" More knocking followed.

Robyn raised an eyebrow. I sighed and sat up. "My brother," I explained as I stood, reaching down to grasp her hand and pull her to her feet.

She nodded and ran a hand through her hair, looking around the room. "Do you have a brush or something?"

"In the bathroom," I said over my shoulder as I walked to the door. Perry knocked again, harder this time. "I'm up, I'm up!" I said loudly and pulled the door open, catching Perry in mid-knock. "Jeez, Per, I'm up already."

"Took you long enough," he said, stuffing his hands in his pockets. His hair was still wet from a shower, and he had what looked like a small nick from a razor on his jaw.

I leaned against the door. "Have a little trouble with the razor this morning, Periwinkle?"

He scowled and pushed past me but stopped dead at the sight of Robyn coming out of the bathroom with a baseball cap in her hands.

"Can I borrow this?" she asked me, flashing a quick smile at Perry.

"Holy shit," Perry said.

I'd had similar reactions on several occasions, so I could sympathize.

"Perry." I pushed the door shut and stepped around him, resisting the urge to go over to Robyn and slip my arm around her. "Close your mouth and don't stare. This is Robyn. Robyn, my brother Perry."

Robyn put the hat on her head, tucked her hair behind her ears, and stepped forward, extending a hand. "Perry, nice to meet you."

He took her hand carefully, staring at her despite my warning. "You're Robyn Ward."

She laughed lightly and allowed him to continue shaking her hand. "That I am."

"Jesus, Perry," I said in exasperation, "would you quit staring?" My sympathy with his reaction was waning.

He dropped her hand immediately and looked over at me with a scowl. "I wasn't staring."

"Were, too."

"Was not."

"Were, too."

Robyn's laughter stopped the argument before Perry and I could make complete idiots of ourselves. I glanced over at her sheepishly. "Sorry," I mumbled.

She just smiled. "I've got three sisters, I've been there." She glanced at her watch and looked over at me apologetically. "I should get to my room. I have a change of clothes and I should take a shower."

Still humming with tension from our earlier activities, the vision of Robyn naked in the shower nearly short-circuited my brain. I blinked, and felt my pulse speed up. Some of what I was thinking must have been plain in my expression, because a slow smile spread across Robyn's face. "Within reason, Miss Harris, within reason," she murmured as she walked past me and patted my stomach.

She stooped to pick up her bag at the door. "I guess I'll see you both downstairs..." She looked at her watch and raised her eyebrows. "And we'd all better hurry. Liz would hate for any of us to be later than she is." She left with a final smile and a lingering glance at me, the door closing slowly after her.

I couldn't have stopped my smile even if I'd wanted to.

Hot damn. What a great way to start the day.

"Damn." Perry's awed voice drew my gaze. He was staring, much as I'd been, at the door that Robyn had just left through. He shook his head. "Damn. I heard you and Liz last night talking about a Robyn, but I had no idea..." He backhanded me on the arm. "You didn't tell me you were friends with Robyn Ward," he complained with a miffed expression on his face.

"Hey, Perry." I feinted at his head with my hand and poked him in the stomach when he raised his arm to cover his face. "I'm friends with Robyn Ward. Now get the hell out of here so I can take a shower."

"Ha-ha." He eyed me suspiciously as he sidestepped over to the door, guarding his stomach. "Jeez, I just about hit the floor when I saw her in here." He frowned. "What was she doing in here, anyway?"

I was tempted to tell him everything. Frankly, I had the urge to run up and down the halls, pounding on doors and letting everyone know that Robyn Ward liked me. Thirty-four years old and I wanted to turn cartwheels and tell everyone my secrets. Sheesh.

I realized, though, that until Robyn and I talked about how open we were going to be about this, I probably shouldn't go blathering on about how Robyn and I had just been rolling around on the bed, making out like teenagers. The thought stopped me for a second — I'd never had to worry about that before.

"Borrowing a hat," I said casually and herded him out the door, feeling a twinge of guilt about the semi-truth. "Now go, I'll see you downstairs. And you might want to warn James. I don't want his head to explode."

Perry was laughing as the door closed behind him.

BREAKFAST WAS AN interesting affair, with lurking photographers, overly solicitous wait staff, and eager autograph seekers. There was also a visit from several police officers under the guise of updating me on the investigation into my stolen truck, but what was more likely an attempt to see Liz and Robyn in the flesh. In addition to that, Liz flirted outrageously with my younger brother, and James continued to cast puppy-dog-like, adoring looks at me despite the presence of Robyn and Liz, two much more worthy targets, in my opinion.

Like I said, breakfast was an interesting affair.

I was also a little bothered by Robyn's ability to act as though we were nothing more than friends, and not particularly close friends at that. I knew she'd had more practice than me in this area, but I didn't know how she was able to act so normal when all through breakfast I was fighting the nearly overwhelming desire to leap across the table and tear her clothes off.

I escaped back to my room after breakfast with relief, and was gathering my things and zipping the last of my toiletries into various pockets of my pack when someone knocked on the door. "Yeah, Perry, I'm almost rea...dy."

Robyn leaned against the doorframe, dangling my baseball cap on a slender finger. "I came to return this." She shrugged off the wall and stepped toward me, pushing me back into the room with a hand on my chest and tossing the cap on the bed behind us. She kicked the door closed with her foot, slid her other hand around the back of my neck, and pulled me into a heated kiss that left me gasping.

"Mmm." She broke the kiss and wrapped her arms around me. "That's all I've wanted to do for the last hour."

I ran my hands up and down her back gently and kissed the side of her head. "Glad it's not just me."

She chuckled. "No, it's definitely not just you."

We stood for a minute holding each other, and then I pulled back, tucking a loose strand of hair behind her ear. "This is a little strange for me. I'm not sure how to act," I admitted. "I don't know who I should tell, who I shouldn't tell..."

"I know, Caid." She sighed. "I'm sorry. Don't take this the wrong way, okay?" I nodded cautiously. "I think we should wait and see where this goes before we start telling people about it. And not," she interrupted as I started to say something, "not because of the gay thing. Although, honestly, Caid, in our business, we do need to be careful. But right now, this is about you and me. No one else. I don't want to jinx this, and honestly, I'd like to have you to myself for at least a little while. Do you understand?"

I nodded slowly, thinking about what she said. What she was

asking for wasn't unreasonable; it actually made a lot of sense. This was going to be complicated enough without getting other people involved — maybe we should take the time to figure out what there was between us before telling people.

"Caid..."

Robyn moved away from me smoothly as Perry knocked and pushed open the door that wasn't quite shut. I stifled a sigh of disappointment, missing the warmth of her body immediately. Kicking the door shut before sweeping me into a mind-blowing kiss had been quite dramatic and more than a little exciting, but next time, she needed to kick harder.

"Are you ready?" He stopped and smiled at Robyn. "Oh. Hi."

She smiled back and walked to the door. "Thanks for the hat, Caid. See you downstairs."

"Yeah," I said, watching her go. "See you."

PERRY, JAMES, AND I stood next to the limo as Liz's driver Walter pulled Robyn's overnight bag from the trunk and started to carry it toward the gate.

"That's okay, Walter, I've got it." Robyn stopped him with a hand on his arm. He looked at her uncertainly and she stepped over and took the bag, slinging it over her shoulder with a smile at the older man. "Thank you, Walter."

"Of course, Miss Ward." He nodded and walked around the car, and slipped into the driver's seat.

The three-hour drive back from Big Bear had been uneventful, but slower than expected due to unusually heavy Sunday morning traffic. Liz spent most of trip on the phone to various people, Paula worked on her laptop, Robyn conversed easily with Perry and James, and I made a few phone calls and tried not to think about how goddamned sexy Robyn's voice was, or how good it had felt to wake up with her that morning.

Robyn turned to face the three of us. "James, Perry," she held out a hand to each, smiling, "it was good meeting the two of you. Try to take it easy on Caid here for the next few days, hmm?"

James blushed. Perry grinned rather stupidly and said, "It was nice meeting you, too, Mi...Robyn. And don't worry. Caid's still pretty spry for her advanced age. I think she'll be able to keep up with us." He quickly jumped back to avoid the swipe I'd taken at his stomach, and ducked into the limo. James followed him with a grin.

"Little shit-head," I mumbled and shook my head.

Robyn laughed lightly and adjusted the bag on her arm, looking up toward the house. I glanced down at the driveway, my eyes following the simple cobblestone pattern, and finally looked up to find she had turned her attention on me. She tipped her head to the house. "Walk me up?"

I nodded and we walked silently through the gate and up the path onto her porch. I didn't know where to go from here, where we stood, or what to expect. We'd expressed an attraction and interest in each other, but now what? Did I ask her out? Did we date? Were we girlfriends?

We stopped at her front door, and she reached inside her purse and pulled out a set of keys. She fit the key in the lock and paused, not looking at me. "I leave on Wednesday. For two months." She opened the door and ducked inside to turn off the alarm and drop her bag, then stood in the doorway, watching for my reaction.

The Lynne Wesson movie. I'd forgotten all about it. *Shit.* "Two months?"

She nodded. "The shooting schedule is going to be crazy, and I'm really going to need to immerse myself into character and try and avoid distractions..." She fidgeted with the doorknob and crossed her arms across her chest. "Listen, Caid. What I'm trying to say, and doing a bad job of it, is that I'm not going to be able to communicate much for the next two months. I know we just...started something here, but maybe it would be a good idea for us to put this on hold until I get back."

Put this on hold? Was she freaking kidding me?

I put my hands on my hips. "Are you going to change your mind in two months? Have you changed your mind already? Is that what this is? A graceful way of backing away again?"

"No, Caid. God, no. Of course not," she said, obviously startled by my anger. "I just..."

"Ah." I said in suddenly realization.

She frowned. "What does 'ah' mean?"

"It means I think I know why you're doing this. You're not going to change your mind, but you think I will. You still don't trust that this isn't just some fad for me, do you?"

"No, that's not it, either." She uncrossed her arms and ran a hand through her hair. "I'm not going to lie to you, Caid. Yeah, I'm scared that once we get involved, you'll decide that it's not for you, and I'll end up hurt. I told you, though—I think it's worth the risk. What I'm talking about now has nothing to do with that." She sighed. "Look. I don't want to mess this up. I know this is new for you, and I don't want us to feel rushed because I'm leaving, and maybe we do something you're not ready for..."

She was doing this because of me. She was concerned about me. I smiled, and stepped forward. "Back up."

"Wha..."

"Robyn, back up. Into the house. I want to kiss you, and I don't think you want Liz or Walter to see that quite yet if they can see us from the car. And I don't want to give Perry and James a cheap thrill."

She took two quick steps back, then another two to her left, so that she was out of the doorway. I followed her into the foyer and swung the door partially shut behind me, then stepped in close and put my hands on her waist.

"Robyn." I kissed her gently. "I've been putting how I feel about you on hold for almost two years. I'm tired of it, and I really don't see the point. I appreciate your concern, but I'm a big girl, and I'm not going to get rushed into something I don't want, or something I'm not ready for." I kissed her again, wanting much more but keeping it light, mindful of the car full of people waiting for me outside.

Her eyes fluttered open as I drew back, and she frowned. "What do you mean, almost two years? I haven't even known you for two years. We only met —"

"September 14th, year before last," I interrupted matter-of-factly. "After the morning shoot. You had on jeans, a rust-colored tank, and tennis shoes. You smiled and I nearly passed out." She blinked in surprise and I smiled slightly. "You're not the only one who started wanting that day. In fact, I wanted so much that I acted like a complete moron whenever you were around. Hence the giggling and saying really bizarre things."

"Oh," she said faintly.

"Now..." I leaned forward to nibble at her lower lip, closing my eyes and humming in pleasure when Robyn pulled me closer and turned the nibble into a slow, gentle kiss. I pulled back after several long moments and opened my eyes. "Will I see you before you leave?"

Her smile was slow and sweet. "You'd better."

I STEPPED OUT onto the large wooden deck of Liz's Malibu beach home, taking a deep breath of moist ocean air. The sun was dipping low in the west, just kissing the watery expanse of Pacific that stretched to the horizon, turning the sky gold and the water a deep purple. The sound of the surf, gently breaking on the beach below, was soothing, and I leaned against the deck railing with a sigh, resting pleasantly tired muscles and enjoying a bit of relaxation after a hectic day.

Showing two college-aged men the exciting sights of greater Los Angeles had turned out to be a full-time job. Mann's Chinese

Theater and Liz's star on the Walk of Fame, dinner at Spago's, and clubbing on The Strip yesterday, and today, a full day at the beach with private surfing lessons. I was wiped out, and we still had a movie premiere that I'd talked my way into later tonight. Tomorrow would be busy as well, with a tour of the network complex and a couple of hours on the set of a currently shooting movie before their afternoon flight back to Madison.

Maybe after all that, I'd finally have a chance to see Robyn. I hadn't seen her in over twenty-four hours, and now that I'd felt what it was like to touch her, I couldn't wait for my next touch. But Robyn's pre-filming preparations and my hectic schedule with Perry and James were combining to make it very possible that we wouldn't see each other before she left, and that was frustrating the hell out of me.

The sound of the door sliding open and closed brought me out of my thoughts, and I glanced over as a glass was placed on the railing beside me.

"I, uh, I asked Perry, and he said you liked scotch..." James said, picking nervously at the label of the bottle of beer in his hand.

"I do," I said with a smile, picking up the glass and swirling it a few times before taking a sip. "Thanks, James."

He watched me drink and, apparently satisfied that I did indeed like scotch, leaned against the railing and faced the water, mimicking my position. We leaned in silence for a few minutes, drinking and watching the sun dip lower. "It's beautiful here," he said eventually. "It was really nice of Liz to let us use it."

"Yeah." I took in another deep lungful of air. "I love it here. I think she's crazy not to use it more. It's a great place to get away."

"Is it..." he paused, and looked over at me. "Is it like that a lot? All those photographers? And those people yelling at you?"

He was talking about the scene that greeted us when we returned to my house after dropping Robyn off the day before. A herd of photographers and news vans blocking my drive, surrounding the limo as we pulled up, making it nearly impossible for us to get to the house. Liz had offered the beach house immediately, knowing how much I hated that kind of attention.

"No, it's not usually like that for me. It's just fallout from this whole...thing." I waved my drink around vaguely. "It'll die down in a couple of days. It's like that for Liz, almost everywhere she goes, and for Robyn sometimes...but, no, I don't usually rate that kind of attention."

He glanced away when I looked over at him. "I don't know why," he said quietly. "You're just as pretty as they are."

I laughed, but quieted quickly when I noticed his wounded expression. "Thank you, that's sweet of you to say."

"Well, it's true," he mumbled.

I smiled and sipped at my drink. "You did great out there today—a real natural," I commented, wanting to change the subject. The day we'd just spent surfing seemed like a safe enough topic.

He smiled shyly. "You too. You're really, uh, athletic. And you, um...look great in a swimsuit."

Perhaps not such a safe topic after all. I think it was time to have a little talk with James about how he had absolutely no chance with his best friend's much older—and most likely a lesbian—sister.

I put my drink on the rail and turned to face him, but before I could say anything, he lunged forward and planted his lips on mine.

To say I was startled would be an understatement, and it took me a moment to react. I put my hands on his shoulders and pushed him away, annoyed that he had tried something and annoyed with myself for not nipping this in the bud.

"James, no," I said firmly when I'd pried his lips off me. He cringed like a kicked puppy and I stifled my annoyance with a sigh. "James, this is not happening."

"But," he started.

I shook my head, stopping him. "But nothing. You're a nice guy, James, but this isn't happening. I'm practically old enough to be your mother, for one thing, and honestly, you're not my type." Okay, so the "old enough to be your mother" bit was a slight exaggeration, but I thought it might help.

"What is your type? I'm not tall enough? Not famous enough? Not rich enough?" he asked, sulking now.

I resisted the urge to roll my eyes. Sometimes men were such babies. "I would hope you know me a little better than that, James." I gave him a sharp look, no longer caring about hiding my annoyance.

He dropped his gaze and had the good sense to look apologetic.

"I'll tell you what my type isn't, James. It's not friends of my brother's who are barely twenty-one, okay?"

He nodded and slumped dejectedly against the rail.

I softened my tone. "I'm sorry if I did something to give you a different impression."

He shook his head. "No, you didn't. I was just..." He shrugged. "I dunno. Hoping, I guess."

"I'm flattered, James. Truly. And some girl is going to be very lucky to get you someday."

Ugh. Did I just say that? Cheesy, cheesy, cheesy. After-school specials, here I come.

"But not you, huh?" His tone was resigned.

I smiled slightly. "No, not me."

We both turned and watched the final rays of sun fade to purple, and the sun dip below the horizon. After a few minutes, I bumped him with my shoulder. "Piece of advice?"

He glanced over. "Sure."

"Next time, save the tongue for the second kiss, hmm?"

He looked embarrassed for a moment, but saw that I was smiling. He laughed and clinked his bottle against my glass. "I'll try to remember that."

Chapter
Eleven

"COME ON, CAID, four more. That's it, three...you've got it. Two...and one more... All right, nice job!"

Shawn plucked the twenty-pound dumbbells from my hands as though they were toothpicks, smiling down at me with a practiced, encouraging smile. "Take a sixty-second break and then we'll go for another fifteen."

I groaned and let my arms dangle behind my head, arching my back over the exercise ball I was lying on top of for tricep curls. "You're evil. You know that, right?"

"That's what you pay me for." He smiled again, and this time, the smile was a little more genuine. "You're the one who wanted a last-minute, butt-kicking workout. I'm just giving you what you wanted."

"Well, I'm an idiot," I mumbled, and I raised my hands up to receive the dumbbells again, blowing out a few deep breaths before lowering the weights behind my head slowly, and then raising them up again.

I was on my tenth rep when the muffled tones of my cell phone interrupted my concentration, and I paused.

"Oh, no, you don't. Five more, Caid, and then you can answer it." Shawn picked up the phone from where it sat on my towel and waved it enticingly in front of my face.

I scowled, too breathless to call him all the names running through my mind, and pushed out five more reps as fast as I could, my arms shaking crazily on the last two. He handed me the phone after taking the weights from my hands, and after a moment of fumbling, I got the thing open.

" 'Lo," I gasped, closing my eyes and draping a sweaty arm across my face.

There was a moment of silence, and then a low, husky voice asked, "Am I interrupting something?"

I didn't think it was possible, but my heart rate picked up even more and it took me a moment before I could respond. "I'm at the gym. Trying to work off some...frustration," I panted finally. I knew the smile on my face was giving Shawn some ideas, but I couldn't help it. "Where are you? I thought you had a dinner thing tonight."

Robyn had called while I was on my way to the airport with Perry and James, to tell me the bad news that her presence was required tonight at a dinner party at her agent's house, and she didn't know when she would be home. Perry and James were in the car with me so I couldn't yell and scream in frustration as I'd wanted to, but the moment I dropped them off, I'd called Shawn and asked for a workout that would leave me exhausted and wanting my mommy.

I could hear the smile in her voice when she answered my question. "I told Mark I'm not feeling well. I think I might have gotten food poisoning this afternoon. So...I find myself suddenly free for the evening."

I sat up. "Tell me you're not kidding."

She laughed. "I'm not kidding. When can you get over here? I'll cook you dinner."

"Give me an hour," I said, reaching for my towel and ignoring Shawn's look of disapproval. "Hour and a half tops."

She laughed again, low and breathless. The sound tickled down my spine as though she were here, touching me. "Hurry."

I snapped the phone shut and stood, giving Shawn a smile that made him blink. "Looks like I won't need that workout after all."

I CLOSED THE gate behind me and headed up the sandstone path, forcing myself to walk instead of sprint like I wanted to. I felt giddy with anticipation, like a teenager with a first crush, and when Robyn opened the door in a sleeveless, button-down shirt, long denim shorts, and no shoes, the smile I gave her made my face ache.

Her return smile was dazzling, her eyes shining with welcome. "Hey, you."

"Hey." I suddenly felt shy, wanting to hug her but not knowing if it would be welcome.

She put an end to my wondering by tugging me into the house by the hand, shutting the door behind us, and pulling me tightly against her.

I sighed and wrapped my arms around her waist, burying my face in her neck. "I missed you."

She tightened the embrace and rubbed her face against my hair. "I missed you too, baby," she whispered. "It's crazy how much."

We stood, just holding each other and not speaking, as long minutes passed. Finally, she pulled back, cradling my face in her hands, and placed a gentle kiss on my lips. I leaned into the kiss, savoring it for what it was; not a kiss for passion's sake, but rather a reconnection — an affirmation — of things already said.

"Come on," she said eventually, stepping away but not letting go of my hand. "Let me get you a glass of wine and you can watch me cook you something fabulous."

I kicked off my sandals and followed her downstairs, where she seated me on a barstool along a counter in her kitchen and handed me a glass of white wine. "Can I help?" I asked

"Nope. Sorry, I'm a bit territorial about my kitchen," she answered with a smile that said she wasn't sorry at all.

I made a mental note to not mess about in her kitchen.

"You like shrimp, I hope?" At my nod, she pulled a bowl of medium-sized shrimp out of the refrigerator and set it on the counter, then splashed olive oil into a pan, added a bowlful of sliced garlic, and set it to heat.

We talked of random things as she pulled various cups of liquid out of the refrigerator, transferred the cooked garlic to a paper towel, and briskly tossed the shrimp with salt and pepper, moving with a confidence and economy of motion that nudged something in my memory.

When I was twenty, I spent the summer on the wait staff of an upscale resort outside Rice Lake, serving pricy dinners to sunburnt tourists. The overall atmosphere of the kitchen had been hectic and chaotic, but the area around the head chef, Jean-Marie, had always seemed calm, and I had admired the way he inhabited the space around him, as though the pots, pans, knives, and other utensils were an extension of his person.

Robyn moved around her kitchen the same way; as though her actions were second nature, an extension of herself.

"You've done this before," I commented, and she raised an inquisitive eyebrow in my direction, not pausing in her preparations. I gestured at the sauté pan now filled with shrimp that she was absently shaking with casual flicks of her wrists. "Cooking. Where'd you learn?"

She smiled, her face softening. "My mom was a chef. Still is, actually, although now she mostly handles front-of-the-house. She and my sister are both restaurateurs — they have restaurants in Santa Barbara and Santa Monica." She gave the shrimp another expert flip. "My sisters and I knew our way around a kitchen before we were out of elementary school."

"Tell me about your family," I requested, realizing that I knew almost nothing about her. We had talked, certainly, but never about our pasts or families.

She scooped the shrimp out onto a platter and placed the pan back on the burner, adding the garlic back in, along with a plateful of some kind of chilies. "My family." She smiled again with obvious fondness. "Well, I have three sisters. One older and two younger. Trish—she's the oldest—is part owner of the restaurants with Mom. She runs the place in Santa Monica now, and lives there with her boyfriend Enrique. Diane, she's two years younger than me...she works in a law firm in San Francisco. The youngest is Lori—she's a stay-at-home mom with two little boys and a third on the way. She and her husband, Will, live in Santa Barbara, near my parents."

A few cupfuls of liquid went into the pan, along with the already cooked shrimp and some spices. She turned the flame down a bit before turning to pull two plates out of a cupboard above her head and unplugging a rice cooker that had been quietly steaming away on the corner of the counter. "Mom...like I said, she's a chef and runs the restaurant in Santa Barbara, and my dad used to model—that's how I got into it—and now he dabbles a little in real estate, plays a lot of golf and tennis, and occasionally helps out at the restaurant."

"So that's where you grew up? Santa Barbara?" I asked, watching the play of muscles under the tan skin of her forearm as she flipped and stirred the contents of the pan a few more times before removing it from the heat. I let my eyes travel from her forearms up over the swell of breast, the long, elegant neck, sharp chin, full lips, straight nose, finally resting on obsidian eyes that stared at me with a heat that caused my breath to hitch.

We stared at each other, conversation forgotten, until finally Robyn blinked and looked away, drawing a shaky breath. "Christ, Caid...those eyes are lethal."

She stood for a moment more, staring at the stove, and then pulled a few large spoons out of a drawer and began doling out generous portions of brown rice topped with the shrimp and chili mixture, along with greens and cooked carrots. Looking over her shoulder at me, her expression now bland, she picked up the two plates and nodded at her wineglass on the counter. "Could you bring mine, and the bottle?"

I nodded and did as she asked, tucking the bottle under my arm and picking up her glass before following her out of the kitchen and into what I'd guess was the living room—the huge room with the wall of two-story windows looking out over the flickering lights of the San Gabriel valley that were just starting to come on. A small table had been set up near the windows, with a deep burgundy tablecloth, two place settings, and two tall candles.

She set the two plates down and took the wine bottle from under my arm, placing it in a ceramic wine cooler on one end of the table. Then she took her wine glass from my hand and placed it on the table, gesturing for me to sit down while she lit the candles. Finally, she sat down across from me and put her napkin in her lap, meeting my gaze for the first time in several minutes.

"This is nice, Robyn. Thank you," I offered, trying to get us back to the ease we shared in the kitchen before she caught me staring.

"I hope you like it—it's something my mom was tweaking for the restaurant last time I went home. Please," she waved at my plate, "eat."

I leaned over the plate and breathed in deeply. "Mmm. If the smell is anything to go by, it'll be fabulous, as promised." I picked up my fork and took a bite. "Oh, God." I closed my eyes and chewed slowly, savoring the heat of the chilies paired with sweet shrimp. It was, indeed, fabulous. "This is wonderful."

I opened my eyes and found her leaning back in her chair, watching me with a slight smile on her face. I paused mid-chew and swallowed. "Aren't you eating?"

She smiled fully now, teasing and light. "It's more fun to watch you. Most people I cook for don't appreciate it quite as much as you seem to. Nice to see so much enthusiasm."

"Well," I speared another piece of shrimp, "then the people you've cooked for are idiots. Honestly, Robyn, this is fantastic." I put the shrimp in my mouth and again closed my eyes at the burst of flavor. I chewed for a moment, and swallowed. "You can cook for me anytime."

She gave me a delighted smile and picked up her fork.

I learned more about Robyn over dinner. I'd always been good at getting people to talk to me, and it turned out that Robyn liked to talk. She grew up in Santa Barbara and had a dizzying number of aunts, uncles and cousins still in the area; she was close with all her sisters, but from how she spoke about Diane, the two of them were especially close; she broke her arm and three ribs falling out of a tree when she was seven; she lost her virginity to Duane Resin on prom night when she was seventeen; and most of her family, like the rest of the world, had no idea that she was gay.

I'd practically licked my plate clean while she talked, and I picked up my wine and leaned back in my chair, pleasantly full. "So only Diane knows?"

She nodded, playing with her food. "I know, sounds strange, doesn't it? It just always seemed easier not to say anything...and it never really mattered. I've never wanted to bring anyone home to meet the family."

I digested that, wondering what it meant for us. The fear that I was going to end up being just another "thing" in an apparently long list of things once again surfaced, but I squashed it as best I could.

"There's a little more, if you'd like it," Robyn said finally, after a long silence.

I shook my head and smiled. "I'm stuffed, thank you. That was great."

I followed her into the kitchen with my plate and silverware; she took the items out of my hands and turned to put them in the sink with hers. I'd wanted to touch her all through dinner, and I finally gave in to temptation, stepping up behind her and snaking my arms loosely around her slim waist, resting my chin on her shoulder.

"Dinner was wonderful," I murmured in her ear, closing my eyes and breathing in the scent of her hair. "And so are you." She leaned back against me, placing her hands over mine. I kissed her cheek, and trailed my lips to her ear, nibbling gently. "You taste good, too."

I could feel her smile, and she turned in my embrace, settling her arms on my shoulders with her hands joined behind my head. "How do you manage to be so sweet," she said, kissing me softly before pulling back, "and so goddamn sexy at the same time?"

I gave her a pleased smile and leaned in to brush our lips together again, meaning for the kiss to be brief but quickly losing myself in the softness of her lips and the feel of her tongue stroking hesitantly against mine. Her hands went into my hair, gently encouraging me, and she purred deep in her throat when I pushed her hips against the counter and deepened the kiss. We kissed for several long moments before pulling apart, breathing heavily.

I leaned into her, touching our foreheads together as I caught my breath. "You're one hell of a kisser, Ms. Ward."

She gave a breathy laugh and ran long fingers through the hair at the nape of my neck. "Oh, honey...I'd say you have some skills of your own."

We stood quietly against each other for a few moments more, and then she grasped my hand and slid out from between the counter and me, leading me into the other room and gesturing for me to sit on a large leather couch in front of the fireplace. I sat down and watched as she put on some soft, instrumental guitar music and turned on the gas fireplace before retrieving our wineglasses and coming back to the couch.

"A fire when it's eighty degrees outside?" I teased, and she paused as she handed me my wine.

"Do you mind? It doesn't put out that much heat and I like

watching it—"

"I was just teasing," I interrupted her. "It's nice."

She smiled, and lowered herself onto the other end of the couch, tucking her feet under her.

I hid a frown at her being so far away—I wanted to touch her, but if she felt the need for some distance, I didn't want to push. We watched the fire for a while, and I had to agree with her that it was nice to watch a fire, regardless of the time of year.

"So what about you?" she asked eventually. "Turnabout is fair play...tell me about your family. I know you have an extremely handsome twenty-two-year-old brother...any other siblings lying around?"

I paused, swirling my wine, before answering. "Just one. I have an older brother, Sebastian. He's a tax attorney, lives in Tampa."

There was no warmth in my voice, and she raised her eyebrows. "You don't get along." It was statement, not a question.

"That would be putting it mildly." I took a sip of wine, trying to think of how best to describe the antagonism between my eldest brother and me. "Would you like the short version, or the long version?"

"I'm not in a hurry to be anywhere...why don't we go with the long version?"

"Okay," I said with a wry smile. "Just remember that you asked for it." I paused for a moment, wondering where to begin. "My father is a doctor. In the late Sixties, he was a family practitioner in Milwaukee. He had married his high school sweetheart and opened up his own practice. Everything was going along nicely until, as a favor, he hired the daughter of a family friend to help around the office. A year later he'd divorced his wife and married his young employee, who was pregnant."

"So, the young employee was..."

"My mom," I answered with a quick nod. "The whole thing was something of a scandal, I guess, since Mom was only eighteen, so Dad sold the practice and moved his young bride and new baby to Madison, where he set up shop again, and they had another kid," I pointed to myself, "and they lived in what seemed to me, when I was young, happy bliss, until I was about twelve. That's when they found out that Mom was pregnant again. Mom was thrilled, but Dad wasn't so happy. They started fighting constantly..." I paused for a moment as the memory of the first time I'd heard my parent's voices raised in anger at each other surfaced, still vivid even after twenty years. I'd been too young to really understand what was happening, but I remembered the sick feeling I'd gotten in the pit of my stomach that night, and the certainty that "Something Bad" was happening.

A gentle brush of fingers along my arm shook me out of my memories and I glanced at Robyn, forcing a small smile that, from the look of compassion on her face, held more remembered pain than I'd intended. I held my glass to my chest and drew my feet up under me as Robyn had done, clearing my throat before I continued. "Anyway, things progressed as they usually do, and eventually Perry was born. A few weeks after Perry's first birthday, Dad filed for divorce and ran off to Chicago with his twenty-four-year-old receptionist. Dad was nothing if not consistent," I said, unable to keep the trace of bitterness out of my voice.

"Oh, Caid...that must have been awful." She scooted over until our knees were touching and took my hand, her eyes full of empathy.

I stroked my thumb across her knuckles, liking the feel of her hand in mine, and the way our hands looked together. "It was...hard for us all, but it was especially hard on Sebastian. Mom asked for full custody, and Dad didn't fight it, basically removing himself completely from our lives. Sebastian worshiped Dad, and after he left, Sebastian just...he completely changed. He was angry all the time, screaming and yelling at Mom and me, saying it was our fault, getting into trouble, picking fights..." I shook my head as more memories surfaced. "That was a really fun time, let me tell you."

She squeezed my hand. "So he never really got over it?"

"Nope, he never did..." I looked into the fire. "And then he married into a rich, incredibly religious fundamentalist Tampa family, and went from being an angry, hurt kid to a bigoted, self-righteous asshole." I shook my head. "It's hard to love someone who hates everything about you, and Sebastian has made it very clear that my job, my life...everything about me is evil. Jesus," I said with a pained laugh, "when he finds out I've...that I'm a lesbian, he will seriously blow a gasket." I shuddered at the thought, and Robyn squeezed my hand again.

"I'm sorry, Caid," she said simply.

I smiled wryly and finished the rest of my wine in a gulp. "Me, too."

"Do you ever...see your father? I can't believe someone would just cut their kids off like that."

"Hard to believe, isn't it? When he first left, I was pretty angry too, but unlike Sebastian, I was angry at Dad, and not Mom. He left when I was thirteen, and I didn't see him again until I was twenty-one. Now I see him once or twice a year, I guess. Sebastian might see him more, I don't know. Dad is definitely a topic I don't want to discuss with him. Perry has met him a few times, but Mom remarried a couple of years after Dad left, and as far as Perry's concerned, his dad is Larry, Mom's current husband."

She shook her head, stroking my hand. "I'm sorry," she said again, and leaned forward to kiss my forehead. "I wish you hadn't gone through that."

"Mmm." I closed my eyes at her tenderness. It had been a long time since I'd told anyone that story—since I'd dredged up those memories—and I was glad it hadn't sent her screaming into the hills. Or maybe it had, and she was just being nice. I opened my eyes. "So...now that you know the whole sordid tale, still interested in starting something with me?" I tried to keep my tone light, and not sound too pathetic.

She cupped my face and forced me to look at her. "I'm not that easy to scare away, Caid. I don't care about your family, I care about you."

I turned my head and brushed my lips against the hand cupping my cheek. "Lucky me."

"And don't you forget it, missy," she said, and tapped my nose, lightening the mood. "I'm going to get a little more wine. Would you like some?"

I handed her my empty glass when she stood, and she crossed to the table and divided what was left in the bottle between the two glasses. I put my feet on the floor and stretched my legs, still feeling the slight pull in my hamstrings from my surfing adventure.

"So where does your mom live now?" Robyn asked from across the room.

"She and Larry are still in Madison, although they travel almost six months out of the year. They run a travel tour company—hiking tours to Switzerland, biking in France, sailing the Greek Islands, that sort of thing. They're out of the country now until August, leading the first of...I think three this year...trekking tours of Nepal."

"Really?" She sounded intrigued. "What a great job. How long have they been doing that?"

"Um, let's see. Maybe eight, nine years? Since Perry was about thirteen, I guess. They used to take him with them."

"Have you ever gone?" She perched herself on the arm of the couch and handed me my wineglass.

"I went on a bike tour through Germany with them once, and part of a New Zealand tour a few years back. By the time they started it, I was just starting to get interested in acting—taking classes, picking up gigs here and there, working a couple jobs—it just never seemed like I had enough time."

She motioned for me to move over, then slid in beside me on the couch, curling her feet up and tucking them under my thigh. I could feel the slight chill through the thin linen shorts I was wearing.

"Comfortable?" I asked with a smile and a raised eyebrow.

"Very." She wiggled her toes and grinned at me, the force of it hitting me like a punch.

I love it when she smiles like that.

This wasn't the practiced smile she gave the cameras and the public, or even the warmer smile that she'd flash occasionally at work. No, this one she gave out sparingly, to a select few, and it lit her entire face up — hell, her entire self. It was open, inviting, and completely captivating. The image robbed me of breath and brought an ache to my chest, and I reached out to trail slightly trembling fingertips down her cheek, shaking my head.

"You're so damn beautiful, Robyn. Sometimes I look at you, and I can't breathe."

Her body stilled, and I wondered if I'd said something wrong. I withdrew my hand slowly. "I'm sorry..."

Her eyes didn't leave my face as she gently placed her wineglass on the table, and then did the same with mine. Her hands went to the buttons of her shirt and she slowly unbuttoned them, one by one, revealing glimpses of tanned skin and peach-colored lace. I watched her hands in equal parts fascination and trepidation, and when she was done, I looked up to meet her gaze. She smiled slightly at whatever petrified, excited, confused look I had on my face, then her expression became serious again and she took my hands in hers, turned them over, and kissed each palm. "I want you to touch me, Caid," she said softly, and placed my hands on the smooth skin of her stomach.

I drew in a shaky breath at the first touch of my hands on her heated skin. I was trembling, and I could feel the echoing tremble under my fingers. "Robyn..." My voice was hesitant, unsure.

"Shhh..." She leaned forward and kissed me, slow and deep, then leaned back against the armrest of the couch, the action parting her shirt completely. "There's no right way or wrong way, Caid. Just...touch me."

I dropped my eyes to take in the sharp angles of her collarbone, small breasts covered by almost sheer, peach-colored material, and the long, flat planes of her abdomen where my hands rested. She was slender — almost too slender, I thought briefly — and my hands looked large around her waist. I brushed tentatively with my thumbs and raised my hands to run my fingers over the ridges of her ribs. The slight tremors under my fingers gave me confidence and I stroked my hands down her stomach, swirling fingertips into the hollows just above the waistband of her shorts, the hollows that had so intrigued me last time I saw them as she walked up my drive three weeks before.

I paused for a moment, remembering in a rush what I had wanted to do then. *Don't think, Caid. Just...do.*

She gave a tiny gasp of surprise and pleasure when I lowered my head and kissed one hollow, then skimmed my lips across her stomach to kiss the other. I felt her hand in my hair, stroking softly and then spasming briefly when I ran my tongue around her navel, dipping in quickly and then sucking gently on the surrounding skin. I laid my cheek against the smooth, warm skin of her belly. "You're so soft," I whispered, letting my fingers play over her skin for a moment before turning and bracing my hands on either side of her, kissing my way up the middle of her body and finally capturing her lips. The gentle kiss soon turned urgent, and when I pulled away, we were both shaking.

Her hands gripped my upper arms tightly, and her breathing was uneven. "God...you make me feel so much..."

I balanced myself on one arm and ran my hand from her shoulder to her chest, hesitantly cupping her breast and lightly stroking my thumb across the material of her bra, feeling her nipple harden in response.

She sucked in a breath and her hands dug into my arms painfully. "Caid...baby, I don't want to rush you...we need to stop..."

I raised my fingers to her lips, silencing her, and replaced the fingers with my lips for a brief kiss. "I want you, Robyn," I whispered. "Jesus, so much it hurts. I want to make you feel." I looked at her pleadingly. "Teach me. Show me."

And she did—helping me slowly undress her, whispering breathless words of direction and encouragement, guiding my mouth to her neck and breasts, and much later, my hand to her sex, holding me tightly against her as she shuddered, muscles tightening in release around my fingers.

She continued to hold my hand against her as she slowly relaxed, and I had no objection, enthralled by the feel of her warmth around my fingers and the slick evidence of her desire. Finally she moved her hand and I withdrew, lowering my body next to hers.

"That was...amazing," I said softly, and kissed her forehead. "Thank you."

She let out a strangled laugh and opened her eyes, looking at me with a slightly dazed expression. "I think it's me that should be thanking you."

"So that's good, right?" I asked hopefully, shamelessly asking for reassurance.

She laughed again, and this time when she opened her eyes,

they were filled with gentle humor. "Yes. Very good. Caid...you did just fine." She smiled at me and stroked my cheek. "Just fine."

"Good." It wasn't the fireworks-exploded-and-I-lost-touch-with-reality kind of praise that every lover hopes for, but it was enough. I smiled contentedly, thinking practice makes perfect, and gathered her up in my arms, nuzzling her hair. "Mmm. You feel good."

She shifted onto her side and laid her head on my chest with a satisfied sigh. "You feel good, too." She reached back and tugged at a blanket that was lying across the back of the couch, pulling it on top of us and settling in once more, her hand making lazy circles on my stomach under my shirt.

After a few minutes the circles moved upward and she brushed her palm across my breast, then came back to circle my hardening nipple with a fingertip. The scrape of her fingernail across the material of my bra sent tiny shockwaves of sensation straight to my groin and I bit back a groan.

"Why is it," she said in a raspy whisper, "that you have so many clothes on?" She tipped her head back and sucked my earlobe into her mouth. "Hmm?"

I could only shake my head as the material of my bra was pushed up, freeing my breasts, and my nipple gently rolled between her fingers. "Oh..." She gave my other breast the same treatment before my shirt was pushed up and her mouth, moist and hot, replaced her fingers. I closed my eyes and sucked in a breath, arching against her. "Jesus...Robyn..."

She rolled until she was on top of me and pushed my shirt up further, sucking and nipping at my breasts, her hands and mouth seeming everywhere at once. I was lost in a haze of sensation and arousal, and when she stopped and lifted herself off me, I whimpered in dismay.

"Caid." Her voice was rough with emotion and need, and my eyes flew open to find her standing naked above me, holding out a hand.

I took her hand and wordlessly followed her as she turned off the gas to the fire, blew out the candles, and led me up the stairs to her bedroom. In the dim lamplight she undressed me, each newly revealed piece of my body eliciting murmurs of wonder and soft, reverent kisses, as though they were gifts.

"Beautiful," she said softly as her eyes roamed my body. She ran her hands up my arms and across my shoulders, pausing a moment to knead the muscles there. "So strong." The hands continued their trek, down over my breasts, tickling along my ribs, and finally coming to rest on my hips. She looked into my eyes, pausing as though to make sure she had my attention. As if there was any doubt about that. "You're beautiful, Caid."

She took my hand again and pulled the covers on the bed back, then pushed me down and slowly lowered herself on top of me. The feel of our naked skin touching for the first time pulled a low moan from both of us.

"So good," she whispered as she settled on top of me, kissing my neck. "I knew you'd feel so good..."

She took her time, her hands stroking and kneading, and her teeth, lips and tongue igniting fires across my skin. Sensation overwhelmed me and left no room for nervousness or doubt. I drowned in the sweetness of it, finally coming with a shuddering gasp as her fingers filled me and she swiped her tongue across my clit.

The tremors of my orgasm still echoed in my limbs as she kissed her way up my body to brace herself on her hands above me. "You're amazing," she whispered, kissing my forehead. "Incredible." She placed a soft kiss on each eyelid. "Perfect." She hovered above my mouth, our breath mingling, and traced my upper lip with her tongue. I groaned and surged up to bring our mouths together, tasting myself on her lips. The wave of heat that rolled through me at the thought made me ache, and I needed, right then, to taste her.

Her eyes widened in surprise when I pushed her over and reversed our positions, but she murmured her approval when I ran my tongue down her neck to her breasts, spending several minutes in languid exploration before continuing down her body, remembering areas where she was most responsive and discovering new ones that brought an intoxicating mixture of moans and tiny gasps.

When I eventually touched my tongue to her wetness she hissed, and grabbed the back of my head, guiding and encouraging as she had done before, with her hips surging against me in unabashed need. Her hand tightened in my hair, at once demanding and beseeching, and long moments later, when she came against me, I needed no reassurance that it had been good.

I circled her waist with my arms and lay my head on her stomach, feeling the fading echoes of her pleasure against my cheek, and listening to her breathing and the gradually slowing beat of her heart. The feel of our bodies together, the smell of her, the heat of her skin on mine, and the taste of her on my lips — it was all a revelation, and I lay marveling at the sense of absolute rightness.

Gentle fingers ran lightly through my hair for a few minutes, and then tugged.

"Come up here, you." Her voice was a purr of contentment,

lazy and sated, and quite irresistible.

I placed a wet, openmouthed kiss between her legs that made her twitch, and inched up her body, placing more kisses as I went. After one final kiss on her smiling mouth, I settled in next to her, propping my head up on my hand, and watched her watch me.

"Mmm..." She sighed contentedly and rolled on her side to face me. "You were certainly right about having the mechanics down," she said with a smile, stroking my cheek. "I thought you said you were new at this."

I smiled slightly and kissed her fingers. "I'm a fast learner with the proper motivation. And you," I kissed her fingers again and caught one between my teeth, biting gently before releasing it, "you are some kind of motivation."

"Lucky me." She leaned in for a lingering kiss and then pulled back, hesitating for a moment before asking quietly, "Stay?"

I smiled and kissed her forehead. "I'd like that."

"Good." Her fingers traced random circles on the skin of my shoulder and a slight push sent me sprawling onto my back. She contemplated my naked form with languid, half-lidded intent, sparking a shiver of anticipation that danced along my skin and set my body humming. "I'm not even close to being done with you."

I grinned.

Hot. Damn.

SOMETIME BEFORE DAWN, an insistently full bladder woke me, and after carefully extricating myself from Robyn's arms, I rose and padded to the bathroom. On my way back to bed I paused, captivated by the sight of her sleeping form visible in the soft spill of light from a floor lamp that we'd been too comfortable and too spent in each other's arms to turn off. She was on her stomach, facing me, one arm curled above her head and the other beneath her pillow. She'd kicked most of the covers off during the night, exposing leanly muscled shoulders, the long expanse of her back, one perfect globe of buttock, and one smooth, slender leg.

I stared at her in wonder.

She was astonishing. Fierce and gentle, delicate and strong—a perfect fusion of sharp angles and soft curves, and truly the most beautiful thing I'd ever seen. I drew in a shaky breath, wanting her with an intensity that amazed me. Sex before had been adequate, often pleasant, and sometimes I'd even considered it very good. But this...this was different. Physically intense, but also tapping into a new, unfamiliar emotional component for me, and the combination was heady, liberating, and addicting.

Even now, exhausted and sated, all I needed was a glimpse of her, a thought of her, to stir my need again. I wanted her — wanted to feel her warmth under my hands, to taste her on my lips... I swallowed hard at the rush of emotion that swamped me, surprised at the overwhelming tenderness accompanying the wave of arousal.

Oh, my. I sighed softly.

I was in deep, deep trouble.

When I had talked with Perry about my feelings for Robyn, I'd been unsure and used the label "love" for lack of a better way of explaining my emotions. But now I was sure. Sometime during the night, the feelings I had for Robyn had intensified into something very deep, very strong, and not a little frightening. I had no doubts about it now — I was in love with her.

So. I was in love. In love with a famous, closeted actress with a boyfriend who wasn't really her boyfriend, who called her affairs "things," and who had never cared enough about any of her past lovers to bring them home to meet her family.

I dropped heavily into the softly upholstered wing chair next to the floor lamp and sighed again. *You sure can pick 'em, Caid.*

I sat for a long time, contemplating my new lover and the plethora of ways she could hurt me. Eventually, I turned off the light and slipped back into bed, wiggling around to get comfortable and draping my arm across Robyn's back. This would either be the best thing that ever happened to me, or a spectacular crash and burn that would fuck me up for a good, long time. Either way, I was happy now, and determined to enjoy it for as long as it lasted.

Chapter
Twelve

THE SOUND OF a shower running, along with quiet singing, woke me the next morning, pulling me from dreams that I couldn't remember but that left me slightly unsettled. I rolled onto my back and opened my eyes, blinking groggily at the unfamiliar, sunlit room around me. My eyes fell on a pile of clothes on the floor and I smiled slowly, remembering the night before and exactly who was singing Prince's "Kiss," slightly off-key, in the next room.

I yawned and stretched luxuriously, humming in satisfaction at the pull from muscles long unused. With any luck, I'd have many chances to whip those muscles back in shape. I tucked an arm behind my head, smiling at the thought. The shower turned off, but the singing continued, and a minute later I watched Robyn exit the bathroom wearing a short, black robe—damn, that woman looked good in black—and toweling her hair dry.

Mumbled words about shoe sizes and doing the twirl stopped abruptly when she realized I was awake and watching.

"Morning," I smiled. "I can't remember the last time I was serenaded in bed."

"Uh...hi." She looked around the room, anywhere but at me, obviously uncomfortable and at a loss for words. I fought back a stab of panic. She couldn't be done with me already, could she?

Not if I could fucking help it.

I pushed the covers off and threw my legs over the side of the bed, never losing eye contact. "Come here." I think we were both surprised by the authority in my tone, and she blinked and dropped the towel to her shoulder, staring at me. "Please," I added, holding out a hand to her.

She hesitated, warring with herself, before finally draping the towel across the back of the chair and slowly approaching the bed. She stopped a few feet from me and I reached out to pull her forward the last few feet until she came to a stop standing between my legs.

I stared up into her face for a moment, looking for a hint of what we shared the night before. *Come on, sweetheart; don't do this to me...*

With careful deliberateness, I untied the belt of her robe and spread the material, drinking in the sight of her. She did nothing as I slowly ran my hands up her thighs and over her stomach, but when I nuzzled the hair at the juncture of her thighs and placed a gentle kiss on the small swell just above it, I felt a tremor run through her body and a shaky sigh escaped her lips.

I wrapped my arms around her waist inside the robe and laid my cheek against her stomach, squeezing tightly. "Please, Robyn," I whispered, "don't pull away from me. Not now. I don't think I could stand it."

She let out another shaky breath and I felt a gentle hand on my head, stroking my hair softly. "Oh, Caid...Christ, you scare the hell out of me. You know that, don't you?"

"I'm scared, too." I mumbled in response, and her hand paused briefly before resuming its stroking.

We stayed that way for a few minutes, and finally I looked up to find her gazing down at me with a tenderness that calmed my fears. She cupped my face with both hands and leaned down to kiss me. "I'm sorry, Caid. I'm not used to someone staying the night...I guess I freaked out just a little. Let's start again, okay?" She kissed me again. This kiss was much more involved, and when she finally pulled away, she was on top of me in a tangle of limbs, her robe discarded somewhere on the floor, and her breasts warm and supple in my hands.

She sighed and lifted off of me slightly. "Good morning." She gave me a gentle kiss. "I had a wonderful, wonderful time last night, thank you."

"I..." I didn't know how to begin telling her what last night had meant to me, and I was fairly certain we weren't ready for declarations of love, regardless of my nocturnal realizations. I settled for a heartfelt, "Me, too," satisfied for the moment with the pleased smile my words elicited.

I raised my head and nibbled along the line of her chin, stroking my thumbs gently along the undersides of her breasts and feeling the answering surge in my body at her sharp intake of breath. "God...." She tucked in her chin, putting it out of my reach, and laid her forehead against mine. "Damn... As much as it kills me to say this, we need to stop. My flight leaves at ten twenty and I have a car coming in an hour, and I still have some things to take care of..."

I dropped my head to the pillow with a tiny noise of distress. "Son-of-a-bitch." Slowly, with supreme effort, I pulled my hands from where they cupped her breasts and laid them, palms down, on the bed. "Unfair. So unfair."

"I agree," she said with obvious regret and kissed my nose before rolling off me and climbing off the bed. "I'm sorry, baby."

I sighed dramatically, but smiled inwardly. I could get used to that voice calling me baby in the morning. Or any other damn time she pleased. I rolled on my side and watched in disappointment as she retrieved her robe and shrugged it on, hiding all that glorious skin from my appreciative eye.

"I trust you'll make it up to me later, Ms. Ward?"

Her gaze swept my naked body, and the smile she gave me could only be described as wicked. Deliciously wicked. "Count on it."

The look didn't do anything to calm the heat in my belly. I groaned and pulled a pillow over my head, hearing her laughter move out of the room. "Right now," she called to me as she moved down the stairs, "all I can do is offer you coffee. Come on down when you're ready, help yourself to whatever you need."

I lay still for a minute, attempting to get this thing—this *amazing* thing—that Robyn did to me under control.

She had a car coming. She was leaving. For two months.

I pulled the pillow tight against my face in frustration.

I wasn't going to see her for two freaking months. Wasn't going to feel what I'd felt the night before for two goddamn months. Wouldn't touch her, hold her, taste her...*Jesus, she's not even gone yet and I already miss her. You've got it bad, Caid.*

The sound of a phone ringing, muffled by the pillow but still audible, stopped the depressing path of my thoughts. I tossed the pillow to the side and rolled off the bed, realizing that I was wasting what little time I had with her, and that I should get my butt downstairs pronto. After a quick perusal of my wrinkled clothing from the night before, I ducked into Robyn's closet and grabbed a faded UCLA T-shirt and a pair of black soccer shorts off the shelves, pausing to breathe in the familiar scent of her before pulling them on.

I started down the stairs, whistling happily, and was nearly run over when Robyn came barreling up the stairs full-tilt with a panicked look on her face. She skidded to an abrupt halt at the sight of me, a brief smile flickering across her features as she took in my outfit.

"Damn. You look good in my clothes." She blinked, and her expression closed. "But you need to leave. Now."

The quip about looking even better out of her clothes died on my lips, and I stared at her. "Excuse me?"

She pushed past me into the bedroom, returning a moment later to shove a bundle of clothes—my clothes—into my hands.

"My sister just called. She'll be here any minute, and you can't be here."

I took the clothes automatically and let her direct me down the stairs, bewildered by the turn of events. We were at the entryway and Robyn was muttering something about her sister's bad timing when I finally snapped out of my passivity. I planted my feet and shrugged off the hand that had been none-too-gently pushing me toward the door. "Why?"

She frowned, glancing nervously at the door. "Why, what?"

"Why do I need to be gone when your sister gets here? You're an adult, Robyn. You own this house. You can have whoever the hell you want here and it shouldn't make a difference to your sister."

Her eyes narrowed, her face becoming cold, and I watched the transformation from lover to stranger happen in seconds. She stepped back and crossed her arms. "Careful, Caid. I don't like to be pushed. A night in my bed doesn't give you the right to tell me how to deal with my family. I'm not coming out to my sister because you're a good lay."

I blinked, and my ragged, surprised intake of breath was audible.

Ouch.

Amazing how much hurt a few careless words could cause. A part of me knew she didn't mean it—couldn't mean it. She was stressed and scared, and would regret those words as soon as she had a chance to think about them. In fact, I could tell she was already regretting them as she closed her eyes and pinched the bridge of her nose, swearing softly.

"Shit, Caid, I'm sorry..."

Knowing she was sorry didn't make her words hurt any less, or dim my flare of anger one bit.

"For fuck's sake, Robyn, I wasn't asking you to come out to your sister, I was just asking you to treat me at least like someone you give a shit about, that's all, and not push me out the door like some stranger you picked up in a bar." Her eyes widened as I stripped out of the T-shirt and shorts I'd borrowed in jerky, angry movements, tossing each item in her direction as it came off.

"What the hell are you doing?"

I shook out my own wrinkled clothes and started pulling them on. "There's a woman I assume is your sister coming up the walk. Wouldn't want her to see me in your clothes, now would we? She might get the wrong idea." I finished dressing and laughed bitterly as I stuffed my bra and underwear into my pocket. "I can't freaking believe this. It's been a long time since I've had to sneak out of someone's house with my underwear in my pocket."

I pulled at the hem of my silk sleeveless shirt in an ineffectual attempt to get rid of some of the wrinkles, and ran an unsteady hand through my tangled hair. It didn't help. I looked exactly like I should—like someone who'd spent the night screwing and was now getting kicked out on her ass.

I gave up with an annoyed expletive and straightened, looking over at Robyn. "Thanks, babe, for turning something I thought was pretty damn amazing to crap. Now I know if I ever need a good knock-down for my ego, you're my go-to gal."

She winced and stepped forward. "Caid—"

I cut her off with a wave of my hand and yanked the door open, startling a blond woman standing on the other side with her hand on the knob. "Morning," I said, nodding politely. "You must be Robyn's sister. Nice to meet you. I work with your sister occasionally and stopped by to say hello. I was just leaving."

"Caid...wait." Robyn reached for my arm but I slipped past her very confused-looking sibling, glancing back when I reached the edge of the porch.

"Safe trip, Robyn. I'm glad, at least, it was good for you."

"Damn it, Caid, I didn't mean..."

I whirled and stomped down the path in very mature, righteous anger, not realizing until I got out the gate and to Twila's door that I didn't have my keys. Or my wallet. Or my cell phone. All of these items were in my bag, on a stool in Robyn's kitchen.

Sonofabitch.

I closed my eyes and leaned my hands against the roof of the car, trying to calm my anger that was now mixed with acute embarrassment. *I cannot go back in that house. I cannot go back in that house. I can not go back...*

I stamped my foot against the cobblestones and my eyes popped open at the sudden pain. I looked down and realized I wasn't wearing any shoes.

Well, fuck.

I threw up my hands. "Isn't this fucking *perfect*! Last night's clothes, no keys, no wallet, no phone, no goddamn shoes..."

"Hey, shhh." Robyn was suddenly behind me, wrapping long arms around my body and pulling me against her. She rested her forehead on my shoulder, tightening her arms. "God, I'm such an idiot, Caid, I'm sorry. I didn't mean it... Please, baby, don't leave. I'm so sorry..."

I struggled against her for a few moments, until finally some of my anger burned away and I realized how panicked she sounded. I sighed and slumped back against her. "Shit." Jesus, weren't we a pair. One step forward, eighteen back.

"I'm so sorry," she whispered, and raised her head to kiss my hair just behind my ear. She tightened her embrace for a moment and sighed. "I'm such a fuck-up, Caid, and I so don't want to be a fuck-up with you. I never, ever wanted to hurt you, or to make you feel like I did. To say that to you, about being a good lay... God, I'm an ass. You're not that..."

"Hey!" I squawked, turning my head enough to frown at her.

"Ah, damn, that didn't come out right...of course you are...great, actually...I mean, not that I think of you that way, despite what I said..."

She looked so flustered, so damn earnest—I laughed.

Her forehead creased in confusion and she turned me around to face her, holding me by the shoulders. "You're not mad?"

I snorted. "Of course I'm mad—it was a shitty thing to say, and a shitty way to treat someone."

She dropped her hands from my shoulders and looked at the ground, shuffling her feet like a scolded child. A gorgeous, six-foot-tall, scolded child, dressed in a slinky black robe that left a whole lot of her on display. "I know," she said quietly and looked up remorsefully through long lashes.

It was adorable.

Damn. No wonder she got away with acting like an ass. Whip that look out and no one had a chance. I sighed, and tilted her chin up with my hand. "I'll get over it, Robyn, but this is the last time you get to use the 'I'm not used to this' card, okay? This is new to both of us, but that's not an excuse to act like a jerk."

"I know, Caid, and I'm sor—"

"Uh, Robyn? What's going on?" Both our heads jerked toward the tentative voice.

Whoops. Forgot about the sister.

Without any urgency, I dropped my hand from Robyn's chin and took a casual step back, moving out of her space. She might have been a bit callous in her phrasing earlier, but Robyn was right. How she interacted with her family wasn't my business.

Yet.

Robyn's eyes flicked over to her sister briefly, then back to me, pinning me as though I might leave. She must not have heard my little tirade about not having my keys, wallet and cell phone. "Sorry, Trish... We'll be right in. Can you give us a sec? There's coffee on."

"Robyn, I need to..."

"Trish. Please. Just give me a minute, okay?"

I felt pressure on my fingers and looked down to see that Robyn had taken my hands in hers. I looked at her in surprise. Ten minutes ago, she had been terrified that her sister would find me at her house and get the wrong idea. Or the right idea. Now she was standing here, holding my hands in her driveway.

There was an annoyed huff and light footsteps retreating back up the walk, but Robyn kept her eyes on me. "So." She absently stroked her thumbs over my knuckles, looking at me intently. "Are we okay?"

I resisted the urge to lean in and kiss the lines of worry from her forehead, settling for a nod and a squeeze of her hands. "We're okay."

Her body sagged visibly in relief, and she blinked slowly and smiled. "Thank you."

"Do it again, though, and I'll kick that lovely ass of yours into the next century." I was only half kidding, and she knew it.

"If I do it again, I'd deserve it. In fact, I deserve it now. I'm truly sorry, Caid. I acted...horribly. If I were in your place..." She shook her head, looking blindly over my shoulder for a moment. "I don't know if I'd have forgiven quite so quickly."

"Hey." I tugged on her hands, bringing her eyes back to mine. "Don't think that because I'm quick to forgive that it didn't hurt me, Robyn. It hurt. But I'm not ready to throw the towel in quite yet, and I hope you're not either."

"No way," she said fervently, shaking her head.

"Good."

We stood smiling shyly at each other, until she bit her lower lip and looked up at the house. Ah, yes, the sister. I kept forgetting about her. Robyn glanced back at me and hesitated, the internal debate surprisingly easy to read in her normally guarded expression.

"Would you come inside? I'd like...I'd like you to meet Trish properly." Some of the surprise must have shown on my face, because she hastily amended, "Not as a someone I...not as my lover, Caid, I don't think I'm quite ready for that yet, but I do want her to know you're more than just someone I work with occasionally."

My lover. The words gave me an unexpected thrill of pleasure and I smiled. "I'd like very much to meet your sister."

"Well, then," she said, and grinned, "let's not keep her waiting."

She turned to the gate, dropping one of my hands but keeping a firm grip on the other as she pulled me through it and up the path.

When I resisted, she stopped and looked at me curiously. "What's wrong?"

"Should we..." God, I couldn't believe I was saying this. I felt like I was fifteen and out past curfew. "Should we get our stories straight or something?"

Her forehead furrowed in confusion. "Stories straight?"

"For your sister. You don't want your family to know about...us, but when you came after me, well, that probably looked a little more than friendly. What are you going to tell her?"

She shrugged. "Nothing."

"Nothing?"

"Yes, nothing, because she won't ask."

"She won't?"

"She won't. My family..." She shrugged again. "Some things we just don't mention."

I had a hard time believing that a half-naked Robyn running out of her house and practically tackling a woman in her driveway would be ignored, but soon found that Robyn was right. When we walked into the kitchen, her sister looked more annoyed than curious, and I got my first lesson in Ward family dynamics.

"Don't ask, don't tell" was alive and well in more places than the US military.

Robyn went straight to the coffeemaker, filled a mug already sitting on the counter and handed it to me. I looked into the mug and smiled at the milky color, pleased that she'd remembered how I took my coffee. "Thanks." I took a sip, using both hands to bring the cup to my mouth in an effort to quell the urge to touch her.

She smiled slightly and turned to her sister. "Trish, I'd like you to meet a very good friend of mine, Caid Harris. Caid, this is my older sister Trish."

Trish was shorter than Robyn by a few inches, with dark blond hair cut in a stylish, chin-length bob. Her features were rounder than Robyn's, and her eyes a light brown instead of the piercing near-black of her sister's, but there was no doubt that they were siblings, and that good looks ran in the family.

She gave me a polite nod over the top of her coffee cup, her eyes curious. "Nice to meet you."

"You, too," I said, trying to remember the different family members that Robyn had talked about the night before. Oldest sister, Santa Monica, restaurant... "You must be...the chef?"

"Yes, I am. I have a restaurant in Santa Monica." Her smile widened, and I congratulated myself on picking a topic of conversation that Trish was obviously fond of. "Keeps me running almost non-stop, but I love it. And you...." Her eyes widened and she put her cup down on the counter. "Wait. *Caidence* Harris? The one who disappeared?"

I stifled a sigh and decided now was not the time to go into a defensive diatribe about how I had *not* disappeared, and how it had been a big misunderstanding. Instead, I smiled. "That would be me. But in my defense," I added lightly, "I knew where I was the entire time."

"Well, whatever happened," she cocked her head slightly to the side and regarded me thoughtfully, "it sure had Robby tied in knots. I'm glad it turned out all right."

"Me, too," I said simply, feeling the weight of Robyn's gaze.

Trish's brow furrowed slightly — exactly like Robyn, I thought fleetingly — and she looked me up and down. "I don't watch a lot of TV, but I've caught your show a few times, when Robby's on it." I could tell that information both surprised and pleased Robyn. "Sorry I didn't recognize you. You look...different."

Wrinkled clothes and bed-head will do that to a girl, I thought dryly, and ran a self-conscious hand through my hair. "Not being recognized is fine with me. On screen I'm normally hidden beneath several layers of makeup and mousse, so it's understandable."

She stared at me a moment, then laughed and picked up her coffee. "With a face like that, I doubt you need many layers." I raised an eyebrow in surprise, and she laughed again. "Don't look so surprised to hear you're gorgeous. All Robyn's friends are. After all, it's what you get paid for, isn't it? Go on camera, look pretty, make a fortune..."

I blinked at the sudden turn in conversation, and wondered if maybe she was kidding.

"Trish." Robyn's tone was a mixture of impatience and warning, and let me know Trish wasn't kidding. She really had gone from complimentary to insulting in the span of a few words, for no apparent reason. Unless her reason was to piss Robyn off. In that case, she had succeeded admirably.

"Well," I said, keeping my voice mild, "I like to think there's a little more to it than that." I smiled coolly at her and picked up my bag, checking the contents quickly before slinging it over my shoulder. "Kind of like being a chef is more than just following recipes. Isn't it?"

Trish opened her mouth, and then closed it again, and a slight blush appeared on her cheeks. "Yes, it is," she said quietly. "I'm sorry, I was out of line."

"Yes, you were," I said evenly, thinking I should just leave it at that. Unfortunately, my mouth, angry at the implied insult to Robyn, had other ideas. "I don't mind so much for myself — hell, I know why I got my job, and it wasn't my acting ability. But your sister is good. Very good. And she's had to work twice as hard to get where she is *because* of her looks, and because of attitudes like the one you just expressed." I put my hands on my hips, my voice angry now. "Were you ever turned down for a job because you're too pretty to possibly be a good chef?"

"I..." She was staring at me, wide-eyed in the face of my

sudden anger.

Shit. Way to make a good first impression. I bit my lip and took a deep breath, forcing myself to relax. "Sorry, I didn't mean to go off like that." My apology was met with silence as I dug my keys out of my bag. "I should probably go. Trish, despite how it might seem, it really was nice to meet you."

She nodded slowly, glancing from me to Robyn, and said faintly, "Yeah, you, too."

"Robyn..." I turned toward her, expecting anger or disappointment but finding instead a warm smile.

"I'll walk you out." She glanced at her sister. "I'll be back in a minute."

"Robby, I'm going to be late..." Trish sighed in obvious aggravation.

"The world will keep turning if you're five minutes late," Robyn said bluntly, shooting her sister an annoyed glare.

Trish pursed her lips. "The world won't fall apart, but my kitchen might. Go ahead, just don't be too long."

"I wasn't asking for your permission, Trish." Robyn's voice was glacial. "Now just sit down, drink your coffee, don't touch my knives, and I'll be back in a minute to discuss whatever it is that's so goddamn important."

Oh, to be a fly on the wall for *that* conversation.

Robyn herded me out of the kitchen with a light hand on my back, and we walked up the stairs in silence. When we reached the front door, I paused and turned to her with an apologetic look. "I'm sorry. I got a little carried away..."

The ferocity of her kiss took me by surprise, and I'm sure the whimper I heard as our bodies pushed up against the door was mine. Her tongue plunged into my mouth and my keys clattered to the floor from fingers that suddenly, urgently, needed to feel her skin. My hands went under the hem of her robe, squeezing the soft flesh of her behind, and she moaned when I trailed them down her upper thighs and then back up, drawn to the heat, dipping briefly into wetness —

"God..." She pulled herself away abruptly and stepped back, leaving my hands grasping air. "You..." She shook her head, breathing heavily.

"You started it," I accused, sagging against the door, trying to get my own labored breathing and wildly beating heart under control. "You can't expect nothing to happen when you kiss me like that. Whenever you touch me..." I shook my head, amazed and a little scared by our loss of control.

"I know. God, I know. It's..."

"Crazy." I finished for her.

"Yeah," she breathed. "Crazy."

She moved forward tentatively and I completed the motion, pulling her into my arms and resting my chin on her shoulder.

After a few moments of silence, she mused, "What is it about us and this door, anyway? I'm going to have to consider some kind of padding if we keep this up."

I smiled and pulled back a little, raising a hand to cup her cheek. We stared at each other for a long time.

"I'm going to miss you," I said finally. "Very much." I hesitated, knowing we had already talked about this, but I needed to ask. "Will you call me when you can?"

"Caid..." She sighed heavily and covered the hand on her cheek with her own. "I thought you might be a distraction before, and now..." She turned her head to kiss the palm of my hand, then pressed my hand more firmly to her cheek. "I want you to understand. What's happening between us—it's very important to me. I don't want to jeopardize it. But I really want this part, Caid. I *need* this part, and I need to do it right. I don't know if I can..."

I stopped her with two fingers to her lips, smiling apologetically. "I know, and I'm sorry. I told myself I wouldn't push, but...two months is just a long damn time."

"I know." She stroked my cheek, her eyes searching my face. "I'll call when I get settled, and then I'll see how things are going, okay?"

"Okay." I nodded and pulled her back into an embrace, holding her tightly. "I should go."

I felt her nod, but neither of us loosened our grip. Finally, I took a deep breath and stepped away from her to slip on my shoes. She bent down and picked up my keys, handing them to me silently.

I leaned in and kissed her gently one last time, lingering for a moment to memorize the texture and taste of her lips before pulling away. "Be safe, sweetheart." The endearment slipped from my lips without thought.

She smiled, slow and sweet. "You too, baby. And, Caid?" she said as I pulled the door open. I stopped, looking at her expectantly. She pressed her hand to my chest. "You were right when you said it was pretty damn amazing. It was."

Chapter
Thirteen

STROKE, STROKE, STROKE, breathe.
Stroke, stroke, stroke, breathe.
Tuck, twist, push, kick...

I pushed off the wall into another lap, settling easily into a comfortable rhythm through the water.

Stroke, stroke, stroke, breathe.
Stroke, stroke, stroke, breathe.

Two weeks.

Stroke, stroke, stroke, breathe.

She'd been gone two weeks, and I'd talked to her three times. Three damn times.

She called from Marathon the night she left LA, and we had an awkward but sweet conversation about her flight, my day, and our night together. I shyly told her I missed her, and she said she missed me, too, and I hung up with a huge, stupid grin plastered on my face. Two days later she called again between takes to bitch snarkily about what an asshole Lonnie Colchev was. She made me laugh and then had to hang up too soon, before anything remotely personal was said. And the final phone call had taken place four days after that and consisted of a stilted conversation about the weather, the island where they were filming, and Josh, who'd made it through the first two rounds of the French Open and looked very strong. I hung up frustrated and unsatisfied, and that feeling hadn't gone away in the seven days since, despite the flower delivery I'd received four days ago and the accompanying note saying she missed me and was thinking of me.

Stroke, stroke, stroke, breathe.

I knew what this part meant to her, and I knew what she felt she had to do to be successful. Her focus when she worked, her dedication, and drive—they were all part of what attracted me to her in the first place. I knew she thought talking with me would be a distraction that she couldn't afford, and I had expected that as she got deeper into filming, I'd hear from her less.

I knew all these things, but hadn't been prepared for how damn frustrating it would be. I missed her, and it was driving me crazy.

I glided into the wall, finishing my last five hundred, and pushed my goggles up. Checking my time by habit, I wasn't surprised to find I'd shaved a good bit of time off my normal workout. I was pushing myself lately, in an effort to keep myself sane, and if nothing else, the next month and a half would put me in better shape that I'd ever been in my life.

After a few minutes of stretching out my shoulders on the diving blocks, I dragged myself out of the water and walked to the locker room, my feet slapping wetly on the concrete. It was mid-afternoon and the gym was sparsely populated, so I took my time showering and changing, having nothing planned until dinner this evening with Liz.

Showered and dressed in shorts, a snug tank top, and a baseball cap, I dropped my locker key at the front desk.

"Thank you, Miss Harris." The dark-skinned, athletically built man behind the desk took my key with a smile. "Would you like to set up something with Shawn for later in the week? He has openings on Thursday or Friday, at one and three."

I nodded, adjusting my gym bag higher on my shoulder. "Let's try for Thursday, three o'clock. And does Toshi have any time after?"

"Let me check." He glanced down at the monitor behind the desk and pressed a series of keys. "Toshi is already booked for that time..." A few more keystrokes. "Colleen has time at five..."

"That'll work."

He entered the information, and looked back up at me. "Okay. I have you booked for a training session with Shawn at three on Thursday, and a massage with Colleen after that at five. Let us know if you need to change any of that around."

"I will. Thanks, Greg, have a good one."

"You're welcome, Miss Harris. You have a great day, too, and we'll see you on Thursday."

I waved and walked through the lobby and out into the smog-filtered sunshine, checking my cell for messages as I walked to where Twila was parked. Two messages from Connie. I frowned, thinking over my schedule for the week, knowing I had nothing, business-wise, scheduled. Instead of listening to her messages I called her back, figuring if she left two, she'd want to talk to me anyway.

She answered immediately, launching into me without greeting. "Caid, hon, I'm all for you seeing someone, but if you're going to end up in a lip-lock on the cover of some tabloid, I'd like a little notice."

My lungs stopped working, and even though physically I knew it was impossible, my stomach fell to the pavement with an audible thud.

Oh shit, oh shit, oh shit...

There was no way someone could have gotten pictures of Robyn and me, but apparently, somehow, someway, someone had.

God, if this doesn't send Robyn to freakville, nothing will.

"Caid? Are you still there?" Connie's slightly chastising tone had turned to one of concern.

"I..." I cleared my throat and took a calming breath. "Yeah, I'm here."

"So, something you'd like to share with me?"

"Uh, well..."

She clucked in annoyance. "Caid, I suppose it's not imperative that you tell me who your gentleman friend is, but since there's a blurry but recognizable picture of you kissing some blond hunk on the front page of *The Hollywood Seer*, I'm going to get some calls. What would you like me to say?"

"Gentleman friend?" I repeated dumbly, going over her words again.

Gentleman. Blond. Kissing.

James.

James and his sneak attack at the beach house.

The relief was so intense that I felt light-headed. I started laughing, not stopping until there were tears in my eyes. "Oh...God...Connie, I'm sorry," I apologized, getting myself under control. "You just...I thought... Never mind." More laughter threatened, and I tamped it down. "Um, I'm not involved with the guy in the picture. It was sort of an accident."

"An accident," she said in disbelief.

"Yeah."

She paused. "Well, do you want me giving out this accident's name?"

I thought for a moment. Despite the fact that James might like to be named as the person in the photo, it would cause more trouble than he realized, and I really didn't need a story circulating about how I was prone to kissing barely legal friends of my brother's. "I don't mind telling you who it was, Con, if you'd really like to know, but I'd rather not name him to the press, okay?"

"Sounds fair," she said cautiously. "Caid, is this going to be something I don't want to know?"

I laughed. "It's not terrible, but I'd rather it not get around. My brother and a friend were staying with me at Liz's beach house, a few days after the whole Big Bear thing, and the friend—James—

kinda ambushed me out on the deck."

There was a pause. "So, you are seeing him, then?"

"God, no!" I said, appalled at the thought. "Connie, he's just turned twenty-one, for Christ's sake. Give me a little credit."

Connie laughed. "You certainly wouldn't be the first actress to take a younger man as a lover, Caid. Happens all the time. Makes good press, usually."

"Yeah, well, not this time. Sorry to disappoint."

"I'm not disappointed, dear. But for future reference, if you do decide to date a younger man, I'm all for it. As long as he's legal, that's gold."

I rolled my eyes. "Would you like me to start trolling the local high school parking lots? Anything particular I should look for? Jocks, potheads, musicians?"

"I don't think that will be necessary." She laughed, and I could hear typing in the background. "So, you're not seeing anyone?"

I didn't want to lie to her. There was a chance she'd be handling fallout from something a lot bigger than me dating a teenager. But I wasn't quite ready to tell the truth, either. "No, the James thing was a one-kiss deal, I'm not dating him."

She was silent for several moments, and I knew she'd picked up on my change of wording. "Caid, let me ask you again. Is there something you want to tell me?"

It was my turn to be silent before finally answering, "Not right now, Connie, no."

She sighed. "Just don't let them blindside me, please. I hate when people know more than I do."

I laughed lightly. "I'll try to make sure that doesn't happen, I promise."

"All right," she said grumpily. "Now back to the kissing bandit. You know if I give them a no-comment, it might get you more attention instead of less, and I know how you hate that."

"I know." I rubbed my forehead with the heel of my hand. "I thought about that, too, but I really don't want James named. It's just the *Seer*, right?"

"So far."

I sighed. "If it gets me more attention, I'll just have to deal with it. They're never interested in me for very long—I live a very boring life. Hell, I disappeared and was possibly murdered by a roaming motorcycle gang, and that died down within a week."

She chuckled. "Okay, it's your call. But how about we say he's a friend and it was just a friendly peck, instead of no comment. Might stir up a bit of interest at first, but less in the long run."

"Whatever you think is best, as long as his name stays out of it. Thanks, Con."

"You are quite welcome. Now, while I've got you on the line, Corporate called earlier. They want you on the network morning show next week before they air the final *9th Precinct* episode, and *Night Talk* right after."

"Ugh." Somehow, in all that had happened over the last few weeks, I'd forgotten about my big primetime kiss. That would bring more press than any teenage lover would. "This is going to suck, isn't it?" I asked, already knowing the answer.

"For you personally, I'm afraid so, hon. But I still think it'll be a good move professionally."

"Like I had a choice," I grumbled.

"What?"

"Nothing. Do you have an itinerary?"

"Of course. The finale airs Tuesday, and they'd like you for the morning show that morning, and *Night Talk* on Wednesday...the four-thirty taping. Do you want to stay over, or shall I book two flights?"

I grimaced, not liking the thought of flying back Tuesday morning just to turn around and fly again on Wednesday. "Staying over is fine."

I heard more typing. "The morning show tapes at seven, and they expect you there at six...you want the redeye, or afternoon flight on Monday?"

"I hate the redeye, especially if I have to function that morning. Put me on the five o'clock, I can have a late dinner at Ono."

"Okay, I'll have Danielle book you for a Monday afternoon flight. Two nights at the Gansevoort, and the...eight o'clock back to LA on Wednesday?"

"Ugh," I repeated, and Connie laughed.

"Sorry, hon."

"Eh, I chose this job, guess I gotta live with the consequences. Oh, you'll be happy to know that Liz is dragging me to Crustacean tonight—she was feeling like a photo op, and somehow talked me into joining her."

"It won't kill you to get a little press, especially with Liz," she said in a scolding tone. "You might get some questions tonight about the *Seer* photo. Try not to be belligerent, okay? Just smile and say nothing, and if they want a quote, they can call me."

"Ugh." I hadn't thought of that. I contemplated canceling, but the wrath of Liz was much worse than a few nosy photogs or reporters. "I'll do my best. Liz says I need to work on my charm skills."

"Liz is right. Now have fun, and wear something with cleavage."

"Yeah, yeah..."

She laughed as she hung up and I closed my phone slowly, thinking about the appointments I'd need to rearrange next week. I also needed to call Perry to get him to talk with James for me — maybe I'd bribe him with the promise of some UW tickets in the fall if he could keep his buddy from bragging. And then, for no particular reason other than she was constantly in my thoughts lately, I thought of Robyn.

My panic earlier had been completely for her benefit, in reaction to any consequences exposure would have had on our relatively shaky relationship. The thought of any other consequences — my family, career, friends — hadn't even crossed my mind, but I thought of them now.

Mom and Larry would be confused but generally supportive. My grandparents might be a little scandalized, Perry would think it was cool, and Sebastian would call me a filthy, whoring, sinner. Nothing new there.

As far as my career went, I felt fairly safe since I had two years remaining on my contract with *9P*. There were, of course, ways to get rid of me if they wanted, but considering the new direction my part was taking, I doubted it would be an issue. Things might be different when I no longer had *9P* to fall back on — there were plenty of gay actors in the biz, but not so many out ones. So future fallout to my career had yet to be seen.

And finally, friends. Old college friends might be a bit thrown; Toby, who I still loved dearly as a friend and kept in touch with, would probably come up with some statistical model that would have predicted this happening, and my friends here in LA probably wouldn't bat an eye. Some raised eyebrows, maybe, and backroom gossip, but general acceptance.

There would be other consequences, certainly, but those were my main concerns. Was this worth a possible risk to my career, and a loss of a few friends? Was Robyn worth it? I thought of how it felt, just to be in her presence. How her smile warmed me, how her skin felt, soft under my hands...

Hell, yeah.

That, and a whole lot more.

I started Twila up and headed home, smiling.

A KNOCK SOUNDED at my door, and I walked down the hall to the front entry, fastening a dangly, gold earring as I went. The sturdy form of Liz's driver, Walter, was visible through the glass block window. I pulled open the door, still fastening the other earring.

"Good evening, Miss Harris. You look lovely." He smiled slightly and crossed his hands behind his back. He wore a black suit with a black shirt underneath and a deep purple tie that shimmered in the light.

I grinned. "Thank you, Walter. Great tie. I'll just be a minute."

He nodded. "Of course."

I ducked into the bedroom for a final check of my outfit. Dark brown slacks with a flared leg, low heels, and a sleeveless, brown and white geometric print blouse that showed plenty of back, and had a neckline that fulfilled Connie's joking request for cleavage. On the way back to the front door I snagged a small brown purse from the hallway table, checked it for keys, cell phone and wallet, and slid the thin strap over my shoulder. "All set."

Walter nodded and stepped back. I closed and locked the door, and followed him to the black limousine idling in the drive.

Liz was already sipping on a glass of white wine when I slid into the cooled interior of the car. She handed me a tumbler with a few ice cubes and a whole lot of scotch as soon as I sat down.

"Hi." She touched her glass to mine. "Cheers."

"Hi." I took in her outfit as I settled into my seat. "You look great." She wore a simple, sky blue cocktail dress that matched her eyes, and her hair was swept back in a carefully mussed coiffure that reminded me vaguely of an exotic bird.

She nodded her head slightly, like royalty accepting her due, but I could tell my comment pleased her.

I gestured with my glass, raising an eyebrow quizzically. "Not that I'm complaining—you know I won't turn down good scotch—but are we celebrating something?"

She smiled, then picked up an item on the seat beside her and handed it to me. "Your first truly scandalous front page, sugar. I'm so proud. Why didn't you tell me you had a new beau?"

I looked at the item in my hand. Three grainy but recognizable black and white newspaper pictures detailing the moments just before, during, and after James laid the kiss on me. James's back was to the photographer and it was hard to recognize him unless you knew him by the back of his blond head, but each shot showed my face clearly. The first picture showed me smiling at him, and the second, the actual kiss. The third showed our faces still close together, with my hands on his shoulders as I pushed him away, but it looked as though I was pulling him closer. The clippings were neatly trimmed and laminated, with the headline *"Was she really camping?"* and the caption, *"Caidence finds more than wildlife on her infamous camping trip."*

"Oh, God," I groaned.

Liz smiled delightedly. "Paula insisted we laminate it. I think it's a nice touch. She sends her congratulations, too."

I scowled at her and threw the pictures onto the seat in disgust. "How sweet," I said sarcastically. I pointed to the pictures. "That was taken at your house, you know. Maybe you better talk to your neighbors about who they let on the beach."

Her smile faded and she grabbed the lamination, studying it carefully. "Well, fuck. I'll have to talk to Mel about that. I didn't pay close to four million dollars for a house that just anyone can snap pictures of whenever they want."

Four million? Sheesh. And that was years ago. That ended any thoughts I had about buying in that area.

"So, if this is my house..." She looked at the photo again, frowning, and then with dawning realization. "Oh, Caid..." She looked at me in disbelief. "*James*? You're doing *James*?" She sat back and laughed, shaking her head. "I never would have guessed that one."

"I am *not* doing James." I snatched the lamination from her hand. "We were out on the deck, watching the sunset, and suddenly he's kissing me." I scowled at the pictures. "Goddamn hormonal little twerp."

She laughed harder, and I glared at her. "Liz, this is not funny."

"Oh, I disagree. It's hilarious. The boy barely spoke, yet somehow he worked up the nerve to kiss you. It's...priceless. Oh, I would have loved to have seen your face." That sent her off into more peals of laughter.

I frowned and tossed the lamination down, crossing my arms and sipping my drink broodily until Liz calmed herself.

"Oh, God, that was good." She magically pulled a tissue out of some dark recess of the car's interior and dabbed at her eyes.

"Glad to be of entertainment value to you, Liz," I said with irritation.

She giggled and patted my leg. "And you're so damn cute when you get all torqued."

I grunted and sipped my drink while Liz repaired the damage her laughing fit had done to her makeup. After a few minutes, she started giggling again.

"Liz..." I said warningly.

"I'm sorry, Caid, it's just so...not like you. To get caught kissing some kid. Although, you know there's a lot to be said about dating younger men. I'm somewhat of an expert at it, myself, so I know what I'm talking about."

I smiled slightly. "That's what Connie said. Not about you, but about younger men. Said she'd be tickled pink if I brought one home some day, because it's good press."

"Well, Connie is right." She drained the rest of her wine in one gulp and smiled knowingly. "And there are several other benefits that I can mention..."

I raised a hand. "Spare me the details, oh, experienced one. I'll leave the young studs to you."

"Okay, sugar." She patted my leg again. "We'll find you someone a little older to play with. You know," she mentioned casually, "Anthony asked about you the other day."

I gave her a look. "Anthony is a cokehead, Liz. And he can't seem to talk about anything but partying and sports cars."

"But you slept with him, didn't you?"

"Jesus..." I wondered how many other people had heard that. Remembering Anthony's big mouth, I was guessing quite a few. "A cokehead with a big damn mouth. Not a mistake I plan on making again."

She took in my angry posture and nodded slowly. "*Okaaay*...that's a big N-O on setting you up with Anthony again, I guess. What about Patrick? Or Cameron?"

"Liz, I don't need you to set me up with anyone."

"Caid, your little tussle with James aside, I bet you haven't even been kissed, much less done anything else, in ages."

I was swamped with memories of soft, demanding lips, warm hands on my skin, and the feel of her inside me... I blinked and drew in a slow, steadying breath, unable to stop my smile.

"You're blushing! And smiling! Caidence Harris, what are you not telling me? Tell me who he is, this instant!" Liz demanded.

I looked over at her and said mildly, "No."

That stopped her and she straightened in surprise. "*No*? Did you just tell me *no*?"

"Yes."

"Wha..." She frowned in confusion, and then her face took on a calculated look. "But that means there's something to tell me, right? You are seeing someone?"

"Maybe." I smiled at the frustrated noise she made, and finished my drink. "We're here."

She glared at me. "We are not done with this conversation."

"Yes, we are," I shot back, stepping out of the car as soon as Walter opened the door.

I glanced around, swearing under my breath when a chunky, balding man leaning against the railing outside the restaurant looked over at me in interest and slowly lowered his newspaper. When Liz stepped out of the car, he straightened and dropped the newspaper completely, grabbing up the camera around his neck.

"Shit."

"Smile, sugar," Liz said softly, flashing a dazzling smile at the man who was snapping shots frantically. "It's why we're here. And we are *not* done talking about this." She swept by me, and I forced a smile and followed her past the photographer into the restaurant.

Inside, we walked atop a glassed-over stream filled with placid black and orange koi, across a tiny wooden bridge next to a gurgling waterfall, and past a huge, floor-to-ceiling aquarium. The *maître de'* greeted us both effusively by name, seating us immediately at a small table in the spacious main dining room which boasted marble floors, skylights, and a grove of what looked like bamboo.

The curious, excited stares we received as we crossed the room and sat down made me nervous, and once the waiter had left with our drink order—more wine for Liz, and sparkling water for me, since I'd knocked back nearly a triple in the car in about fifteen minutes—I grumbled that we should have sat upstairs in the private dining room.

"Caid," she said with an exasperated sigh. "This is why we came here. I certainly didn't do it for the food—you know I don't like seafood."

"So you're going to spend fifty bucks for a plate of fish that you don't want, just to get some new photos circulating?"

"Yes, Caid, that's exactly what I'm going to do. It's not like I can't afford it, and I know you're not a pauper either. But if it makes you feel better, I'll buy your dinner." She opened her menu and began studying it.

"Damn straight you're buying my dinner—this was your damn idea." I looked around nervously.

She lowered her menu and stared at me, frowning. "I take back what I said about you being cute when you're torqued. It's not cute at all. It's downright annoying."

"So sorry I'm not the light evening entertainment you were hoping for," I said sarcastically.

She regarded me for a moment, then returned her eyes to the menu. "I'm not going to let you pull me into your bad mood, Caid. I'm feeling good tonight, and I'd like to have fun. If you're going to be like this the whole night, I can have Walter take you home. It would save me some money, and I wouldn't have to spend my evening with an overgrown baby."

I scowled, knowing she was right. I was being a big baby. A big, grumpy baby. *Suck it up, ya big weenie.* "Sorry," I sighed and gave her an apologetic look. "I'll behave."

"Glad to hear it," she replied mildly, without looking up.

I watched her for several moments before asking sweetly, "Can I get the lobster, Mom?"

She paused, and looked up slowly. "You can get whatever you

want, sugar. But don't ever, *ever* call me Mom again." She smiled slightly, and I knew I was forgiven.

I grinned and looked down at the menu, studying the choices. I'd heard wonderful things about the food here, and I hoped it wasn't all hype.

"Oh, look, Caid," Liz started innocently. Whenever Liz used that tone, I knew to be wary. "They've got *James* Bay shrimp." She smacked her lips. "Young and tasty."

"Shut up," I muttered, but couldn't stop my lips from curling upwards into a smile. Liz's ringing laugh drew more attention to us than we had already been getting, but I forced myself to ignore it.

"There's the Caid I know and love," she said softly and winked.

I tilted my head to the side, watching her read the menu. "You *are* in awfully good spirits this evening. It can't all be the excitement of my first truly scandalous rag headline — what gives? Or is Bruce just satisfying your needs?"

She looked up from the menu absently. "Who?"

"Bruce. Pretty-boy from Scotty's party. Big lips, nice butt, vacant stare..."

"He did have a nice butt, didn't he?" She smiled in fond remembrance, and waved her hand in front of her. "No, he's history."

"So, who?"

She looked at me and smiled secretively.

I closed my menu and laid it across the table. "Why, Liz Ann Stokley. I do believe you're keeping secrets from me." I was charmed and intrigued by the thought. Liz normally couldn't keep a secret to save her life.

The waiter came with our drinks, and when he left, Liz leaned toward me. "You tell me yours and I'll tell you mine." She raised her eyebrows suggestively.

"Well, I think..." I pretended to ponder. "No."

"No?"

"No."

She sat back. "You're really not going to tell me, are you?"

I reached over and patted her hand before opening the menu again. "Nope."

"I can't believe you're not going to tell me." She pouted and took a sip of wine. "Fine, then. I'm not going to tell you either."

I shrugged, not looking up from the menu. "Okay."

A bewildered silence followed my statement, and I tried to hide a smile.

"Caaiiidd..." The petulant tone was right on cue and I burst out laughing. She frowned.

"God, Liz, you're so easy." I grinned at her and took a swallow of water.

"Bitch," she huffed good-naturedly.

My smile widened. "You know you love me."

She sighed resignedly. "Yes, for reasons I can't recall at the moment, I do."

I laughed and leaned back in my chair. "And you say I lack charm."

She smiled and looked down at the menu again.

After the waiter took our orders, conversation turned to other topics. The show, my upcoming trip to New York for the talk show circuit, Liz's summer plans, and the good-looking men in the landscaping crew working at her house. Liz could always make me laugh, and we chatted easily over dinner, occasionally interrupted by autograph seekers but mostly left alone.

We ordered a dessert to split, and I sipped a cognac while Liz decided on some foofy coffee drink with lots of whipped cream.

"You want that *and* lime whatchamacallit? You glutton." I leaned back in my chair and crossed one leg over the other.

"You'll be eating most of the whatchamacallit," she told me, blowing ineffectually on her coffee through a mountain of whipped cream. "I just want a taste."

"You always say that, and then I look down and *poof!* The plate is clean."

She pursed her lips and continued blowing.

I smiled into my cognac. "So. Is it one of those handsome gardeners who's got you so chipper? Isn't that a little cliché for you? Hollywood starlet seduces gardener..." I frowned slightly. "Or are you supposed to seduce the pool boy?" I mused, taking a drink as I pondered the question.

She glanced up from her blowing. "No, I haven't seduced a gardener. And the pool boy..." She sighed dramatically. "I did try to seduce him once, but alas, he loves his wife and even I couldn't tempt him into unfaithfulness."

I smiled. Liz's "pool boy" was a gregarious, leather-skinned sixty-two year old named Raoud. He was an incredible flirt, quite charming, and had the most beautiful laugh—Liz adored him, and I could see her tossing out a proposition, just to get him to laugh. "So, if it's not a strapping young gardener, and Raoud can't be swayed, who is it?"

She picked up her spoon and dipped it in the whipped cream. "Not until you tell me yours."

I shrugged. "I can wait. Can you?"

She put the spoon down slowly, her mouth set in a stubborn line. "Of course I can."

Oops. I'd just ruined any chance of finding out anytime soon. I should have known better than to challenge her. That was like waving a red flag at a bull.

There was a commotion near the back of the restaurant and the room suddenly seemed charged with electricity. People were muttering and craning their necks to see, and I admit to doing the same for a moment before stopping myself. I glanced self-consciously at Liz, but she was busy rubber-necking with the rest of the room.

"Caid," she said and touched my arm. "Isn't that Josh Riley?"

My head turned so fast I heard my neck pop. It was indeed Josh, smiling and making his way through the dining room toward us, looking scruffily elegant in dark pants, a crisp white shirt under a black jacket, and several days' growth of stubble on his face.

He caught my eye and his face broke into a warm smile.

"My," Liz breathed. "Isn't he pretty."

And he was. I hadn't seen him since the night of Scott Ziem's party, and I'd forgotten how affecting his mix of incredible good looks and charisma was. I found myself unconsciously smiling back, sincerely glad to see him.

He reached our table and leaned down to brush his lips across my cheek. "Caid. It's great to see you." He took my hand in his and held it, smiling down at me.

"Josh." I smiled back, and squeezed his hand. "Nice to see you, too." I glanced over at Liz who was looking at me impatiently. "Josh, this is my good friend Liz Stokley."

He dropped my hand and turned to Liz with a charming smile. "Of course I recognize you, Miss Stokley. It's a pleasure to meet you."

"Call me Liz, please," she said breathlessly, "and it's an honor to meet you, Josh."

"Thank you, Liz." He smiled again at Liz and glanced back at me. "Sorry to interrupt your dinner."

"It's fine," I told him. "I'm glad you came over. You played great in the Open...when did you get home?"

Josh had made it to the semis, a very respectable showing, but he shook his head in disgust. "If I'd played great I would have won, but thank you anyway." A waiter materialized beside our table with a chair. Joshed hesitated, but at my nod and Liz's, he murmured his thanks and slid into it. "I just got back yesterday," he continued when he was settled. "I made a quick stop in Florida first..."

An unexpected ball of anger surfaced at his words.

Josh had actually seen Robyn, in person. Touched her, talked to her, laughed with her — while I couldn't even talk to her over the fucking phone. With effort, I kept a relaxed smile on my face, but from Liz's curious expression, and Josh's dropped gaze, it appeared that my effort wasn't very successful.

"The Keys?" I tried to keep my voice neutral. My frustration and jealousy weren't Josh's fault.

"Yes."

I nodded slowly. "Nice for you."

Yeah, okay...maybe not doing such a good job of keeping my feelings to myself.

He shrugged helplessly. "Caid..."

"I think..." Liz said uncertainly, and stood quickly. "I think I'm going to find the powder room. It was nice meeting you, Josh."

He smiled easily at her. "You too, Liz."

When she left, he reached out and touched my hand. "You look wonderful, by the way. I can understand how you'd be considered a distraction."

"That's nice of you to say, Josh, but you'll understand when I say that's not really what I need to hear right now."

"Well, how about this then." He leaned forward, lowering his voice. "She said, and I quote, 'tell her I miss her so damn much, it's crazy.' "

I closed my eyes at the words. "Yeah." I blew out a breath in an explosive sigh. "Crazy." I opened my eyes. "God, I miss her, too."

Josh smiled softly at me and leaned back. "I'm glad I ran into you. I was going to call later in the week to see if you wanted to have dinner."

"With you?" I asked, startled.

He smiled. "Yes, with me."

"Sorry, I just..." I shrugged and smiled, embarrassed. "That would be nice, thanks."

He squeezed my hand and stood up. On impulse, I stood and gave him a hug.

"Thank you, Josh." I stepped back and punched him lightly on the arm. "I'm jealous as hell, though. You know that, don't you?"

He grinned and leaned in to brush my cheek again with his lips. "From the looks of things, I'm the one who should be jealous," he said softly before straightening. "I'll call you, okay?"

"Yes, I look forward to it."

He smiled his million-dollar smile. "Me, too."

Liz was just making her way back through the dining room as Josh left, and the two stopped and talked for a moment before Josh continued on and Liz came back to the table. "Sweet, isn't he?" She slid back into her seat, her eyes on his retreating back.

"Yeah," I agreed, scratching my cheek absently where his stubble had grazed, thinking more of Robyn's words about missing me than about Josh being sweet.

Robyn. I smiled slowly. *Damn, I love that woman.*

"Robyn's a lucky woman," Liz continued, turning her attention from Josh when he finally moved out of sight.

My smile grew wider. "Uh-huh."

She frowned, and picked up her spoon to stir her coffee. "Caid...you and Robyn are friends, right?"

She sounded so serious, and my smile faded. "Yes," I said cautiously. "We're friends."

She tapped the spoon against the side of her cup, then began stirring again. Liz was fidgeting, and Liz rarely fidgeted.

I watched her stir for a few more moments and rapped my fingers against the table. "Looks like you've got something on your mind, Liz. Spit it out."

She looked up and met my gaze for the first time since she'd returned to the table. "You and Josh seem kind of...close. How does Robyn feel about that?"

It finally dawned on me what she was probably thinking, and what she was getting at. "Oh." I stifled the urge to laugh. Laughing would be bad. "Um, no, Liz. I think I know what you're thinking, and it's not Josh."

She gave me a skeptical look. "You seemed upset that he'd been in Florida...that's where Robyn is shooting, isn't it? Why were you upset that he'd been to see her?"

"Well..." How to explain, with out really explaining? I gave up and shrugged my shoulders. "Honestly, Liz. Josh is just a friend, I swear."

We were quiet while the waiter set down the dessert we were splitting. Liz sighed and pushed her well-stirred coffee away. "Promise?"

"Promise."

I almost told her then. I wanted so badly to grip her hand and tell her how I'd fallen in love with this amazing woman who thrilled me, pleased me, made me feel alive, and made me happier than I'd ever been. Christ, I wanted to tell *someone.*

Instead I just smiled.

"I..." She paused, and picked up a fork to try the lime dessert we'd ordered. She looked at it in surprise, and took another bite. "Damn. This whatchamacallit thing is great."

I picked up my fork and tried some, and had to agree with her. It was damn good.

We spent a few minutes demolishing the dessert, and after Liz had taken a final swipe of the plate with her finger and licked it clean, managing somehow to make the action look polite, she looked at me again. "Sorry, it just seemed like an impossible situation, and I don't want to see you hurt."

She really could be very sweet.

"Thanks, Liz. But no need to worry about Josh."

Let's hope you're as supportive when you find out what's really going on.

Chapter
Fourteen

JOSH'S COACH, ELADIO Sabatis, kept up a stream of heavily accented chatter as he hit ball after ball in a steady rhythm over the net at Josh. "Yes, yes...good. Cross to the corner now..."

Josh returned each ball with a powerful, spinning backhand, each shot varying only inches in placement along the baseline. His short, blond hair was dark with sweat, and moisture glistened on his skin. I watched his fluid movements in appreciation from my spot on the courtside bleachers, my elbows propped against the bleacher bench behind me and my legs stretched out on the bench below. Seeing the game from this distance was completely different than watching on television. Everything seemed faster and more intense, increasing my already healthy admiration for Josh's talent.

"Good. Now. Show your beautiful friend how fast you can run." Eladio grinned at me, his teeth very white against dark skin. He sent a ball deep into the opposite corner of the court, forcing a swearing Josh to scramble after it.

"Damn it, Eladio..." Josh chased the ball down in a few long strides and sent a sizzling forehand down the line. He turned immediately to sprint the other way when the dark-haired man hit the next ball into the other corner. That ball was crushed by a backhand down the line, and Josh was off and running again to chase Eladio's next offering.

"Cross, Josh, not line," Eladio chided, sending another ball into a corner. "We work the cross today."

Josh grunted and continued to chase down balls for another ten minutes, hitting deep cross-court returns on each ball Eladio sent him. After a final forehand that had enough velocity on it to raise even Eladio's eyebrows, the coach called an end to practice.

"Good, Josh. You move your feet and your form is very good today." He glanced over at me and flashed another brilliant smile. "I think you are showing off for your lady friend, yes?" He laughed at Josh's scowl and waved him forward. The two men talked quietly at the net for several minutes then Eladio slapped Josh on the arm, waved at me, and turned away to begin collecting balls in a green wire ball basket.

Josh put his racquets in a large bag, and grabbed a bottle of water and a towel before walking over and sitting down on the bleacher next to my outstretched legs.

"Very impressive." I smiled down at him, shading my eyes against the late afternoon sun. "A lot different than watching on TV."

"Thanks." He wiped his face with the towel and took several deep gulps of water. "I was surprised when you said you wanted to come by early and watch — not many people like to watch practice."

I raised an eyebrow and nodded at the small crowd of about fifteen people slowly vacating the bleachers on the other side of the court behind a barrier, most of them watching us with open curiosity. "Looks to me like you've got a nice little cheering section."

He drained his water bottle and wiped his face with the back of his arm, glancing across the court. "Yeah, we usually have some watchers for my afternoon court time. Mornings are always closed, but we have afternoon time at least once a week and people come and watch, and I sign some autographs...and here they come now." He smiled wryly.

I looked up to see several people being escorted past the barriers and across the court by a young, painfully cheerful-looking woman dressed in club whites. Josh swiped his hair one last time with the towel, pushed himself off the bench, and stepped away from the bleachers to meet the oncoming group with a wide smile.

They gathered around him, some pushing forward eagerly while others hung back shyly, but Josh greeted them all with a friendly smile, chatted briefly, signed whatever item they gave him, and posed for pictures. A middle aged couple — two of the first to push forward and get Josh's attention — turned to me when he had signed a few tennis balls and a hat for them, and looked at me speculatively.

"Are you someone?" the woman asked after taking a few hesitant steps in my direction, eyeing my reclining form doubtfully.

I'd stopped for a run along Manhattan Beach on my way to Josh's club in Torrance and I was dirty, sweaty, and not a little rough-looking in loose T-shirt, running shorts and shoes, a baseball cap, and wrap-around sunglasses. I smiled slightly and crossed one leg over the other. "No, no one important."

The husband frowned, looking at me intently, but the woman just nodded, her original opinion confirmed. I watched in amusement as she latched onto his arm and dragged him back across the court, chattering about who they might see in the dining room. The rest of Josh's group lost interest in me after watching the couple talk to me and leave without an autograph, and no one else approached me until the group was gone and Josh himself came over.

"No wonder the public loves you so much." I sat up and handed him my half-full water bottle. "You have the patience of a saint."

He took the bottle with a nod of thanks and drained it quickly, picking up his towel and wiping the back of his neck. "I honestly love the attention. Robyn will tell you, I'm a complete and total attention whore."

Just the mention of her name caused a flutter in my stomach and a slight hitch in my breathing. I scowled at my body's reaction and my inability to control it.

"Caid? You okay?" Josh's voice was questioning, pulling my attention back to him.

"Oh, yeah. Sorry. I just...listen, Josh. About Robyn..." I trailed off as he held out a hand to help me off the bleachers.

"How about we both get cleaned up and I take you to that dinner I promised? Chelsea can show you where you can shower and change, and I'll meet you out in the front lobby when you're ready." He gestured behind him and I realized that the staff member who had led the group of autograph seekers across the court was waiting respectfully several yards away.

I gripped his hand automatically and let him pull me up. When I was standing, he leaned in and said softly, "We can talk there, okay?" I nodded and he turned, not dropping my hand. "Chelsea, can you show Miss Harris to the locker rooms and make sure the bag she dropped at the front desk gets to her?"

"Of course, Mr. Riley." She stepped forward, glancing quickly at our linked hands before favoring me with a professional smile. "If you'll just follow me, Miss Harris?"

I resisted the urge to drop Josh's hand like a hot potato, annoyed at the vague feeling of guilt her furtive look produced. "Thank you, Chelsea. See you in a bit, Josh." I squeezed his hand and let it drop slowly before following the young woman across the court and into the main club building. We stopped at the main desk and I picked up my bag and a locker key, then Chelsea directed me to the locker rooms and gave me a polite, "Have a nice day" before hurrying off to another duty.

I showered and changed quickly, hoping that Josh's idea of "casual" jived with mine and the well-worn sandals, denims, and black silk halter neck top would be appropriate wherever we were going for dinner. After drying my hair for a few minutes and gathering up my things, I returned the key to the front desk.

"Thank you, Miss Harris." The desk attendant was a fit, twenty-something blonde with a deep tan and a near blinding smile. "Mr. Riley is waiting just outside for you. Through the doors to your right."

"Thank you..." I glanced quickly at her nametag, "Bridget."

Her smile, if possible, got brighter. I returned her smile with a smaller one of my own, and turned to the doors she had indicated.

"Miss Harris?"

The tentative voice stopped me; I turned back to Bridget and found her looking around cautiously. "Yes?"

She licked her lips nervously, not meeting my eyes. "Um...I really like your show. Do you...do-you-think-I-could-get-an-autograph?" she finished with a rush, looking up at me with a hopeful expression.

"Sure." I smiled at her encouragingly, and her nervousness disappeared.

"Oh, thank you!" She produced a pen and piece of paper from behind the desk, handing them to me. "I *knew* you'd be nice in person. I mean, I could just *tell*. Those stories in the paper about how you're mean—I just *knew* they weren't true. I watch *9th Precinct* every week, and..."

I blinked. Mean? The papers said I was mean? Belligerent, possibly. Surly, maybe. I'd never been particularly friendly with the press, but I always tried to be at least polite...and they thought I was mean? It bothered me how much that thought...bothered me.

Bridget was still chattering on when I focused my attention back onto her. "...I had no idea you were dating Mr. Riley. Did he and Miss Ward break up? She's come in several times, you know. She's very...intimidating in person. Not like you. You're not intimidating at all. At least, not now. A little when you first came in, maybe, but now I feel like we could be great friends."

I started to correct her about me and Josh when I recalled something Liz had told me more than once. *Nothing gets people's curiosity up quicker than a good denial, and curiosity draws the press like ants to a picnic.* I closed my mouth and hastily scrawled my signature across the paper before shoving it back at her, my smile turning slightly brittle. "There you go. You have a nice evening, okay, Bridget?"

Not waiting for a response, I strode to the side doors and pushed my way outside, looking around for Josh and spotting him climbing out of a white, low-slung Jaguar coupe parked at the curb. I waved in acknowledgement, and walked over as he rounded the car and held the door open for me.

"Thanks." I ducked into the car, tossed my bag in the tiny back seat, and settled into plush leather as Josh walked around to the driver's side and slid in beside me. He pulled away from the curb and maneuvered the car out onto the main road at a speed that had me glad I'd put on my seatbelt.

A few more quick turns and we were on the entrance ramp to 405, and I gripped my seat as casually as I could as we merged onto the freeway. "So, where are we heading?"

Josh sped up even more, sending the car zipping in and out of traffic. He crossed three lanes of traffic with a casual flick of the wrist and glanced over at me. "Santa Monica."

I waited, watching him, using the opportunity to keep my eyes off the scenery flying by at an alarming rate. When nothing further was forthcoming, I quirked an eyebrow at him. "That's a little vague — want to narrow it down a little?"

"It's a surprise." He grinned like a little boy, and I was reminded of another reason he was so popular with the press.

I shook my head, unable to keep from smiling back. "As long as I'm not underdressed, that works for me. You did say casual, right?"

He perused my outfit with a quick glance and nodded in approval. "You'll do."

"Gee, thanks." I tossed him a crooked grin. He was wearing khakis and an un-tucked light blue and white striped bowling shirt, so I guessed casual was indeed okay. "You know, the desk attendant at the club thinks we're dating," I told him idly as I turned my attention back to the road, bracing my feet against the floor and settling as far as I could into the seat.

"Does she?" He looked over at me with raised eyebrows and laughed. "Damn, I'm good. I'm dating two beautiful women." He passed a slow-moving truck, muttering to himself as he glanced behind him and changed lanes, "...and don't have a chance with either of them."

There was no bitterness in the words, only an underlying sadness. I said nothing for a moment and then decided to go ahead and ask what I'd wanted to ask since I found out that he and Robyn weren't a couple. "Why do you do it, then?"

He changed lanes again and sped around a bus. "Why do I do what?"

"This...thing that you and Robyn do. I can understand why she does it — to keep the press off her back about her sexuality — but you..." I waved a hand, gesturing at him. "Jesus, Josh, you're gorgeous, famous, wealthy, charming...you must have women falling over themselves to be with you. Beautiful women who would do just as much for your image as being seen with Robyn does. So..."

"So you want to know what's in it for me," he stated, not taking his eyes off the road.

I winced slightly at how callous that sounded. "Well, yeah. You could have any woman you want. Or two. Or six..." I quirked a grin to take the sting out of my next words. "I think you're a nice guy, Josh—really, I do—but I have a hard time believing a guy would give up the possibility of all those fawning women because their lesbian best friend needed a date. Once or twice, maybe, but for years?"

He actually smiled at that. "No," he said with a soft laugh. "I'm not doing this out of the goodness of my heart. Believe it or not, the reason is actually because of those fawning women." He glanced in his rear view mirror, and then at me quickly before focusing his attention back on the road. "I'm twenty-nine, Caid. In tennis, I'm practically an old man. There's a very small window of opportunity when you've put enough years into the game to have the benefit of experience, and you're still young enough that your body is able to do what you want it to do." He gestured at himself. "I'm in that window now. I don't make it into the top five in the next year or two, it's not going to happen. Doing the 'thing me and Robyn do,' as you call it, allows me to keep my focus. I do what's expected of me to keep the sponsors and advertisers happy, but I don't have to worry about getting involved with someone, getting caught up in something like that, which I know from past experience messes with my head. We keep each other out of trouble, and get to spend time with someone we enjoy being with. It's basically hanging out with a friend, with some added benefits."

I pondered that for a moment, and then hesitantly asked, "Do you still love her?"

He glanced at me in confusion. "Of course I love her. She's my best friend..." His eyes widened in sudden understanding. He turned his attention back to the road. "*Ohhh*. You mean, am I *in* love with her? That whole straight-boy-pining-away-after-his-lesbian-best-friend thing?"

Well, when he put it that way, it did sound kind of silly...

At my slow nod, he smiled wryly. "No, I'm not in love with her. I used to be, a long, long time ago. And I like to think she was in love with me, too." He slowed a little and looked over at me. "Lord knows it would certainly be simpler if we were both still in love with each other, but we're not." He glanced in his rear view mirror, and then at me. "I'm not competition, Caid. As long as you make Robyn happy, I'm on your side."

I shook my head. "That's not what I meant..." Then I stopped myself and sighed. "Oh, hell, maybe it was. You two are just so close—you know each other so completely, and all I have are these little...pieces of her. It's frustrating."

We were quiet for a minute before he reached over and patted my knee. "If it makes a difference, Caid, she doesn't give those pieces up easily, and she's given more to you than anyone else has gotten in a long time."

I turned my body to face front again, thinking of the brief glimpses I'd gotten behind dark, guarded eyes. "I want them all," I said quietly, watching the traffic around us. "I want every last piece."

He squeezed my knee and I looked over at him. "Good," he said, a smile spreading on his face. "Good."

Conversation moved onto different topics, and we quickly regained the comfort level we had shared the night I joined him and Robyn for dinner. The twenty-minute trip went by swiftly, and soon we were pulling into a parking spot on Main Street in Santa Monica.

We walked a few blocks, commenting on the art displays in various windows until we arrived at a restaurant called *Sophie's* where Josh held open the door and gestured for me to enter. Inside was an airy, brightly painted, café-style restaurant decorated in a curious mix of Southwestern and Mediterranean décor; I glanced around, appreciating the mix of colors and textures, and the appetizing smells wafting through the air.

Along one wall was a long counter with several glass cases displaying an array of desserts and other goodies. Behind the register at the end of the counter stood an elegant woman, her dark hair shot through with silver, writing in a notepad. She looked up when we entered and piercing dark eyes took me in, then traveled to Josh. Her face lit up in an open, welcoming smile, and the jolt of recognition left me momentarily speechless.

"Joshua!" She moved from behind the counter and the two kissed each other on both cheeks and embraced.

"*Buenas tardes,* Sophie." He stepped back and gave her a warm smile. "This is an unexpected pleasure. What are you doing down here? Checking up on your temperamental chef?"

The woman laughed and patted Josh on the arm. "Eh, you know my Patricia. She does as she pleases, no matter what her mamá says." Her English was precise and slightly accented. "No, Marcy is on holiday for a few days and I have volunteered to help until she returns." She paused, and then winked. "And it is also good to keep an eye on my temperamental chef."

The two shared a laugh, and the woman looked over at me curiously. "Where are your manners, Joshua?" She prodded him with an elbow. "Who is your friend?"

Looking properly chastised, Josh placed his hand on my back

and gestured to the woman. "I'm sorry. Sophie, this is my friend, Caidence Harris. Caid, this is Sophie Ward, Robyn's..."

"Mother." I finished for him, reaching out to grasp Sophie's outstretched hand. "*Encantada, Senora.*"

Mom would be so proud that her emphasis on languages finally paid off.

Sophie raised an eyebrow at my greeting, the gesture so achingly familiar that I couldn't stop a tiny laugh of delight. She frowned slightly, and I hurried to apologize. "I'm sorry, *Senora*, for laughing, but I've just realized where Robyn got..." I raised my own eyebrow and tapped it with my finger, "...that."

Her frown turned into a wide smile. "You know my Sabina?"

"Ah...Sabina?"

"Sabina is Robyn's first name," Josh explained. "Robyn is actually her middle name."

Sophie waved her hand in a graceful, dismissive gesture. "Eh, she prefers Robyn, but she will always be Sabina to me." She leaned in and added conspiratorially, "And it drives her *loca,* so of course I call her that."

I smiled, easily picturing the exasperated look on Robyn's face. "I can imagine, *Senora*, how that would definitely drive Robyn *loca.*"

Sophie raised an eyebrow again and looked at me speculatively. "Please, call me Sophie. And I will call you Caidence," she announced. "So tell me, Caidence. How is it that you know my daughter?"

I'm completely, utterly, helplessly in love with her...

I cleared my throat. "She and I work together. Well, sometimes we work together."

"You work on this lawyer, defense show with her?"

"No. I mean, yes. Sometimes." I shook my head at my sudden inability to communicate. Apparently, Robyn wasn't the only Ward that left me tongue-tied. "I work on a different show, but sometimes I work on Robyn's show, and sometimes she works on mine."

"Ah...the police show. *9th Patrol*, is it?"

"*9th Precinct*," I said automatically, and then felt slightly silly for correcting her.

She nodded slowly, her eyes sweeping me from head to toe. "You are the friend who became lost," she said bluntly.

I kept the explanations to myself and replied with a simple, "Yes."

"My Sabina, she was very upset. I have never seen her so..." she searched for a word, "distraught. I am very glad you were found, and I am very glad to meet you. We do not meet Sabina's friends often, so it is good to meet a friend of my *hija* who she must care for very much." She glanced at Josh. "It is good, Joshua, that you brought Caidence to meet me. Thank you." She stepped between us and linked an arm through each of ours. "Now, come. I will seat you, and Patricia will make you something special."

She seated us in a private corner and brought a bottle of wine before hurrying off to seat another group who had just arrived. It was still early — only five thirty — and the restaurant wasn't full, so Sophie came by our table often over the next half hour, asking me questions about my family and work, and telling a hilarious story about catching Josh and Robyn in a rather...compromising position when the family had visited Robyn one weekend while she was at UCLA.

"And then Elora, in the way only teenagers can, told her sister that Joshua, he had a very nice ass..."

"Sophie!" Josh flushed an interesting shade of red and excused himself, murmuring something about seeing someone he knew. Sophie and I watched him stride quickly across the room before turning to each other, smiling.

"He is such a good boy," she said fondly, looking over to where he was talking to a couple seated on the other side of the restaurant. "My *hija* is very lucky to have him in her life."

"Yes." I swirled my wine, watching the deep, red color coat the glass. "They are lucky to have each other. They are both wonderful people."

I felt a light hand on my arm and looked up into dark, intelligent eyes so like Robyn's. "I think, Caidence, that she is lucky to have you, also. You care for her very much."

I hesitated, and then nodded. "Yes, very much," I said quietly.

"Yes, I can see. You smile always when you talk about her, and your eyes...they show much. It is good, what I see. Sabina...she has not been happy for some time. Yes, she is famous, and knows many people, and likes what she does, but she has lost her smile. I would like to see her smile again." She patted my arm and stood up. "I think, Caidence, that perhaps you can make her smile again."

I stopped swirling my wine and stared at her. *Did Sophie just give me approval to be in a relationship with her daughter?*

"I..." I looked up into her face and saw nothing but openness and warmth, and a hint of amusement. "I would like to try," I said carefully, watching for any change of expression, "if she will let me."

She smiled widely, and reached across the table for the wine bottle, deftly filling my glass. "*Bueno*. If she is smart, she will let you, but sometimes, she is stubborn. She gets that, of course, from her father." She set the wine bottle down and placed a hand on my shoulder. "You will have patience with my Sabina, eh, Caidence Harris?"

I could only nod, overwhelmed by the conversation and not sure whether to be elated or terrified.

"We will keep this conversation between you and me, yes? When Sabina is ready, she will talk to me." She moved her hand from my shoulder to cup my cheek and stared into my face, nodding briskly. "Yes, you are very pretty. My Sabina always did have excellent taste." She patted my cheek and walked off, leaving me blinking and speechless.

I slumped back in my chair, absently sipping my wine and staring sightlessly out the restaurant's front window, thinking over the conversation. I was sure I wasn't reading anything into it. Robyn's mother knew she was a lesbian, seemed fine with it, and wanted me to make her daughter happy. But Robyn didn't know her mother knew, and her mother didn't want her to know that she knew, and wanted Robyn to tell her herself...

I sighed. *Jesus. Ward family dynamics just got weirder...*

"My mother is quite taken with you."

I nearly spit out a mouthful of wine as a woman in a white, short-collared chef uniform appeared seemingly from nowhere and slipped into the chair Sophie had recently vacated.

I swallowed deliberately and set down my glass. "Trish, hello. Nice to see you again." I nodded and gave her a friendly smile, hoping she didn't hold the other morning against me. "Your mother is quite charming, and I'm quite taken with her as well."

"Yes, *Mamá* can be very charming." Her expression was bland, the smile pleasant. "She likes to see the good in people."

"Trish, about the other morning..."

She leaned forward abruptly, her face now anything but pleasant. "I'm not fooled by you, not for one minute. I know what you want from my sister."

Guess that answered my question about whether she was still pissed about the other morning. And for fuck's sake—did her whole family know about us?

"Josh is with Robyn," she continued fiercely, "and you weaseling in on him while she's gone isn't going to work."

...and that answered that question.

There were several ways I could have handled the situation, and of course, I chose the worst way possible. I laughed. Still reeling from my conversation with her mother, the incongruity of Trish's accusation struck me as funny, and I laughed.

I stopped myself almost immediately, but the damage was done. Trish's eyes narrowed, sparking with anger and she leaned in even closer. "Stay away from Josh," she hissed through gritted teeth, and then stood abruptly and stalked away, ignoring my attempts to call her back to apologize.

"Well, shit." I slumped back in my chair, glancing around and noting that our altercation had drawn some attention. I forced a polite smile and nodded at the on-lookers, casually glancing around for Josh and spotting him crossing back to our table with a worried expression on his face.

"What was that?" He sat down in his chair and looked in the direction Trish had gone.

I rubbed my forehead and then ran a hand through my hair. "That was Robyn's sister telling me in no uncertain terms that my obvious plans to get you into bed while Robyn is gone are not going to work."

"You're shitting me." He turned his head to stare at me, his mouth slightly open.

"I shit you not. I seriously think she might come back with a meat cleaver or something. She was pretty pissed off. And I didn't make things any better by laughing at her."

He winced. "You laughed at Trish?"

I shrugged apologetically. "I'm sorry—she accused me of wanting to get into my girlfriend's ex-boyfriend's pants. Right after her mother told me she thought I could give Robyn her smile back. It just seemed...funny. At least at the time." I finished lamely.

"Damn, I'd better go talk to her." He started to stand and then stopped and sunk back into his chair. "Wait. Her mother told you *what*?"

I shook my head. "Never mind. It was kind of a private conversation and I shouldn't go into it. But, believe me, it made what Trish said seem funny."

I could tell he wanted to press me for more details, but a waiter had arrived with a flat skillet piled high with a rice, seafood, and vegetable mixture, along with a basket of tortillas and small bowls of pureed gazpacho.

"The chef's special *paella* for two and Sophie's gazpacho..." the server announced with flair as he set the sizzling skillet in the middle of the table and set warm, empty plates in front of us. After dishing us both up generous portions, he stepped back. "My name is Tom, please let me know if you need anything else."

We asked for a large Pellegrino to split and I immediately picked up my fork and started eating, more relieved than I should have been that the *paella* was for two. I doubted Trish would try to poison Josh along with me.

After the first bite, I let out a contented sigh. Great cooking, as well as great looks, ran in the Ward family, and I happily dug in for more, enjoying each and every bite for its subtle difference in flavor and wondering what spices she used.

"Those Ward girls can cook, can't they?" I mumbled, rather impolitely, around a half-chewed mouthful of rice when I noticed in embarrassment that Josh hadn't picked up his fork yet but was instead just watching me eat with a tiny grin on his face.

I finished chewing, swallowed, and took a sip of water. "What?"

He gave a quiet laugh. "When I saw Robyn last, in Florida, we were talking about you—we didn't talk about much else, to be honest—but anyway, she was extolling your many virtues, and then she got this really goofy smile on her face, and when I asked her what she was smiling about, she said she loved how you ate. Said you ate like you truly enjoyed it, and like every bite was special, and it really turned..." He stopped, looking slightly uncomfortable, and cleared his throat. "Um, anyway, now I see what she meant."

I looked down at my food, not bothering to hide my own goofy grin, ridiculously pleased that not only had she talked about me favorably, but that a quirk of mine that annoyed more than a few people was something she actually...liked.

He picked up his fork with a smile and took a bite, chewing slowly. "Mmm. Yes, those Ward girls sure can cook."

We ate our meal slowly, talking about Wimbledon, which he was leaving for on Monday, recent movies we'd seen, and my worry over how the *9P* finale would change facets of my life I'd rather not change. He told me stories about run-ins he and Robyn had had with the press, and talked about his recent visit to her— about how excited she was to be working with Lynne Wesson, and how the rumors about Lonnie Colchev being an arrogant prick were absolutely true.

Talking about her made me miss her, and I sighed discontentedly. "Damn, I miss her. I wish she'd at least call me a little more often."

He took my hand across the table. "I know, Caid. Just give her a little more time. I think she's going to realize soon that she's more distracted from missing you than she would be if you two were talking, or even if you'd visit."

"I hope you're right. God, I'd love to see her, but I'd be happy with just a damn phone call."

"Just be patient with her, she'll come around."

I smiled. "That seems to be everyone's advice when it comes to Robyn."

Patience had never been a particular strength of mine, but I guess I'd have to learn some, because I wasn't letting this go.

The restaurant filled up with Friday night diners and we were approached by a few autograph seekers, but in general, we weren't bothered. By the time we finally decided to leave, darkness was falling and the restaurant was packed. I argued good-naturedly with Sophie about the bill while Josh went into the kitchen to try to reassure Trish that I was not looking to jump his bones, but the slight frown on his face when he returned didn't give me much hope that he'd been successful.

My argument with Sophie hadn't changed her mind and she flatly refused to let us pay for dinner. She also extracted a promise from both of us to come to Santa Barbara when Robyn got back and let her cook for us at her restaurant. She kissed and hugged us both goodbye, ignoring the curious stares we were getting, and told me softly, "I am glad to have met you, Caidence. Bring her smile back, please."

I smiled in response and squeezed her hand. "I'll do my best, Sophie." I placed my other hand on my chest. "*Prometo.*"

She smiled warmly and then pushed me gently at Josh, who was eyeballing the desserts. "Go, or you will never get him out of here."

I laughed and tugged him by the arm toward the door. "Come on, Josh, let's get out of Sophie's hair." He looked longingly at the desserts, even though he'd finished off his own huge piece of flan and half of my cheese tart. I grabbed his hand when he hesitated and physically pulled him out the door, laughing.

The flashbulbs going off as we stepped outside blinded me for a moment and I stumbled a bit, throwing up a hand in an automatic defense. Josh's arm went around my waist in support, and he mumbled, "Let me handle this..." before the barrage of questions started, followed by another round of flashes.

Oh, shit.

"Mr. Riley, how long have you and Miss Harris been seeing each other?"

"What is your relationship?"

"Miss Harris, over here!"

Josh stepped slightly in front of me, keeping a hand resting lightly on my back. "What's all this?" he asked with an easy smile, sending the photographers into a frenzy of clicking and whirring. "Slow news day?"

"Does Robyn know you're here with another woman?" someone yelled, shoving a microphone into Josh's face, and it was then I realized this wasn't just photographers. There were video cams as well, and reporters from TV tabloids.

Shit, shit, shit.

"Caidence is a friend of both Robyn and me..." Josh tried to explain, but another volley of questions and yelling drowned him out.

"Over here! Josh, Caidence, over here! Give us a smile..."

"Josh, when did you and Robyn break up?"

"Miss Harris, what will it be like to work with Miss Ward now that you've stolen her fiancé?"

"Oh, hell," Josh said under his breath, "I think that's enough of this — come on."

We pushed through the throng, and walked as quickly as possible down the block with the group trailing behind us, still yelling questions and taking photos. I kept my eyes to the front, so I didn't get an exact count, but there must have been at least twenty, if not more.

"Josh, is it true that you, Caidence, and Robyn had a threesome?"

Oh, Liz would have loved that one...

"Caidence, were you actually with Josh when you 'disappeared'?"

Goddammit, how many times do I have to say it — I didn't disappear, I didn't get lost...

"We have a source that tells us you're trying to weasel your way between Robyn and Josh to break up their relationship. Is that true, Miss Harris?"

My steps slowed. *Weasel?* Now how was that for a coincidence? I felt my jaw tighten and my temple start to throb in anger.

I was never a big believer in coincidences.

I slowed even further, ready to go back into the restaurant and kick some elder Ward sister ass, but Josh tugged at my hand, urging me on. I quickly decided he was right, and kicking Trish's ass, with twenty-some reporters and photographers as well as her own mother looking on, wasn't the best idea right now.

Maybe some other time.

I lengthened my stride to keep up with Josh, and soon we were slipping into the car and slamming the doors behind us while the group continued to film, yell, and take pictures.

"Goddammit!" Josh jammed the key into the ignition in disgust. "What the hell was all that? Shit, I hate when they get like that." He started the car and jammed it into gear, backing swiftly out onto the street and scattering reporters as he went.

I fastened my seatbelt, remembering Josh's penchant for speed, and gripped the seat with shaky hands, holding on tightly as Josh led a determined news van and a few photographers on a merry chase. We squealed onto Pico at dizzying speed, our pursuers still on our bumper, but a harrowing left onto Lincoln lost two of them, and when we hit the Santa Monica Freeway and Josh opened up however many horses that little car had under the hood, they didn't have a chance.

After a few more minutes of white-knuckle driving that would have made Dale Earnhardt Jr. proud, Josh slowed to a more sedate speed — if you can call ninety sedate — and I loosened my grip on the seat and the door.

"God damn," Josh said finally, and flashed a smile at me. "That was kick ass."

I frowned at him and punched him in the arm. "Jerk. You coulda killed someone. Someone like me, for instance."

He just laughed. I grunted and rubbed my face with my hands, hiding a smile.

He glanced over at me, caught the smile, and laughed again. "Admit it. It was kick ass."

I smiled and shook my head, relaxing back into the seat. After a few minutes of driving in silence, I asked curiously, "Does that happen to you a lot? The press just waiting for you like that?"

He shrugged. "Sometimes, when it's a publicized event and I'm with Robyn, it can get a little crazy, but they're usually a little less...nasty." He paused, and looked thoughtful. "This was kind of strange."

When I'm with Robyn... That brought up a whole set of insecurities I didn't feel like dealing with at the moment. Robyn and Josh did the public couple thing for publicity and for their careers. What happened if — *when*, I corrected myself — things got more serious between Robyn and me? Where did I fit into her life? Or did I? Did she assume things would just stay the same, and she would continue to be with Josh publicly while keeping me on the side? I pushed the thought away with an annoyed shake of my head, concentrating instead on whether I should tell Josh my suspicions about Trish.

"Josh..." I started hesitantly, still not sure of how to bring it up. "Did you hear one of those guys ask me if I was trying to weasel my way between you and Robyn?"

He nodded. "Caid, don't let it bother you..."

"No, no, it's not that." I shook my head. "Although it does bother me that people think that." I paused. "When I talked with Trish earlier tonight, her exact words were, 'Josh is with Robyn, and you weaseling in on him while she's gone isn't going to work.' "

He swore softly and shook his head sadly. "Goddamn Trish. She said something tonight when I went back to talk to her about how I'd better be honest with Robyn, because she was going to hear about this whether I told her or not. So instead of just calling Robyn, she calls the press." He hit the steering wheel with his palm.

"Jesus. She's such a fucking drama queen — you'd think she was the actress instead of Robyn. I can't believe she'd do that! I know she likes to give Robyn a hard time, but this is ridiculous. Damn, Robby's going to kill her..."

"Not if I get there first," I mumbled. "What's with those two anyway? One minute she's defending Robyn and acting like the proud sister, and the next, she's cutting her to shreds..."

"Yeah, they've always had a strange relationship. I think Trish is totally jealous of Robyn's fame, but at the same time she's incredibly loyal..." He looked over at me curiously. "You got all that from her tonight?"

"No." I shook my head. "Trish came by to see Robyn the morning she left for Florida. I'd just spent the night... When Robyn introduced us, she talked about watching *9th Precinct* whenever Robyn was on, and then proceeded to basically call her, and every other actress, a pretty face with no talent. It was bizarre."

"You spent the night? At her house?" He asked in surprise. I nodded. "And she introduced you to Trish?"

I nodded again, and smiled wanly. "Not quite as simple as it sounds — there were some...issues. But yes, I stayed the night, and yes, she introduced me to Trish."

He let out a low whistle. "You've got more pieces of her than you think, then, Caid. She never lets her women stay over. Never even invites them to the house. Never."

The words hit me like a punch, and I let my head fall back against the headrest. *Her women.*

Jesus.

I couldn't even be glad about the other things he'd said. All I heard was *her women...*

He looked over at me apologetically. "Ah, shit. That sounded bad. I..."

I held up a hand, stopping him. "No, no. Don't apologize. I pretty much knew about," I waved my hand vaguely, "that. I just..." I shook my head. "Let's just change the subject, though, okay?"

He looked at me worriedly, but obliged. "So, ah, you said you were going to be in New York next week?"

"Yeah. Monday through Wednesday, probably. Connie is still working out the details."

"My dad lives upstate...I'm stopping over for a couple of days on my way to England. Do you know where you're staying? Maybe we could have dinner or meet for a drink or something."

I looked over at him and laughed lightly. "I love ya, Josh, and enjoy your company, but do you really think that's a good idea after what just happened?"

He frowned. "I'm not going to let the press dictate who I do things with, Caid, and neither should you."

The irony of the statement wasn't lost on me, since in essence he and Robyn had been doing exactly that for two years. But I knew what he meant.

"I have a feeling we're going to be doing a lot together in the future, Caid," he continued. "The press is going to have to get used to it sometime."

"Ugh." I rubbed my forehead with the palm of my hand and then ran my hand through my hair. "I know, I know, and I might as well get used to it, too, since it's going to be a little crazy for a while after the finale airs." I sighed. "How about a compromise? I'll be at the Gansevoort—I fly in on Monday night, and was planning on a late dinner at the hotel restaurant. Want to join me? It would keep the press to a minimum. They're good about security."

"That works for me. How about I call you later this weekend to firm things up?"

I nodded. "Thanks, Josh...and, can you call Robyn and tell her about all this? You can call her, right? I don't want her to be surprised, or to think..."

"I'll call her, but she's not going to think anything bad, Caid — not about you and me. I doubt she'll even hear about it. She's pretty wrapped up in the movie, and it's a closed set." He patted my leg. "You shouldn't worry so much. They'll lose interest in no time."

I desperately hoped he was right.

Chapter
Fifteen

HE WAS WRONG.

No one lost interest. If anything, the recent mix of stories about me — my disappearance, the photos of me kissing an unidentified blond man, and my dinner with Josh — combined to set the press into something of a feeding frenzy.

My flight out of LA the afternoon before had drawn a good bit of interest from the lurking LAX celebrity photo corps, and my arrival in LaGuardia had been just as well documented. Annoyed by the growing group of press following my every move, I wasn't as friendly as I could have been as I made my way through the cadre of photographers at the hotel that evening, or the next morning on my way to the morning show taping when I was swamped again outside the network building.

"Shit." I grunted in disgust, tossing the paper I'd been looking at onto the table nestled in the bay window seating nook of my hotel room. It skidded across a stack of other papers and Internet printouts already there, scattering them and knocking several to the carpet.

Pictures of Josh and me at Sophie's, smiling and laughing over dinner.

Pictures of Josh with his arm around my waist as we left the restaurant and others of us as we hurried to the car ahead of the press, our hands linked. I don't even remember holding his hand, but there it was, in full color.

Pictures of the two of us at dinner the night before at Ona, again smiling and looking very chummy. The security at the hotel was good, and to my relief, we hadn't been bothered once during dinner, but they couldn't stop every enterprising diner with a camera-phone.

The pictures taken on the balcony of Liz's Malibu house of James kissing me.

Grainy covert photos from the supposedly "closed" set of *Lost Key*, showing Robyn looking gaunt, pale, and unkempt, with accompanying stories of her rumored breakdown. I knew she was playing an addict in the film, and I applauded her makeup artist, but the photos gave me a twinge of concern—the thinness was real, and she was too thin already. I hoped she wasn't taking this looking like an addict to the extreme.

Scattered throughout the pages were pictures of Josh and Robyn, looking happy and beautiful together, gazing at each other with obvious affection and adoration.

And then there were the headlines.

Home-wrecker. Temptress. Seductress. Back-stabber. Harlot. Conniver. Schemer.

Basically, a thesaurus of words meaning nasty, deceitful bitch.

I sighed again and dropped heavily onto the couch, staring out the window at the Hudson River and the cityscape beyond it, leaving the papers where they lay. Seemingly overnight, I had become a certified jezebel. A prickly slut who had broken up one of the most recognized celebrity pairings of the last several years, and caused a nervous breakdown in the process.

Fantastic.

Josh had tried to reassure me, telling me that this would blow over, that some other celebrity would do something shocking or just plain stupid and the press would forget all about us, but to me it seemed doubtful. I'd never been the focus of so much press, nor did I ever want to be again.

Ever.

I'd have to examine that wish carefully, considering the relationship I was fumbling around in with Robyn. If the press ever got the points of the triangle of Josh, Robyn, and me connected correctly... I shook my head, not even wanting to imagine the kind of frenzy that would provoke. What was happening to me now was quite enough to deal with.

And I still have the fallout from the season finale to go through, which should be just about...I checked my watch...halfway through right now.

I ran a hand through my hair, still slightly damp from the recent shower I'd taken after making use of the rooftop pool and the very fancy exercise facility the hotel boasted. The workout had helped my stress levels a little, but not as much as I'd hoped. The tumbler of scotch and ice I was sipping on was the next step in trying to relax enough to sleep.

The buzz of my cell phone vibrating against the glass-topped bed stand interrupted my next sip, and I rolled my eyes, thinking it was probably Connie. Again. She'd been calling me almost hourly to give me pep talks, advice on what to say and more importantly what *not* to say to the press, and updates on what steps the agency was taking to get things back under control. While I appreciated her concern and support, more press-talk was the last thing I wanted to hear right now.

I pushed myself reluctantly off the couch and crossed to the phone, not even bothering to check the display. "Connie, I think you're the best damn agent in the world, but honestly, I don't need to be babysat. I'm fine, really."

There was a pause, and then a low chuckle that sent my heart pounding and made breathing suddenly difficult. "I'm glad to hear it," the familiar voice rasped, and I closed my eyes, savoring the riot of emotions that voice produced.

"Robyn..." I steadied my breathing and sat down on the bed. "Hey."

"Hey, yourself."

Neither of us spoke for several moments—I was happy just listening to her breathe, knowing she was at the other end of the line, finally connected to her again in some way. I lay back on the bed and closed my eyes, trying to picture where she was, what she was doing, what she looked like. Was her hair loose around her shoulders or tied back? Was she dressed for an evening out, or in casual clothes—jeans and a T-shirt maybe?

"Goddamn, I miss you," I said finally, gratified at the slight catch in her breathing.

"I miss you, too," she said softly. "I think I might have a remedy for that."

"Do you?" I smiled slightly. "Why, Miss Ward, are you suggesting..."

"Open the door, Caid."

My eyes popped open and I sat up fast enough to make myself dizzy. "What?"

There was a soft tapping on the door. "Open the door."

"Holy shit." I tossed the phone down, scrambled off the bed, and flew to the door, fumbling with the different chains and locks before finally throwing the door open and staring dumbly at the sight that greeted me.

Damn, she looked good.

Faded jeans, tennis shoes, and a blue hooded UCLA sweatshirt pulled up to cover her head...

"Surprise." She smiled hesitantly. "Can I come in?"

I blinked and shook myself out of my frozen state. "I...oh...uh, sure. Yeah." I stepped back to let her in, annoyed at my inarticulateness. I thought I'd gotten past that reaction to Robyn, but apparently not. She brushed past me, closer than necessary in the wide door, and the slight contact and accompanying hint of her perfume set my skin and senses tingling.

She moved further into the room, looking around curiously. I flipped on a light to dispel the gloom I'd been sitting in and followed her across the room. She stopped in front of the bay window and looked out over the city.

"Nice." She turned to me, pulling back the hood of her sweatshirt to reveal a loose tumble of dark hair. Her movements stopped and her lips parted slightly as she looked at me. I was dressed — or rather undressed — for bed, and her eyes wandered my body, starting at my bare feet and moving up from there, taking in my bare legs, baggy cotton boxers and snug tank top. When she reached my face and our eyes met, the emotions on display there had me moving toward her without a thought about my previous awkwardness — I just wanted to immerse myself in what I saw.

We came together furiously, desperately, no finesse or tenderness, just raw need and instant, overwhelming arousal. I was dizzy from it, dizzy from the ferocity of her kisses, from her tongue seeking mine, from her lips and teeth on my neck...it was overwhelming and held an underlying desperation that, even in my brain's addled state, set off warning bells.

I tried to slow it down, to get things back in control by breaking the kiss and pulling away slightly, but Robyn took the opportunity to quickly pull the sweatshirt over her head and the T-shirt beneath it — *does the woman ever wear a bra?* — tossing them haphazardly to the floor as she kicked off her shoes and worked at the buttons of her jeans. In seconds, she was naked, and any thoughts of slowing things down to ascertain the reason for her desperation vanished when she took my hands and laid them on her skin.

"Oh, yeah..." she breathed. "Christ, Caid, I need you to touch me. I just need to feel you..." Another heated kiss pushed me backward and I fell onto the bed; she came after me and straddled my waist, grasping my hand and guiding it to her sex. "Inside...please, Caid. I need..." She pushed my fingers into her warmth and groaned, falling forward and bracing herself above me, with one hand next to my head and the other against the headboard. Her eyes closed and she threw her head back, moving against me with increased urgency.

Oh, my God...

It was wildly erotic, to be inside her like this as she moved above me. My own hips moved in response, rising to meet her thrusts and drawing low moans from both of us. With my free hand, I grabbed her waist and pulled her against me harder.

"God..." Her breaths were almost sobs, her eyes shut tightly, and I felt a flicker of uncertainty. I needed to see her eyes, needed to know she was here, with me.

"Look at me, baby. Don't close your eyes, look at me..."

She slowed her movements and lowered her head, her hair cascading over one shoulder and tickling the skin of my chest. Her eyes opened, so dark they looked black, staring intently into mine.

"Caid," she whispered, raising her hand from the bed to cup my cheek. "I...oh, God..."

Her eyes widened when I gently stroked her clit with my thumb, and I watched in wonderment and reverence as her breathing stopped, only to be let out in a rush as her body stiffened and release washed over her face.

There were no words to describe it, watching her at that moment.

It was terrifyingly personal, so intimate that I had to force myself not to look away, even though it had been at my request. I continued the stroking and the gentle push of my fingers until she stopped my hand and slowly collapsed against me, burying her face in my neck, her breathing harsh and labored in my ear.

I slowly withdrew my fingers and wrapped both arms around her tightly, pulling her closer and kissing her temple. I held her as her breathing returned to normal and her trembling stopped; held her as her body relaxed in my embrace.

"Hey," I said finally, and kissed her hair. "You okay?" I felt her nod, and stroked her hair with one hand. "Honey..."

She raised her head and kissed me, silencing my words. "Shhh," she said softly, and kissed me again. "No talking. Just let me touch you."

Her hand had already worked its way under my shirt, stroking the skin beneath my ribs, and I made no protest as she pushed herself up and straddled me again, pulling the material over my head and tossing it to the floor. As much as I wanted to know what was going on in her head, something told me to keep quiet and let her control things. She needed this somehow, and to be honest, so did I.

So I said nothing as she sat back and her gaze raked my naked torso, claiming it as hers. I said nothing as her mouth licked and sucked at my neck and breasts, and a hand tugged my boxers down over my hips and off my legs. I said nothing as she kissed her way down my body with infinite tenderness, so different from her desperation of minutes before. I said nothing until I breathlessly gasped out her name as her tongue brought me to climax once, and then again, and I lay exhausted in a tangle of sheets, with her dark hair spread out across my stomach and her lips soft against my thigh.

"Jesus," I breathed when I'd gotten my breath back. I stroked her head. "Come up here, please."

She did as I asked, placing gentle kisses as she went, her hair brushing softly against my skin as she moved up my body. She looked into my face for several long moments, her eyes swirling with emotions I couldn't decipher. I almost told her then. Almost said the words, almost blurted out *I love you*...but she broke eye contact, kissed my chin and laid her head on my chest, and the moment slipped away.

My arms went around her automatically, and I touched my lips to her hair. "Rob..."

"Shhh..." she quieted me again. "I don't want to talk right now, okay? Just hold me."

I hesitated, wanting very badly to know what was going on, but not wanting to spoil the moment.

"Please, Caid."

I sighed and kissed her head again, rubbing a hand up and down her back. She felt my acquiescence and draped an arm across my waist, turning her head to kiss the skin below my collarbone. I closed my eyes and relaxed, enjoying the feel of her weight on me, and the heat of her skin. As I drifted off to sleep, she whispered something and I stirred, fighting against a dragging tiredness caused by sleepless nights, stressful days and recent physical activity. A soothing hand on my stomach calmed me, and I gave up and let sleep come.

"I DON'T REALLY give a flying fuck about what the studio's normal policy is for handling the press at the building entrance, Connie," I snapped. "I just want to know if they're going to do anything about it *today*."

The silence on the other end of the line told me that I'd again let my nasty mood get the better of me. *Damn*. First it was the poor room service guy this morning—the first person I'd seen after waking up alone. Then the concierge, who had asked me, innocently, if I'd enjoyed my stay. And now I'd jumped all over Connie. I sighed, and leaned my head back against the leather interior of the network furnished limo.

"Shit, Connie, I'm sorry. Pay no attention to the raving lunatic on the other end of the phone. She's had a bad couple of days, and wants nothing more than to be home and away from this damn city."

Connie laughed lightly, but her voice held concern. "You seemed okay when I talked to you last night, Caid. Did something happen? You didn't go out, did you, and run into more press?"

"No." *My lesbian lover stopped by for a lovely fuck and then snuck off without a word while I was sleeping. But she was nice enough to order me croissants and coffee before she left.* "I'm just tired, and ready to go home."

"Well, you're almost done, kiddo. Just charm the pants off Brandon Marcus and you'll be home in no time."

I barked out a laugh. "I'll do my best, but if he starts taking his pants off, I'm outta there. That is *definitely* not in my contract."

Connie giggled and I smiled in relief, glad I'd been forgiven for my previous outburst. "You could do worse than Brandon Marcus, Caid. He's kind of cute in a..."

"...geeky, teddy bear sort of way?" I finished for her, and laughed. "He actually kind of reminds me of an ex-boyfriend I had in college."

"Really?" I rarely spoke about my personal life or my life before she'd been my agent, and I could tell she was intrigued.

"Really," I told her, and laughed again. "But I still don't want to see him without his pants. And what's with you trying to hook me up lately? Teenagers last week, and now nerdy talk show hosts..."

"Well, lately your choices in men could have been better—" She stopped herself and there was heavy silence. "Ah. Damn. I'm sorry, Caid, I shouldn't have said anything. It's none of my business."

The beginnings of an improved mood dissipated instantly, and I rubbed my forehead vigorously with my palm. I'd assumed, when Connie didn't ask questions about Josh and immediately put out a press release that we were just friends, that she actually *believed* we were just friends. Apparently not.

"No, I don't suppose it is your business, Con, but you could have asked, and then you wouldn't have had to think you've been lying about it for the last four days." I was disappointed but not surprised. I had implied recently that I had a big secret that I wasn't ready to tell her. I couldn't really blame her for jumping to conclusions. "Josh and I are friends. That's it. There is nothing romantic between us. Nothing."

"And Robyn..."

"Robyn and I are friends, too. She's aware that Josh and I are friends and do things together—she introduced us, for God's sake. And she knows I would never do something like make a play for Josh."

For more reasons than you realize, Con, I thought, and frowned.

Robyn *did* know that, didn't she? Could that be the reason for her desperation last night? I shook my head. If she entertained that thought for even a second, I was going to have to smack her upside the head.

Right after I kicked her in the ass for leaving me this morning without a word.

"I'm sorry," she said quietly. "I should have asked if I had doubts."

"I'd rather you didn't have doubts, but I guess I don't blame you."

"Caid..."

"Don't worry about it, Con. It's all right. Now...can you find out about the entrance for me? Maybe there's a back way or something?"

"Yes, I'll find out and let you know. Where are you now?"

"Oh, hell, I don't know this city." I squinted at a passing street sign. "Uh, Ninth and...Thirty-second, I think."

"Okay, you've got a fair bit to go yet. I'll call you back."

"Yep." I hung up and leaned my forehead against the glass. Watching the people and cars around us as we crawled through traffic, I thought back on the morning.

A KNOCK ON the door and a muffled, "Room service!" pulled me from sleep just before eight. After a surprised glance at the clock, I sleepily reached behind me, expecting a long, warm body but finding a cold, empty space. I wondered, briefly, if I'd dreamed the entire thing, but the smell of her lingered on the pillow, and my body — my body remembered.

I called out for her, thinking she was in the bathroom or the shower, not even considering the possibility that she was just...gone. The room service waiter received the brunt of my disbelief and anger when I realized Robyn had indeed left, and after stammering a confused apology for something he certainly had nothing to do with, he scurried off with his cart, taking the silver serving tray of pastries and coffee with him.

I called her cell phone — my resolve to honor her request of no contact flew out the window the minute she showed up at my hotel room in New York — but I was immediately sent to voicemail. I left a sarcastic, scathing message that made me feel a little better for about two seconds, but didn't change the fact that she'd left.

She hadn't even left a note. No note, no message, nothing. Once again, she'd managed to astonish me with her passion and her touch, and then make me feel like just another lover in a long line of lovers. If this was what loving Robyn Ward was going to be like, maybe I could live without it.

I rapped my forehead against the glass a few times, and shook my head.

No, I can't.

"*YOU ASSAULTED ME, Detective. I could have you thrown in jail for that.*" The voice was low and smoky, doing its normal number on me even though it wasn't live, and I was thoroughly pissed off at the woman generating it.

"*Why didn't you?*" I winced at the breathiness of my reply.

Some big, tough cop I was.

I watched from behind the stage curtain as the clip of our now infamous finale lip-lock rolled to its conclusion on the screen behind the host's desk. The audience erupted in whistles and loud applause, and I took a deep, calming breath and tilted my head from side to side to relieve the tension.

Unlike other talk shows I'd been on, the rotating hosts of *NightTalk* didn't meet their guest beforehand, and that sense of unfamiliarity was making me more nervous than usual, especially with all the press I'd drawn lately. I was hoping Brandon Marcus was as amiable as he appeared to be. My mood had yet to improve today, and I wasn't particularly confident I'd be able to hold my temper if he started picking at me about all the things that the press had accused me of. What great headlines *that* would make. *Slutty Man-Stealing Seductress Brains Talk Show Host With Coffee Mug and then Steals Stage Manager's Husband. Film at 5:00, 5:12, 5:20, 5:25...*

"From the hit series *9th Precinct*, please welcome Caidence Harris!"

I brought my mind back to business and shook the tension out of my body one last time before plastering a smile on my face and walking out onto the set. I gave the audience a quick wave, then stepped up onto the stage and shook the host's hand. He was about my height and just shy of heavy, with a neatly trimmed goatee and a mop of dark curly hair that looked about to spring free, at any minute, of whatever hair product was keeping in place. Up close he reminded me even more of my ex, Toby—aside from his green eyes and a suit that Toby wouldn't have been caught dead in—and I flashed him a genuine smile as he gently shook my hand.

I sat down in the overstuffed armchair he indicated, and he sat behind a curved wooden desk. "It's great to meet you, Caidence. Really a pleasure." He sat back in his chair. "So, how ya doing? How's our fair city treating you?"

In an effort to look non-temptressy, I'd gone casual with low-rise denims, a stretchy, dark green and white zip-up mock tee and black, thick-heeled oxfords. I was comfortable, and glad for it now as I crossed my legs and rested my elbows on the arms of the chair, swinging my foot a little. "Well, let's just say it's been an interesting stay..."

He was funny and amiable, and we talked easily for a few minutes, alluding to my current status with the press and moving into how I'd gotten started in acting. I talked about the Ballentine campaign — my days as a "beer bitch" I'd called it, and got a good chuckle from the audience — and my work on *9th Precinct* and *In Their Defense*.

"So I have to tell ya, I watched that finale last night, and I think it took a lot of people by surprise. Is that something that had been in the works for a while, or was it kind of a last-minute thing?"

"The finale script never changed from the first time we saw it," I answered, "but I guess you could say it was a relatively recent storyline."

"Was it hard for you at all, or strange, to do that scene? Do you get, like, performance anxiety during a scene like that? I mean, you were kissing Robyn Ward!" He waggled his eyebrows, and the crowd laughed. "I guess I shouldn't assume my male fantasies apply to you, right?"

Oh, you'd be surprised...

I smiled. "I was nervous, for sure... God, it seemed like a million people showed up for the taping. The crew can tell you that I was maybe a little, ah, touchy on the set. But I was incredibly lucky to be working with Robyn — she's such a professional, you know, as well as being just a damn nice person. She really kept me sane."

Okay, just a *teeny*-weenie lie. Sane was something I rarely felt in the company of Robyn Ward.

"Well, I'm glad to hear you say that..." he grinned at me and winked, "because I've got a little surprise for you."

I forced a smile. *Crap.* Surprises on late-night TV talk shows were rarely good. At least not for the surprise-ee.

He stood up and gestured toward the curtain I'd recently stood behind. "Ladies and gentlemen, as an extra special treat tonight, another *9th Precinct* regular, and also star of the popular series *In Their Defense*, give it up for my good friend Robyn Ward!"

A quick blink was my only reaction.

Oh, goody. What a great surprise.

I'd had quite a bit of practice over the last few days at keeping my emotions hidden, and I needed every bit of that practice to keep my expression pleasant and smiling while I was flooded with the contradictory emotions of fresh anger and the elation that seeing Robyn always produced. I pushed up from my chair, clapping with the rest of the crowd as Robyn appeared from behind the curtain and crossed the set toward us.

She wore a long suede skirt in deep burgundy that had tiny black buttons down each side, with more than half of them undone to show plenty of thigh as she walked, and black, knee-high lace-up boots. Top that off with a black silk camisole...

The whistles and cheers from the crowd were raucous. I chuckled to myself. And people thought little ol' me could seduce Josh Riley away from this woman.

How completely and utterly ridiculous.

Brandon moved from behind his desk and greeted Robyn with a one-armed hug and a light kiss on the cheek. She smiled as he said something into her ear, but her eyes were on me, hesitant and shy, full of guarded pleasure.

I couldn't help myself. I smiled at her.

Yes, she'd left me alone without a word that morning. Yes, I was angry. Yes, every damn thing she did seemed to confuse me more, but I couldn't help myself. I smiled, and admitted that despite everything, it was very good to see her.

She stepped around Brandon and grasped my hands in hers, brushing cool lips across my cheek. "Surprise," she said softly as the audience continued to noisily voice their approval.

I let out a short, soft laugh with no humor, and kept my voice low and even. "Think you might stick around after this one, and not run off like last night?" I felt her stiffen and start to pull back, but I held on tightly. "Never mind...it's good to see you." I kissed her cheek and squeezed her hands, leaning in until my mouth almost touched her ear. "You look incredible."

I felt a tremor in her hands, and I pulled back, releasing her. She gave me a tiny smile that spoke volumes, and turned to the still rowdy audience to wave, her professional smile firmly back in place.

I moved over a seat and Robyn sat down in the chair I'd just vacated. The crowd finally quieted, although there were occasional whistles and yells, and a loud "I love you, Robyn!"

"I love you, too," she said with a grin and crossed her legs, showing enough thigh to set off another round of shouts and whistles. I willed myself not to stare at the exposed skin that was close enough to touch, and instead focused my attention on Brandon.

He smiled and sat back in his chair, obviously pleased with the reaction his surprise had gotten from the crowd. "Hi, Robyn," he said when the crowd quieted again.

"Hiya, Brandon," she replied with obvious fondness. She pushed a strand of long, loose hair behind her ear.

"I've just been chatting with your co-star here. She's got some good things to say about you."

Robyn looked over at me and smiled. "I heard, and I'm completely flattered. I'm the lucky one to get to work with Caidence on this..."

The three of us chatted back and forth for another ten minutes, hitting all sorts of topics that seemed natural, but I quickly realized were carefully chosen to create opportunities for Robyn to mention things like "Caid and I did this," or "Josh, Caid, and I did that," subtly but determinedly emphasizing the friendship between the three of us and her obvious trust in Josh and me as friends, without coming right out and saying Josh and I weren't sleeping together.

Nothing gets people's curiosity up quicker than a good denial...

Robyn and Liz must have read the same handbook of how to handle the media. *I need to get myself a copy of that book some time soon. I wonder if they sell it on Amazon?*

Just before the second commercial break, Brandon wrapped up the interview, thanking us both and announcing his next guest. As soon as someone yelled, "And...we're clear. Three minutes!" we all stood, and Robyn gave Brandon a warm hug.

"Thanks, Brandon—I owe ya." She touched him gently on the arm.

He grinned. "No problem, beautiful. Always great to see you, and my boss is loving me right now. Can you stay a bit after the show?"

She shook her head and glanced at her watch. "I'm going to be cutting it close as it is...sorry. I'll see you at the Open, though, right?"

"Wouldn't miss it." He turned to me and shook my hand. "Caidence, it was so nice meeting you. I enjoyed talking with you."

"You too, Brandon." I nodded and smiled.

He looked behind us with a frown, and waved a young woman over. "Sorry to dash, but Mike is waving frantically and I'd better go see what's up. Sherri will show you back to your dressing rooms."

He gave Robyn another quick peck and left, and we followed the fast-moving assistant backstage.

"Miss Harris, this is you," she gestured at a door. "Miss Ward, you're down this way—"

"Thanks, Sherri, I can find it," Robyn interrupted with a courteous smile. After a second of hesitation, Sherri nodded and hurried off down the hall.

I pushed open the door to my dressing room and stood aside to let Robyn in before closing it behind us. She immediately moved toward me, but I held up my hands and backed away.

"No-no-no." I pointed to the other side of the room. "You stay over there. I can't be pissed at you when you touch me, and I need to be pissed at you right now."

A look of hurt confusion passed over her face. "Caid, why are you so angry with me? I thought...last night we were so close..."

"And then this morning, after all that closeness," I said

sarcastically, "I woke up alone."

Her brow furrowed at my tone. "Caid, I'm sorry about this morning. I had a string of interviews, and had to get back to change. I didn't realize it would upset you so much. I was on my way to the airport when I finally got your message this afternoon, and you sounded so angry. That's when I called up Brandon and asked to get on the show. I wanted to talk with you before I left."

"Why couldn't you have just told me that?" I asked in frustration, shaking my head. "You couldn't just tell me that you had interviews, and that you would have to leave in the morning?"

She looked at me and raised an eyebrow. "And when exactly was I supposed to tell you that, Caid? We weren't doing much talking last night, if you remember correctly..."

"I remember," I said quietly. "And I also remember waking up alone this morning."

"And I'm sorry about that, truly I am." She took a step toward me. "I wanted to stay this morning, more than anything, but I had those damn interviews. You didn't seem to mind when I said goodbye, and I told you in the note why I had to go — "

"Whoa, whoa! Wait. Told me goodbye?"

She looked at me strangely. "You don't remember? I know you were a little out of it, but I thought you were awake. You mumbled something about me smelling good, said goodbye, and smiled when I kissed you..."

Shit.

On more than one occasion when I was with Toby, he'd said he kissed me goodbye in the morning and I'd responded, but had had no recollection of it later.

"And the note?" I asked hesitantly. "You left a note?"

She gave me another strange look. "Of course I left a note. Didn't they deliver breakfast this morning? I wanted to be there when you woke up, but I figured that since I couldn't be, I'd try to start your day out with something nice. I know how stressed-out you must be about all this..."

"The note was with breakfast?" I asked in a small voice, remembering the uniformed waiter practically sprinting down the hall to get away from the crazy, pissed-off lady in 7210.

"Well, yeah." She smiled sheepishly. "I know, kind of corny, right? It seemed — I don't know — sweet and kind of romantic at three in the morning, but..."

I rubbed my forehead with my palm and shook my head. "Jesus Christ. I'm an idiot."

"What — "

"I never got the note," I told her softly. "I thought you didn't leave one. And I don't remember you saying goodbye. I thought you'd just...gone."

She frowned. "Come on, Caid, you can't believe I'd do that..." She looked at me for a moment, and read the truth. She shook her head sadly. "But you did, didn't you? You really thought I'd do that to you." She took a few steps across the small room and studied a framed poster on the wall, hugging her arms to her body defensively.

Shit. I ran a frustrated hand through my hair. *Shit, shit, shit.* What was it with the two of us? If it wasn't one of us letting our fears and insecurities get in the way, it was the other.

I walked over to her and after a moment's hesitation, put my arms around her from behind and rested my chin on her shoulder. "I'm the idiot this time," I whispered. "I'm sorry."

She was unyielding for several moments, but eventually relaxed against me and shook her head. "We're both idiots." She let out a short, cynical laugh. "I don't know why I got so offended. You had good reason to believe I'd just leave. Lord knows I've done it in the past, many, many times."

Ouch. Was it really necessary to add the second 'many'? Wouldn't one have sufficed?

Feeling me stiffen reflexively, she turned in my embrace and rested her forearms on my shoulders, running her fingers through the hair at the nape of my neck and waiting until I met her gaze. "The keyword is *past*, Caid. You and I..." She looked away from my face to where her fingers played in my hair. "This thing between us, it happened so quickly, and then I had the film shoot, and we never got the chance to talk about anything. About expectations, what we wanted out of it...anything." Her eyes came back to mine. "You have to know that I want you, Caid. That physically," she placed a hand on the side of my face, stroking gently with her thumb, "you make me so crazy I can't think. But I also want you to know that I honestly care about you. You're my friend, and I respect you so much—I would *never* purposely hurt you. We haven't had much time together, and my track record isn't so great, but I hope you believe that."

So...we're friends with benefits? I knew that wasn't what she was trying to get at, but my mind couldn't help but get stuck on it. I didn't want to be her fuckbuddy, I wanted to be her...everything.

Great. I was quoting Andy Gibb songs. That couldn't be a good sign.

I forced a smile that I hoped wasn't tinged with disappointment. "I do believe you. I know you care about me...as a friend, Robyn, and you'd never purposely try to hurt me. I'm sorry I doubted that."

She frowned. "That's not exactly what I meant, Caid...of course

I care about you as a friend, but—"

"Miss Harris?" Sherri's voice and tentative knock on the door interrupted, and we both jumped a little. Robyn made a cute little noise of frustration as we reluctantly pulled apart.

I smiled. "I guess this isn't the best place to be having this conversation anyway, is it?"

She glanced around and shook her head. "No, I don't suppose it is."

Another knock came and I walked to the door and opened it. "Yes?"

"Hello, Miss Harris, sorry to bother you, but do you know where Miss Ward went? There's a driver here waiting for her, and she's not in her dressing room..." her voice trailed off as Robyn stepped up behind me. "Oh. Miss Ward. There you are. Your driver—"

Robyn nodded. "Is waiting for me, yes, thank you, Sherri. Can you tell him I'll just be a moment? Maybe you can let him grab a sandwich or something from the green room? I'll find him there."

She nodded, and rushed off in what seemed like the only other speed she possessed besides Stop.

I closed the door again and turned, and the two of us stared at each other for several seconds.

"Damn," she said finally, pushing her hair behind her ear. "I wish I didn't have to go. I feel like we're leaving things hanging." She chewed on her lip. "Are we okay?"

I pulled her into a hug, running my hands up and down her back, and kissed her hair. "Yes, we're okay," I whispered.

We stood in each other's arms for nearly a minute, and finally I kissed her lightly on the neck below her ear and pulled away. "I know you want to concentrate on the film, but do you think we could at least talk on the phone a little more often? I think—"

She quieted me with a long finger against my lips. "Yes. Definitely. Trying to keep myself from thinking about you isn't working anyway. I'll call you when I get back tonight."

"I'll probably be in the air..."

"Tomorrow, then, after filming?"

"Any time. I'll take what I can get."

She frowned a little at that, before her expression cleared and she leaned forward to kiss me lightly on the mouth. "I'll talk to you soon, then. And, Caid, thank you for last night. I needed to reconnect, to feel you..."

I smiled. "I needed it, too, and I enjoyed every second." I took her face in my hands and kissed her slowly and deliberately. "But, next time," I said quietly after I pulled away and waited for her eyes to flutter open, "I don't want to rush, and I don't want to

wake up alone."
    She smiled softly. "You got it."

Chapter
Sixteen

I LEANED OUT of my car and pressed the intercom buzzer outside Liz's gated estate in Beverly Hills, pulling back and saluting the camera mounted above the intercom.

"Good afternoon, Miss Harris," came a disembodied voice that I recognized as belonging to Risa, Liz's housekeeper.

"Afternoon, Risa. Is Liz in? I know she's not expecting me, but I'd like to see her if she's around."

There was a long pause, presumably while Risa checked with Liz, and I glanced in my rear-view mirror, noting that the green sedan and orange, early model Volkswagen Beetle that had been tailing me most of the day were pulled up on the side of the road a safe distance behind me.

"Persistent little buggers," I muttered, squinting behind me and hoping neither car would try to follow me through the gate.

There was a loud click and the gate started creaking open. "Come on through, Miss Harris. Miss Stokley is most happy to see you."

"Thanks. Ah," I glanced in my mirror again, "Risa? I've got some paparazzi on my tail—I don't want them to follow me in..."

"Don't worry, Miss Harris. Miss Stokley's lawyer made the last photographer who tried to sneak in very sorry. They won't follow you."

I drove through and the gate closed behind me with a solid clang, leaving my lurking paparazzi friends on the other side. At times like these, I understood the attraction of a gated property. I had no such barrier around my house, and I'd been dealing with groups of photographers and reporters hanging around my yard, as well as the wrath of my neighbors at having their lives disrupted, since returning from New York four days earlier. The neighbors had all been thrilled when I first moved in, excited to have a TV star in the neighborhood. This recent group of campers, following so close on the heels of the crowds of press generated by my disappearance, had changed their minds, and I'd been seriously considering relocating just to get them off my back.

I pulled up in the circular drive and climbed the steps to Liz's door, pushing my sunglasses up on my head and shifting the bag I carried into the opposite hand. I rang the doorbell, and a few moments later Risa opened the door, her graying blond hair in its habitual severe bun, and a slight smile on her stern face.

"Miss Harris, nice to see you. How was the trip?" She stepped back and gestured for me to enter.

"Hi, Risa." I smiled and stepped past her, then reached into the bag and pulled out three eight-by-ten publicity stills of the anchors of the networks morning show, *America AM*. "Jane Lee, Ruben Halstrom, and Jim Yorn." I handed her the photos. "Oh, and this, too." I pulled out a rolled-up polo shirt with the morning show's logo embroidered on the chest. "Lindsay Dole wasn't there, so I couldn't get all four...sorry."

The small smile she'd given me at the door got noticeably bigger, a rare occurrence for the normally stoic woman. "Oh, thank you, Caidence." She took the items carefully, handling the stills with extra care.

"You're welcome." I grinned, pleased at her reaction. The use of my first name meant I'd scored big points. "Where's the mistress of the house?"

"Miss Stokley is in the atrium," she informed me, still looking at the pictures. I nodded and headed in that direction, frowning when she called out after me, "Careful of the dogs."

I frowned. Dogs? Liz didn't have any dogs.

Puzzling over her warning, I walked past the stairway and rounded the corner—and let out a girlish scream when two large, hairy, furiously barking bodies threw themselves against the sliding glass door leading into the glass walled atrium that overlooked Liz's immaculately kept back lawn.

"What the fuck!" I leapt back, nearly dropping the bag I was carrying.

"Bonnie! Clyde! Down!" Liz spoke firmly, rising from the couch where she'd been reading, and walked to the door. The two slobbering creatures from hell immediately quieted and lay down, morphing into two attentive and almost harmless-looking German Shepherds.

Liz slid the door open, her eyes glinting with amusement. "Hi, sugar. Now did I, or did I not, just hear you scream?"

"You did not," I said firmly, and stomped past her into the atrium, keeping a close eye on the two Shepherds in case they morphed back into the devil's spawn. "And whose dogs are these anyway? I thought you hated dogs."

"I hate yappy dogs," she corrected. "I love big dogs. Don't I,

Clyde?" she said in a baby-talk voice I'd not heard from her before. She leaned down to scratch one behind its ear, triggering vigorous tail-wagging. "Did you make Caid scream, sweetie? Hmm?"

"I did *not* scream."

With a final pat on the beast's head, Liz straightened. "I distinctly heard a scream."

"You were mistaken. I don't scream."

She laughed, raising her eyebrows. "That's between you and...whoever, Caid, and more information than I really need to know."

I scowled and, to my annoyance, blushed.

"Don't worry, sugar." Liz patted me on the arm and walked past me. "Your secret's safe with me."

The dogs followed her across the room and lay down on the floor near her feet when she reclaimed her seat on a short leather sofa. I eyed them suspiciously and lowered myself into the armchair to her right. One of them sniffed my sandaled foot, and then licked my toes and wagged its tail. I set my bag on the floor and tentatively reached down to stroke its head.

"That's Clyde," Liz told me, watching the interaction. "He's a big baby. Loves attention."

Jealous of the petting Clyde was receiving, the other dog sat up and shoved its nose under my hand. I scratched its ears while still petting Clyde.

"And that's Bonnie. She's usually a little shyer, but she seems to like you."

"You never did tell me—whose dogs are these?" I asked, continuing my ministrations. They weren't so bad, now that they weren't hurling themselves against the glass with bared teeth.

"Danny's. I'm watching them for a few days while he's out of town."

I stopped the petting and looked up. "Our Danny? Danny DeLorenzo?"

She nodded.

I straightened slowly, and tried to keep the incredulity out of my voice. "You're...dog sitting? For Danny? You?"

"Yes, me." She gave me an annoyed look. "Don't act so surprised."

"I'm..." I almost said *I'm not*, but I was. Very surprised. It didn't seem like something Liz would do. "I'm sorry, I just didn't know you liked dogs."

She gave me a pointed look, knowing that wasn't the main reason I was surprised, but let it go. "Come on." She stood quickly, and the dogs scrambled up, one of them clawing the top of my foot in the process. "Let's sit outside; there'll be some shade by now."

I picked up the bag and limped after her, smiling along with her when she opened the door and both dogs pelted down the steps and onto the lawn, growling at each other playfully.

We followed at a more dignified pace, strolling around a long, skinny pool where I knew Liz did laps most mornings, and settling into padded metal gliding chairs under a looming Chinese Pistache tree. One of the dogs came jogging up with a beat-up plastic buoy hanging from a tattered rope in his mouth. I watched in amazement as Liz took the toy and chucked it into the pool, and both dogs followed it in with a gigantic splash.

There were so many things off about this picture, I didn't know where to start. Liz taking care of someone's pets. Liz obviously enjoying taking care of someone's pets. Liz touching a ratty toy that had been drooled on, chewed on, buried, and dug up again. Liz tossing said ratty toy into her pool, and laughing when hairy animals jumped into the pool—where she swam—to retrieve it. It was just so...not Liz.

I shook my head and wondered what was going on.

Both dogs had a hold of the buoy now and were tugging in opposite directions, splashing and growling, neither willing to give it up. None of their efforts brought them anywhere near the end of the pool where the steps were to get out, but Liz just smiled fondly, not seeming overly concerned that the two looked tenacious enough to keep it up until one of them drowned. I shrugged and dug around in the bag. I pulled out a bottle of wine and an ashtray.

"For your collection." I handed her the ashtray, and she took it and turned the heavy smoked glass over in her hands with a delighted smile. She ran her fingers over the hotel logo inside the dish and frowned, rubbing her fingers together and then holding them up to show me the black smudge of ash.

"Ew, Caid, it's been used. Were you smoking?"

"Crap. Sorry about that, I didn't even think to check. No, I wasn't smoking. I'll have you know I went through great lengths to get that for you—they don't sell them at the hotel shop."

"So you got this one how? Stole it from someone's room?"

"Mmm, sort of." I took the ashtray from her, pulled up a handful of grass, and used it to wipe the glass clean before handing it back to her. "I talked someone in housekeeping out of one."

She raised her eyebrows. "You?"

I frowned. "I can be very persuasive."

"Uh-huh."

I reached for the ashtray again. "Well, if you don't want it..."

"Ah-ah-ah..." She held it away from me. "I never said that. I was just concerned that it was previously used."

"That's what people do with ashtrays, Liz, they put out

cigarettes in them. The fact that it's used just makes it more authentic. The lead singer of the Black Dolls was staying at the hotel while I was there...maybe it was hers."

"The lead singer of who?"

"Yeah, I hadn't heard of them either. But apparently they're very big in certain circles."

"Uh-huh."

"And it's very possible that that ashtray was used by the lead singer."

"Uh-huh."

I gave her a look. "Now is typically the time in the receiving of a gift where the recipient, that would be you," I pointed to her, "tells the giver," I tapped my chest, "that would be me, in this case, 'oh, thank you so much for making the special effort to get this lovely, famous-in-certain-circles used ashtray for me.'"

She laughed, and placed the ashtray on the table between us. "Thank you, Caid, for getting this for me. It's really quite lovely, and will fit nicely into my collection."

"You're welcome." I smiled slightly.

She looked down at the wine. "And what's this?"

"Ah, that." I picked it up and looked at it for a moment before handing it to her. "Did you know there's 'wine country' in New York? I had no idea. Anyway, it's a late harvest Riesling from a little winery in the Finger Lakes that Josh recommended. Well, actually his dad recommended it. He says it's a very nice dessert wine."

She looked at the bottle and then up at me, the ghost of a frown on her face. "Josh's dad? As in Josh Riley? The Josh Riley that you swore you weren't involved with?" She lowered the bottle. "You met his father?"

I sighed. "Yes, that Josh Riley. And I'm still not involved with him, and, no, I didn't meet his father. Josh just told me his dad liked this wine, so I looked around for it and bought some. Again, you're welcome."

"I'm sorry, Caid, I just—" We both yelped as we were hit by a shower of water from the two dogs, who'd returned from the pool and were shaking off excess moisture. "Ah, damn." She wiped her face and flicked the water off, laughing. "I hate when they do that. Com'ere, Bonnie." One of the dogs trotted over to Liz and dropped the wet, slimy buoy in her lap. "That's a good girl."

I watched for a moment and then threw up my hands. "All right, Stokley, what's up?" I demanded, unable to keep quiet anymore. "A wet dog just dropped a drooly plastic toy in your lap, and you're laughing? Who are you, and what have you done with Liz?"

She set down the wine bottle and rubbed Bonnie's ears, looking up at me. "I like these dogs, is that a crime?"

"No, it's not a crime, it's just...weird. Come on, when Jules brought her dog onto the set last time, you wouldn't even be in the same room. You said it was dirty or smelly..."

"Because it *was* dirty *and* smelly. I swear she'd just walked that dog in a cow pasture. And it was out of control. Did you see him take off across the parking lot after the squirrel? And I was wearing white, for God's sake — it was a black lab!" She gave Bonnie's ears a final scratch and threw the buoy into the pool again, sending both dogs barking after it. "These dogs are sweet, well behaved, and don't smell. I like them." She leaned back in her chair and pushed it back and forth a few times, watching the dogs. "And I like their owner, too."

"Well, hell, Liz, I like Danny too, but I don't know that I'd let his two huge dogs invade my house..." Liz looked over at me pointedly, and my eyes widened.

"Oh." I blinked. "Oh! You mean, *like* him, like him?" She nodded and I blinked again and settled back in my chair. "No shit. You and Danny?"

She looked across the lawn, then back at me, and smiled softly. "Yeah, me and Danny."

It wasn't a pairing I would have predicted, but it somehow fit. Danny was loud and occasionally obnoxious, but he was also one of the sweetest men I'd ever met, and Liz's cool exterior held a surprisingly fragile, and sometimes insecure, woman who could use someone being sweet to her.

I smiled hugely, and reached over to smack her on the leg. "You little vixen. I think that's great."

She gave me a relieved smile. "Really?"

"Yes, really. I think Danny's a great guy. When did all this happen?"

She laughed a little. "Actually, it all started the night of Danny's party...when you didn't show up, and I called and you said you'd crashed? The way Robyn flew out of there when she found out, like you were dying or something...it made me feel pretty shitty about myself when I hadn't done anything." She shook her head at the memory and then smiled slightly. "I was all ready to call Walter and charge over to your house like some...I don't know...whatever Robyn was trying to be, but Danny talked me out of it, saying Robyn could handle it, and that she'd let us know if there was something seriously wrong. Anyway, the two of us proceeded to get drunk as cooters, and I fell asleep on his bed..."

"Why, Liz Ann." I touched a hand to my chest in mock shock.

"You *are* a vixen. A drunken night in Danny DeLorenzo's bed? I'm scandalized!"

She frowned at me, without any real censure. "Nothing happened, Caid. Get your head out of the gutter," she said primly, and I held up my hands in apology. "We spent the next morning together, since neither of us was due in the city to shoot until after noon. I helped him clean up, we hung around the pool..." She smiled a satisfied smile that was much more like the Liz I knew. "*Then* things happened."

That would have been the day after my accident, when they'd brought over pizza. There had been nearly another two weeks of shooting and seeing both of them every day, our dinner at Crustacean, and the many other times I'd seen or talked to her since. And Liz had kept it to herself the entire time.

More completely non-Liz behavior.

"Damn, Liz, that was more than a month and half ago. You two have kept it quiet this whole time?"

"Well." She brushed ineffectually at a wet spot on the leg of her cream-colored capris. "It hasn't been that whole time. We both felt a little weird about it at first, and didn't see each other for a while, but we've worked it out." Her smile was reflexive and one of the happiest I'd seen grace her face in the whole time I'd known her. "And now everything is...wonderful."

I smiled back, genuinely happy for her, and leaned forward to squeeze her arm. "I'm happy for you, Liz. It looks really good on you. Danny's a lucky guy."

She tilted her head back and laughed. "I don't know about that. But he's being very patient with my quirks, and I'm trying to be patient with his, and in between all that, we're having a fine time together."

"I'm glad. And now I know the secret you were keeping from me at dinner the other night. Danny is who has you in such good spirits." I relaxed back in my chair. "Who'd a thunk it?"

"No one at the moment, and we'd like to keep it that way for a while, okay? It'll probably get a lot of attention from the press...we just want some time without that, you know?"

I gave a tiny snort. "I've had plenty of experience recently with what kind of feeding frenzy that can be, and I don't blame you one bit. I'll keep your good news to myself, I promise."

"Uh-huh." She paused. "About that, Caid... Now that I've spilled my secret, why don't you come clean with yours? That was our deal, after all."

"That was *your* deal," I corrected. "I never agreed to anything."

She ignored me and picked up the wine bottle, brushing her

thumb across the label as she studied it. She looked at me and cocked her head to the side. "What's really going on between you and Josh?"

"Liz." I shook my head in exasperation.

"Caid, just wait. Hear me out, okay?" I quieted, and with exaggerated politeness, gestured for her to continue. "I know you're not romantically involved with Josh. I know you — fairly well, I think — and you're just too damn nice to do something like that to Robyn, especially now that you two have gotten to be friends." She smiled ironically. "Kind of funny, that — you've been painted as the bitch in this, and you're by far the nicest of the three of you. And the most innocent."

"Yeah," I muttered, "real funny, that." I frowned. "Innocent?"

"Yes, innocent." The dogs came running up again but Liz stopped them and had them lie down before they got close enough to give us another shower. When she'd dealt with them, she turned back to me. "Josh and Robyn both know how to work the system. They're not darlings of the press by accident, Caid — no one ever gets that much good press by accident." She set the wine down and gave me an affectionate smile. "You, on the other hand, are just...you. You say what you mean, you do what you want, not thinking about how you're perceived, because you just don't think that way. People think you're manipulative, Caid, because you don't play the game, and they don't know how to take that." She waved a hand. "Anyway, that's beside the point."

My frown deepened. "And what, exactly, is your point?"

"My point is this. You may not be involved with Josh Riley now, but that doesn't mean you don't want to be. I think you have feelings for him. I saw something between you two at dinner that night, how you were so angry he'd been in Florida and seen Robyn. I know jealous when I see it, and, sugar, that was definitely jealous."

I started to speak, but she held up a hand. "I also know you're so damn noble, you'll never do anything about it, and you're going to end up getting hurt." She sat back and crossed her arms, regarding me seriously. "I think you need to remove yourself from the situation, Caid, and get as far away from Robyn and Josh as possible."

I raised my eyebrows. "That's what you think, hmm?"

"Yes, that's what I think."

"Interesting theory."

When I didn't elaborate, she made a tiny noise of frustration. "Am I close?"

"No, not really. But I give you an A for effort, and I appreciate your concern."

In what I thought was rather freakish timing, my cell phone
started ringing, and I held up a hand to forestall whatever tantrum
Liz was about to throw. I checked the display, and couldn't hide
the smile of pleasure I felt spread across my face. I stood and
walked a few yards away before answering. "Hey."

"Hey, yourself," came the raspy reply. "Did you know that I
had a miscarriage because you're sleeping with my boyfriend? You
bitch." She was eating something crunchy, and I heard voices in the
background, along with intermittent beeping.

Robyn and I had talked daily since I'd returned from New
York, never really getting into anything serious, just talking about
our days and getting to know each other better since we'd sort of
skipped that step in our relationship. As we'd become more
comfortable with each other, I'd found out that she was adorably
goofy at times, and had a somewhat twisted sense of humor.

I laughed. "Yes, I think I read that somewhere. I also read that
you threatened to scratch my eyes out, and, um, I think you put a
hit out on me. Or did I put a hit out on you?" I pondered. We both
chuckled, and were quiet for a few moments. "Where are you?" I
asked eventually. "Did they let you out of the asylum?"

"In line at the grocery store. We had a break, and I had a
craving for potato chips."

"You're just standing in line in the grocery store, eating potato
chips, and no one's bothering you?"

"Uh-huh." More crunching, and a swallow. "I'm in disguise."

"Disguise? And just what are you disguised as?" I asked
curiously, hard-pressed to think of any kind of disguise that would
cover up someone that looked like Robyn.

"Soccer mom," she said between crunches.

I laughed, sure she was kidding. "Uh-huh. Yeah, that's some
disguise for you."

"It's not what you look like, Caid," she said distractedly, and I
heard voices in the background, "it's what you want them to see.
One sec..."

I'd seen her slip in and out of character on the set of *9P*
enough to know what she was capable of, and my admiration of
her talent went up another notch. I shook my head and listened
with an absent smile as she interacted with the cashier, paying for
her items and making the woman laugh about something. "Okay,
I'm back," she said eventually around more crunching. "Whatcha
doing?"

"I'm at Liz's. I had some gifts for her, and we've just
been...chatting."

"Oh, well, tell her hi."

I heard a splash, and looked over to see Liz had gotten up and was tossing the buoy to the dogs again, the expression on her face clearly annoyed. "I don't think that's such a good idea at the moment."

She stopped crunching. "Caid, what's wrong?"

I smiled at the concern in her voice. "Nothing. Liz has just finished telling me that since I obviously have a thing for Josh, I should stay away from both of you."

A pause. "You have a thing for Josh? And just when were you going to tell me about this?"

"Ha, ha," I said sarcastically, and she laughed and bit down on a particularly crunchy chip.

"You know, Caid, it's okay with me if you tell her," she said after swallowing.

"It is? I thought we were still in stealth mode."

"Well, I'd rather not announce it in a full-page ad in the *New York Times*, but I know it can make things...difficult...when you can't be honest with someone. I told Josh right away, remember?"

"Yeah..."

"I'm not telling you what to do, Caid, I'm just telling you it's okay. Okay?"

"Okay," I agreed, looking over at Liz thoughtfully. She looked back and I smiled, but she didn't return the smile, instead throwing the buoy with added viciousness across the pool. Yeah, maybe it was time to have a talk with Liz.

"So," Robyn's voice pulled me from my musings, "you're probably wondering why I'm calling in the middle of the day?"

I actually *had* been wondering that—the routine over the past few days had been a phone call around eight PM LA time, just before Robyn went to bed. Not that I minded a call in the middle of the day. Not at all. "You missed me so desperately you just had to hear my voice?" I said flippantly, and then kicked myself at the resulting silence.

"There is that," she said finally, without a hint of teasing. "But," she added in a lighter tone, "that's not the only reason I called. Do you have big plans for the weekend?"

"Hmm, let's see. I have some laundry to do, and I suppose I should wash my hair. Oh, and sleep with Josh, I should fit that in somewhere, too..."

"Come spend it with me."

I sucked in a breath. "What?"

"Spend it with me," she repeated, and then rushed on nervously. "They don't need me over the weekend, I was thinking about renting a house on the beach—something private, and quiet, and we could, you know, just spend some time together..."

"Yes."

She paused in her nervous rambling. "Yes?"

"Yes. Of course, yes." I heard her soft sigh of relief, and shook my head. Had she actually thought I'd say no? Crazy woman. "When and where?"

I could hear the smile in her voice. "I'll call tonight with details."

"Okay."

"Okay."

We were quiet for several moments. "I should go. Liz is going to bust if I don't let her yell at me soon."

She chuckled. "Best not keep her waiting, then. I'll talk to you tonight?"

"Yeah. And, Robyn? Thanks. I'm looking forward to it."

"Me, too," she said softly before she hung up.

I stared at the phone for a full minute, a stupid grin plastered across my face, and didn't hear Liz until she was practically in my face.

"Goddammit, Caid, tell me what's going on or I'll toss you in the pool for the dogs to fetch!"

I smiled at the picture her threat conjured in my head, and waved her into her seat. "Okay."

Her eyes narrowed and she looked at me suspiciously. "Okay, what?"

"Okay, I'll tell you. Just sit down."

She slowly did as I asked, eyeing me warily. "That was him, wasn't it? You don't smile like that for anybody, Caid. I was right, wasn't I?"

I tucked my cell phone in my pocket and sat down. "You were half right. Sort of. Yes, that was the person I'm...involved with, but it wasn't Josh."

She popped up out of her chair and threw up her hands. "Then who the hell is it? Damn it, the way you're keeping it a secret makes me think it's someone else you shouldn't be with—"

"It was Robyn." I dropped the name and sat back to watch the reaction.

She stopped and frowned as though she hadn't heard correctly. "What?"

"Robyn. It was Robyn on the phone just now."

"What does Robyn have to do..." she trailed off, still looking confused.

"Remember our conversation about kissing women?"

She nodded slowly. "You said you hadn't, but you wanted to..."

"And now I have."

"Oh. *Oh.*" She sat down heavily. "Really? Robyn?"

"Robyn."

"But she seems so..." She motioned vaguely with her hand. "And she and Josh..."

I frowned a little. "Are you telling me you don't think a feminine woman can be gay? Come on, Liz, you know better than that. And as far as she and Josh go, you said yourself, they know how to work the system. I won't get into particulars, but trust me when I say that what's between Robyn and me isn't interfering in anything romantic between the two of them."

"I'll be damned." She stared into space for a moment, and looked over at me. "That explains some things, I guess. I'd heard things about Robyn, but always just figured it was just random gossip."

"You heard gossip about Robyn being gay?" I asked in surprise. Now, why hadn't I heard that gossip? "I never heard anything..."

She gave me another affectionate smile, like I was a small child who'd just told a cute, albeit stupid, joke. "Because it was gossip, sugar, and you never pay attention to it, so no one ever tells you anything good. And it wasn't about her being gay, necessarily, just...flexible, maybe."

"Flexible?" Well, she certainly was that, but I doubted that's what Liz was talking about.

"Yes, flexible. Occasionally seen at a women's bar, spotted with women known to be gay, that sort of thing. But, hell, the majority of industry people in this town end up in a gay bar at one time or another, and it doesn't mean anything. I guess this time it did."

I smiled slightly. "I guess."

She was quiet for a moment. "So is this...is this just messing around, just for fun, or is it for real?"

I shrugged. "I can only speak for myself, but for me, it's as real as it gets."

Her eyes showed surprise at the words, but she didn't reply, instead looking away across the lawn to where the dogs were lying in the sun, panting.

We were quiet for a while, watching as the dogs began to wrestle. Eventually Liz looked over at me, her expression serious. "You're happy?"

I didn't try to stop my smile. "Yes, I'm happy."

She nodded. "I'm glad for you, then." She smiled wickedly and leaned forward. "Now 'fess up, sugar—was I right? Is she a screamer?"

Chapter
Seventeen

"MILE MARKER..." SQUINTING against the sinking afternoon sun, I slowed and double-checked the name of the road before turning. I kept an eye on my rearview mirror after the turn, half expecting cars to follow me as they'd done all over LA the past week. No other car turned behind me, and I gave a satisfied nod that the precautions Liz suggested seemed to have been enough to throw the press off, at least for the time being.

Instead of flying out of photographer-laden LAX, I'd left my house at an ungodly hour of the morning and made the four-hour drive to Yuma to catch a commuter flight to Phoenix, then from Phoenix to Fort Lauderdale and onto a tiny prop plane that took me to Marathon. Connie hadn't batted an eye when I'd told her I needed to get away for a few days and asked her to arrange a car without using my name, and it had been waiting, just as she promised, in long-term parking with the keys under the floor mat. From Marathon, it had been another thirty miles to this turnoff. I'd been traveling for nearly fourteen hours and was more than ready for my traveling day to be over.

"Follow for a quarter of a mile..." I muttered to myself, looking around with interest at the tall palms and shrub trees that kept the road hidden and essentially secluded from the nearby overseas highway.

I followed Robyn's directions and turned into a small break in the foliage just before the turnaround, and the car sluggishly churned through the loose sand of a narrow lane lined with shiny-leaved brush and dwarf palms. The lane opened up into a wide, sandy driveway, and I pulled my practical, mid-sized sedan up behind a bright yellow Mercedes convertible, smiling at our role reversal. If we went anywhere this weekend, Robyn was definitely driving.

The house was white and boxy, and Robyn's little convertible was nestled in an open-air carport that took up half of the lower level. I got out of the car and stretched, looking through the carport, surprised to see how close the ocean was to the house. No one came to greet me but I noticed curtains billowing through an open sliding glass door on the second floor, so I pulled my backpack and small suitcase from the trunk and climbed the stairs to the wrap-around deck on the second story, pushing up my sunglasses as I stepped through the door and looking around curiously.

The house was clean and neat, with a small living room opening into the kitchen on one side, and a hallway that I assumed led to the bedrooms on the other. The walls were white, the tile floors gray, and the comfortable-looking sofa and loveseat facing a wooden cabinet housing a television and other electronic equipment had a subdued, floral print. The kitchen was large and connected to a screen-enclosed area of the wrap-around deck, and a delicious aroma of garlic and spices filled the house.

"Robyn?" I set my bags down and listened for a response. "Hello? Anyone home?"

My stomach grumbled, and I followed the smell of food into the kitchen. A fresh loaf of French bread wrapped in paper sat on the counter, and a note was taped to the handle of the oven.

> *I knew this would get your attention. I'm down on the beach—come watch the sunset. There's beer in the fridge, bring one for me.*
> R

I smiled and shook my head. The woman had my number.

After taking a quick peek in the oven to find a bubbling pan of lasagna with white sauce, I picked up my bags and carried them down the hall, hesitating momentarily at what was obviously the master bedroom before walking past to the next room and depositing my bags on the bed. I was dressed in jeans and a sleeveless, V-neck blouse—I'd always disliked wearing shorts when I flew, there was something about the thought of my skin against the airplane seat that made me queasy—and I quickly changed out of my traveling clothes and into shorts and a tank top.

Back in the kitchen, I snagged two short, squatty bottles of Negra Modelo from the fridge and rummaged around in the kitchen drawers for an opener that I finally found attached to the fridge door with a magnet. Laughing at myself, I plucked it from the door, pulled the caps off, and walked out onto the deck facing the ocean.

The beach was sandy—something I'd been told was rare in the Keys—with low vegetated dunes bordering the stretch below the house and making it quite secluded. A hundred feet from the house, near the water, two lounge chairs were set up looking out over the ocean. One was empty and the other occupied by a familiar, dark-haired figure in a wide-brimmed hat.

A frisson of excitement and happiness ran through me at the sight of her, and I forced myself to keep a sedate pace as I walked down the stairs and out onto the beach. I came to a stop beside her chair, taking a moment to just look and allow myself the pleasure I'd missed the last time we were together.

Her dark hair was fastened in a long braid that spilled from beneath her straw hat and over one shoulder onto her chest. She wore a white, gauzy, button-down shirt with the sleeves rolled above her elbow and most of the buttons undone, showing off a black bikini top and plenty of deeply tanned skin. My eyes took it all in, from burgundy-colored toenails, up long legs, over the brown sarong wrapped around her waist, along her flat belly, lingering momentarily on small, high breasts in black fabric visible through the outer shirt, and finally up to the classic lines of her face. Black, oval-framed sunglasses hid her eyes and expression, but the tip of an arched eyebrow was visible just above the black rims, and a small smile curled the corners of her mouth.

"When you're through objectifying me, you're in my sun."

"I was admiring, not objectifying," I said mildly, taking a few more moments to drink her in. "And unless the sun suddenly started setting in the north, Princess, I'm nowhere near your sun." I moved anyway, lowering myself into the chair beside her. "For you, Madame." I handed her a beer, which she took with a nod of thanks and a murmured "*Merci.*"

She seemed content to sit in silence and watch the ocean, and I was content to let her be content, so we watched the ocean and occasionally sipped at our beers as the sun sunk lower on the horizon. After several minutes she reached for my hand and brought it to her lips, kissing each knuckle and sending little sparks of pleasure shooting up my arm. She rubbed my hand against her cheek, and then rested it, palm down, on her stomach and let out a long, contented sigh.

I smiled but let the silence continue, tracing tiny circles on the skin of her stomach with the pads of my fingers until she stilled my hand with a gentle slap. "Tickles," she said softly, and pulled my hand back up to her lips to place an open-mouthed kiss on the pulse point of my wrist, following it up with a little nip. I shivered, her action doing much more than tickle, and heard a low chuckle. My arm was bent at the elbow, my palm resting against her cheek. I moved my hand up to cup the back of her head and leaned over at an awkward angle to bring our mouths together in a soft, exploring kiss.

"Hi," I whispered when I'd pulled back a few inches.

She smiled, and lowered her sunglasses to rest on the end of her nose. "Hi." The smile on her face matched the one in her eyes, and I kissed her again lightly before sitting back and letting out my own contented sigh. I found her hand and laced our fingers together, and we sat in silence, holding hands, watching until the last sliver of sun sunk below the sea.

She stirred as the sun disappeared, squeezing my hand before dropping it and pushing herself out of her chair. "Hungry? Dinner should be just about ready."

"If you're cooking? Always. Whatever you have in the oven smelled wonderful."

"Cajun seafood lasagna." She walked around to the other side of my chair and held out a hand to help me up. "You like spicy, right?"

"I love spicy." She pulled me to my feet, and our faces ended up inches from each other.

I gave her a friendly peck on the lips. "And I love..." I stopped myself before the words I'd been thinking tumbled out of my mouth. "...that you don't mind cooking for me."

Whoa. Close one. Good recovery, Harris. Things were so relaxed, so easy between us, that my mouth was running off without my mind's permission. I'd have to watch that. I wasn't going to screw this up by scaring her away.

She smiled. "And I love that you enjoy my cooking."

"Hmm. Sounds like we make a good pair." We started toward the house, swinging our loosely linked hands. "Maybe we should hang out."

We walked a few steps in silence, and I caught the flash of her smile in the falling darkness. She raised my hand to her lips. "Maybe we should."

"TIRED?" ROBYN ASKED and kissed my hair, running her fingers lightly up and down my arm. "Been a long day for you."

"Mmm. A little, maybe." I leaned my head back to look at her. "This is nice, though."

"Yes." She kissed my forehead. "This is very nice."

We were sitting on the wooden porch swing in the corner of the mesh-enclosed area of the deck, swinging idly back and forth and listening to the sound of the ocean and the distant murmur of the highway. I was half sitting, half reclining against her, a position we'd gradually come to over the last two hours since retiring to the swing after dinner. We drank a bottle of wine and cautiously felt each other out on topics of politics, religion, and musical tastes, and save a few glaring discrepancies in the latter, we were surprisingly in synch. I suppose, in the grand scheme of things, the fact that she still liked Eighties hair bands was something I could live with, and my fondness for twangy hill country music was something she could overlook. Our conversation had wound down into sporadic comments, then to comfortable silence, and Robyn's question had been the first to break the silence in at least ten minutes.

I stopped the fingers that were rubbing my arm, interlaced them with my own, and brought the hand to my lips briefly. "I'm on LA time, though, and you're not—maybe we should get you to bed."

I moved to get up, but the arm around my shoulder tightened. "Caid?"

I relaxed back against her and tipped my head up again to see her face. "Hmm?"

"I noticed that you put your bags in one of the other rooms..." Her expression was uncertain.

"I..." I didn't think this was the time to get into my insecurities about this relationship meaning more to me than it did to her, or to ask for a definition of exactly what the relationship was. Sometime before Sunday afternoon I meant to get answers to those questions, but not tonight. I sat up and brushed a hand across her cheek. "I just didn't want to assume anything."

A look that was a mixture of annoyance and hurt flashed in her eyes, and she stared out the screened window behind me for a moment before looking back at me, smiling tightly. "Am I so hard to read?"

"Rob—"

She stopped me with a finger across my lips. "I think we need to have a talk, you and I, about what this is, and where this is going, but we've done enough talking for tonight. Right now, I'd like to go to bed, and I'd like very much for you to be with me when I do." She stood and pulled me up beside her, smiling slightly. "And for future reference, I think that if there's anything you can assume about all this, it's that I'll always want you in my bed. But if that's not what you want..."

"Oh, no," I said quickly. "I want."

"Come on, then." She smiled shyly—a look I'd never associated with Robyn—and took my hand. "Let's go to bed."

At her words, I realized that for the first time, that's what we'd be doing. Going to bed. Not falling or stumbling into bed as the final destination of frenzied love-making, or happening to fall asleep together as we'd done in Big Bear. This was actual washing-your-face, brushing-your-teeth, and putting-your-pajamas-on kind of going to bed. It sounded so domestic, so normal.

It sounded wonderful.

I smiled to myself and allowed Robyn to pull me through the house, turning off lights and locking doors as we went. When we reached the door to the master bedroom, she paused, looking slightly nervous. "Ah...the bed in here is bigger, is that okay?"

I kissed her lightly and pushed her into the room. "It's fine. I'll be just a minute."

I used the second bathroom to brush my teeth and get ready for bed, and then stood in the bedroom where I'd put my suitcase, frowning at the boxers and silk tank in my hand. "Oh, very sexy, Caid," I muttered in disgust. What the hell had I been thinking? I obviously hadn't been, or I would have packed something a little more...alluring. *I'm sure I still have that red nightie thing that Toby liked so much...*

"Caid? Are you lost?" Robyn's teasing voice floated into the bedroom.

I caught the undercurrent of worry in her tone and, after a last annoyed sigh, quickly stripped off my clothes and pulled on the boxers and tank. I crossed the hall to the other room, hit immediately by an attack of awkwardness that brought me to a stop just inside the door.

Robyn was sitting against the headboard with the sheet tucked loosely around her chest, flipping absently through a magazine. She looked up as I entered and her movements stilled, her eyes taking me in from head to toe.

After several moments of silence, I finally laughed nervously and gestured at my sleepwear. "I know, sexy, right? I guess I should have brought something more...I don't know, lacey, maybe—"

"Caid," she interrupted with an amused smile, "shut up."

I closed my mouth and blushed.

"Come here, you," she said softly, tossing the magazine on the floor and motioning me forward.

I hesitantly walked over, feeling stupid as well as awkward.

When I stopped next to the bed, she waited until I met her gaze. "Although the thought of you in lingerie is...highly intriguing," she said with a tiny smile, "this is you, and it's you that I find incredibly sexy, not your clothes." She tugged lightly on the leg of my boxers. "You won't be wearing them long, anyway."

I crossed my arms and raised a skeptical eyebrow. "Kind of cocky, aren't you?"

In a move I wasn't expecting, she grabbed me around the waist and half pulled, half tossed me onto the bed, pouncing on me with a mock growl and attacking my neck with her lips and teeth. An honest-to-God giggle escaped my lips, increasing the volume and enthusiasm of her assault. I laughed and wrapped my arms around her, caught between amusement and arousal.

"Oh..." I breathed in pleased surprise when my hands encountered nothing but the warm skin of her back. "Hey, you're nekkid."

Her laugh vibrated against my neck and she raised her head, her dark eyes twinkling in humor. "I like that you're so quick."

I smiled and scraped my fingernails gently up her spine; her eyes fluttered shut and I kissed her, taking advantage of her momentary distraction. The slow burn that had started the moment I saw her on the beach instantly flared white-hot, and she groaned deep in her throat and responded with matching fervor, rolling us over until I was on top, and then tugging at my shirt. "Off," she commanded hoarsely.

The demand rippled through me, turning on every switch I had but also reminding me of a promise. "Whoa. Hang on." With effort, I pulled myself up and sat back, straddling her waist. She reached to pull me back down, and I gently slapped her hands away. "Just...wait."

She let out a huff of frustration and lay back. "Jesus, Caid, you're driving me crazy. What's wrong?"

"Nothing's wrong," I said, and ran a finger lightly along her lower lip, taking a moment just to look. *God, she's beautiful.* She'd taken her hair out of the braid and it was fanned across the pillow in a dark wash of color, framing her striking features and making her eyes seem even darker than usual. Eyes that stared at me with an undisguised hunger. I shifted slightly, swallowing hard. "...but I remember someone promising me slow."

She looked at me like I was insane. "Please tell me you're kidding."

I shook my head.

"You want slow?"

I nodded.

"Now?"

I nodded again.

"Screw slow." She shook her head and reached for me.

This time I caught her hands and fell forward, letting my weight pin her wrists above her head. I leaned down and nuzzled her ear, grazing my teeth across her earlobe. "That's the idea." She shivered under me and I moved down her neck, nipping gently. "Now, is it really so terrible," I murmured, moving to the other ear and tracing the outer edge with my tongue, "to go slow?"

"Uh..." She sucked in a breath when I switched my grip to hold her wrists in one hand and used my free hand to pull the covers down below her chest, circling a taut nipple with my fingertip and leaning down to follow with my tongue. "Well," her voice was faint, breathless. "Maybe I can work with slow..."

I WOKE THE next morning lying on my stomach with soft, lingering kisses being planted along my spine and fingers tracing lazy patterns across my back, drawing me pleasantly from dreamscape to wakefulness.

"Mmm...s'nice."

The fingers paused for a moment before resuming their tracing. "Sleeping beauty awakes," she breathed huskily in my ear, and kissed my shoulder. "I thought you might sleep the day away." Her hand swept down my back and up again, stopping occasionally to knead at a muscle. "God, I love your body."

"And my body loves you," I mumbled, too sleepy to care what that might sound like. I pried one eye open and blearily focused on the bedside clock. "It's seven thirty. Seven thirty is sleeping the day away?"

She moved over to kiss the opposite shoulder, her breasts pressing into my back. "The sun's up and there's a big wide world out there to explore."

The gentle caresses changed to light scratching and I closed my eyes again, sighing in contentment. "I'm not going anywhere if you keep doing that."

The nails moved lower, scraping up the back of one thigh and over my butt. "Doing what?" she whispered in my ear, repeating the action on the other thigh. "That?"

My body arched into the touch and I knew, with just that touch, that voice, that I was wet again. I spread my legs slightly in reflex and heard the small hitch in her breathing near my ear.

She trailed fingertips across the inside of my thigh, brushing lightly against coarse hair. "What do you want, baby?" She brushed again, her touch more firm. "That?"

"Yes..." I hissed, my breath coming faster. "Yes."

"Tell me."

"Ah...God, Rob..." I tried to push against her to increase the pressure, but she pulled away.

"Tell me, Caid. What do you want?"

"I want you to touch me," I whispered. "Please..."

She responded with a firm stroke through liquid heat, trailing up for a fleeting touch across my clit, her breath hot in my ear and as unsteady as mine. "Tell me," she whispered again.

"More..." I managed through clenched teeth. "Ah, Jesus...yes, there..." I gasped as her fingers came back to where I needed them, and I bucked up against her. She groaned and fastened her lips to the back of my neck, sucking hard. The tiny pinpoints of pain seemed to heighten sensation—I made a strangled noise and clutched at the pillow under my hands. She stroked insistently and then lightly, bringing me to the edge of orgasm and keeping me there until I surrendered to it with a loud moan.

I buried my face in the pillow, slowly loosening my grip on the cover as my breathing eased and my body relaxed.

I could hear the smile in her voice when she breathed "Good morning" in my ear and tenderly kissed the spot on my neck where I was sure she'd left a mark.

I let out a muffled chuckle, but didn't raise my head, embarrassed by how blatant I'd been.

"Caid?" she questioned after a few moments of silence, resting her hand on my back. "What's up, baby? You okay?"

"Mm-hmm," I mumbled into the pillow, and then slowly rolled onto my side, giving her a shy smile. "A little embarrassed, maybe, about acting like a cat in heat, but I'm fine." I reached out to tuck a loose strand of hair behind her ear, wondering how she could look so damn good when she'd just woken up. "Better than fine. Stupendous, even. That was one hell of a 'good morning'." I leaned forward and kissed her lightly. "Good morning to you, too."

She gathered me in her arms and rolled onto her back, pulling me with her. I rested my head on her chest and draped an arm across her stomach, liking the rumble of her voice under my ear. "Don't ever be embarrassed about wanting to be touched, Caid, or about wanting sex. I love touching you and being with you. How you respond to me is one of the sexiest things I've ever seen. I...it's a huge turn on for me."

Feeling strangely self-conscious considering what we'd just done, I kept my head down and traced small patterns with my fingertips on the skin of her stomach. "I guess I'm just not used to it."

"Not used to what?" The fingers that had been sifting idly through my hair as we talked stilled. "Sex?" She gave me her best southern drawl, which was a pretty damn good one. "Because, honey, you sure don't seem like no novice to me."

I pinched her lightly on the arm in response to her teasing, trying for my own southern accent and failing miserably. "Well, goodness, Miss Scarlett, I'm so glad you approve..."

"Oh, I definitely approve." Her voice was low and husky, whispered directly in my ear, and sent my body humming yet again, highlighting the truth of my next words.

"I'm not used to...wanting so much."

She was quiet, and I listened to her heartbeat beneath my ear, the steady rhythm lulling me into drowsiness. "Neither am I," she said finally, and brushed her lips across the top of my head.

We were quiet for another few minutes, and I thought maybe now would be a good time to have "The Talk" she'd spoken of, but before I could start, she kissed my head again and said briskly. "Cheese omelet okay for breakfast?"

I guess our little tête-à-tête would have to wait. I tapped her belly with my fingers. "You're serious about this whole getting up and exploring the big wide world thing, aren't you?"

" 'Fraid so. We need to be on Big Pine Key by ten."

I rolled onto my side and propped my head on my hand. "We do?"

"Mm-hmm." She reached forward and brushed a hand through my hair, the obvious affection in her gaze making me smile.

"Well..." I sighed and leaned forward to kiss the tiny cleft in her chin. "If we must, we must. So. How far away is Big Pine Knot, and do I get a hint as to why we need to be there in," I checked the clock, "an hour and forty-five minutes?"

She rolled over, bracing herself on her arms above me, and kissed my forehead. "It's Big Pine Key, not Knot." She kissed my nose, which I wrinkled in response. "About thirty minutes." She kissed me soundly on the lips, lingering long enough to make me forget what we'd been talking about in the first place. "And no, you don't." She climbed off me, leaving me with diminished brain capacity to match her answers to my questions, and padded across the floor to the bathroom.

"So..." I tried to get my brain to concentrate on something besides the feel of her lips against mine and the resulting havoc they'd caused. The sight of her nakedness as she crossed the floor was not helping. "Uh..." I pulled my eyes from the door as it partially closed behind her and stared at the ceiling. "So, what do I need to wear on this exciting outing?"

I SHOOK THE excess water from my hair and flicked it out of my eyes, just in time to see Robyn emerge from the calm blue water like some fantasy brought to life, her body long and tan in a brief black bikini and her dark hair sleek against her head, glossy with moisture.

"God. Damn," I muttered, enjoying the view as she walked through the shallow water toward me like a runway model at a Milan show. I shook my head in sheer amazement that this woman was here, with me, of her own volition.

She cocked her head to the side as she walked up, accepting the towel I handed her. "What's the headshake and funny look for?" She looked down at herself. "Do I have a lamprey hanging off me or something?"

"No..." I let admiring eyes travel up her body. "You're perfect. I was just wondering how in the hell I ever got so lucky."

Her face showed pleased surprise and her lips quirked in a crooked grin—one of my favorites in her smile repertoire. With a flick of her wrists, she looped her towel around my neck, grabbed the other end, and tugged, pulling me against her body gently. "Funny," she gave me a quick kiss, "I've been thinking the same thing all day."

I splayed my hands across her bare back, pulling her against me harder, and dropped my hands to cup her behind. "You say the nicest things," I murmured, and sampled the skin of her neck with my lips, tasting the saltiness of seawater. "So." I nipped lightly. "How private is this beach?"

She chuckled breathlessly and tried to push me away. "Not that private."

"Mmm." I nibbled on her neck some more, then up along her chin, catching her lower lip between my teeth and tugging gently before releasing her. "Too bad."

"Uh-huh," she answered, staring at my mouth, which curled into a knowing grin. She pushed me away with a mock scowl and I laughed, happy to see I wasn't the only one whose brain became scrambled when we were together.

I dropped onto the closest lounge chair, stretching my arms above my head to loosen the muscles of my shoulders, leaving them in that position when I realized how comfortable it was. The late afternoon sun felt good on skin still chilled from my recent swim and I closed my eyes with a contented sigh, letting the rays slowly warm me.

It had been a wonderful day.

It had started with the scenic drive west on the overseas highway, the top to Robyn's little yellow convertible down and the light blues and greens of the shallow waters on either side of us stretching out to the horizon. When we reached Big Pine Key, a grumpy, weathered old man had met us at the marina with a motorboat and silently taken us to a destination in the channels of the backcountry, leaving us with a double-kayak, a map, a radio, and gruff instructions about getting back by sundown or they'd send someone after us.

We paddled leisurely through the day, past mangrove forests, sponge and grass flats, and an abundance of wildlife, talking occasionally but mostly enjoying the beauty and the quiet. A small island that was nothing more than a spit of sand became a picnic lunch spot, and after we'd eaten our fill of the sandwiches and fruit

Robyn had packed, we continued our explorations, making it back to the marina by three.

Back at the house, we'd decided on a swim and some sun before figuring out what we would do for dinner.

"Damn, Caid, you sure don't make it easy on a girl, do you? All day long I had that beautiful back in front of me, and now this?" Her words and frustrated sigh pulled me out of thoughts of our day, and I cracked open an eye to find her staring down at me. I was wearing a red tankini that left a few inches of my midriff bare — not nearly as much skin as she was showing, but apparently it was enough to get her attention.

I turned my head to the side and opened both eyes, looking her up and down with a lazy smile. "Look who's talking, Miss Show-off." I reached up to pluck at the material of her bikini bottoms, and then slid my hand up the back of her thigh, my fingers brushing lightly between her legs. "And if you keep looking at me like that, I'm not going to give a good God-damn how private or not private this beach is."

"Hey!" She jumped away from my hand with a tiny squeak and wagged an admonishing finger at me, smiling. "Behave, Harris, or I'll be forced to punish you."

"And this would be bad...how?"

I'd said it as a joke, but instead of laughing, the smile on her face faltered and she looked away pensively, patting her neck and chest with the towel. "Is that something you like?"

"Huh?" was all I could come up with as a reply.

She looked back at me, searching my face. "Being punished."

Oh. I blinked. The intense look on her face told me this was important, and the flippant remark on the tip of my tongue would not be appreciated. I sat up and swung my legs over the side of the chair, motioning to the space beside me. She lowered herself slowly, her eyes wary, and I took her hand, lacing our fingers together.

"Are you asking if I'm into pain?" I asked carefully. She nodded, and I thought for a minute and then answered as honestly as I could. "I don't know."

She tensed and withdrew her hand from mine, turning her gaze from me to look out over the water for a moment before returning her eyes to mine. "I'm willing to...explore a lot of things with you, Caid. I want you to be happy with me, with what we do..."

Was she crazy? "Honey, I am happy —"

She shook her head and held up her hand. "Just let me finish, please." I quieted, and she took a breath. "I'll do just about anything for you, Caid, but..." She stared down at her hands. "I was involved with someone once, and she asked for things..." She shook her head vehemently. "I don't think I could do that again."

"Hey." I grabbed her hand and held it fast when she tried to pull away. "Robyn, honey, look at me." Slowly her dark eyes rose to meet mine and I saw old hurts and new fears, and wanted to strangle whoever this person had been. "Rob, I said I don't know, because honestly, I don't. It's not something I've ever done, or ever had a lover who wanted something like that. I *can* say that it's not something I've ever had the urge to explore, and while that might not mean I wouldn't like it if I did, it's probably a good indicator."

She frowned, looking perplexed, and I thought back over my last statement. Hell, I barely understood it myself, and I'd come up with it. I touched her cheek. "What I mean is...no, I'm not into pain. At least, not the pain I think you're talking about—we're not talking about a little love bite, like you gave me this morning..." I rubbed the back of my neck, and the still-tender skin.

She blinked, and looked stricken. "I didn't...God, Caid, I'm sorry...I—"

"Shhh." I placed a finger against her lips. "I'm not complaining. Far from it. This morning was wonderful, just like every time we're together. Believe me, you've never done anything I haven't enjoyed the hell out of. But I don't think we're talking about love bites, are we?"

She looked away and shook her head.

I tugged her hand, bringing her attention back to me. "Then, no, Robyn, I'm not into pain. And I could never, ever take pleasure from hurting you. I swear I won't hurt you like that person did."

She raised my hand and kissed it absently before putting it in her lap with the other. "She didn't hurt me, Caid. At least not how you mean. Inflicting pain wasn't her thing." She looked past me, her eyes clouded. "Receiving it was. She wanted *me* to hurt *her*."

She shifted restlessly and started to stand, but I held her hands in mine firmly. "Tell me?" I asked, stroking a thumb across the back of her hand. "Please?"

She sighed heavily and sat back down, staring at our joined hands. "It was all a long time ago."

"That doesn't make it any less important. It obviously still affects you."

She sighed again and looked out over the water for several long moments. "I met her in Paris, at a party...I was about twenty-three, I guess, and just starting to realize that women were more my thing than men, and I fell for her hard. God," she shook her head sadly, "I was so in love with her, and for a while, everything was so perfect..." She paused, her mind far away, and I stayed quiet, hoping to encourage her with my silence.

"She started asking me to do things. Light stuff, at first." She glanced at me quickly and then away. "Holding her down, being a little more...aggressive." She shrugged, avoiding my eyes. "It was new and I'll admit, it excited me, the control — or what seemed like control at the time — but it wasn't enough. I wasn't enough." She paused, and then said quietly, as though speaking to herself, "I was never enough."

I could tell this story wasn't going to have a happy ending, and squeezed her hand in a show of support, despite the inappropriate and completely irrational stab of jealousy at hearing how much she had loved someone else. Again I kept quiet, knowing there was more to the story, and realizing that what she was telling me had a lot to do with why she hadn't let herself love since.

After a moment, she continued, her voice stronger. "I was doing a lot of speed — a lot of us did — and chasing it hard with vodka. The more she wanted me to do, the more fucked-up I had to get to do it, because it wasn't exciting anymore. I hated it, hated myself after...but I loved her so much and I tried, I really tried to be what she needed."

She stood abruptly and took a few steps away, folding her arms across her chest and looking out toward the ocean. "Finally she asked for something that I just couldn't do...I couldn't do it anymore, and when I told her..."

I could see her body tense at the memory and I rose to stand beside her; not touching, but there if she needed me. "What happened?"

She stared at the water for a long time before answering. "She laughed. She laughed and said she knew I would break soon, but she'd gotten more from me than anyone expected, and it had been great fun taking me as far as she had." She looked over at me and smiled bitterly. "It had all been a big game. Let's see how far the stupid, naïve American will go for love...I had never been in control at all."

She shook her head in disgust, and this time I did touch her, slipping my arms cautiously around her waist from behind and resting my chin on her shoulder. "I'm sorry." It seemed a wholly inadequate response to what she'd gone through, but it was heartfelt, and when I felt her relax against me and her hands cover mine, I knew it was enough.

We stood like that for several minutes, Robyn lost in memories, and me thinking of how Robyn's past experience shed some light on her present-day tendency to keep people at arm's length and not become emotionally involved. It also made me realize why it had been so hard for her to accept what was happening between us, and just how much she'd risked when she told me, in that hotel room in

Big Bear, how much she cared about me.

Eventually she patted my arms. "So that's *my* sordid tale, and probably explains all sorts of things about what an emotionally stunted slut I've been since then."

I felt a little guilty, having been thinking along similar lines, although not quite that harshly. I gave her a quick kiss on the cheek. "Thank you for telling me."

"You're welcome." She turned in the circle of my arms and rested her forehead against mine. "I suppose you should know what you're getting into...maybe I should have told you sooner."

"Oh, pish. Wouldn't have made a bit of difference. I don't scare away that easy."

She pulled back with an amused grin. "Pish?"

"Pish-posh, out with the wash," I recited, and her smile widened. I shrugged. "It's a Grandma thing."

She laughed and hugged me hard. "God, you're cute."

It was good to hear her laugh, and I was pleased to be the one to cause it, even if I hated being called "cute." Puppies were cute. Kermit the frog was cute. That little four-year-old kid that rapped was cute. Creepy, I'll admit, but cute. I disliked being thought of as cute, but from her, I'd take it.

"Thank you for listening," she murmured in my ear, "and not freaking out, or thinking badly about me..." She pulled back and looked at me intently. "You don't, do you? Think badly of me?"

"Of course not. Why would I?"

She dropped her eyes. "Some of the things I did..."

"Robyn." I tucked my fingers under her chin and raised her gaze back to mine. "The only person I think badly of is the woman that you were with. And that's because of what she did to you, and how she hurt you, not because she got off on pain. I want to hurt her because she hurt you."

She smiled weakly. "I'll point her out next time I see her and you can have at it, then. My money's on you. I bet you could snap her like a toothpick."

I frowned, and dropped my hand to her chest, rubbing lightly. "You see her?"

She tilted her head back and forth in a nonchalant gesture, but the eyes that looked past me flared briefly with emotion before settling into feigned indifference. "Every once in a while. She has a house in LA, and we still have mutual acquaintances. I see her at parties, benefits, openings..."

"That must be...difficult."

She took a moment to answer. "It's gotten easier, over time, but yes, sometimes it's still hard. Especially if she's in a...playful...mood." She said the word with obvious sarcasm. "Then it gets especially fun. She calls me her *petit sadique* and wants to talk about old times."

"I'm sorry, baby." I kissed her gently.

"Thank you." She kissed me back, just as softly.

We stared at each other, and she slowly leaned in and kissed me again. When we pulled back from that kiss, minutes had passed and anyone watching our not-so-private beach had gotten quite an eyeful.

"Inside?" she asked hoarsely.

"God, yes." I grabbed her hand and dragged her toward the house.

She tripped after me, struggling to get her footing in the sand. "Dinner..."

I stopped and rounded on her in exasperation. "Do you want dinner, or do you want me?"

She grabbed my face in her hands and kissed me. "Stupid damn question."

We didn't even make it to the couch, ending up in a tangle of limbs on the carpet just inside the door.

Chapter
Eighteen

I WOULD HAVE been perfectly happy with leftover lasagna, cheese and crackers...hell, bread and water would have worked, as long as Robyn was with me, but at her request, and for what she called "counter-propagandaism," we drove a few miles into Islamorada for oysters, stone crabs, and clam chowder at a popular waterside restaurant. In Robyn's words, "What better way to show them we're not squabbling over Josh than to be seen having dinner together?"

I couldn't fault her logic; the only better way I could think of showing we weren't squabbling over Josh was perhaps for some media outlet to get film of that kiss we'd shared on the beach, and the gymnastics that had followed once we were safely inside the house, but I didn't think either of us was ready for that. We had a nice meal — as nice as a meal could be with numerous interruptions by autograph and photograph seekers — and then we'd come back to the house, and Robyn had shown me how appreciative she was of my patience.

Dinner had been well worth the aggravation.

Robyn stirred and I reached out to run gentle fingers through her hair. She was on her side, facing me, one arm curled around her pillow and the other stretched above her head. I had been awake for nearly an hour, just watching her sleep. It was like every damn cliché about love that I'd ever heard. I felt full, bursting with love, like it was a palpable force, radiating out of me. I looked at her and my chest felt tight with emotion; I felt like crying and laughing at the same time. It was exhilarating, wonderful and not a little frightening.

Dark eyes blinked open, regarding me sleepily. "Mmm...hey."

"Morning." I leaned in and placed a gentle kiss on her forehead.

Her mouth curled into a smile and she rolled onto her back and stretched. "Been awake long?"

"A little while." I scooted closer and tucked myself in beside her, laying my head on her shoulder and draping my arm across her stomach. Her arms went around me immediately. "I was enjoying the view."

"The view of me drooling, and my hair looking so pretty?"

I turned my head slightly and kissed the skin near her collarbone. "It is very pretty. And you don't drool...much."

I felt her chuckle and a brief touch of her lips across the top of my head. After a minute of quiet she asked, "When do you need to leave?"

I sighed, not wanting to be reminded that I would be heading home soon. "Around one or so. The flight is a little after three."

She kissed my head again and tightened her arms briefly. "I wish we had more time."

"Me, too." I raised my head and kissed her, sighing in pleasure when strong fingers threaded through my hair and she deepened the kiss, turning a brief peck into a slow, gentle investigation. She rolled onto her side and pulled me closer, tangling her legs in mine, and we spent long minutes in unhurried kisses, neither of us escalating the passion of the exchange.

"Mmm." Robyn eventually broke the exchange, dropping light kisses on my cheeks and forehead before pulling away. She put a finger on my lips. "Stay. I'll be right back."

She unwrapped herself from our embrace and rolled off the bed; I watched her retreating form in languid appreciation until she disappeared behind the partially closed door of the bathroom.

Her slightly muted voice came from behind the door. "You have a long travel day. I was thinking maybe we could go for a run later this morning, get you some exercise before you have to sit all day. Interested?"

"When?" My tone was noticeably petulant, and I scowled at myself. It was a good idea, and would certainly be good for me, but I was enjoying our closeness this morning and didn't want it to end quite yet.

I could hear the smile in her voice. "I'm not in any hurry. Just...later."

Satisfied that she was coming back to bed, I nodded, and then voiced my agreement when I realized she couldn't see me. "That sounds good. If you promise not to kick my ass."

"Well, I really wanted to *run*," came her muffled reply after a beat, "but I guess a walk would be okay."

"Hey!" I protested, and heard her answering laugh. "Damn, Ward, that was cold. And to think all the people who read the rags think *I'm* the bitch."

She laughed again. "If only they knew that you're actually the sweet one."

I smiled and threw my legs over the side of the bed, stretching my back as I sat up. "That's what Liz said, too. I guess I'm destined to be misunderstood."

I heard the toilet flush, and water running. "So, did you tell her? About us, I mean." Her voice was still muted by the door, but I heard the tentativeness of her tone.

"Yep."

I didn't say anything else, and she poked her head out the door a few moments later, a toothbrush in her mouth. "An? Wha' she sa'?"

I looked at her questioningly and she rolled her eyes and ducked back into the bathroom to spit out the toothpaste before opening the door wider and leaning against the jamb. "What did she say?"

"Huh?" Distracted by her nakedness, it took me a moment to respond. I blinked and dragged my eyes up to meet her smug gaze.

"I asked what Liz had to say," she motioned with her hand, "about us."

"Oh. Um, let's see...she said 'wow', and something along the lines of 'I'll be damned' and 'holy shit', and then she asked....um, what it was like."

"Did she?" Robyn sounded entertained by the idea and went back into the bathroom, her voice taking on a slight echo. "And just how did you answer that one?"

I leaned back on my hands, watching her through the bathroom door as she washed her face, and pondered just how honest I should be about what I had told Liz. *What the hell, let's start our day out with a little shot of honesty.*

"I told her it was none of her damn business..." She grinned at that, and patted her face with a towel. "And then I told her that even if it was her business, I couldn't tell her anyway because I couldn't think of words to describe how totally amazing it is to be with you."

She gave a strangled laugh and pulled the towel away from her face. "Oh, aren't you a sweet talker..." Her eyes widened in surprise when she saw the look on my face. "You're serious."

"Of course I'm serious."

She placed the towel gently on the counter and turned toward me. "You really told Liz that?"

"Yes, I told her. And I meant every word," I added, trying to keep the nervousness out of my voice.

Her mouth formed a tiny "O" of surprise. "Caid, I..." She stared at me for a moment, and then started toward me slowly, her gaze never leaving mine.

Now that you've started, you might as well finish it. I pushed myself off the bed, wanting to be face to face with her when I told her the rest.

She crossed the room and stopped in front of me, reaching out to brush my cheek. "You really told Liz that," she repeated, but this time it was a statement and not a question.

I cupped her face in my hands and laid the gentlest of kisses on her parted lips before taking a deep breath and stepping off the cliff. "I told her it probably had something to do with the fact that I'm crazy in love with you."

"Wha...?" Our faces were close enough that I could actually feel the whoosh of air as she drew in a sharp breath. She blinked and a myriad of emotions ran across her face, surprise the most immediately recognizable. She tried to pull back, but I held her in place, my hands still cupping her face.

"I love you," I said again softly, surprised at how easily the words came, now that they were out. I placed another kiss on her stunned lips. "I am totally, completely, head-over-freaking-heels in love with you, Robyn. I don't want to scare you, but I wanted you to know. You don't need to say anythi—"

The rest of my words were swallowed abruptly as Robyn crushed her mouth to mine, and the next thing I knew I was flat on my back in the middle of the bed, with six feet of warm, naked, and very amorous Robyn Ward on top of me, raining kisses on my face, neck and chest.

"Say it again," she demanded suddenly, pulling back to look at my face intently, as though judging my sincerity.

I wondered, as she searched my face for proof, just how many times she'd been told those words. Considering her fame, her looks...more than a few times, I'd guess. How many others had told her they loved her in hopes of getting something from her? I knew of at least one who had professed love and lied, hurting her badly. How many others had there been?

It was yet another reason for the walls she'd put up around herself, and I felt a moment of intense gratitude that she'd let me in as far as she had. I met her gaze squarely, wanting her to see everything I was feeling, needing her to believe me. I brushed her cheeks with my thumbs and ran my hands through her hair. "I love you, Robyn," I said clearly, bringing her head down for a soft kiss. "I love you," I said again and trailed my lips over her chin and down the long column of her neck. "I love you," I murmured, nipping at the skin just below her ear and feeling a slight shiver in response. I tilted my head back and found her eyes again, willing her to believe me. "I. Love. You."

She touched my face, trailing her fingers over my eyebrows and down my cheeks. "Oh, Caid..."

Her voice, to my ears, seemed apologetic, and I fought back panic. Now, when faced with her response, my brave statements did not seem like such a bright idea. I pulled her head down and silenced her with a kiss, not wanting to hear what she had to say right now, not wanting her to feel pressured or obligated, and especially not wanting her to tell me she didn't feel the same. She could tell me how she felt later—right now, I wanted to *show* her how I felt.

I rolled us over, kissing her hard, and pushed my hands into her hair, tilting her head back so that I could kiss along the underside of her chin and down her throat.

"Caid..." Her words stopped in an expulsion of breath when I settled my thigh between her legs and pressed against her while I covered her nipple with my mouth, sucking and biting gently. I trailed my hands down her body and braced my arms on either side of her chest, lifting my body off of her slightly, pushing my thigh against her again. Her fingers threaded through my hair, tightening almost to the point of painfulness when I held her nipple gently in my teeth and flicked the tip back and forth with my tongue.

"Ah...Christ..." She arched against me, lifting her leg and pushing against me roughly. I groaned and pushed back automatically, quickly falling into the rhythm she set. I let go of one nipple to move to the other, giving it a few minutes of attention before she dragged my head up and brought our mouths together in a panting, openmouthed kiss, her tongue meeting mine in time with our thrusts. Gradually the rhythm increased and our kiss slowed until we were just breathing in each other's air as we concentrated on the movement and feel of our bodies.

"Oh, yes," she whispered, her lips moving to my forehead and her hands to my hips, urging me into her. I kept up the rhythm of my leg against her, riding her thigh, feeling the slickness of sweat and desire where our bodies touched.

"Oh...God, Caid..." Her leg shifted again and pushed into me harder. "I'm..." she sucked in a breath, "come with me, baby..."

Our movements became frantic; labored breathing interspersed with whispered nonsensical words and gasps, and I slipped one hand between us, drawing my fingers through her warm wetness and teasing the hardened nub of her clit with gentle strokes. She hissed out a breath and her body stilled at the contact, then jerked, and I felt the slight sting of her fingernails as she tightened her grip convulsively on my ass. Her head was thrown back, the muscles in her neck corded and tense, and I watched, enthralled, as I continued my movements, amazed as always by how beautiful she was. Suddenly her hand was between my legs, and her fingers inside of me, just as she arched further and let out a shuddering moan, jerking inelegantly against my hand. The moan, her movements, her fingers...it was all enough to send me tumbling after her into orgasm, whispering a final "love you" before collapsing in a very ungraceful heap on top of her.

After several moments, she withdrew her fingers and her arms circled me in a loose embrace. We lay without speaking as the thundering of her heartbeat beneath my ear returned to a steady thump-thump, and the rise and fall of her chest slowed to evenness; as the sweat dried on our skin and the rising sun cast ever-changing shadows on the bedroom walls.

It was a peaceful, blissful silence and I was loath to break it, but eventually the jangle of a ringing telephone broke the complacent stillness, the sound so incongruous after two days of quiet that it took my brain a moment to understand what it was.

Robyn tensed underneath me and swore softly. She started to move, but I shifted my weight, stopping her. "Don't."

She sighed, and ran her hand up and down my back. "I'm sorry, baby, I have to. It must be something on the set...the only way I could talk Lynne into letting me have this weekend was if I let her know where I would be and promised to come in if they needed me. She's the only person I gave this number to."

I slid off of her reluctantly and she climbed out of bed, giving me an rueful look before snagging a T-shirt—mine, I noticed—draped across the back of a chair and pulling it on as she trotted from the room.

"Damn." I sighed and rolled onto my back, listening to the sounds of Robyn's voice, raised slightly in annoyance, in the next room. I doubted they'd be calling to chat about the weather—it looked like our little weekend was coming to an end even sooner than expected.

I sighed again and rolled off the bed, annoyed to feel a twinge of relief at being given a reprieve from Robyn's reaction to telling her I loved her. Jesus, I was such a chickenshit.

A few minutes later, after using the bathroom and throwing on some clothes, I found Robyn out on the back deck, phone still in her hand, looking pensively out at the water. I walked up behind her and slipped an arm around her waist, brushing the hair from her neck with my other hand so I could kiss the soft skin below her ear.

She turned her head and gave me a distracted smile, holding up the phone up. "Sorry."

I put my other arm around her and rested my chin on her shoulder. "Now it's my turn to ask. When do you have to go?"

"As soon as I can get there...they got a permit to shoot on-site in Key Largo, but we've only got today."

"Damn." I wasn't surprised, but I had hoped for a little more time. I kissed her cheek with a sigh and held her tighter. "Thank you for this weekend."

She turned in my arms and ran both her hands through my hair. "Caid..." She stopped and looked at my face searchingly. I could see her struggle for words. Finally, she looked away. "You're welcome. I had a great time."

A great time.

I'd used that exact phrasing to brush off a mediocre date more than once. I inwardly steeled myself, waiting for the "but..." It never came, but neither did the hoped-for profession of love.

Jeez, Caid, what do you expect? A minute ago you were relieved to not know, and now you're frustrated?

I hid my disappointment, and tugged her into the house. "Come on. Why don't you jump in the shower, and I'll fix you breakfast for a change." I hesitated, not wanting to push things, but deciding that there were still questions that needed to be answered, and I was going to get those answers before she left. "Maybe we can talk a bit over breakfast, okay?"

Something flickered in her eyes briefly, and then a seductive smile curled her lips. She pulled me back against her body. "How about you join me in the shower, and we skip breakfast?" she murmured, laying a light line of kisses along my neck.

I quashed my immediate reaction to her words and nearness, feeling a certain hollowness in her offer. My body was willing, but at the moment, my heart just wasn't in it, and I wasn't sure hers was, either. "We'd never make it out of the shower," I joked lightly in an attempt to ease the disappointment and confusion that flashed across her face as I pulled away. "You have a long day ahead of you and need to eat." I pointed to the hallway and pushed her gently in that direction. "Away with you."

"Caid..." She frowned, her expression still betraying her confusion.

"Go on." I tilted my head up and kissed her lightly on the forehead before pushing her toward the hallway again. "I'll have something ready for you when you get out."

She hesitated a moment longer, staring at me intently, then nodded slowly and walked past me and down the hall.

I sighed and walked into the kitchen, taking stock of what kind of ingredients we had on hand to make breakfast. Eggs and some leftover seafood mixture from Robyn's lasagna would make a decent enough filling for an omelet, and French bread for toast... I nodded to myself and pulled the items out of the refrigerator. I rooted around in the cupboards and drawers for a skillet and a small mixing bowl, my movements getting slower and slower, until they stopped altogether.

What in the hell was I doing?

The woman I was in love with was naked in the shower, and I was about to make an omelet? I shook my head in disbelief. Robyn asked me to share the last of our time together making love, and I had said no.

Caid, you are a dumbass.

I put the food back into the refrigerator and walked down the hall, a smile building on my face until I entered the master bedroom and saw that Robyn wasn't naked in the shower at all. In fact, she was standing in the middle of the room, fully dressed, and apparently fully packed. The small duffel she had brought was slung over her shoulder, and she looked to be in the process of checking for any stray items she might have missed.

I stopped abruptly in the doorway and stared at her stupidly. "Wha...what are you doing?"

"Leaving," she said briskly, taking one last glance around.

"But...you were showering...we were going to have breakfast..." I frowned in confusion. "Why are you leaving?"

She hitched the bag higher on her shoulder, finally looking at me. It was then I realized how angry she was. "I won't be manipulated."

That did not help my confusion at all. "What are you talking about? I'd never try to manipulate you."

"That's what I thought, too, until a few minutes ago." She shook her head sadly. "I really thought you were different, Caid. Stupid of me."

She moved to the door and I stopped her with a hand on her chest. She gave the hand a look of disdain that made me cringe, and looked at me coolly. "Get out of my way."

"Not until you tell me what the hell I did wrong!" I was starting to worry now; I'd been on the receiving end of that look before, the night at her house when she'd told me nothing could happen between us. It was cold and resolute, and just like that night, I had no idea how to counter it.

"I won't let you use sex to manipulate me into saying what you want to hear. I enjoy you, Caid — I enjoy being with you. But sex is sex, and I can find it elsewhere. Remember that." She moved my hand and brushed past me roughly.

I didn't stop her, too shaken by the thought that maybe she was right. Not about the sex-is-sex part; that was a bunch of crap. I knew whatever was between us was something special, and went much deeper than physical. But her accusation of my withholding sex because she hadn't told me what I wanted to hear...*was* that why I had refused her? As some kind of punishment for not returning my feelings?

I thought back to what I'd been feeling, and shook my head. No, that hadn't been the reason. I'd refused because it felt...wrong. Like...she was trying to distract me, to avoid having to discuss issues that needed to be discussed.

She had been the one that tried to use sex to manipulate.

My worry was displaced by anger, and I followed her into the living room, grabbing her arm and turning her around. "I told you I loved you, damn it, because I do. Very much. And I thought you should know. I'm not trying to manipulate you, regardless of what you think. I didn't, and still don't, expect anything from you except honesty."

She glared at my hand, but I continued to hold on to her—I wasn't finished. "Maybe you should take a look at your own behavior before you go accusing me of manipulation. I tell you I love you, and you don't want to deal with it, so what better way to distract me than to drag me off into the shower? You know the effect you have on me, and you tried to use it to your advantage. So don't give me righteous lectures about using sex as a weapon."

She shrugged my hand off angrily and grabbed her purse and keys from the table. "The cleaning service comes at three; make sure you're gone by then. Leave the key in the mailbox," she told me icily, and stomped to the door.

"Robyn." I had one more thing to address.

To my surprise, she stopped at the door and turned back, her expression stony.

She wouldn't be manipulated, but I wouldn't be threatened. "If you do find sex elsewhere...despite how much I love you, you'll never be with me that way again. I told you before that I don't like to share. Remember *that.*"

A muscle in her jaw twitched, and she stared at me for a long moment, and then she was gone.

I THOUGHT—I hoped—that she would come back.

I actually sat on the couch for another half an hour, hoping. Finally, I was forced to face the reality that Robyn's fight-or-flight tendencies were going to take a lot longer than a weekend to counteract. I wasn't giving up quite yet, though—we didn't get this far to allow a misunderstanding as stupid as this to tear us apart.

I started planning my assault on Fortress Robyn as I changed into my running clothes, and as I set off down the hard-packed sand near the water, heading east and hoping the beaches connected for at least a few miles, my head was filled with nothing but thoughts of how I could get her to talk to me.

I waved at a man with binoculars on the beach one house over, nodded sympathetically to a couple overseeing four children building sandcastles several houses after that, and patted a few friendly dogs on the public beach I ran onto that ended sooner than I'd hoped, but was far enough to make it worth the run.

The run back went quickly, and once I'd gotten back to "our" beach, I stood for a long time, looking out at the water, remembering what an amazing weekend it had been, and vowing to do everything in my power to make it happen again.

Eventually, I started back to the house, but stopped when I saw the man with binoculars from next door limping slowly over the dune between the houses, leaning heavily on a gnarled, black walking stick as he struggled through the deep sand. He looked to be in his sixties, with a wide-brimmed hat and the bright tropical print shirt and Bermuda shorts that seemed to be the uniform of the older tourists in the area.

Curious as to what his mission was, and wondering if I could somehow help in his struggle through the sand, I started toward him. "Hi." I called out, but he made no response, just continued his resolute progress over the dune and onto the beach in my general direction. When I got closer, his face finally lifted to meet mine, and I realized he wasn't as old as I thought—late forties, maybe—with pale blue eyes that stared at me with an intensity that made me uneasy.

"Hi," I said again when I was within a few yards. "Can I help you with something?"

He stopped and smiled, watching me approach. "As a matter of fact, you can."

If I hadn't had other things on my mind, if I'd been in the city, if I'd been expecting trouble, maybe things would have gone differently. As it was, I smiled expectantly, and watched as he flipped the walking stick into the air, caught it in both hands, and swung.

I realized what was coming at the last second—not nearly enough time to dodge the swing or even get my arm up in defense. Pain exploded in my head as the stick struck me across the jaw, spinning me around and sending me stumbling across the deep sand and dropping to my hands and knees.

What the...

Stunned from the blow, I stared dumbly at the blood on the sand beneath me, unable to comprehend what was happening. Another blow came down hard on my back and I hissed as pain shot from the point of impact and down my legs.

That can't be good.

A foot in my stomach knocked the wind from my lungs and I collapsed onto the sand as he kicked me twice more, and took several more vicious swings with the stick.

All six of the main cast members of *9th Precinct* had gone through a modified police academy curriculum, with self-defense and subduing techniques a large part of the training. I'd been good at it, and confident that I could use the knowledge if the need arose in real life, but none of that training had prepared me for the violence of this attack. It had been too swift, too unexpected. The only thought in my mind was to get away.

I struggled clumsily in an attempt to get back to my hands and knees, but a hand yanked my head back by the hair, and I stared into wild, feverish eyes.

"I saw you with her. I saw you touch her, you filthy bitch. You're sick! I saw you touch her!"

He punched the side of my face, driving it into the sand. My vision blurred, and my face throbbed — I felt the grit of sand in my mouth and watched, helpless, as he drew back his hand again.

Thank God Robyn left... It was the last thought to flit through my brain before another blow struck hard across the back of my head, and then — nothing.

Chapter
Nineteen

SO MUCH NOISE...so many voices...and pain...

"Caid, baby, stay with me. Damn it, don't you leave me..." The frantic voice came from far away. It was familiar. I knew the raspy tones, wanted to respond...

"...we need to load her in the ambulance now, ma'am..."

My body jolted and pain erupted in my head. I slipped back into blackness.

"...NURSE, I SPECIFICALLY said family only. Why is this...woman...still here? Call security, right now."

The loud, unwelcome voice pulled me groggily from unconsciousness.

Who... The voice was familiar. Sebastian?

My mind slowly came back into the land of the living, and once it did, all I wanted to do was to go back to nice, pain-free darkness.

God, I hurt. And I was so, so tired.

"Mr. Harris, calm down. I'm sure we can work something out," an unfamiliar female voice said soothingly. I could have told her that wouldn't do any damn good—Sebastian always got his way.

I kept my eyes shut, cataloging the hurts. The pain in my head was excruciating. Nauseating. It made it hard to think, hard to hear, hard to breathe. And other areas of my body were chiming in on the pain meter, too. My lower back, my stomach, my left wrist... I winced, and the movement brought a whole new set of aches to my attention—my nose, cheek, and jaw felt painfully swollen.

What happened? Why...

"Go ahead and call security. I'm not going anywhere." The voice was low and husky, tinged with irritation.

Robyn.

I wanted to giggle. No one talked to my brother like that.

At the sound of her voice, the throbbing in my head eased to a somewhat tolerable level and I let my eyes flutter open a little, finally finding something in this situation worth sticking around for. Bright light and colors hit sensitive eyes and I shut them again as my stomach roiled. After a moment, I took a shallow breath and tried again. When my head didn't explode, and my need to hurl up whatever might be in my stomach passed, I opened them wider. Or at least as wide as I could, since I could feel that one was nearly swollen shut.

Christ, what happened to me?

The blurred images around me gradually gained focus, and I stared in dazed bewilderment at my surroundings. I was in a long room—a very white room—and weak light streamed through several narrow windows. On either side of me, stacks of instruments and machines beeped and pinged regularly, and a pale blue curtain stretched across the space to my left, bunched on a ceiling rail at the end of the bed. My eyes dropped to my arms and I felt my brow furrow in confusion. My left wrist, the one that ached, was wrapped in some kind of splint, and there was an IV line running out of the back of my other hand and something clipped to my finger.

Hospital. Something happened. I tried to get my brain to work, to piece together what was going on, but couldn't make any sense of the jumble, and trying made the pain in my head worse.

I shifted my gaze and focused on the man speaking across the room. Sebastian. My brother. This I remembered, but not why he was here. His dark hair was beginning to gray at the temples, but the square, strong jaw, thin, pinched mouth, and intense brown eyes were the same. He stood stiff with anger and outrage, glaring down at a dark-haired woman slumped in a chair.

Robyn. I let my gaze linger on her. I loved her. This I remembered, too.

A woman in brightly patterned scrubs hovered next to Sebastian, looking worriedly from one to the other. A nurse, I assumed, but didn't recognize her.

"Don't think I won't," Sebastian was saying. "I don't care how famous you are or what connections you have..."

Robyn's eyes wandered in apparent boredom as my jerk of a brother railed at her, eventually coming to rest on me and widening in sudden realization. She was out of her seat and across the room in seconds. "Caid? Baby?" Her voice was hopeful and desperate, and she reached out a hand to touch me, but drew back and grabbed onto the rail of my bed instead.

I blinked slowly. "He..." I croaked, my voice weak and raspy. I swallowed, and licked my lips with a tongue that felt three times too big for my mouth, flinching when I passed over a tender area that felt split. I tried again. "Hey."

Her face broke into a beautiful smile, and a tear slid slowly down her cheek. "Oh, baby," she whispered, gripping the rails of the bed tightly. "I'm so glad you're awake. God, you scared me..."

I tried to smile back, but it hurt, and I closed my eyes again.

"Caid?"

I was so tired—her words flowed around me and I let the beckoning darkness washed over me again.

"...I DON'T WANT visitation changed. I don't care who she is, Perry, she's not family."

"But she's her friend! She sees her a lot more often than we do—it might help her to hear her voice..."

"I said no, and that's final! She doesn't need to be around those kind of people right now. She needs her family, and our faith in God..."

The arguing voices drew me rudely from the safe, pain-free arms of unconsciousness into the distinctly non-pain-free world of consciousness. I groaned involuntarily in disapproval. *Jesus. Those two never stop arguing.* My eyes fluttered open, and blurry images gradually gained sharpness. Three startled sets of eyes were staring at me: two familiar, one not.

I tried out my voice—it was weak, but audible. "Will you...two...shut up."

"Caid! You're awake!" Perry hurried forward to hover uncertainly by my bedside.

"Hard...to sleep...with you two...ragging...at each other," I croaked out, and swallowed, wishing for some water and some more nice, pain-free darkness.

He smiled tremulously. "How do you feel?"

I would have laughed if I wasn't sure it would have hurt like hell. Instead I grunted.

"Jesus Christ, Caid, you scared the shit out of me."

"Sorry," I whispered, although I wasn't sure what I was sorry for.

Sebastian moved up beside Perry, frowning in disapproval. "Perry, you will not take the Lord's name in vain."

I winced at the volume of his voice, and the pompous tone. "Jesus Christ...Sebastian...shut up," I told him wearily, and thought I heard a titter of laughter from the room's other occupant, who I assumed was a nurse.

The disapproving eyes turned to me, narrowing in annoyance. My brain might be muddled, but pissing off Sebastian was second nature. "Well, hello to you, too, Caidence. Nice to see the attitude survived intact. And you're welcome. I dropped everything to come down here to be with you, and this is the thanks I get?"

I met his glare without remorse. We hadn't been civil to each other in years, and I didn't see any point to starting now. Whatever his reasons for being here, I doubted my welfare was one of them.

The nurse pushed both men out of the way with practiced ease and moved up beside me. She glanced over at a console of machines to my left and smiled down at me. "Hello, there. Glad to have you back with us. How are you feeling?"

I blinked slowly. "Crappy."

She smiled and patted my hand gently. "Yes, you took quite a beating. You look a lot better than you did two days ago, if that's any consolation."

Beating? Two days?

"Wh-what happened? I don't remember..." I frowned, trying to concentrate. The pain in my head intensified. I hissed softly in pain and closed my eyes.

"Shhh, don't worry. It'll come back to you. Just relax, and I'll be back a little later with the doctor."

I nodded, sleep already tugging at me again, and heard her move away.

"Gentlemen, could I speak to you outside, please?"

"MISS HARRIS? CAIDENCE?"

My eyes jerked open and I flinched in pain, blinking up at a blond, athletic-looking woman in maroon scrubs with a stethoscope looped around her neck. She flashed a wide, friendly smile while light brown eyes swept over me in quick, professional perusal. "I'm Doctor Reese. How are you feeling?" She looked down at a clipboard in her hands, flipping through pages, and then back up at me.

I coughed slightly and winced at the resulting twinge in my back. I cleared my throat carefully. "I've had better days."

She put the chart back with a chuckle. "I bet you have. Would you like some water?"

"Please."

She nodded across the bed and I noticed another person in the room, the nurse from before. "Gail, could you grab that?"

The woman picked up a small pitcher on the table next to me and filled a plastic cup, dropping a straw into it and handing it to me. I drank gratefully, the liquid trickling down my throat in blissful coolness.

The doctor pulled the stethoscope from around her neck and fitted it into her ears, speaking briskly as she gently pulled aside the neck of my gown and laid the cool metal against my chest.

"Gail tells me you might be a little confused about what happened. Do you remember anything at all?"

I shook my head slightly. "Not about how I got here, no. Nothing. My head — everything is so fuzzy."

She nodded. "I'm sure Gail told you that that's normal. You took quite a knock on the head. What's the last thing you remember?"

I frowned, trying to gather my stray memories into some kind of order. *A paddle in my hands, turning my head and laughing at Robyn behind me...* "I...we went kayaking." *Robyn across the table from me, smiling sweetly at a young girl and her mother who asked for an autograph...* "We went into town for dinner..."

A possibility suddenly occurred to me and I straightened, trying to sit up and grimacing at the pain in my back. "Where's Robyn?" I ground out. "Is she okay? We were together..."

"Whoa, there." The doctor gently pushed me back on the bed, her hands on my shoulders. "Just relax. Your friend, Miss Ward, is fine. A little steamed at your brother right now, and worried sick about you, but she's fine." I relaxed, and after watching for a moment to ensure I wasn't going to try to jump out of bed again, she released my shoulders and straightened. "Let me fill you in a little, okay, and maybe it will help a little with your memory."

I nodded gratefully.

"You're at Mid-Key Medical Center in Marathon, Florida. The ambulance brought you in at around eleven on Sunday morning."

"Sunday?" I forced myself to concentrate. Kayaking had been...Saturday. Sunday... What had we done Sunday? I'd been scheduled to fly out early that afternoon, and Robyn was due back on the set...

A throb of pain that seemed to engulf my entire head stopped my memory-gathering and I shut my eyes for a moment, before opening them again. "How long..."

She glanced at the watch on her wrist. "It's nine forty-five PM, Tuesday."

Nearly three days. *Whoa.* "What happened?" I asked slowly. "Why..."

"You were attacked and severely beaten. Miss Ward came with you in the ambulance, but she wasn't hurt — she apparently found you."

She found me? Oh, honey. I couldn't even imagine what that must have been like. "Beaten?" I said slowly. A flash of memory: an object coming at my face and a flash of pain along my jaw. Another flash: my hand on Robyn's arm, pleading with her, her face cold and angry...

"Is any of this sounding familiar?"

"Maybe..." I scowled in frustration, and she nodded sympathetically.

"I wouldn't worry. I'm confident your memory will right itself in time. Now," she hung the clipboard up and gestured to the nurse, "we'll just do a quick examination, and then we can talk about your injuries, and you can ask any questions, okay? I'm sorry, but some of this is going to hurt."

She was right. They poked, prodded, and maneuvered my body, and by the time they were finished, I had long since stopped trying to hide tears of pain and I was exhausted. She finished with a light test to my eyes, and a few simple questions. After writing in my chart for a minute, she gave me her attention. "Well, Miss Harris, it might not feel like it right now, but you're one very lucky woman."

"I'd hate to know what it would feel like if I'd been unlucky," I mumbled grumpily.

She looked at me seriously. "Quite frankly, you'd be dead."

Oh.

"You've got multiple contusions on the head, face, abdomen and back, but it doesn't appear that there will be any lasting physical damage from any of it. You're concussed, which is to be expected, but not severely, according to scans. That's what's causing the confusion and memory loss you're experiencing. It should be temporary. You have a very hard head." She smiled slightly. "Despite the amount of trauma to your face, no bones were broken, although you sustained a couple fairly deep cuts...luckily we have a plastic surgeon on staff and he stitched them up nicely. If treated properly, they should heal without noticeable scarring. Your abdomen is heavily bruised, but amazingly no ribs were broken and no internal damage...and we were concerned about spinal bruising from a large contusion on your back, but all of your reflexes and sensation seem to be within normal limits. A pelvic exam showed no signs of vaginal or anal trauma, and your clothes were intact when you were brought in."

I sucked in a sharp breath. *Jesus!*

She glanced at me sympathetically and her tone softened. "You weren't raped, which is good news in an attack like this. The most serious injury, besides the head trauma, was a fracture of the ulna in two places above the left wrist. You've got a small plate and a couple of screws in there to keep it together while it heals. All in all, very lucky, and you're in excellent physical shape, which should speed the recovery process."

I nodded slowly and suddenly felt very lucky indeed. "How long..." I gestured at my body with my good hand.

She crossed her arms and cocked her head to the side. "A few weeks for the bruises to fade, five or six days before we take the facial stitches out, and then several weeks for those to heal completely, six to eight weeks for the wrist, and we'll have to see how the back feels when we get you up and around. Your head injury, it's hard to say — we'd like to keep you here a few more days for observation, and once you're released, you might experience headaches, dizziness, light-headedness anywhere from a couple of weeks to months after. You'll definitely need to take it easy for a while, and you might need a little help for a bit when you're released.

"The best thing for you right now is to rest," she continued. "I'm going to restrict visitors for you for a little while. We've had some...issues, and you need the quiet. I've got you hooked up to a morphine drip — now that you're awake, you can manage that yourself. This button here," she pressed a button on one of the machines by the bed, and a moment later I could feel a tingling in my hand and a delicious lethargy flow through my body, "releases the drug into your system. It's set up to allow you a certain amount an hour. Do you have any questions for me? Anything we can do for you?"

They both looked at me expectantly.

I put processing the information about what my body had gone through on hold, and contemplated her question, fighting fatigue and the slowly encroaching haziness brought on by the morphine. There was something I wanted to ask...about Robyn...

I closed my eyes to concentrate and sleep took me again.

I WOKE BRIEFLY on and off over the next several hours, long enough for a nurse to ask me how I felt and for another hit of morphine before drifting off again.

When I finally woke with my head clear of haziness and my body rested enough that fatigue and pain didn't make me want to go right back to sleep, I was in a different room — a much smaller room — and the array of machines beside me was much less impressive. The sharp odor of antiseptic was overlaid by something sweet and floral; I looked around curiously and found that nearly every available spot of counter space, along with some floor space, was taken up by flower arrangements off all sizes, and even a stuffed animal or two.

I tried to chuckle at that, which ended up as more of a wheeze, and a nurse who was scribbling something on a clipboard at the end of the bed looked up. She smiled. "Oh, good, you're awake again. How do you feel?"

Jesus. They kept asking me that. *How do you* think *I feel, honey?*

I wanted to ask. If I looked even half as bad as I felt, it should be freaking obvious how I feel —

"Miss Harris?"

I managed to suppress my first response, realizing, even in my somewhat groggy and grumpy state, that being a bitch to the people who were trying to help me wouldn't accomplish anything. Instead, I took a moment to catalog my hurts and give her an honest answer. "Not great," I croaked, and cleared my throat. "But...better," I added, surprised that it was true. My head still throbbed, but the nausea was gone, my face didn't feel quite as tight and swollen, and my mind was much clearer.

She glanced at the display of one of the machines beside my bed and wrote something down, then looked back at me. "Good." She poured me a glass of water and I nodded gratefully when she handed it to me.

"What time is it?" I asked, noticing weak gray light coming in the room's one window.

She looked at her watch. "It's about a quarter after six. Wednesday morning," she added before I could ask. She hung the clipboard on the end of the bed and refilled the water glass I'd set down. "How does some food sound? Maybe some toast, some juice?"

I nodded slowly. I wasn't hungry, but now that the nausea was gone, I thought I could probably handle some food. "I could eat."

"Great. I'll go fetch you something, and your brother was just in here...he went to find some coffee, I think. I'll let him know you're awake."

"Which brother?" I asked bluntly, not wanting to deal with Sebastian quite yet.

She smiled slightly. "Perry. He's been here most of the night." She motioned to the corner of the room where a messily folded blanket lay across the back of a chair. "I'm Kara, by the way. I'm on until eight. I'll be back in just a bit with your breakfast."

"Thank you, Kara."

She smiled and pushed out of the room.

A few minutes later Perry poked his head hesitantly through the door, smiling uncertainly. "Hey. Morning, sleepyhead."

I gave him a wide smile in greeting, happy to see a familiar face, and flinched slightly at the pull on my right cheek. I raised my hand curiously, feeling the swollen tightness of my skin and the evenly stitched welt that followed the line of my cheekbone beneath my right eye. Exploring further, I found another welt running along my jaw from below my right ear to the middle of my chin, and a small, painful knot on my forehead above my right eye. The left side of my face felt smooth in comparison, with only a few tender areas of scraped skin.

"Caid, you okay?" I blinked and glanced over at him. He had entered the room and was looking at me worriedly.

"Yeah...sorry. Just hadn't...felt the damage before. How does it look?"

He looked at me uncomfortably, "Uh, well..."

"That good?" I asked dryly. Perry looked at the floor and bit his lip. "It's okay, Per. I know I probably look like the bride of Frankenstein, but they tell me it'll all heal up fine."

He shoved his hands in the pockets of his jeans, still looking at the floor.

"It'll be fine, Per, I promise. Didn't the doctor talk to you?"

"Yeah." He nodded after a few moments of silence. "She's been really cool."

"She seemed very...competent."

He was quiet for a bit longer, then looked up with a tiny grin. "She's a hottie, too."

I raised an eyebrow — my left one. "Is she?"

"Oh, come on, Caid — I woulda thought you'd notice something like that, after your recent...discovery." His grin widened.

"My brain was a little scrambled when I met her." I smiled slightly, happy to move the subject of the conversation away from what had happened to me, and glad for Perry's brightened demeanor. "I'll try to pay attention next time."

He grabbed the chair in the corner and dragged it over next to the bed, dropping into it with a chuckle. "She's got some balls on her, too. Sebastian's trying to pull his crap on her, but she won't take any of it. And I heard that when he had Robyn tossed from your room, the Doc turned around and tossed him, too. Oh, I would have loved to have seen the look on his face. Man, he can be such an ass."

I frowned. "Robyn was here?" A vague memory of her worried, tearstained face surfaced, and her voice telling me to stay with her, and then another of her staring Sebastian down, with a nurse looking on. "And Sebastian tossed her out of my room? Why?" I shifted restlessly, feeling the stirrings of anger and letting it come. It felt good to vent a little after lying around so damn helpless for the last few days. "If he's chased her off, I'm going to kick his sanctimonious, preaching butt. And why the hell is he here, anyway? He should be in church thanking God that his sinning sister got what was coming to her — "

"Whoa, Caid." Perry held up his hands in surprise at my outburst. "Hey, calm down. He didn't chase anyone off," he said, and frowned at me. "And I think you're being a little harsh. He seemed genuinely concerned. He's an asshole, but you're still his sister."

"Uh-huh." It was nice to think that maybe somewhere, deep down, Sebastian still carried around familial feelings for me, but too much had passed between us and too much had been said for me to lay any bets on it.

Perry watched me for a moment and then sighed. "It's kind of my fault he's here anyway. When I got the call on Sunday about what happened, I tried Mom and Dad's cells without any luck — they'd mentioned before they left that their reception wouldn't be so good on this trip, so I just left them a message to let them know I'd fly down to be with you and not to worry...and, um, then I called Steve." He glanced quickly at me to gauge my reaction. "I thought he should know, too..."

"And he called Sebastian," I finished. Steve was our father, although Perry had never called him such. The fact that Dad had called Sebastian meant he wouldn't be coming down himself. It also explained why Sebastian was here — not for me, but for his father. Our father. My father. Who couldn't be bothered to leave his cozy little life in Chicago to come visit his only daughter in the hospital. I felt the prick of unexpected tears and angrily gave myself a mental shake, annoyed that after all this time, it still could hurt.

After a moment of silence, I deliberately moved conversation away from the topics of Sebastian and Steve, and moved to the opposite end of the spectrum: our often times over-reactive mother. "Did you ever get in touch with Mom?" I asked, and then groaned. "Please tell me Larry didn't let her jump on a plane?" I was already feeling guilty for worrying her, and right now, I could do without the added guilt of having her fly halfway across the world to see that I was going to be fine.

Perry grunted. "Well, if there'd been a plane anywhere close, I doubt that even Dad could have stopped her, but since there wasn't, between the two of us we managed to get her calmed down, and then the doctor pretty much said you were out of the woods by the time I got here Monday night...they've been calling a couple of times a day, so you can talk to them when they call this morning."

"You've been here since Monday?"

Perry nodded. "I couldn't get a flight out until the afternoon, but since Sebastian's in Tampa, he got down here Monday morning." He smiled slightly. "That's when Doc Reese kicked him out. I guess he found Robyn in the room with you — the nurses said she'd been with you since you were brought in — and he threw a fit about visitors being family only. Since he's a blood relative, and the oldest sibling, they let him have his way and asked Robyn to leave, but the doc made him leave, too. I tried to get him to lighten up about Robyn, but you know how he is."

"Pompous dickhead," I muttered, and shifted restlessly. "How do I fix that? I should be able to make those decisions myself now, right?"

"Um, I don't know. I guess the nurse would know, or the doctor—"

"Good. I'll ask when she gets back. I don't want him to have any say in who can see me." The thought of him having any control over my life, ever, made my head throb. "Where is she? Did she leave?"

He frowned. "Who, Doctor Reese?"

"No. Robyn. I'd like to see her."

"Oh. Uh, she left last night, after she heard you'd woken up for real and were doing good. I talked to her a little before she left, and she mentioned something about her director threatening to replace her...she said she'd try to make it back tonight."

I closed my eyes. *Damn.*

Since I'd talked to the doctor about what happened, more and more of the puzzle pieces that made up my memory had fallen into place. Memories of our weekend—good and bad—had surfaced and I desperately wanted to see her, to know where we stood. She'd stormed out after our fight, but she must have come back—for some reason—since she was the one that found me. That gave me some hope.

"She said that she's been talking to Liz, to let her know you were all right, and some people from the show, and...Connie, I think it was?"

I nodded, my eyes still closed. "My agent."

"Oh, right. Yeah, I guess you'd have one of those, huh?"

I smiled slightly. "Mmm-hmm."

"Yeah, well...it's good she made all those calls, since I wouldn't have known who in the hell to call. Shit, Caid, I realize I don't know crap about your life..."

I opened my eyes at his aggravated tone. "Per..." I looked at him searchingly.

He shook his head and held up a hand. "Sorry. I didn't mean for it to sound like that. I'm still a little on edge, and I..." he blew out a long sigh. "You really scared me, Caid."

"I know. I'm sorry," I said, not knowing what else to say.

He stared at his hands for a moment, and I let him have his time. Finally, he sighed. "You scared a lot of people. Hell," he looked up with a tiny grin, regaining his good humor, "I didn't realize you were so damn popular. From what I hear, they've had about a million calls asking how you are, and Robyn...shit, it was scary how worried she was about you. I was kinda surprised that she actually left, but it was probably best that she did, anyway. A lot of the media people left when she did."

I scowled so deeply that it pulled the stitches along my jaw. "Media?"

"Uh, yeah. I guess they tried to keep it quiet and managed to for a while, but..." He shrugged.

Just what I needed — more media scrutiny.

Fan-fucking-tastic.

The pain in my head went up another notch, and I rubbed my forehead with my palm, forgetting about the IV line and nearly jerking it out of my hand. "Shit," I muttered in frustration.

The door swung open and Kara pushed in, back first, with a tray in her hands. "Here we are." She smiled at Perry as he scooted the chair aside to give her room to place the tray on my table. "Toast and juice, as ordered, and some eggs, if you're feeling adventurous."

I gave her a weak smile and looked at Perry. "Is Sebastian here?"

He shook his head. "He went back to his hotel last night after Robyn left."

I nodded, and looked at Kara, doing my best to keep my tone neutral, despite my anger at Sebastian. "Kara, could you let someone know that I'd like to make my own decisions about who can and can't visit me? My brother Sebastian doesn't need to be involved in that anymore."

She blinked in surprise at my abruptness. "Um. Yes, sure —"

"Do I need to talk to Dr. Reese, or sign anything?"

"No, I can take care of it —"

"Great. And Robyn Ward is welcome to visit any time," I finished, and resolutely reached for a piece of toast, even though the pain in my head was making me nauseous again.

She nodded hesitantly. "Okay."

"Thank you." I took a bite and chewed slowly, managing not to immediately throw it back up again. After a few minutes, after the pain in my head subsided a little, it was easier.

Perry sat quietly as I ate, and Kara asked me a few question about my injuries. When she left, I glanced over and found him watching me thoughtfully. I paused in my chewing and swallowed. "What?"

He just shook his head and laughed.

I shrugged and took a cautious sip of juice before reaching for another triangle of toast. The eggs...I tried not to even look at them.

"It's Robyn, isn't it? The woman you were talking about on the trail. The one you're in love with?"

I stopped with the toast halfway to my mouth. Even as crappy as I felt, I couldn't stop the smile that came to my face. That must have said it all.

"Holy crap," he said, and laughed again.

I bit into my toast, amused at the expression on his face.

"Holy crap. I can't believe I didn't figure it out before. She was in your room in Big Bear, you're always talking about her, and the way she's been freaking about you being hurt..." He shook his head again. "I guess she changed her mind about not being interested, huh?"

I just smiled, and hoped he was right.

"Holy crap."

I grinned, feeling better than I had in days, and finished my breakfast.

SEBASTIAN VISITED LATER that morning, and with Perry's words about his concern in mind, I did my best to be civil and quelled the immediate urge to jump all over him for being such a prick to Robyn. We actually conversed for at least three minutes before we ran out of safe topics, and he started in on my choice of careers and how the assault was basically my own fault—a direct result of my association with "those people," and in particular, "that woman." I asked him to leave and not bother to come back, at a volume that brought nurses running, and with language colorful enough to even impress Perry, who had to step between the two of us, and finally escorted Sebastian out.

The run-in shook me up as well as exhausted me and I slept for several hours, until Perry woke me gently in the early afternoon to tell me the police had sent someone to talk with me. He gave me a few minutes to wake up, and then ushered the two police detectives into my room.

One was in his late twenties, tall and well-built, with dark hair cut in a military style buzz, and sharp brown eyes. The other was older, in his mid-forties maybe, short and fit, with thinning brown hair and a reddish mustache that he pulled at often. As they took places at the end of my bed, Perry hesitated at the door. "Want me to stay?" he asked quietly.

I gave each detective a brief glance, and then shook my head slightly. "No, I'll be fine. Thanks, though. Why don't you get out of here for a while? Go grab a burger or something. You've been here for hours."

After another moment of hesitation, he nodded. "Back in a bit, then."

"Bring me some fries!" I called to his retreating back, and smiled when I heard his laughter as the door closed behind him. Using my non-splinted hand for leverage, I carefully shifted myself further up on the bed and then gave the two detectives my attention. "Perry said you wanted to talk with me?" I prompted.

"Yes, ma'am. I'm Detective Fischer," the shorter one said, "and this is my partner, Detective Linden. We're with the Monroe County Sheriff's office." His voice held a hint of the South and reminded me of Liz, which in turn made me wonder how she was taking this whole thing. I was grateful to Robyn for calling her, and made a note to try to call her myself when the detectives left.

I realized the two men were watching me expectantly, and brought my mind back into focus. "Sorry," I told them with a wry grin. "I was just sleeping. I'm still a little out of it."

They both nodded, and this time the tall one, Detective Linden, spoke. "Not a problem, ma'am. We're sorry to bother you. How are you feeling?"

"Like some crazy man beat the crap out of me with a stick," I said dryly, drawing a slight grin from Linden and the barest flicker of what might have been sympathy from Fischer.

"Can you tell us what happened?" he asked and pulled a small notebook from his pocket. "We have a good idea, but we'd like to hear it in your words."

I carefully reached out for the cup of water on the table by my side and took a few sips, gathering my still slightly jumbled thoughts. As my mind had gotten clearer over the last several hours, I'd remembered the attack, and the wild-eyed man who did it, but this would be the first time I'd put it in words.

"I was down on the beach. I'd just gone for a run, and was cooling down. I started back to the house, I saw this man—I'd seen him before, on my run. He was on the beach, one house over. He had a walking stick, and was limping, looked like he was having trouble getting over the dune, there, between the houses. I thought I could help him, and wondered what he was doing, what he wanted..." I paused for another sip of water and to clear my throat as the memory of his face came vividly to mind. I took a breath. "I said hi, and asked him if I could help him...he said yes, and started swinging with that damn stick." I shook my head and fought down a wave of nausea, closing my eyes until it passed. I blinked them open again. "Took me completely by surprise, knocked me down, kicked me a few times...I tried to get up and he grabbed me and punched me...then I got hit in the head, and that's pretty much all I remember until I woke up here."

"Did he give you any indication why he attacked you?" Detective Fischer asked.

I nodded slowly, choosing my words carefully. "I was staying with a friend for the weekend. Robyn Ward. Just before I was knocked out, he said, 'I saw you with her'...how he said it, his face...he meant her, I think. He was angry with me for spending time with Robyn."

Both men nodded, as though I'd confirmed something, and Linden pulled a small envelope from his jacket. "We'd like for you to look at some pictures for us, and tell us if you see the man who attacked you?"

I nodded, and he opened the envelope and pulled out four mug shots, lining them up neatly on the table beside me. Familiar, pale, wild-looking eyes looked back at me from the third picture, and I sucked in a sharp breath. Seeing him made everything much more real. I pointed at it with a shaky finger. "Him. That's the guy. Who is he?"

Linden hesitated, shooting a look at Fischer, who nodded at him. "His name is Todd Massey." He glanced at me, his expression asking if the name meant anything. I shook my head slightly, and he picked up the pictures and slid them back in the envelope. "We picked him up in a public restroom on Long Key after we had a call about suspicious behavior...thought he was just some tourist off his meds, but as soon as he started talking, we knew he was the guy."

"He confessed?"

"Yes ma'am, and then some. Guy won't shut up now, he's being pretty vocal, ranting about what he did to you, seems proud of it even. Turns out he's got a history of stalking...nothing violent in those, although NYPD was looking at him in an assault case, but couldn't make anything stick. Even though he wasn't good for the assault, it sounds like it was just a matter of time until this guy cracked. Three restraining orders against him in the last five years for harassing his subjects. He's a photographer for *World Weekly*, based out of New York. Paper says he was sent down here to get shots of Lonnie Colchev, but if the stacks of photos found in his hotel room are anything to go by, our guy seems to have developed a fixation with your friend, Miss Ward. Looks like he's been following her for a few weeks, developing some kind of fantasy that they're together...keeps saying he was protecting Miss Ward from you, which matches with what you told us he said during the attack."

From the carefully neutral looks I was getting from both detectives, I was betting Todd Massey had been saying quite a few other things about me and Miss Ward. And he was a photographer.

Damn it.

I closed my eyes wearily. I really wanted to talk to Robyn about this, but I wasn't going to lie if they asked me — they'd been honest with me and I owed them the same. I waited for the expected questions, but they didn't come. Instead I heard a rustle of clothing and opened my eyes to see both men had put away their notebooks.

"Sorry to have kept you so long, Miss Harris. We'll let you get back to your rest. Thank you for your time. If you need to get in touch with us for any reason, here's my card." Detective Fisher laid a card on the table, and stepped back. "We'll let you know if we have more questions." He hesitated a moment, and tugged at his mustache. "Miss Harris. I want to assure you that we're aware of the...delicacy of this situation, and all the information gathered in the course of the investigation will be handled with discretion."

I blinked slowly. *So they definitely know. And they're going to try and be discreet about it.* I wasn't very optimistic about this kind of thing staying discreet, but I appreciated the gesture. "Thank you," I said faintly, unable to think of anything else to say.

He nodded and the two moved to the door, where the shorter man paused and looked back at me. "Hope you start feeling better soon."

HE STRUGGLED SLOWLY *over the rise between the houses, laboring in the deep sand and leaning on his walking stick, limping painfully...suddenly his intense, pale eyes were just inches away, and I could feel hot breath on my face. "You touched her..."*

I jerked awake, my eyes wide, fear still coursing through me even as the apparition from my dream faded, and reality—helped along by the throbbing in my head and the knot of pain in my back—took its place.

Hospital. Florida. Safe.

I blinked several times and took a deep, shaky breath, willing the last, foggy remnants of the dream away and consciously relaxing muscles that were rigid with tension. As the pain slowly subsided, I let out a slow sigh of relief and reached for the cup of water on the table next to my bed, taking a few small swallows to wet my parched throat.

I heard movement across the room and the cup jerked slightly in my hand, sloshing water over the edges and onto the table. My eyes darted to the source of the noise, expecting to see Perry, but instead I found Robyn staring at me, her dark eyes filled with more naked emotion than I'd ever seen, taking my breath away. She looked pale and exhausted, and her eyes were dark and haunted. Seeing her brought an ache to my chest and for a minute, I just stared.

"Hi, baby," I said softly, smiling as much as I could. "You look like hell."

She let out a muffled sound that was part laugh, part sob, and closed her eyes, sending a trickle of tears sliding down her face. When she opened her eyes again, they told me everything I needed to know. She might not be able to say it, but she loved me, I was sure of it.

We stared at each other for a long time, until finally she whispered, "I thought you were dead. You weren't moving, and there was so much blood..." She shook her head and looked down at her hands.

"I'm sorry," I said after a moment of quiet. "I'm sorry you were the one to find me, to see me like that..."

She shook her head vehemently. "I'm not. The police think it was the sound of my car pulling up that scared him off...if I hadn't realized what a shit I'd been and come back to apologize...he could have killed you. He would have." She stood and paced the room. "Fuck. If I hadn't have been such a shit in the first place, maybe this would have never happened."

She stopped pacing, her back to me, and said softly, "God, Caid, I'm so sorry. This is my fault...I should have been there...it should have been me."

"Robyn." She slowly turned to look at me. "Come here." She didn't move. "Please," I added softly. Slowly she crossed the room to stand next to the bed. I held out my non-splinted hand for her and she took it hesitantly. The feel of her hand in mine was better than any drug, and I sighed and rubbed the back of her hand lightly with my thumb. She was looking at me as though she didn't quite believe I was real, and I tugged on her hand, pulling her forward a little more. I caught her gaze and carefully laid her hand on my chest in a spot that wasn't bruised. "I'm okay, baby," I told her, and covered her hand with mine. "See? Alive and well, just a little banged up."

She didn't move for several moments, just stood looking at our hands together. Finally, some of the tension went out of her body and she sniffed and wiped at her face with her free hand. Her eyes ran over my face and down to my splinted arm. "Just a little?" she said skeptically, the corners of her mouth turning up into a slight smile.

Relieved that she could joke and that the haunted look was gone from her eyes, I did my best to smile back. "Yep, just a little. Doc says I'll be good as new in no time."

She opened her mouth to say something, and then closed it.

"What?" I asked curiously.

She shook her head and gently extracted her hand from beneath mine and raised it to trail her fingers lightly along my left cheek, the tenderness in her gaze nearly making me cry. "I was going to say I'm glad, which I am." She found my hand with her free hand and squeezed, looking at me intently. "But that seems so...trivial, compared to what I really feel." She took a deep breath and leaned forward, carefully brushing her lips across mine in a feather soft kiss. "I love you, Caid. So damn much..."

The words ran like electricity through my body, and I took a shuddering breath, blowing it out slowly. I stared at her, knowing my eyes were filling with tears. My first reaction was to pull her down and kiss her until neither of us could breathe, but in deference to my somewhat incapacitated state, I slowly reached up and ran my fingertips across her cheek. "I love you, too, sweetheart," I whispered, and threaded my fingers into her hair, pulling her down into another gentle brush of lips.

For a minute I forgot my injuries and tightened my grip on her hair, increasing the pressure of the kiss, and lifting my other hand to cup her cheek — and a stab of agony from my wrist brought my movements to a halt with a hiss.

"Ow. Damn." I froze, and so did Robyn, which is how the nurse found us when she walked in a moment later.

"Oh, hello, Miss Ward. I didn't realize you were in here." She breezed in with nothing more than a curious glance in our direction.

I expected Robyn to pull away quickly, to make excuses, to explain away what the nurse had seen, but instead she barely flinched and stayed where she was, hovering above me with our lips nearly touching. "Are you okay?" she asked softly, her eyes full of concern. "Did I hurt you?"

I swallowed convulsively at the intimate feel of her breath across my lips, and shook my head wordlessly. She nodded and slowly straightened, flicking a glance at the nurse. "Hi, Gail."

Gail smiled at her and picked up my chart, transferring her attention to me. "Just coming to check in. How are you doing?"

"Um, good, I think."

"And how's the head? Any nausea, dizziness, light-headedness?"

"Head hurts, but none of that, no."

"Great, great. Anything I can get you?" I shook my head. "No? Okay, then, just let me know if you need anything. You really should be resting now." She glanced at her watch, and then looked pointedly at Robyn. "Miss Ward..."

Robyn held up a hand and flashed a winning smile at the woman. "I'll let her rest, I promise."

Gail hesitated, looking between Robyn and me briefly. "Okay, then," she said with a nod. She flashed a smile at Robyn and told her, "Nice to see you back, Miss Ward," before pushing out of the room.

I smiled slightly when she'd left. "You've made yourself quite a fan club. Of course, that doesn't surprise me — I'm rather fond of you myself."

Robyn toyed with the thin blanket on my bed, staring down at it. "The staff here—especially the nurses—they've been great to me, letting me sit with you when it was against the rules, keeping me in the loop about what was happening. Gail even let me stay after your brother laid down the family-only policy, but when he saw me in your room..."

"Sorry about Sebastian," I said with a wince. "He can be...trying."

She chuckled and stroked my hand. "That's very diplomatic of you." Her face turned concerned and she looked up at me. "I heard you two went at it this morning. Are you okay? Sounds like it was quite the argument."

I shifted on the bed. "Let's just say no one can push my buttons quite like Sebastian. He's my brother, so on some level, I love him, but mostly I just want to kick his teeth in."

She raised a surprised eyebrow at that, and then looked down at our hands, picking mine up and bringing it to her lips before placing it carefully back on the bed and meeting my gaze. "I also hear that he was blaming me for this." She stepped back from the bed and wandered over to the window. "And, really, he's right. If you hadn't known me, if I hadn't left..." She paused, looking out the window, and shook her head. "I'm sorry, Caid. I'm so, so sorry."

"Sorry for what?" I asked with a frown. "For inviting me to spend the weekend with you? For loving me?"

She turned quickly and her eyes flew to mine. "No! God, no! Loving you...it's not something I was looking for, but I'll never, never be sorry for that. It's the only thing I've done right in this whole mess."

I smiled slightly, trying to lighten her sudden melancholic mood. "I hardly consider it a mess, and I can think of a few other things you've done right."

I was rewarded with a tiny smile before her face saddened. "I just feel like this is my fault somehow."

Well, that line of thinking definitely had to go. We had enough problems without her dragging a truckload of unnecessary guilt around for God knows how long. "Damn it, Robyn, that's bullshit and you know it. Did you attack me? Club me with a walking stick? Kick me? Punch me?"

She visibly flinched.

"Did you?" I pushed.

She shook her head. "No," she said in a voice that was barely a whisper, "but..."

"No!" She blinked at the vehemence of my voice. "No buts.

This is no one's fault but the man who did it. He did this. Not you. Do you understand me?"

After several long moments, she finally nodded.

I released a slow breath, suddenly very tired. "Good. Now get over here and kiss me."

A small smile played on her lips as she moved to the bed and looked down at me. "So demanding," she murmured, and leaned in to brush brief kisses across my forehead, cheek, and finally my lips.

I closed my eyes and sighed. "God, I love you."

When I opened my eyes, she was smiling that smile — the one that made it hard for me to breathe. "I love you too, baby. I'm sorry it took me so long to say."

"And now you've told me twice in ten minutes..." I reached for her hand. "I feel like I've won the lottery or something."

She laughed quietly and raised my hand to her lips. "I love you, Caidence Harris."

I closed my eyes and relaxed back into the pillow with a smile. "Oh, my," I murmured. "Three times in ten minutes. Look, Ma, I'm a millionaire."

She chuckled. "I don't know about that..." She paused, and I felt her lips touch my forehead again. "But I know of one who's available if you want her," she whispered.

I opened one eye. "A millionaire, huh?"

She shrugged nonchalantly. "Not as big a deal as it used to be, but yeah."

I opened the other eye and regarded her thoughtfully. "She hot?"

She blinked and let out a surprised bark of laughter. "Depends on who you ask."

"Uh-huh." I pulled her forward against the bed and released her hand so I could rest mine on her hip and brush my thumb lightly against the warm skin just above the waistband of her jeans. "Depends on who you ask?" I repeated skeptically. "Just who are you asking? Dead people and live people?"

She laughed again and I closed my eyes with a happy sigh, loving the sound of her laughter and the contented warmth it caused. She brushed a hand through my hair soothingly, and I relaxed under the caress.

I jerked awake a little later, not knowing if it was seconds that had passed or minutes, but the warmth of Robyn's skin was still under my fingers and I stroked absently, opening my eyes to find her looking down at me pensively.

"So," she asked hesitantly. "Do you want her?"

It took me a second to realize what she was talking about. When I did, I smiled slightly. "The hot millionaire?"

She smiled, but her eyes were worried, and I could tell she was unsure of my answer. She actually thought I would say no? Crazy woman.

I squeezed her waist. "Yes, I definitely want her. More than I've ever wanted anything in my life."

"She'll be very happy to hear that," she told me with a wide smile, and leaned down to kiss me lightly on the lips. "Now close your eyes and go to sleep."

"M'kay." I let my eyes flutter shut. "Love you."

"I love you too, Caid."

I smiled and snuggled into the pillow.

"CAID, BABY. WAKE up." Soft lips pressed against my forehead. "Let me see those gorgeous eyes."

The low, husky words were whispered in my ear, drawing me from sleep and bringing an involuntary smile to my face. I did as I was asked and opened my eyes, rewarded for my efforts by a soft smile and dark eyes hovering inches from mine.

"Ah, there they are. Good morning." She kissed my forehead again. "I need to head to the set, but I wanted to tell you I was leaving. Are you really awake? You're not going to go all *Fatal Attraction* on me because you didn't remember I said goodbye, are you?"

I blinked sleepily at her, my smile widening as I remembered what she had told me...she loved me. Robyn Ward loved me.

Hot damn.

I yawned carefully and lifted my hand to stroke her hand. "I'm awake. Your rabbit is safe." I looked around the room. "What time is it?"

"It's four thirty."

I furrowed my brow. "You stayed all night? Did you get any sleep?"

"Some," she said with a shrug, but I doubted it. She looked tired and drawn, but her eyes were shining happily as they looked down on me. "I wanted to be here when you woke up. I'm sorry I have to go. I'd rather stay with you, but I'm walking on thin ice with Lynne as it is."

I gingerly shifted my body on the bed, twisting until I was facing her. "Rob, you know I understand. I'm just sorry if all this has screwed things up for you..."

"Shhh." She reached out and let two fingers hover just above my lips. "No sorrys, okay?" I nodded and she leaned in for a brief kiss before pulling back. "Everything's fine, I just don't want to push any more than I have to. Can I come back tonight?"

I glared at her. "If you promise not to ask stupid questions like that one."

"*Ohhh.*" She smiled. "Kinda feisty at four thirty in the morning, aren'tcha?"

I did my best to waggle my eyebrows, despite the pain it caused. "Stick with me, baby, and you'll find out just how feisty I can be at four thirty in the morning."

She suppressed a chuckle and a dark, elegant eyebrow inched up her forehead. "Is that so?"

"Uh-huh."

"Well, I certainly need to stick around for that. Guess you're stuck with me for a while."

"Lucky me." I smiled up at her.

"Lucky *me.*" She grinned down at me. Our eyes locked, and both of our smiles faded as electricity sparked between us, along with something deeper. "I love you," she said softly.

"I love you, too."

She closed her eyes and took a deep breath at the words, smiling radiantly. "I wonder if I'll ever get used to it."

"To what?" I brushed my fingers across her cheek, and she opened her eyes. "To hearing someone loves you?"

"No, baby..." She leaned down to brush her lips across my cheek. "To actually believing it."

Chapter
Twenty

"EROTO—WHAT?" LIZ gave me a blank look and the normally smooth, flawless skin of her forehead furrowed in perplexity.

"Erotomanic Delusional Disorder," I repeated. "With..." I scrunched my face up, trying to remember what Detective Fischer had said. "Uh, attached Narcissistic Linking Fantasies."

She blinked. "Uh-huh. And is there an English translation for that? Something us simple folk can understand?"

We were sharing a carafe of coffee on the small back patio of the guest cottage on Liz's estate, talking and enjoying the cool morning air as had become our habit over the past few weeks since I'd been released from Mid-Key Medical Center. Liz had insisted I use her cottage as a place to rest and recuperate out of the public eye, and I had taken her up on her offer with very little argument. Since then, these early morning coffee sessions had become something of a ritual. Every two or three days Liz would show up at the cottage door after my morning walk—running was still too painful—and her morning swim, carafe in hand, and we'd talk for an hour or so until the coffee was gone. This morning when Liz knocked on my door, I'd just gotten off the phone with Detective Fischer.

I smiled slightly and took a sip of coffee. "Mm-hmm. Basically what it means is that Todd Massey thought he had some kind of relationship or friendship with Robyn, and the stories about Josh dumping her for me...apparently it was insulting to Robyn, and since he thought he had this relationship with her, it insulted him, too. Which really 'angered' him," I continued, trying to keep the bitterness out of my tone. Some unstable guy reads a bunch of completely untrue tabloid crap, and I end up beat to a pulp. I shook my head, getting my mind back to my conversation with Liz. "So anyway, that anger had been building up for weeks, and when he saw her with me—the supposed reason Josh had dumped her—he just...snapped."

She blew on her cup idly and nodded, her eyes flicking from my face to my splinted wrist. I had done a lot of healing since leaving the hospital—my face had returned to its normal size and shape, the welts from the cuts on my face had gone down and lost the angry, swollen red of a new injury, the large metal-and-bandage splint on my wrist had been downsized to an easily removable light-weight vinyl-and-canvas splint, and most of the bruising had faded to a faint, slightly jaundiced yellow—but evidence of Todd Massey's "snap" was still very visible.

"And they're just going to ship him off to some loony bin? No trial for what he did?" She wrapped both hands around the mug, tapping gently with one long, blood-red nail.

"It's not official yet, but that's what it sounds like, since they doubt he's fit to go to trial. And he's continued to be violent in custody, attacking two cell mates before they transferred him to a mental health facility that deals with that kind of thing." I delivered the information as dispassionately as possible, suppressing the churn of emotions that talking about Todd Massey and the attack brought on.

"And how do you feel about that?" Liz said carefully, watching me with concern.

I was quiet for a moment, then let out an explosive sigh and rolled the tension out of my shoulders. "Oh, hell, Liz, I don't know. On one hand, I guess I'm mad, because it seems like he's getting away with it, you know? But the detectives and the DA think that with the violence of the assault and his behavior since the arrest, it will be a long, long time before anyone has to worry about him walking the streets—longer, they think, than what he might get if he actually went to trial."

"Maybe that is better, then."

I shrugged. "Maybe. Yes, it probably is. And when I look at it realistically, I guess I'm...relieved. I wasn't looking forward to living through it again, and the media attention a trial would have brought." I shuddered for emphasis. "I'm finally starting to be a nonentity again with the press—I'd like to keep it that way for a while."

I had thought the amount of attention I garnered for "dating" Josh Riley had been intense, but I'd learned that being attacked by a clinically insane erotomanic delusional with narcissistic linking fantasies ranked much higher on the scale of newsworthy things a celebrity could do to get attention. And add the extra titillation factor that the object of the attacker's fantasies and obsession was Robyn Ward, whose boyfriend I had recently stolen, and who I had been spending the weekend with when I was attacked...the fervor had been insane, and the speculation, mind-boggling. Rumors of a lesbian affair between Robyn and me had surfaced, but seemed to stem from previous rumors fueled by the season finale kiss, not by any new information. With nothing new to keep them alive, they never gained a good foothold, and although they never disappeared altogether, there was far less speculation in that area than I had expected. I was glad to be proven wrong about the Monroe County Sheriff's Office's capacity for discretion.

"Yes, things do seem to be calming down," Liz mused. "Paula said you two swung by your house yesterday when you were out, and it was relatively press-free."

I nodded. "Nary a photog in sight. My hydrangeas are decimated, and the front landscaping is a mess, but it was a beautifully empty mess."

"And the rest of the trip?" she asked casually, although her eyes searched my face intently for my reaction. "Everything go all right?"

The attack had taken its toll psychologically as well as physically, and since getting out of the hospital, I'd been battling nightmares, bouts of insomnia, and a hair-trigger startle reflex that made even using the toaster in the morning an adventure. I'd also been very anxious at the though of being in crowds and having people around me that I didn't know, and yesterday's trip with Paula was only the second time in twenty-three days that I'd left the fenced confines of Liz's estate. I knew Liz was concerned by my reclusiveness, but she hadn't pushed, and for that I was grateful. Last week, I'd finally forced myself to leave the property, accompanying Risa on a brief trip to the grocery store, and yesterday, I'd tagged along with Paula as she ran some errands for Liz at a crowded shopping center, just trying to get accustomed to being surrounded by strangers again.

"Everything went fine. Better than fine, really. I'm still a little on edge, but it wasn't as bad as I expected, once I got over the initial weirdness of having people in my space. I'm actually thinking that I should move my ass home and stop hiding out here, especially now that my house is press-free. I've taken advantage of your generosity for long enough. I was thinking of going back early next week."

Liz paused in mid-sip and lowered her cup, reaching out with one hand to touch my arm. "Caid, you're not taking advantage of anything. You know you're welcome to stay as long as you want." She pulled her hand away and returned it to her cup. "I've enjoyed having you around, actually." She smiled. "The only other person who stays in this cottage is Mama, and you're much easier to deal with."

"Liz, I've met your mama. Being easier to deal with than her isn't much of a feat."

She gave me a mock frown. "Are you bad-mouthing my mama?"

I laughed. "No, ma'am. I'd never do that." We shared a smile and I reached out and tapped her cup gently with mine. "And I've enjoyed being here, Liz. Thank you again. I think I would have gone a little crazy if I'd have been at home."

"Caid, you've already thanked me a hundred times..."

"So now it's a hundred and one." We were quiet for a moment. "Speaking of Mama Stokley," I asked curiously, "how'd she take the news?"

Two weeks ago, in an announcement that had surprised pretty much everyone, Liz and Danny not only went public with their relationship, but also announced their engagement. The resulting media flurry had done just as much, if not more, than my seclusion to get stories of my attack out of the limelight, and despite Liz assurances to the contrary, I still wasn't convinced that the timing wasn't deliberate.

Liz laughed. "Oh, she's a little concerned that he's Italian, and Catholic, and that I'm rushing into things, but she's already talking to caterers and florists and bugging us to set a date."

"Well, it was kind of quick," I said absently, remembering my own surprise at the news, even though I knew Liz and Danny were together. Liz looked annoyed at my comment and I hastily amended, "I'm not saying it's good or bad, Liz. I'm just saying things happened very quickly, and you surprised a lot of people."

"God, if I had a dollar for every time someone's told me we're rushing..." She shook her head and looked out over the lawn, and then back at me. "I've been with a lot of men, Caid. A lot," she said matter-of-factly. "I knew right away it was different with Danny, and he knew it too, and we figured, why wait? Because other people think we should?"

I held up a hand in apology. "I'm sorry, I didn't mean to sound like I think you're making a mistake—I don't. I've seen you two together, and I think it's good, Liz. Really good."

She contemplated my apology while she poured herself more coffee. Finding it satisfactory, she moved on to other topics. "So, when is Robyn getting back?"

Robyn's filming had taken her to New York for soundstage work the day before my release from the hospital. We talked daily, but she hadn't been able to make it back even for a quick visit, and I missed her intensely. To say I was looking forward to her return to LA would be something of an understatement—I'd been thinking of little else for the past several days.

"She's not positive yet, but sometime this weekend if everything stays on schedule." I nodded my thanks as she filled my mug.

"Bet you're looking forward to that, hmm?" she asked.

"You could say that," I said dryly.

"Uh-huh." She laughed. "Well, I don't know what y'all's plans are when she gets in," she raised her eyebrows suggestively, "but please make sure she knows she's welcome here any time—I've told Risa to expect her."

I blushed, but managed a smiled at her thoughtfulness. "Thanks, Liz."

She laughed again, and patted my hand. "Of course, sugar."

Liz left a little while later, and I passed the morning with a light free-weight workout and nearly an hour and a half of careful stretching, followed by lunch, some business-related phone calls, and another walk. It was late afternoon before I grabbed a book and settled into a large overstuffed armchair in the cottage's living room, tucking myself in sideways with one leg draped over a padded arm and the other stretched out along the floor to ease the pressure on my still-tender back. I'd become completely engrossed in the story when the shrill jangle of a phone sounded, tearing through the silence of the house and scaring the crap out of me.

"Shit!" The initial jerk of surprise sent the book flying across the room and brought a lance of pain from my lower back. After taking a few calming breaths, the pain eased and I carefully lifted my leg from where it was draped over the arm of the chair and pushed slowly to my feet. I straightened with a wince and crossed to the table where the phone sat in the foyer, picking up the book on my way.

"Yes?" I answered curtly, trying and failing to hide my annoyance both at the pain the intrusion had brought and the interruption to my lazy afternoon.

"Hi." Liz's melodic voice came over the line. "Sorry to interrupt your busy day, sugar, but your girlfriend's here, and I'm going to assume she's here to see you and not me."

"My wha...?" I blinked.

"Your girlfriend. Robyn. Remember her? Tall, dark, and broody? The one you haven't seen in three weeks? I just told Risa to let her in...so I hope you've showered today, and please tell me you're not wearing those atrocious holey sweat-pant things I saw you in earlier today. If you are, you have about three minutes to change into something that doesn't make you look like a reject from the cast of *Rent*."

"Robyn's here?" I repeated dumbly and looked down at my clothes, even though I knew that, yes, indeed, I was wearing those holey sweat-pant things—once-black, bleach-spattered cotton sweats, raggedly cut off at mid-thigh—along with a faded T-shirt with the neck and arms ripped out.

Lovely.

"You are wearing those things, aren't you?" I could hear the amusement in her tone, and scowled. "And I was wrong about the three minutes; the woman must be in one hell of a hurry, 'cause I can see her car already. I give you about thirty seconds. Maybe you've got time to brush that rat's nest you call a hairdo?"

"Liz, you're a shit."

She laughed. "Tick-tock, sugar. Twenty-nine seconds, twenty-eight, twenty-seven—" The countdown continued until I hung up with a shake of my head and a slight smile.

I thought about trying to change quickly but dismissed the idea, since my body wasn't able to do anything quickly at the moment. I used the hall mirror to try and put my hair into some kind of order, and then opened the front door and leaned against the frame with my arms crossed, watching the green SUV roll past the main house and start down the narrow gravel lane to the guest cottage.

She pulled up twenty feet from the door and turned off the ignition, pausing for a moment to stare at me before slowly climbing out of the car and walking up the short path to the door, a grin building on her face that I knew was mirrored in my own. A moment later I was engulfed in her arms, surrounded by her scent and drowning in the feel of her body against mine.

"Hi," she whispered into my hair.

"Mmm, hi." I melted into her with a groan of pleasure. "You're early."

One of her hands went to the base of my neck and kneaded gently. "There was some screw-up with the scheduling of one of the studios, and we're not going to be able to get in until Saturday. Lynne gave everyone a couple of days. I have to fly back Friday night, but I wanted to see you."

"I'm so glad you're here." I kissed the side of her neck and snuggled in closer. "God, I missed you."

"I missed you, too," she said in a husky whisper, and tightened her arms around me. It caused a twinge from my back, but I didn't care. I could have stood right there, in her arms, for days.

And we did stand that way for several minutes, gently rocking back and forth, just soaking each other in. My good hand crept under the hem of her soft cotton tank top and splayed across the heated skin of her back, pulling her closer. She let out a sigh and buried her face in my neck.

At the sound of footsteps on gravel, we finally pulled apart, but to my surprise and pleasure, Robyn didn't pull back very far, keeping one arm draped over my shoulder as we turned to face Liz, who was walking up the drive with a smirky grin on her face.

"Looks like your early arrival was well received," Liz called to Robyn as she approached.

"Looks like." Robyn glanced over at me with a smile and I wrapped an arm around her waist and squeezed.

When Robyn looked back at Liz, the two shared a grin, and I sensed some kind of collusion.

"You knew she was coming?" I asked Liz curiously as she walked up.

"She called this morning when you were on one of your little hikes. It was my idea to surprise you. You would have been a basket-case all day if you'd have known."

She was right, of course, and right now I was too damn happy to make a fuss.

Liz stopped in front of us and slipped her hands into the pockets of her long shorts. "Danny's coming over for dinner in a little bit...I was coming by to invite you to join us."

I felt Robyn stiffen slightly, and she looked at me and then at Liz. "I...uh, actually brought some dinner for us. I thought..."

I looked at her in surprise. "You did?"

"Mm-hmm. Indian."

"I love Indian," I told her and smiled.

She grinned back. "I thought you might."

We kept smiling at each other, and probably would have continued to do so indefinitely, if Liz hadn't pulled her hands from her pockets and clapped happily. "Great! We'll be over as soon as Danny shows up. Do you have any wine, or should we bring some?"

I knew Liz well, and recognized the playful glint in her eye, but Robyn had obviously not been exposed to Liz's more...mischievous side. The look on her face was priceless. I bit my lip to keep from laughing, but Liz had no such compunction, and let out a delighted peal of laughter.

"Liz, you're a shit," I told her good-naturedly, and gave Robyn's waist a squeeze. "Don't worry, Rob, she's joking. She abhors Indian food, and I'm sure she and Danny have something much more interesting planned than dinner in with us."

Robyn looked between the two of us in consternation.

"Caid's right, Robyn, I was just joshin'," Liz said when her laughter had died down. She wiped the moisture from the corner of her eyes delicately, then favored Robyn with a friendly smile. "I wouldn't dream of horning in on y'all's reunion. Actually, Danny's taking me to Matteo's, and then we're going to see what kind of trouble we can get into."

"Watch out, LA," I murmured, and Liz laughed.

Robyn regained her equilibrium and smiled along with us. "Congratulations, by the way, Liz. On the engagement. Danny's a good guy."

Liz smile softened. "I think so, too. Thanks." She glanced over at me, and back at Robyn, smiling slyly. "Congratulations to you, too."

I glanced furtively at Robyn, wondering how she'd react to our relationship being compared to Liz and Danny's engagement. All I could do was grin stupidly when Robyn gave me an adoring look, kissed me on the cheek, and then flashed a dazzling smile at Liz. "Thank you."

She kissed me again, this time on the temple, letting her lips linger and breathing in with a gentle huff of air, as though she were inhaling me. I closed my eyes and wrapped my other arm awkwardly around her waist as tightly as I could.

"I think that's my cue to leave," Liz said with a chuckle, and my eyes popped open guiltily.

"Sorry."

"Oh, don't be." She waved my apology away. "Welcome back, Robyn. You two have fun tonight." As she walked away, she called over her shoulder, "Don't do anything I wouldn't do."

I let her walk a few more steps, and then said in a loud stage whisper, "Don't worry, honey, that covers just about everything."

Liz's laughter floated back to us, and she waved without turning around. I smiled and watched her for another few yards before turning back to Robyn.

"She's a lot...different off the set, isn't she?" Robyn asked, still watching Liz's progress thoughtfully. "I always kind of wondered why you two were such good friends — you seem so different — but now I guess I can see why."

I glanced affectionately at Liz's retreating figure, and then back at Robyn. "Yeah, she just doesn't let many people see it."

She turned and draped both arms over my shoulders. "I look forward to getting to know her better, then," she told me, and kissed me briefly on the nose. As she pulled back, she paused and looked at my face with concerned eyes. She brought a hand to my cheek and slowly traced just below the two scars with gentle fingers. "Do these still hurt?"

I turned my head and kissed her hand. "A little tender still, but not too bad. I have to rub this scar-be-gone goop into them every day, and that hurts like hell, but most of the time they don't bother me."

"They're kinda sexy, now that the stitches are out," she told me, tracing the lines again and quirking a grin. "Especially in this outfit. Very tough."

I gave her a dubious look.

"I'm serious." She leaned in and kissed the scars lightly. "*Muy caleinte*. And the rest of you? How's your back today?" She paused, and stepped back from me quickly. "Ah, shit, I nearly crushed you when I hugged you...that had to hurt. Damn, I'm sorry, Caid, I wasn't thinking."

I stepped close again and put my arms around her waist, pulling our bodies back together. "It didn't hurt much, and it was well worth it. Honest," I assured her when she looked unconvinced. "Now, what was this I heard about dinner?"

"Ah," she said, tentatively returning her arms to my shoulders and running a hand through my hair. "Dinner is in the car. And a few movies to choose from, if you want..."

"You brought movies, too?"

"Yeah." She looked almost shy. "I thought a night in with you, dinner and a movie, sounded...nice."

"It sounds better than nice." I smiled and let my hand drift under her shirt again, scratching gently across her back. "It sounds perfect."

She sucked in a breath and blinked rapidly, then dropped another kiss on my nose and stepped out of my arms. "Good," she said briskly, "the stuff's in the car. I brought some beer, too. Indian is always better with beer—I never could find a wine that went with it. Are you still on pain meds? You shouldn't drink if you are. I didn't know what kind of movies you liked, so I got a mix...some action, some drama, and a foreign flick..."

I shook my head, bemused by what I realized was nervousness. I watched her walk to the car and fumble around with a few bags and a six-pack of beer. "Need any help?"

"No, thanks." She straightened quickly and hit her head on the inside of the car door. "Shit."

I walked to the car and wordlessly took the beer from her. She gave me a sheepish look and immediately used the newly freed hand to rub her head. "Ow. Damn, that hurt."

"Poor baby." I stepped in close. "Let me see." She stopped rubbing and with a slight pout, bent her head. I inspected the spot for a moment, and stood on my tiptoes to kiss it. "There. All better."

"Thank you." She smiled, the nervousness of before gone.

I stepped back and tilted my head, gesturing toward the cottage. "Come on, Ward, I'm starving."

The cottage was a modified loft, with the large living room, kitchen, two bedrooms and bath on the lower level, and the master bedroom and bath on the upper level overlooking the living room. Robyn glanced around curiously, pausing in the foyer while I continued on to the kitchen.

"This is the guest cottage?" she asked with a laugh. "She must like her guests a hell of a lot."

I smiled as I put the beer in the fridge and walked back to join her. "She said, way back when, that it used to be a barn, but I think that's a load of crap." Robyn was still gazing around in appreciation, and I took the bag of food from her unresisting hand and went back into the kitchen.

"Well, whatever it was way back when, it's damn nice now."

"Uh-huh. Why do you think I agreed to stay here? This place is way nicer than my house." I started unpacking different containers of food and placing them on the counter.

"I like your house. It's cute."

I glanced over to see she'd finished her perusal and was leaning in the entryway of the kitchen, watching me. "I like it too," I said, and turned back to the food. "Although I think I'm going to look for something else soon. My neighbors are ready to lynch me." I popped one of the containers open, breathing in the exotic spices. "God, Rob, this smells great. Where'd you...*ohhh*..." My voice trailed off into a tiny gasp as Robyn came up behind me, her body as close as she could get without actually touching me, and kissed the exposed skin at the base of my neck.

"God, I missed you," she murmured, the heat of her breath washing over my skin. She moved her lips to my shoulder, and then trailed them up under my ear. "How you smell." She brushed her nose against my ear, then sucked lightly at the skin of my neck. "How you taste..."

The slam of arousal took me by surprise, and I closed my eyes, gripping the edge of the counter tightly with my good hand and laying the other palm down on the counter.

Jesus.

She laid her hands on the counter on either side of mine. I could feel the hardness of her nipples brush against my upper back, and feel how she moved slightly from side to side, her breath quickening as she rubbed against me.

"God, Caid." Her voice was ragged in my ear. "I can't believe how much I want you right now."

I groaned, and she kissed my neck again, and nipped gently. I let my head fall to the side, giving her better access, and she took advantage of it immediately, sucking and kissing all along the exposed skin, up under my jaw, and back to my ear where she traced the inner curve with her tongue.

Through it all, she kept the steady rhythm of her breasts across my back, some strokes firmer than others, but always the same, steady rhythm. The array of sensations was overwhelming and I could barely breathe. My whole body was trembling, and I reached to steady myself, gripping the counter tightly with my splinted hand and yelping in surprise as pain shot from my wrist up my arm, bringing tears to my eyes.

"Fuck," I hissed, and pulled my arm to my chest, cradling it. "Fucking fuck fuck fuck..."

Robyn jerked away from me as though she'd been slapped, taking a few quick steps away before hesitantly coming back to my side and hovering worriedly. "Oh, shit. Oh, God, Caid, I'm sorry!"

"S'all right," I said through gritted teeth, breathing slowly through my nose until the pain faded to a dull ache.

"No, it's not," she said angrily, and ran a trembling hand through her hair. "Jesus, you just got out of the hospital, you're hurt, and all I can think about is getting you into bed..."

I smiled slightly. She might think that was a bad thing, but I was inordinately pleased by her zeal to get me horizontal. It meant that, despite all I'd been through, and the possible permanent changes to my appearance, she still wanted me. I didn't even realize I had been worried about the alternative until her actions allayed my fears.

Still cradling my arm, I turned and leaned against the counter. "Rob, it's okay."

She took a step back from me and shook her head, staring at the floor.

"Honey." I took the steps to close the distance between us and cupped her cheek with my good hand. "Baby, look at me." After a moment she lifted her head and met my gaze, her dark eyes full of apology. I stroked her cheek. "Robyn, you didn't do anything wrong. I'm relieved, actually, that you still want me, after everything that's happened." She started to protest and I moved my fingers to gently cover her mouth. "Let me finish." When she settled down, I continued. "I love you, and I want you as much as you want me. I've missed you so much, missed your touch and the closeness we had that weekend... I want that back, and I hope you do, too."

I moved my fingers back to her cheek so she could answer, and she turned her head to kiss them before speaking. "More than anything," she said softly.

"Good." I smiled leaned in for a quick kiss. "We just need to be a little careful for a while, that's all. But please don't pull away from me. Please."

She nodded slowly. "Okay."

I slid my hand down her arm until I held her hand in mine and squeezed. "Okay. How about we eat, watch a movie, and see what happens?"

She smiled slowly. "I can live with that."

WHAT HAPPENED AFTER dinner was that I fell asleep.

Drowsy from two beers, settled comfortably on the couch in the vee of Robyn's legs and leaning back against her, I fell asleep to the soothing rhythm of her breath on my cheek, the solid warmth of her at my back, and the feel of her fingers running gently through my hair.

When my eyes fluttered open, the DVD logo was bouncing slowly around the television screen, reminding me of a lazy game of Pong, and sending flickering patterns of light across our sprawled bodies. I lifted my head and turned slightly to see if Robyn was asleep, too, and found her watching me with a tender smile.

"Hey." She kissed the side of my head gently.

"Hey." I let my head fall back onto her chest, and lifted a hand to rub the sleep from my eyes. "Sorry. I'm being one hell of a date, aren't I? How long has it been finished?"

I felt her shrug. "A while. I'm not complaining. It feels great, just holding you like this."

I grinned and tilted my head up to kissed the underside of her chin. "Robyn Ward, you're a sweetheart."

She chuckled and began to rub gentle circles on my stomach. "I've been called a lot of things, Caid, and sweetheart was never one of them."

"Times are changing," I said firmly, and laid another sloppy kiss on her neck before snuggling back into her body.

"That they are," she said softly and gave me a gentle squeeze. "We should probably get you to bed, hmm? Are you upstairs, or down here somewhere?" My body stilled, and the gentle circles on my stomach stopped. "Caid?"

"Will you stay?" I asked quietly, trying to keep from sounding too hopeful.

She resumed her caress. "I'd like to, but only if you want."

"Oh, I definitely want." I shifted my body around carefully and looked her in the eye. "Remember that thing you said in Florida about always wanting me in your bed? That works both ways, honey."

I emphasized my point with a hard, fast kiss. Her eyes widened in surprise and I patted her cheek lightly with my splinted hand before sitting up and cautiously pushing myself off the couch. Once I'd straightened gingerly, I reached out my non-splinted hand to where Robyn was still sprawled on the couch, watching me with ill-veiled concern. When she didn't move, I wiggled my fingers at her. "Come on, woman. Time's a wastin'."

One dark eyebrow rose at that, and I couldn't help but grin. "Have I ever told you how much I adore your eyebrows?"

The other eyebrow went up to join its sibling. "I don't believe so, no."

"Well, I do. They are truly wondrous things."

She smiled and took the offered hand, rising smoothly from the couch without any extra help from me. "*You* are a truly wondrous thing." She leaned in for a quick kiss. "Odd, but wondrous."

I smiled, taking it as the compliment it was meant to be. I tugged her toward the wide stairs, turning off the television and DVD player as we walked past. Robyn followed obediently for a few steps, and then stopped.

"I've got a bag in the car." She looked slightly embarrassed. "I brought it just...hoping, I guess. I've got some stuff to sleep in..."

"You won't need it."

That stopped her for a moment, and she looked at me uncertainly. "Caid, I know we talked about this earlier, but I don't know..."

"Robyn, please. Stop thinking so much and just come with me." I tugged on her hand. After a slight hesitation she followed, and I led her up the stairs that ended in a spacious bedroom with soft, thick carpeting and a huge, low-lying bed.

At the top of the stairs I paused and fumbled a little at a row of switches, surprised when I hit the one I wanted—the one that turned on only the four wall sconces positioned around the room—on the second try. I took a few steps toward the bed, pulling Robyn with me, and then turned back to her and raised her hand to my lips. She watched with hooded eyes as I released her hand and ran light fingers across her abdomen, feeling the ripple of reaction in the muscles beneath, and stopped at the hem of her shirt. "I want to undress you," I said softly, and held up my splinted arm, "but I think I might need some help."

She took a small step back, her eyes not leaving mine, and her hands went to the fastenings of her shorts. She undid the button and zipper and pushed the shorts, along with her underwear, down her long legs, kicking them to the side when they hit the floor. In one quick motion she pulled her shirt over her head and dropped it on top of the shorts, and her bra quickly followed.

My eyes followed the final garment's progress to the floor, and then slowly traveled back up the tan, smoothly muscled length of her legs, pausing briefly at the neatly trimmed thatch of dark hair at the juncture of her thighs, and continuing upwards, over the long, flat expanse of her belly, small, firm breasts tipped with dusky brown, and up her long, elegant neck. She met my gaze with no sign of embarrassment or discomfort, her posture self-assured, and almost arrogant, and she had every right to be.

"You're amazing," I whispered reverently, stepping forward to run my hand up her side, across her breasts, and down across her stomach, stopping with my hand just above her navel. "So beautiful..." I ducked my head and tasted the skin of her chest with my tongue, slowly moving lower until I captured a pebbled nipple in my mouth and sucked gently.

Robyn let out a growl of pleasure and her hands went to the back of my head, pulling me closer as I sucked hard on her nipple, and then dragging my mouth away and dropping her hands to the hem of my shirt. "Now you. Arms up," she rasped, and I compliantly lifted my arms to let her pull my shirt over my head. She tossed it to the side and eyed my front-closure bra with a professional eye, making quick work of it, and kissing the top of each breast as the scrap of material dropped carelessly to the floor. She slowly knelt and dropped a chain of kisses across my stomach, untying the drawstring of my shorts and letting gravity do the rest. Then she sat back on her heels and just looked. I stood quietly as she had done, trying for the same confidence and finding that the way she looked at me made it easy.

Love, desire, tenderness—all of it and more shone in the dark depths of her eyes. I smiled gently down at her and touched her cheek. "Come here, you."

She slowly climbed to her feet. "I'm scared of hurting you, Caid," she told me softly. "I don't want to hurt you."

"You won't, baby." I smiled. "We'll figure something out."

And we did.

We lay face to face on the bed, sharing long, soft kisses and gentle touches, hands gliding over warm skin, reacquainting ourselves with each other.

"I've missed this, so much," Robyn murmured, skimming her palm from my thigh up over my belly to cup my breast, squeezing gently.

"Mmm." I sighed deeply and mirrored her movements, brushing a thumb across her nipple and leaning in to initiate another long kiss.

The pace was slow and gentle, with no rush or urgency, and when our fingers finally found each other, the release was unexpectedly intense. We clung to each other, my face buried in her hair and hers pressed against my neck.

"God, Robyn..." I choked out in a half sob, half laugh, overwhelmed by emotion and how much she made me feel.

She pulled back and stroked my cheek with an unsteady hand, gazing at me in wonder. "How did I not know it could be like this?"

"Oh, baby..." I kissed her softly and pressed my face into her shoulder, unable to find any other words.

She carefully rolled onto her back and wrapped her arms around me, and after I maneuvered my splinted wrist to a more comfortable spot between us, I settled my head onto her chest and snaked my other arm around her waist, pulling us closer together.

She kissed my head, her fingers making lazy patterns on my back. "I love you, baby."

I turned my head a little and kissed her chest. "I love you too, sweetheart."

ROBYN SPENT THE entire two days of her break with me.

I kept expecting her to tell me that she needed to go home, or she had things to do, but she stayed, and we fell into a routine of sorts. A short walk in the morning, reading the newspaper over long, drawn-out breakfasts, another longer walk off Liz's property in the afternoon, a quiet dinner and a movie or television in the evening, and gentle love-making before falling asleep in each other's arms.

It was idyllic. As close to perfect as I'd ever managed to get, and I knew with overwhelming certainty that this was what I wanted. I'd never thought in terms of forever before, actually scoffing at the idea of one person making me happy for the rest of my life, but for the first time, I could imagine it. I'd found someone who could make forever possible, and when she was ready, that's exactly what I would ask for.

Chapter
Twenty-One

"WELL." CONNIE BLINKED her light-brown eyes once, very slowly, her face expressionless. She pulled off thin, gold-framed reading glasses and tapped one earpiece against her lower lip, regarding me speculatively. Sinking back in her chair, she dropped the glasses to hang from an intricate gold chain looped around her neck and steepled her fingers. "Well, well, well."

I smiled slightly and took a sip of the espresso her assistant had brought in a few minutes before, watching her reaction carefully while acting like I wasn't—like the possible repercussions from what I'd just shared with her didn't worry me one bit.

"You've certainly had an eventful summer, haven't you?" She swung her chair slightly to one side and stared at the wall for several moments. The question sounded rhetorical, so I didn't answer, taking another sip of espresso and waiting. She swung the chair back and pinned me with sharp eyes. "You know," she tapped the tips of her steepled fingers together, "four months ago, you were by far my easiest client. Steady gig, liked your privacy, stayed out of the public eye, rarely needed anything..."

I grimaced apologetically. "Yeah, Con, I'm sorry to be such a pain all the sudden."

She waved an imperious hand. "Oh, goodness, Caid, don't be sorry. This is what I do, and I quite like what I do. I also quite like you, which I can't say about many of my clients, but I'll tell you, it makes what I do even more fun for me." She smiled, and some of the tension that was knotting my shoulders drained away. "So." She leaned forward and rested her elbows on her desk. "How do you want to handle this? I'm assuming that's why you told me. And thank you, by the way. For telling me."

I nodded and let the corners of my mouth turn up in a tiny grin. "I know how much you hate it when people know more than you do."

"Damn right I do," she said huffily, and we both smiled.

I set my cup down on the corner of her desk and sat back,

crossing my legs. "That's one of the reasons I told you—Robyn is about done with shooting on *Lost Key* and due back in LA soon, and I don't really know how things are going to play out, but I'm planning on spending as much time with her as possible. I wanted you to be prepared in case this whole thing leaks somehow. I wanted to have some kind of...game plan, I suppose you'd call it."

She nodded. "And the other reasons?"

"I guess..." I shrugged helplessly. "I guess I'm looking for some advice."

Pencil-thin eyebrows crept up her forehead. "About your...love life?"

I laughed softly. "No. About how to keep my love life *mine*."

"Ah. Okay, then." She leaned back again and cocked her head to the side. "Let me ask you first, is this something you want to go public with?"

"God, no," I said with an emphatic shake of my head. "At least, not like going on *20/20* and coming out to Barbara Walters kind of public—certainly not right now, anyway." I suppressed a shudder at the thought of the media attention that would draw. "I don't want to outright lie about it, but I also don't want to make a public statement. Gah!" I ran a frustrated hand through my hair. "It pisses me off that I even need to worry about this. This isn't news, it's my damn life!" I said angrily, and she raised an eyebrow at my vehemence. I calmed, and gave her a wry smile. "Sorry."

She waved the apology away. I sat for a moment, then leaned forward, resting my elbows on my knees. "Connie, this relationship is extremely important to me. There are already enough...complications," I said carefully, "without bringing the public into it. If things don't work out, I want it to be because Robyn and I just couldn't make it work, not because of media interference or public opinion. I want to be able to work on this without the world looking on, and I want you to tell me how I can get the space to make that possible."

She searched my face for a moment, nodding slowly. "Okay." She picked up a pen and tapped the desk. "This is how I see it, Caid. You've got two things that need addressing. One," she waved the pen at me, "you're gay." She gave me another sharp look and added, "Or at the very least, bisexual, and although you don't want to lie about it, you also don't want it to be public knowledge at this time."

She waited for me to confirm her statement with a nod before continuing. "Now, if that was all we were dealing with, that's not nearly as hard as people think, especially now that you've been off the front pages lately. Ron Chandler, Tara Sun, Rena Kohlakis, Owen Lucio...all gay celebrities who have managed to be 'out' in their lives, without outing themselves to the entire world. A combination of keeping a publicly low profile and being discreet is usually all it takes, and I know you are very capable of both."

I nodded again. It was common knowledge in the industry that the people she listed were gay, but the press never mentioned it.

"What complicates things somewhat," she continued with a wry smile, "is issue number two: the fact that you have decided to embrace your newly found lesbianism by becoming romantically involved with an extremely visible public figure who, last I heard, was publicly involved in a relationship with another extremely visible public figure." She tapped the pen against her chin, frowning, and said carefully, "Mmm. What exactly is her involvement with Josh Riley, Caid?"

I smiled slightly, amused by her sudden delicacy. "You mean is Robyn cheating on Josh, and am I the 'Other Woman'?"

"Well." She squinted her right eye, the only sign that my question had flustered her. "Mmm, yes."

I let out a chuckle. "Robyn and Josh are not romantically involved, and Josh is very aware of our relationship."

She sighed in relief. "I figured as much about those two, but I wanted to make sure."

"You figured..." I blinked. "You did?"

"Sure." She shrugged slightly. "I've been on the coordinating end of enough merks to spot one when I see one, although it's tricky with those two since they obviously like each other— sometimes it's so damn obvious that the people involved can't stand each other, it's pathetic."

"Um." I frowned, stopping her rambling. "Uh, merks?"

"Merkins," she clarified at my baffled look, giving me the same fondly indulgent look that Liz did when I showed my utter lack of entertainment business savvy. "As in, a woman dating a man to cover up her sexual orientation. If the man is gay, it's called a beard."

"You're joking." I stared at her. "There's a *name* for that?"

"Of course there is. We have a name for everything. And that kind of thing is fairly common practice."

Well, I knew that. I'm not completely clueless. I just would never have guessed they'd have a *name* for it. I reached for my cup and sipped absently. And what in the hell was a merkin, anyway? Did someone just pull that name out of their ass? Sounded like some kind of termite exterminator.

"...this front with Josh Riley something that Robyn plans to continue? Because that might throw a little hitch in your plans for privacy..."

"Huh?" I said, jerked from my pondering of merkins.

She tapped her pen on the desk. "I was asking if those two planned on continuing their front. Because, really, Caid, since she's the one in the public eye, it's going to be her actions more than yours that dictate the amount of privacy you'll be able to have. To lead a private life, you need to be a private person, which means keeping away from clubs, premieres, parties, and events with lots of paparazzi and reporters. If she can pull herself out of the public eye, and manage to do it without creating too many waves, then you might be able to get that space you want." She put the pen down and steepled her fingers again. "But if she continues her public involvement with Riley, that will continue to make her a top commodity to the press, which amounts to more scrutiny, and would certainly make any kind of privacy hard to manage."

"I..." I chewed the inside of my lip, embarrassed that I didn't know the answer to that question. "I don't know," I said finally, and sighed. "I don't think they will, but we haven't really talked about it."

A tiny tic in her left cheek was the only outward reaction to my admission. "And would you be okay with it, if they did continue?" she asked bluntly.

"I..." I stopped and shook my head. "No. I wouldn't."

"I didn't think so." She put her pen down softly, staring at it for a moment before looking up at me. "So," she said after a slight pause, "what you need to find out is what Robyn is willing to do, and then ask yourself what you can live with."

I held her gaze for a moment, and then looked out the window behind her. "Yeah," I said quietly. "I guess that's the question, isn't it?"

THE SUN HUNG low over the ocean to our left and a sluggish breeze had begun to blow in off the water, cooling the sweat on my skin and countering the oven-like effect of the sand on either side of the path that radiated swirls of hot, dry air up at us. The steady slap of my feet on the asphalt was soothing, and I took a deep breath and held it through several strides, feeling a smile of satisfaction form on my face.

It felt good to run.

I'd only been out a few times since the attack, each time able to go further, and today I was pleased that the slight ache in my back that had accompanied my last two attempts had yet to develop, even coming into our second mile.

I glanced over at my running companion, noting with a twinge of jealousy his easy, athletic stride and barely increased breathing. With chrome bug-eye sunglasses, a white backwards baseball cap, white tank, and long navy shorts, he looked barely twenty, and if his shirt hadn't revealed a few dark spots of perspiration, I'd almost have thought he wasn't even sweating.

Show-off.

Josh's bid for the Wimbledon title had been cut short by a stomach virus that had hit him late in the second round of play, leaving him dehydrated and fighting cramps, nausea and fatigue. He'd struggled through the third round and eked out a win but his weakened state finally caught up with him in the fourth round against a spry young Australian, and he'd lost badly in straight sets. We'd spoken a couple of times since his return to LA the week before, always talking about getting together, but today was the first time we could manage it. Josh had suggested dinner, but I'd wanted to get outdoors after the first day of shooting for the new season of *9P*, so we'd compromised with a run along the Parkway, which we planned to follow up later with take-out at his house in the hill section of Manhattan Beach.

I signaled it was time to turn around, and we turned a tight circle and headed back to the parking lot and Twila. "I know you can kick my ass, Josh." I zigzagged around a pair of walkers along the busy path. "You don't have to wait up for me. When you asked me to go for a run with you, I didn't actually expect to be running *with* you."

He grinned at me and shook his head as we dodged more pedestrians. "This is good, Caid. I'm still feeling some after-effects from whatever bug I picked up, and I don't want to push it just yet, especially in this heat." His gave me an appraising look. "How are you holding up? Back okay?"

I nodded. "Feels great. I think the heat is good for it, actually."

"Good. Robyn said she'd whomp my ass if I let you over-do it today."

"You talked to her today?" I asked curiously as we detoured through the sand to get around a large family strolling along the path.

"Yeah, she wanted to let me know she'd be back Thursday." He glanced at me. "You knew that already, right?"

I nodded and couldn't stop my wide grin. "Yep."

Josh caught the smile and laughed, shaking his head. "God, you two..." He made a snapping motion with his hand. "Whipped, whipped, whipped."

"Eh, *shaddup.*" I backhanded him lightly on the arm, but my smile didn't fade. "You're just jealous," I said jokingly.

"Damn right I am," he replied seriously, and smiled wryly at my surprised look. "I know I said all that stuff about focus and not letting myself get distracted by being involved with someone." He paused when a nearly naked man on inline skates shot past. "...that doesn't mean I don't want to be," he finished, shaking his head at the tiny Speedo, and pelt-like back, skating away from us.

"I'm sorry...whoa!" I yelped as a biker with long blond dreads and no shirt flew by, close enough that I felt the brush of handlebars against my arm. I jerked and swerved a little in reaction, and Josh held out a steadying hand, gripping my elbow lightly until I settled back into stride. I glanced down at his hand on my arm and then back up at him, and flashed a wide smile of thanks. As recently as a couple of weeks ago, my reaction to the biker would have been far more severe, and I probably would have flinched and pulled away from anyone taking my arm unexpectedly. I didn't know if it was Robyn's visit, moving back into my own home, or just the result of time, but lately the jumpiness seemed to be calming down, and my nights were nightmare free. I was slowly but surely taking back control of my life, and the relief was tremendous.

Josh was watching me with a curious expression, and I cast back for what we'd been discussing before Mr. Dreads had flown by. "Uh. Oh. When we talked about it before—about you not wanting to get involved—I guess I just thought you weren't...into that kind of thing." I waved my hand. "Dating, a relationship, or whatever."

"Oh," he laughed, "I'm into it. Too much so, which is why I get so distracted. I tend to forget about most everything else..." He trailed off with an embarrassed look.

"That doesn't sound like a bad thing, Josh." I smiled warmly at him. "Lucky girl, I'd say."

"We'll see. Thanks to you," he poked me in the arm, "it looks like I'm going to be diving back in to the dating pool again soon. Robyn told me she is no longer available to be my escort around town."

I blinked and almost stopped running. "She did?"

"She did." He confirmed. "She said it felt all wrong to even think about it."

"She did?' I repeated, a slow smile spreading across my face.

"Of course she did," he said, rolling his eyes at me. "Did you really think she'd keep doing things with me when she's crazy about you?"

"Well," I hedged, feeling guilty now about my insecurities and that I'd actually thought it was a possibility. "I'd hoped not, but we didn't talk about it..."

"Did you ask her?"

"Um, no." I looked over sheepishly. "Neither of us is what you'd call communicative. We talk a lot, sure, but not about us. I don't want to push her..." I paused as I realized the strangeness of what I was doing — talking about my relationship issues with my lover's ex-boyfriend. The weirdest thing was that it felt completely comfortable. And probably no one knew Robyn better than Josh. With an internal shrug, I continued, "I'm afraid that if I do, she'll pull away. I don't want to lose her because I asked a question she wasn't ready to answer."

He shook his head as we detoured through the sand again, this time around a woman walking a pack of poodles. They yapped noisily at us as we went by. "I don't think you need to worry about losing her, Caid. She seems all-in as far as your relationship goes. But it's obvious that you have some unresolved concerns...you really need to talk to her about them. I know she's not big on emotional discussions, but if you ask straight out, she won't put you off. "

All-in? Unresolved concerns? "What are you, a poker-playing shrink?" I asked with a slight smile.

He grinned. "Just call me Dr. Josh."

I laughed, then unstrapped the small water bottle I was carrying on the belt around my waist and took a few gulps. "So." I offered him the bottle and, when he declined, strapped it back in before continuing. "I shouldn't worry about Robyn backing off if I bring up these unresolved concerns of mine. Is that about right?"

"Uh-huh." He used his shirt to wipe at the perspiration on his forehead, and the resulting glimpse of well-defined abs sent a group of teenage girls in bikinis tittering as we ran past. I couldn't blame them, really. The guy was awfully well put together. "Caid," he said after flashing a smile at the girls and causing hearts to pitter-patter, "Robyn loves you. The fact that she's admitted that to me, and to you, is huge. I don't think you could get rid of her now if you tried. If you need to know something, just ask."

"You make it sound easy," I grumbled good-naturedly.

"I know." He grinned. "Isn't it annoying?"

"Extremely." I snorted, but I was smiling, both at his humor and what he'd told me about Robyn.

The parking lot came into view and I eyed the distance speculatively. I grinned at Josh, and slapped him in the stomach. Hard. "Race ya!" I yelled as I took off down the path, happy enough to believe I might even win.

Chapter
Twenty-Two

"SETTLE, PEOPLE," NATE said crisply, and a hush fell over the crew gathered in the makeshift alley the production designer and art crew had created between two out-buildings on the complex's back lot. "We're rolling..."

For a few seconds, only the faint sound of steady, drizzling rain falling in the surrounding puddles could be heard. I closed my eyes, trying to relax and ignore my surroundings. Ignore the cold drizzle soaking my skin and hair, and the moisture from the wet pavement beneath me seeping into my clothes. Suppressing a shiver, I cursed whatever stupid childhood dream had made me want to go into acting.

Please, please, please let this be the last take.

It had been six weeks since the assault, five weeks since I got out of the hospital, ten days since I'd moved from Liz's cottage back into my house, and three days since the start of shooting for the new season of *9P*. My body had healed well, and I hadn't had any problems with the physical aspects of my job or schedule, but my adventure in Florida was still causing problems because of the caps, blending, and covering necessary to hide the slowly healing damage to my face. The complicated application took an extra hour and a half each morning, forcing Jules and me to be on set by five AM. The additional time needed for touchups during shooting was throwing everyone off schedule, and triggering all sorts of trauma within the cast and crew. When enough people complained, Grant talked to Dorn, Dorn talked to his writers, and the next day, the season opener was rewritten to create a reason for my character to have scars.

The opener spanned two hours, one of those "to-be-continued" episodes people bitched about, but that drew great ratings. The script brought all seven main characters into an investigation of a series of execution-style murders that seemed to be linked to the Mexican Mob, *La Eme*. The original script called for the final scene of the first hour to be an assault by an unknown assailant on a witness in an attempt to keep her from testifying. The writers switched the assault victim from the witness to my character Rita, and added a few bordering-on-sappy hospital scenes to the start of the second hour, where Liz would get to act distraught, the guys would get to act stoic yet caring, and everyone would get to act confused when Robyn's character, Judith, showed up at the hospital to visit Rita.

The new scenes had been scheduled during the second week of filming, but Nate, in his infinite director's wisdom, had decided that this unseasonably cold and wet night would be the perfect backdrop for the mood he wanted to set for the scene. And that was why, at nearly midnight after a full day of shooting, I was sprawled in a soggy heap in a dark, dirty "alley." I was cold, wet, and thoroughly annoyed that my plans for the night with Robyn, who I hadn't seen in two weeks and who was finally coming home tonight after delays on the *Lost Key* shoot, had to be cancelled.

"Scene eleven-C, take five...mark!" someone called, and her words were followed by the distinct snap of a clapboard.

"Ready," Nate spoke again, "...and, action!"

I forced myself to stay limp as rough hands gripped the front of my shirt, lifting me slightly off the ground and hot, cigarette-tinged breath blew across my face. "Drop the case, bitch." The words were harsh and grating, underlined by another shake that I suffered bonelessly. "Forget you ever heard of the name Julian Hernandez."

My eyes fluttered open briefly, enough to see the cruel sneer and the dark, pockmarked face above me. The day-player who'd gotten the part of my attacker — David something or other — really was quite...intimidating, and I experienced again, as I had in the takes before, a moment of unease when I opened my eyes and found his face so close to mine. I fought the accompanying urge to strike out in defense, reminding myself that Todd Massey was safely locked away in the Intensive Psychiatric Service unit of Laurel Beach Psychiatric Center in Tampa, and the man above me was not a threat. I gritted my teeth and forced out a soft moan, lolling my head to the side and exposing the fake blood on my cheek to the cold rain. The gooey mess immediately began to drip down my neck and into the collar of my shirt, tickling slightly.

"Rita?" a muted voice called, and sharp, quick footsteps echoed nearby.

The man swore unintelligibly and gave me one more shake before dropping me unceremoniously back to the wet pavement. I hid a wince and lay still as the splash and slap of his footsteps receded into the night.

The quick footsteps came nearer, stopping abruptly near my

head. "Rita! Oh, God...Rita..." Warm fingers brushed my forehead and then were gone in a rustle of clothing. A click, several beeps, and the voice came again. "This is Detective Jennifer Hastings, badge number 54162. I have an officer down at..."

Liz's voice rattled off a fictional address and other information while she knelt beside me, and I willed myself not to move as the tickle on my neck from the rivulets of fake gore and rain became harder to ignore. From the hours spent setting up, blocking, and rehearsing this scene, I knew the dolly camera was slowly pulling away, widening the shot, and soon we'd be done, if I could just keep still a bit longer.

A fat drop of water dribbled from my hair onto the side of my face, and I felt it start a slow slide toward my ear. I *hate* getting things in my ears. They're extremely ticklish, and just the thought of that big fat drop trickling into one...

Not my ear, not my ear, not my ear, I chanted silently, keeping myself still with supreme effort. *Goddammit Nate, cut already...*

Just as the drop trickled exactly where I didn't want it to, Nate yelled "Cut!" and lights and movement erupted around me, turning the seemingly deserted area into a hive of activity.

"Gah!" I jerked into a sitting position and shook my head wildly, spraying water and film blood everywhere, frantic to get the water out. I dug into my ear with my pinky and shook my head again, finally clearing my ear with a shiver and a sigh of relief. "God, I hate that..." My voice trailed off when I glanced over to find Liz staring at her red-spattered hands and clothes with appalled dismay.

"Oh. Shit." I bit back a laugh and reached out hesitantly to flick a drippy red chunk of gore from her forehead, and another from her cheek. "Sorry. It was dripping into my ear..."

She scowled and rose swiftly to her feet, wiping her hands on her pants in annoyance. "Ew. Just, ew. Until about thirty seconds ago, I was actually feeling sorry for you." She turned and yelled over to where Nate was huddled under a clear plastic tarp with two other people, watching a replay of what we'd just filmed on the monitors. "Nate! We'd better be finished, 'cause Caid just...exploded all over me."

"And I'm freaking freezing!" I called grumpily as I crawled to my feet, careful to not put too much weight on my newly healed wrist. The orthopedic specialist had given me the green light to take the brace off if I was careful, but it was still fairly weak and prone to aching. Especially, I was finding, in weather like this.

Nate waved a vague hand, not looking up from the monitors. "Get out of the wet for a minute, and let us take a look at these. I think we've got a print, but give me a sec."

I grunted and followed Liz toward the improvised tarp shelter they'd thrown up to cover our chairs, a small table with a few empty trays of crumbs, and an urn of coffee. I slumped into my chair and a barely recognizable crewmember draped in a yellow rain poncho handed me a towel. I took it gratefully, leaning over to rub vigorously at my wet hair, and when I straightened, Liz was perched in the chair beside me. Her eyes cut to me with a frown as she sat patiently while Jules wiped away the last traces of the blood that I'd splattered all over her.

"You really did get soaked." She took in my soggy jeans and the short-sleeved, cotton shirt that was plastered to my body, and so soaked it was nearly transparent. *Figures wardrobe would dress me in a white cotton shirt the night I have to lie out in the cold rain.* I felt like a contestant in a wet T-shirt contest, and had already fielded several sniggered comments about my "points of power" and "twin weapons of mass destruction."

"Yes, I really did get soaked," I agreed, shivering, and wiping at my arms and neck. I avoided my face, although the sticky mixture of wet adhesive and makeup clinging tenaciously to my cheek was driving me crazy.

Jules sighed in aggravation and stepped over to peel off the oozing red acrylic appliance that had previously been attached to my jaw to simulate a wound. She dropped it into a container in her set kit with a wet slap, then peeled the other one off my cheek. I winced when it stuck to the still-tender skin beneath. "Sorry," she muttered as she worked, although she didn't sound or act particularly sorry. She stepped back and nodded at my towel. "You might as well just wipe the rest off—it's ruined now anyway."

As she stalked off, I sighed and carefully began to swab my face, cleaning away the film blood and whatever else Jules had smeared on me. I hoped that in a few weeks, when all this extra effort wasn't necessary, she'd stop being so damn cranky at me all the time. The thought of going through the rest of the season with the makeup specialist pissed-off at me was too depressing to ponder.

"New beau," Liz stated, her voice startling me out of my thoughts.

"Pardon?" I glanced over at her and held the towel away from my face, cocking a questioning eyebrow.

"Jules. Has a new beau. Some musician, apparently." She tilted her head slightly and tapped her cheek, just in front of her ear. I wiped at the offending spot on my own face, and she nodded. "Having to be at the set so early is interfering with her love life. That's why she's being such a bitch to you lately."

I shook my head and stood, dropping the crimson-spattered

towel into my chair. "You mean she's treating me like shit because she's not getting laid?" I was annoyed that I was being blamed for the current disruption to the schedule. It wasn't like I went out and got the scars on purpose—I'd been attacked, for fuck's sake. It was, however, slightly heartening to hear that the cold shoulder might end when the schedules settled, and regular nookie could commence.

"So says Drew, anyway," Liz said, and handed me the coat that had been hanging on the back of my chair. "Here, put this on before you freeze to death."

I nodded my thanks and pulled the jacket on, shuddering at the initial feel of the cold material against my already ice-cold skin. I zipped it up and rubbed my arms a few times, hoping my body heat would soon make wearing the coat warmer than not wearing it. "I guess Drew would know. Hell, if this script change gets things back to normal with everyone, then it'll be well worth lying in a puddle in the rain for three hours. But next time, you get the puddle." A violent shiver shook my body to emphasize the words. "At least you got a coat during takes."

The script had called for the assault to take place in the alley behind a bar that the squad frequented. The assailant nabbed Rita on her way to the bathroom, hence no coat for me. Liz had lucked out in that the writers and wardrobe had deemed Jen smart enough to put on a jacket before searching for her partner, and that had kept Liz fairly dry throughout the drizzly shoot.

"Sorry," she said contritely and handed me a cup of coffee. "I promise, next time, I'll lie in the puddle."

I took the coffee it in both hands, holding it for several seconds to warm my fingers and smiling slightly at the ludicrousness of that statement. Her sentiment might be genuine, but the chances of a script ever being written that called for Liz Stokley to lie in a puddle were slim to none. "I'll remember that," I said, and sipped at my drink, feeling almost warm for the first time in hours.

I nodded to David, the day-player, who came under our tarp for a coffee refill. "Nice job tonight, David."

He seemed startled that I had spoken to him, and his hands jerked, coming precariously close to tipping the coffee urn over. "Uh, thanks." He smiled sheepishly, righting the urn and finished filling his coffee without further incident.

"You look familiar...you had a part last season, didn't you? You worked with Micah and Henry."

We chatted idly for a few minutes, Liz interjecting comments occasionally, until Nate finally decided he had what he needed. He thanked us, and told us we were through for the night, and I heard audible sighs of relief throughout the crew, mine included. Several crewmembers started breaking down the set and light rigging, while Liz, David and I, along with the remaining the crew, headed *en masse* toward the soundstage building's rear entrance, the parking lot, or the trailers — all of which were in the same direction.

The drizzle let up as we walked along the side of the administration building, and we rounded the corner, chattering and joking about crappy timing. As the large crowd broke up into smaller groups bound for different destinations, Liz and I waved and headed for the row of actor's trailers which were set up as a subtle reminder of the *9P* cast pecking order — Liz's was first in the row, and mine was last. I stopped at her trailer to finish the conversation we'd been having, ribbing her gently about being willing to pay five thousand plus dollars for a wedding cake.

"Christ, Liz, I've heard you whine about paying a buck fifty for a muffin..."

I could tell she was gearing up for a good comeback, and looking forward to it, when a wolf-whistle and several calls of greeting from the crew drew our attention to a tall, raincoat-clad form emerging from a green SUV that I hadn't noticed, parked in the lot's front row.

I hadn't recognized the car in the dark, but I certainly recognized its passenger. Even bundled in red Gortex from the waist up, her form was unmistakable, and a pleasant warmth stole through me at the sight of her.

"Isn't that Robyn?" Liz asked curiously. "I thought you had to cancel your plans tonight."

I nodded vaguely at both questions. I had called Robyn and left a message about Nate's rearranging of the shooting schedule, telling her that I would call her in the morning. I hadn't expected to see her until then, and I was touched and pleased that she'd wanted to see me badly enough to brave the rain and the late hour. A grin spread across my face as she splashed through numerous puddles, coming in our direction. She waved casually, and returned the crew's greetings and comments, but didn't pause to talk to any of them.

Soon she was standing in front of me smiling widely, her near-black eyes alight with pleasure. She pushed the hood of her coat back, freeing her hair from the confines of the hood and letting it cascade down her back. "Hey," she grinned, and moved toward me, hesitating when I instinctively flicked a glance at the several crewmembers who were suddenly not in such a hurry to get out of the wet. They watched us avidly, not even trying to conceal their interest.

I glanced back at Robyn nervously, not sure how public she wanted to be, and honestly not certain how public I wanted to be, either. She watched me carefully, as though waiting for some clue, and finally said softly, "I'm dying to touch you, Caid, and right now, I don't really give a damn who's watching. But I'll understand if you're uncomfortable..."

Her words melted my indecision instantly, and I stepped forward to wrap my arms around her before she even finished speaking.

"Whoa," she chuckled as her arms closed around me. "Guess that question is answered."

"Hi," I murmured into her shoulder and her arms tightened briefly. Then, as if by some unspoken accord, we both stepped back. Other, more involved greetings could wait until later. "I didn't expect to see you until morning," I said, unable to stop myself from stroking her arm lightly. "I'm very glad to be wrong."

She smiled and shrugged slightly. "I got your message, but decided I didn't want to wait until tomorrow, when I knew exactly where you were tonight." She hesitated, and then leaned forward and pressed her lips to my cheek, letting the kiss linger far past what could reasonably be construed as a friendly peck. "Hi," she whispered as she pulled back.

I blinked in surprise, both at her boldness, and the sweetness of the gesture. She squeezed my hand and glanced behind me with a friendly smile. "Hi, Liz."

"Hi, Robyn," Liz's amused voice replied. "Good to see you. Finally finished, hmm?"

I turned, embarrassed to have forgotten that Liz was standing there. I met her amused look with an apologetic one.

"Yeah, finally." Robyn put her hands in the pockets of her jacket and rocked back and forth on her heels. "It was a cluster-fuck there at the end, but supposedly things are all done. And perfect timing, too — they're in the middle of a heat wave in New York. When I flew out today, it was ninety-eight degrees and something like ninety percent humidity."

Unthinking, I snaked an arm around Robyn's waist as she talked, and when I realized what I was doing, slowly started to withdraw it. She casually pulled a hand out of her pocket to snag the retreating limb, and put it back on her waist, keeping it there with a gentle pat. "I was ready to get back to something at least a little drier." She laughed and waved at the rain around us. "This is somewhat unexpected."

"No shit," I mumbled, suddenly reminded that despite the warmth of Robyn's presence, under my coat I still wore a soaked cotton shirt and wet jeans. I shivered, and Robyn looked over at me with a frown, seeming for the first time to notice my bedraggled state.

Liz made a shooing motion and pushed us both down the line of trailers. "Go. You've been bitching about being cold for two hours—you don't need to stand out here and get even colder. Robyn, I'm glad you're back, and Caid, I'll see you in the morning."

I groaned, remembering that despite tonight's late shoot, we still had a seven thirty call-time in the morning. That meant that I had to be there at five thirty. "Shit," I muttered, and sighed heavily. We said goodbye to Liz, and trudged down the row of trailers to the last one. I mounted the steps and unlocked the door, pushing it open and letting Robyn enter first. My brain was still grumbling about the early call-time when I was yanked into the trailer, the door slammed behind me, and Robyn's deliciously warm, demanding mouth descended on mine.

After overcoming my initial surprise, I gave as good as I got, even pushed up against the door as I was. Her kisses were, impossible as it seemed, even better than I remembered— scrambling my brain and sending heat surging through me. We fought for dominance of the kiss until eventually I directed us across the room and onto the couch, where we fell, laughing, in an ungraceful heap with Robyn on the bottom.

I straddled her body and propped myself up on my hands, smiling happily down at her. "Hi."

"Hey." She grinned and ran her hands along my thighs, her smile turning to a frown as she rubbed my legs. "Caid, you're soaking wet."

I contemplated an innuendo-laden response, but settled for the facts instead, giving her a quick kiss before sitting up. "I've been lying around in the rain for three hours—of course I'm soaking wet." I unzipped my coat and shrugged it off, tossing it onto a neighboring armchair. "And I'm freezing. I was planning on taking a shower to warm up, but someone distracted me." I smiled to show her I wasn't at all upset by the distraction.

She reached up to finger the collar of my shirt. "Please tell me that's fake."

I looked down at my shirt, realizing that the collar and chest were stained with red, and there were red splatters dotting the rest of it. "Yes, it's fake." I plucked at the collar and sighed. "Shit. Now Zoe's going to be pissed at me, too."

She rested her hands on my thighs, rubbing soothingly. "What scene were you guys shooting tonight, anyway? I thought I had the most recent script, but I don't remember anything that called for you to lie around in the rain, or get bloody."

"They must not have sent you the 'new and improved' script, then. Not too surprising, since I think they only made the changes yesterday, and we got the new sides today. Your scenes with me in the first half won't change, I don't think, but you've got some new ones in the second half." I rubbed the raised skin along my cheek and jaw. "Covering these ended up being a butt-load of trouble, so they changed the script and had someone beat the crap out of Rita, to give her character the same scars. That's what we were shooting tonight—the scene where Rita gets attacked."

Her hands tightened on my thighs. "They wrote an attack on you into the script?" she asked angrily. "Could they be any more insensitive? Christ."

I stopped her outburst with another quick kiss. "It's okay, baby. I told them it was fine. And if it gets things back to normal, I'm more than fine with it." She looked unconvinced. "It wasn't so bad...the damn rain and cold were the worst of it. Which reminds me..." I kissed her again and wiggled off of the couch, unbuttoning my shirt as I stood. "I need to get out of these wet things and take a quick shower." I pulled the tail of the shirt out of my pants to finish unbuttoning it, letting it hang open as I bent down and unlaced my boots. I toed them off and kicked them into a corner, then worked at the buttons of my jeans. I glanced up from my unbuttoning and stopped, held immobile by the naked heat in Robyn's gaze.

"You are a beautiful, beautiful woman, Caid," she said quietly, pushing up off the couch and crossing to where I stood. Warm hands pushed aside the edges of my shirt and rested on my hips, stroking gently. I closed my eyes, enjoying the gentle caresses, and her lips claimed mine in a kiss that managed to be incredibly tender and soft, yet intensely passionate at the same time. She broke the kiss and leaned her forehead against mine, and we both sighed softly. "Missed you."

"I missed you, too, baby." I put my hand on her chest, realizing she still wore her damp jacket. I tugged lightly on the material and stepped back. "Why don't you take this off and get comfortable? I'll just be a few minutes, and then maybe we can grab something to eat. I haven't eaten since lunch."

Robyn took off her jacket and tossed it onto the chair with mine, cocking her head at me with a tiny smile. "You do realize it's midnight, don't you?"

I shrugged. "It's LA. There's always something open...ah, shit!" I smacked my forehead with my hand. "I have a five thirty call time in the morning. Damn it, I keep forgetting."

She crossed her arms and looked genuinely annoyed. "You have to be in at five in the God-damn morning after shooting this late?"

I looked at her apologetically. "I'm sorry, baby."

"No, no." She waved her hand. "I'm not mad at you, Caid, I just..." She slumped onto the couch and gave me a wry grin.

"Damn. I had plans for you."

I quirked an eyebrow. "Did you, now?"

"Mm-hmm." Her eyes perused my half-clothed state. "Definitely. But," she added, leaning back to spread her arms across the back of the couch and crossing one leg over the other, "I'll take a rain check. How about instead, I take you home, feed you, and put you to bed?" She suddenly looked uncertain. "You were planning on spending the night with me, weren't you?"

Her apprehension was misplaced, but kind of cute, and I crossed the room and leaned down to capture her lips in a fast, rough kiss, pulling back a few inches and stroking her cheek. "Yes, I was planning on spending the night with you, and I still am. We just might be getting to the sleeping part sooner than I originally planned."

She grinned lazily and hooked a finger in the waistband of my pants, pulling my mouth back to hers for another quick kiss before pushing me away. "Go, or this couch is going to get some action."

I laughed and stepped back, gesturing at the back room. "There's a perfectly good bed..."

"Caid..." she said warningly.

"All right, all right, I'm going," I said, laughing.

After shutting myself into the small bathroom, I stripped out of my wet clothes and stepped into the shower. I set the water hot enough to make me wince and stood under the blissful heat for a few minutes before starting to scrub at the red streaks on my neck and chest.

"What are you doing tomorrow night?" Robyn's question came from the other side of the shower curtain, startling me so much that I fumbled with the soap and nearly dropped it.

"Uh..."

"You don't mind me coming in here, do you?"

"Uh. No, that's fine." I slowly resumed my washing, very conscious that Robyn was only three feet away.

"So, did you have plans tomorrow night?"

"I didn't have any set plans, no." I dunked my head under the spray and wiped the water out of my eyes. "Although," I added, trying to keep the uncertainty out of my voice, "I had hoped to be doing something with you." *Tomorrow night and every night for the foreseeable future...*

I tried to keep in mind what Josh had said — that I wasn't going to lose her by pushing — and I told myself that wanting to spend the evening with someone you're in love with, who says they're in love with you too, after two weeks of not seeing each other, wasn't too presumptuous.

Christ, Caid, stop analyzing everything and just go with it.

I was so intent on my little internal dialogue that I didn't notice I had company in the shower until soft, warm skin pressed up against my back and long arms wrapped possessively around my waist.

"I hope you don't mind me joining you, but the thought of you in here, naked, was just too inviting to pass up. I'm only human, after all."

Her throaty voice, so close to my ear, sent waves of sensation through my body and I jumped a little, then relaxed back against her, humming at the feel of her skin against mine. I laid my arms across hers and squeezed, letting my head fall back against her shoulder with a smile. "No... I don't mind."

"Mmm. You feel good," she murmured, sucking lightly at the back of my neck, making me shiver. She held her lips there for a moment, then rested her chin on my shoulder. "I have to go to a sort of party tomorrow night...I was hoping you would come with me."

I turned my head slightly. "A sort of party?"

Her hands began to stroke my torso lightly where the spray was hitting, from the top of my hips, to just below my breasts, and down my sides. "Trish and Mom opened the Santa Monica restaurant five years ago this week. Trish is closing for the night and having a little celebration in honor of the occasion. Diane is coming down, and Lori, and Mom and Dad..." She hesitated, and kissed the side of my head. "I'd like you to come with me."

Stuck in a strange but pleasant limbo between arousal and utter contentment, it took a moment for the words to sink in. When they did, I turned slowly in her arms and stared at her. It sounded suspiciously like she had just told me she wanted me to meet her family. The invitation certainly wasn't unwelcome, just surprising.

"Are you sure?" I asked cautiously.

She smiled slightly and ducked her head to press light kisses along my collarbone. "Yes," she mumbled into my skin, moving me forward so the spray wasn't hitting her face. "I'm sure." After one final kiss on my chest, she raised her head and looked at me hopefully. "Will you come?"

I stared for a second longer, and shook myself. "Of course," I told her, and she smiled widely.

"Good." She ducked her head again, this time focusing on my neck, and I shut my eyes and stroked my hands up and down her back, thinking about her invitation. I guess she wasn't actually bringing me home to meet the family, but it was a step in the right direction, both in becoming more involved in her life, and her willingness for me to be involved.

A thought struck me. "You know I'm not Trish's favorite

person, right? I don't want to cause problems..."

She stopped me with a long kiss, and I'd almost forgotten what we were talking about by the time she answered. "Josh told me something like that." She dropped more light kisses along my chin and down my neck. "It'll be fine. Trish is more bark than bite."

"She really doesn't like me, Rob," I protested weakly, and gasped softly when her warm mouth closed over my nipple. I braced one arm against the shower wall and threaded the other through the hair at the base of her neck, increasing the pressure of her mouth on my breast. "God..."

"Caid?" My eyes fluttered open at her muffled voice, and then closed again with a groan as teeth scraped lightly across sensitive flesh. "I don't want to talk about Trish anymore."

Who needs sleep anyway? I thought dimly before her hands and mouth pulled me easily into a maelstrom of sensation.

Chapter
Twenty-Three

ROBYN WALKED TO the large window and stood with her back to me. Her arms were crossed, and her posture wary and defensive. "I don't know what you want from me," she said abruptly. Her charcoal gray suit and nearly black hair were stark against the light coming from behind the glass panes, adding to the bleakness of her tone and appearance.

I admired the effect for a moment before speaking. "*You* kissed *me*, Counselor." I walked up behind her and stood to one side, reaching out a hand to touch her back, hesitating as though I thought better of it, and then stuffing my hands in my pockets. "That should be my question to ask."

She leaned slightly — almost imperceptibly — away from me, crossing her arms even tighter. "I don't recall hearing any objections from you, Detective," she said coolly. "In fact, you seemed quite amenable at the time."

I turned and leaned one shoulder against the wall, careful to not lean too heavily, despite assurances that the flimsy set wall would easily hold me. "I'm not saying I wasn't. And I'm not saying I'm at all unhappy that you kissed me. I'm just saying you started this, and you must have had something in mind when you did. So, Counselor," I lowered my voice, leaning forward into her space a bit, trying to catch her eye. "What is it *you* want from *me*?"

"I..." She looked over at me, confusion and fear plain on her face, and then looked away quickly. "I don't know." Her voice was quiet, almost a whisper.

I nodded slowly, not saying anything for a moment, regarding her thoughtfully. "Lunch," I said finally.

She turned slowly, her arms still crossed, but some of the defensiveness was gone. "Lunch?" she repeated, cocking an eyebrow.

I so love that eyebrow. "Yes, lunch. It's eleven thirty. Have lunch with me, Counselor. Consider it a warm-up...like pre-trial preparation. And if we manage to get through an entire hour without killing each other, perhaps you'd consider going to dinner with me sometime this week."

"I..." She blinked and scratched her arm nervously, then seemed to realize what she was doing and gripped her arm tightly instead. "Um." She cleared her throat and her eyes darted around the set before finally landing on me again. "Yes."

God, she's good, I thought, and just stopped myself from beaming at her in admiration. "Yes to lunch, or yes to dinner?" I asked, allowing a small smile to flicker across my face.

"Lunch, for now." She returned the smile with some of her normal, cocky flair. "Ask me again in an hour, Detective."

"Fair enough." I nodded, letting my smile widen as I pushed off the wall. "And maybe, if you don't feel like it's too much, too soon...you could call me Rita."

She smiled.

"Cut!" Nate yelled from where he was watching the action on the monitors behind the flimsy plywood barrier that acted as one of the walls to Judith Torrington's office. "I like it! Let's get the camera set up over here—I want to shoot a couple from this side of the window. Robyn, Caid, can you take your marks by the window, so we can get the focus and lights?"

We both nodded and turned back to the window, standing casually while the operator pulled the boom mike back and people began scurrying purposefully around the set. Jules's assistant Kylie hurried over, eyed both our faces and hair, found them acceptable, and hurried off again. When she had gone, Robyn glanced over at me with a warm smile and I resisted the urge to put my arm around her waist and pull her into a long, unhurried kiss.

It was strange to think that this morning I'd woken in her bed, our limbs so tangled up in each other's that I could hardly tell which were mine and which were hers, and now I had to be cautious about even the most casual contact. Robyn hadn't seemed to mind the crew seeing us together the night before, but today things seemed to be different. It probably had more to do with professionalism than any concern about sparking gossip among the crew, but I still wasn't completely sure of the rules of public conduct I was supposed to follow. I had a feeling that the kind of contact I was wanting right now was well outside the rules.

I fell into buddy mode, which seemed to be acceptable behavior, and bumped her shoulder lightly with mine. "Nice take."

She smiled slightly. "You, too. The lean-in was a nice touch."

I grinned, pleased she had noticed. "Thanks."

She slipped her hands into her pockets, glancing around casually. "How you holding up?"

I resisted the urge to grin again and glanced around as she had done, lowering my voice although I doubted anyone could hear us over the commotion going on around us. "You mean, considering I only got two hours of sleep last night?"

Not that I was complaining. Despite my tiredness, the late hour, and the distinct lack of space to work with, last night's romp in the trailer's tiny shower stall was definitely the most fun I'd had in a shower in, well, ever. And crawling into her bed to fall asleep in her arms, that hadn't been half-bad either.

Her smile turned self-satisfied. "Mm-hmm."

I couldn't help but laugh, drawing a few curious stares. I waited a moment, until people lost interest. "Proud of ourselves, are we?"

"We are," she said smugly.

I laughed again, quietly. "As well we should be," I murmured.

"Caid," Mariel, the Second AD called, popping from behind the wall, "can you go to the second mark?"

I nodded, then took a step to my right and leaned against the wall, rolling my shoulders a bit.

"Will you be okay tonight?" Robyn asked quietly when again attention was no longer on us. "If you don't want to go..."

"I'll be fine," I reassured her quickly. "And I definitely want to go." I wasn't about to pass up the chance to meet her family.

"Great." The smile she graced me with was one of those she seemed to save just for me, and the urge to touch her became overwhelming. I blinked and looked away for a moment, and when I looked back, she was staring at me intently, apparently reading my look correctly. Her eyes dropped to my mouth. "Lunch in the trailer later?" she said huskily.

I nodded quickly, and drew a calming breath as Mariel came from behind the wall again. "Okay, let's do it. Places, everyone."

I snuck a glance at my watch.

Ten thirty.

It was going to be a long two hours.

IN FACT, IT was four interminable hours before we were allowed to break for lunch, and by then, the "lunch" I'd been looking forward to was reduced to a brief, heated kiss in the trailer before Robyn had to rush back to the *ITD* set for an afternoon table read and cast meetings. The morning delay in shooting caused the afternoon schedule to shift out as well, and as a result, Nate didn't let us go for the weekend until well after seven o'clock.

By the time I drove home, I was exhausted and cranky and pondered calling Robyn to tell her I couldn't make it, but I quickly dismissed the idea. I told myself to buck up, took a cool, rejuvenating shower, and was dressed and out the door, headed for Santa Monica, by eight thirty. Robyn had wanted to go to the restaurant early to have some time with her family, and had long since left for the party. I called her when I knew I was going to be late, and she assured me that I should just show up as soon as I could. As I slipped in and out of traffic along I-10, I hoped that nine o'clock wouldn't be too late.

Main Street, Santa Monica, was crowded at nine o'clock on a Friday night in August, but I managed to find a parking spot along the street, only three or four blocks from the restaurant. I climbed out of Twila and nervously smoothed my clothes, taking one last glance down at the simple halter dress of cranberry material shot through with thin strands of silver, and low-heeled sandals. It was too late to change now, so I hoped I wasn't underdressed and I didn't look as tired as I felt.

Taking a few deep breaths, I skipped across the street, avoiding puddles from the recent rain, and headed for the restaurant, trying to remember all that Robyn had told me about the different members of her family. I needed to make a good impression, or at least get through the night without embarrassing myself or Robyn too much.

A tall, bald man dressed in a well-cut tuxedo and sporting a smile that didn't reach his eyes stopped me just inside the door, politely asking my name, and even asking to see my ID. He checked me off a guest list and asked me to wait a moment while he talked into a small microphone on the cuff of his jacket. He nodded at whatever response he got and waved me on to another tux-clad, muscle-bound man, who quickly checked me over with a metal-detecting wand, asked me to please turn off my cell phone if I had one, and told me that if I'd brought a camera or camera phone, I would have to surrender them for the duration of the party. I assured him that I had neither of those items, and after giving me a slightly suspicious once-over, he mechanically wished me a nice evening.

I shook my head, having been through that kind of security several times in the past at various industry gatherings, but curious as to why they'd need it here. At the top of the wide steps down into the main dining room I paused, running an appreciative eye over the changes made for the party. Swaths of rich colored fabrics hung from the high ceiling and covered the walls, combining with an intricate array of filtered lights to create a rippling effect, as though the cloth were caught by some phantom breeze. Several tables had been removed, and the remaining rearranged to allow for serving stations and a bar along one wall, and a jazz trio played in the corner, intent on their music and oblivious to the noise and crowd nearly drowning them out.

I was startled to see that the place was noisy and packed, with at least a hundred people standing in pairs and small groups, eating, talking, and drinking at what Robyn had called a "sort of party." While I hadn't been expecting her family only, I certainly hadn't been expecting this many people, and I found myself a little annoyed that Robyn hadn't specified. The necessity for the tight security became clear, too, as I scanned the crowd and recognized numerous celebrities. Local politicians, athletes, musicians, authors, and of course, several familiar faces from movies and television, along with many of the area's rich and idle were present, several of them dressed to the nines. I still wouldn't consider myself underdressed, but I was glad I'd decided on a dress, and I made a mental note to remind myself to ask Robyn a few more questions next time we went to a party together. Our ideas of what constituted pertinent information were apparently very different.

I stood scanning the crowd, searching for a glimpse of her, and smiled involuntarily when I spotted her across the room in animated conversation with a couple I didn't recognize. She was dressed in a tight black sheath dress, with her hair gathered atop her head in an artfully messy pile, and looked stunning, as usual. The dress was cut around the neck and arms like the wet suits I'd seen triathletes wear, showing off her well-defined shoulders, the long, graceful sweep of her neck, and plenty of tan, delectable skin. I noticed a hand resting casually on that skin, and followed the hand to where it met an arm that was draped across her shoulder.

Josh. Standing next to her, laughing with her, his arm around her possessively as thought they were together. With my woman.

Whoa there, Tarzan.

I frowned at myself and watched the two of them together, feeling a brief stab of jealousy. *For people who aren't going to be a public couple anymore, they certainly look like one,* I thought irritably, and then squashed my annoyance, thinking that Josh was going to have to rein in his touchy-feely impulses in public, or I was going to have to rein in my Neanderthal-like possessiveness. Probably a little of both was in order.

"Caidence!" a feminine voice exclaimed, just as I was about to go smack Robyn over the head with my club and drag her back to my cave. I paused and turned to find Sophie standing beside me, looking up at me in delighted recognition. She gripped my arms lightly and kissed me on both cheeks, then pulled me into a warm embrace. When she let me go she looked at me fondly, and I smiled back, very glad to see her.

"Sophie, *buenas noches.*" I leaned in and kissed her on both cheeks, as she had done. "It's lovely to see you." I took in her flowing black dress, careful makeup, and elegant chignon. "You look *muy hermosa*, Senora."

She smiled and held my hands in hers, squeezing gently. "Ah, you flatter an old woman, but I will accept your flattery gladly." Her smile dimmed slightly as she caught sight of the still-healing marks on my face. I'd spent several minutes in front of the mirror this evening, contemplating whether I should try to cover them up or not, and decided on not. People were going to look for them regardless—I figured I might as well make them easy to find. Sophie glanced around and pulled me into a less-crowded space away from the stairs, then reached up and touched the scar on my cheek gently. I forced myself not to flinch, standing quietly and letting her trace the line with light fingers. "I am very sorry for your pain, Caidence," she said sincerely, and laid her palm against my cheek.

I smiled gently and pulled her hand from my face, holding it in mine. "Thank you, Sophie. And thank you for the flowers. They were beautiful."

"You are well?" she asked, still staring at me intently.

I nodded and squeezed her hands. "I am very well."

"Good. I was so worried for you. And Sabina..." she shook her head. "She was so terribly upset. I am glad she was there with you."

"Me too," I told her honestly, and squeezed her hands again.

"And speaking of my *hija*, I know she has been anxiously waiting for you. She has told us all to behave and not tell embarrassing stories, so of course we have all thought of some to tell..." She smiled widely and for a split-second it was Robyn smiling at me. I blinked away the vision as Sophie tugged at my hand. "Come, I will help you find her, and then there are people I know she wishes for you to meet."

I let her pull me back toward the steps, smiling bemusedly.

"Miss Harris?" The deep voice and polite inquiry were accompanied by a hand on my arm, and I shied away violently, yanking out of Sophie's grasp and nearly bowling over a tiny woman in a bright yellow dress and precariously high heels who was coming up the steps near me. I steadied her with a hand and got a bleary thanks in response, then took a breath and turned to find another tuxedo-clad member of the security team standing beside me. This one was tall and lean, with less obvious muscle, but no less intimidating, despite the contrite expression on his face.

"I'm sorry, ma'am. I didn't mean to startle you."

I forced a smile and tried to calm my wildly beating heart. "Can I help you?"

He stood carefully with his hands clasped behind his back.

"Miss Ward would like to speak with you for a few moments. Would you mind following me, please?"

"What is this?" Sophie said sharply from behind me.

"It's okay." I eyed the man for a moment, then turned and gave Sophie an encouraging smile. "This will only take a minute."

She frowned and gave the security man a hard look, but to his credit, he seemed impervious to the glare and stood watching me expectantly.

"It's okay," I repeated and squeezed her arm gently before turning back to the man. "Lead on," I told him, and followed after giving Sophie one last smile.

He led me along the edge of the dining room and through a set of swinging doors into the kitchen, past the cooks and wait staff and down a narrow hallway, stopping finally in front of a nondescript door where he motioned me into a small but well-appointed office.

I wasn't surprised to see Trish leaning against the desk, thumbing through a stack of papers and looking casually elegant and feminine in a navy blue pantsuit with a very masculine cut. As she raised her eyes to watch me enter the office, I acknowledged briefly that Trish wore clothes nearly as well as Robyn did, and wondered if she'd spent time as a model as well.

Her expression was carefully neutral as she looked at me for a moment, and then flicked a glance at the man behind me. "Thank you, John."

The man nodded and backed out of the room, leaving the door partially open behind him.

When he was gone, Trish looked back at me and said politely, "Caidence."

"Trish." I acknowledged, matching her even tone. "Congratulations on five years. You and your mother should be very proud. And the place looks amazing."

That seemed to surprise her, and she paused before responding with a slight inclination of her head. "Thank you."

"You're welcome." I crossed my arms over my chest and leaned back against the doorframe, waiting for her to get to the point of this little chat.

"I asked security to let me know when you showed up—I'm supposed to let Robyn know, too, but I wanted a chance to talk to you first." She put the papers down and circled around behind the desk, straightening random things as she went. Finally, she stopped tidying and looked up at me. "It seems I owe you an apology. My mother, my sister, Josh...they all tell me I'm wrong about you."

If that was an apology, it was definitely one of the least

enthusiastic I'd ever received, and I nearly laughed. "Your sincerity is touching," I said dryly and cocked my head. "But why don't you tell me what *you* think? That's really the issue here, isn't it?"

"What I think," she mused, and let her eyes wander over me briefly before meeting my gaze again. "I think *Mamá* is easily swayed by good manners, Josh is a pushover for a pretty face and a pretty smile, and Robyn..." She shrugged. "I haven't quite figured out why she's so taken with you, but then again, she always was a little too trusting."

I held in the burst of anger her words caused, and instead raised a slightly quizzical eyebrow. "Not giving them much credit, are you? Your mother is an intelligent woman and seems quite capable of making the distinction between good manners and good deeds, and far prettier faces than mine have tried to sway Josh, I'm sure, and have not been successful. And Robyn...you don't know your sister very well if you think she trusts easily." I shook my head and *tsked* softly. "It sounds like you don't know any of them very well."

I was cranky and had added that last bit just to piss her off. It worked nicely. She leaned both hands on the desk and dropped the polite act, staring at me with obvious hostility. "I think I know them a hell of a lot better than you do, *Caidence*." She practically spit the name out. "I promised I would be nice to you, so I will be, but if they're wrong, and you end up hurting them..."

This was being nice? I'd hate to see her on a bitchy day. I didn't know exactly what I'd done to earn her suspicion, but I was starting to think it had more to do with the possibility of me stealing her family away from her than me stealing Josh away from Robyn. Whatever the reason for her attitude, it wasn't endearing her to me at all, and my patience was running low.

"Or what?" I threw up my hands in exasperation. "Is this where you warn me to stay away from Josh again? Or, better yet..." Anger I didn't realize I'd been harboring bubbled to the surface and I pushed off the wall and stalked to the desk. I grabbed the handset of the desk's phone and thrust it at her. "Here. Is there someone you need to call with the press? To let them know that I'm here, about to steal Josh away from poor, trusting Robyn?"

Trish was taken aback by my outburst, opening and closing her mouth a few times like a fish, but not saying anything.

The more I thought about it, the angrier I got. I dropped the phone back in the cradle and stepped back from the desk, crossing my arms. "You have no frigging idea the amount of trouble you caused that night, do you? And not just for me, but for Josh, and Robyn, too. Your own damn sister, for God's sake! Did you think about maybe *asking* her if she needed to be protected from me before passing judgment and telling the whole Goddamn world something that was completely untrue? Did you think about her at *all* before you made that call? Think about the crap she'd have to put up with?" My voice had risen steadily and I took a deep breath to calm down before continuing in a quieter, but still intense, voice. "Do you realize," I turned my head slightly and pointed at my face, "that after what you stirred up, this could easily have happened to Robyn, instead of me?"

She visibly paled, and I realized that maybe that had been unfair. She hadn't caused Todd Massey's attack; ultimately no one but Todd Massey was responsible for that. I couldn't bring myself to feel sorry for saying it, though. Her actions had set in motion a chain of events that certainly had contributed to his state of mind on that day, and it could have easily been her sister, and not me, who suffered for it.

"Do you want to tell me what the hell she's talking about, Trish?" Robyn's raspy, deceptively mild voice came from over my shoulder, causing us both to start. She stepped into the office and flashed a smile that nearly melted me on the spot.

"Hi. You look fantastic," she murmured as she put her hand on my back and brushed her lips across my cheek. "*Mamá* said you were here—that some security person had whisked you away." She gave Trish a hard look. "What's going on? I thought I asked you to let me know when she got here."

Trish looked uncomfortable, but stood up to her sister's glare. "I wanted to talk to her first."

"About what? And what exactly was Caid talking about before?" Robyn crossed her arms and raised an eyebrow in question.

"I..."

A thunderous crash from the kitchen, followed by a voice yelling curses in Spanish and an answering voice yelling in English, saved her from having to respond. "Damn it." Trish was by us in the blink of an eye, pushing past me none too gently and striding down the hall, hollering for someone named Julian.

When she was gone, Robyn asked, "What's going on, Caid? What did Trish want? If she's being a shit to you..."

I shook my head. "I think she was trying to apologize, actually, but things got a little off track. It's okay, Rob. It's just going to take a little while for me and your sister to get along." She frowned, and I rubbed her back soothingly. "Don't worry about it, really. Now," she watched as I pushed the door shut with one foot, "do you think I could at least get a hug hello?"

"I think I could do that." She smiled and tugged me forward into her arms, her sister forgotten for the moment. She sighed. "I'm so glad you came," she murmured into my hair as we stood holding each other. She pulled back with a shy smile and grabbed my hand, reaching for the door. "Come on, I'd like to introduce you to a few people. Oh, and Josh is here, too."

"Yes, I saw," I said dryly, with more bite than I'd intended.

So much for reining in my possessiveness.

Her hand slowly dropped from the doorknob and she turned back to me, one delicate eyebrow arched in surprise. "You're angry."

I blew out a breath and shook my head. "No, I'm being an ass. Forget it."

"Caid." She took my other hand in hers and watched me closely. "Something ticked you off. Talk to me, please?"

Way to go, Caid. Now you have to tell her what a jealous twit you are. I sighed resignedly. "Keep in mind that I'm tired, and I'm in kind of a pissy mood, okay?"

"Okay," she said and nodded, frowning slightly.

"When I walked into the party, the first thing I saw was Josh with his arm around you." I squeezed her hands to stop her when she seemed about to interrupt. "I know you're not...dating him anymore, or whatever. I know that, you know that, Josh knows that, but no one else knows that, because the two of you still *act* like you are. Plain and simple?" I shrugged. "I was jealous."

She blinked. "You were jealous? Of *Josh*?"

"Yeah." I pulled my hands from hers and stepped back with another shrug. "I was jealous of Josh. Silly, huh? Well, not of Josh, really," I clarified, "but of what he's able to do that I can't. Like stand around in a crowded party with his arm around you...touch you...*be* with you, and not have to worry about what people might think..." I trailed off and ran a hand through my hair in frustration.

She didn't respond for a moment, then stepped forward and took my hands in hers again, her dark eyes watching me intently. "Is that what you want, Caid?" she asked slowly, stroking her thumbs gently across the backs of my hands. "To be public? About us?"

"I..." I shook my head and let out a frustrated breath, looking down at our hands. This was probably not the time or place to have this conversation, but now that I'd gotten the ball rolling, I'd better just get on with it. After a deep breath, I met her gaze again, hoping what Josh had said about not losing her was true. "To be able to be with you publicly, without concerns...yes, someday I want that. I want that very much. But right now? Right now, we still have some things to work out, and I don't want the attention that kind of declaration would create while we're in the middle of trying to figure out how to be together. Because, in the end, *that's* what is most important to me. To be together, with you." I brought her hands to my chest and covered them with mine. "I hope that's what you want, too, Robyn. If it's not," I shook my head and looked at her searchingly, "then I don't know what we're doing."

Please, please, please be what you want.

"Oh, baby." She freed her hands from my grasp and wrapped her arms around me, pulling me close. "I can't believe you're worried about that," she murmured into my ear, rubbing my back gently before pulling back a little and cupping my cheek with one hand. "Of course, that's what I want." She kissed me softly. "I love you, and I told you before that if you wanted me, you had me. I wasn't talking about a few days. I was talking long-term. As in a life together. I don't want to scare you, baby, but I've got plans for the future, and they all include you. Every last one."

I blinked. "You don't want to scare me," I repeated slowly, and almost laughed. She didn't want to scare me, I didn't want to scare her...we should have done this talking thing a long damn time ago. Would have saved me a lot of anxiety.

She frowned slightly, looking perplexed at my reaction. "I didn't want to push you into something you weren't ready for, no matter how much I wanted us to...mmph..."

I stopped her explanation with a kiss, and, after a moment of surprise, she responded wholeheartedly. When we broke apart, her hands were tangled in my hair and mine were wound tightly around her body.

"What was that for?" she asked, looking slightly dazed. "Not that I'm complaining."

"Because I love you, and there is nothing you could do that would scare me away."

She smiled slowly and leaned in again, her grip tightening in my hair.

Our lips had just met when the door swung open. We moved apart, but not very quickly, and not nearly in time.

"Oh. My. God."

I looked over Robyn's shoulder to see Trish staring at the two of us, her eyes wide with shock.

Shit. I sighed and started to move away from Robyn, but she turned to face Trish and put her arm around my waist, holding me where I was.

"Stay," she said quietly. "Please."

I glanced at her quickly in surprise, but stayed where I was.

"Robyn, what the hell?" Trish looked at Robyn, then at me, and back to Robyn. "Are you..." she sputtered, and looked between us again.

I felt Robyn take a deep breath and let it out slowly. "Yes,

Trish, I am. And yes, we are." I could feel the tension in her body, but there was no evidence of it in her outward demeanor as she gave Trish a lopsided smile. "So, now you know. Sorry, I didn't really mean for you to find out this way...that's one of the reasons I wanted to meet for coffee on Monday, to tell you about us..." Her voice trailed off when she saw that her sister wasn't listening.

Trish was too busy glaring at me in naked dislike. "I knew you were trouble. I knew it."

Robyn stiffened at the words and tone, and I rubbed her back soothingly. I bit back the "told you she didn't like me" that was on the tip of my tongue.

"This has nothing to do with Caid, Trish," Robyn said flatly. "I've been into women long before I met her."

"This has everything to do with her!" Trish exploded, moving into the room and waving an accusatory finger at me. "She's using you, Robyn. Using your celebrity, your money..."

"Patricia, there you are!" We all jumped as Sophie came steaming through the door, her agitation at her eldest daughter very plain. "People are asking for you—" She stopped abruptly when she saw that both Robyn and I were also in the room and looked at the three of us curiously. "I am interrupting?"

Robyn's hand left my hip for a moment, and then settled back more firmly than before, as though she were anchoring herself. I felt her take another deep breath, but Trish spoke before she could.

"Oh, no, Mamá, you're just in time. Robby was just explaining her...relationship...with Caidence."

"Trish, don't," Robyn said quietly, the warning in her voice clear.

Sophie looked from a scowling Robyn to a smug Trish, and frowned deeply. She settled her gaze on her eldest daughter and placed her hands on her hips in the universal mother-scolding-her-offspring posture. "Patricia Elizabeth, why can you not be happy for your sister?"

Trish blinked and did her fish impression again. "Mamá, I..."

"No." Sophie shook her head. "Do not Mamá me. Sabina has embraced your Enrique with open arms, why can you not do the same? Your sister has found someone who makes her happy, and you do everything you can to spoil it. This behavior you have toward Caidence, it is unacceptable. Your father and I, we did not raise you to be this way."

Sophie could not have shocked her daughters more if she'd told them she was an alien raised by dingoes in the Australian outback. If the situation hadn't been so tense, it would have been funny. Hell, it was funny anyway, but I managed to stifle inopportune laughter. My sense of humor has always been a tad off.

"You...you knew?" Robyn said faintly, her hand tightening reflexively on my hip.

I leaned into her and put my arm around her waist in support. Sophie glanced at me with a nearly imperceptible smile as she moved forward and reached up to cup Robyn's cheek, giving her a look of fond irritation. "*Querida*, I may not be young anymore, but I am not blind. Of course I knew. I am your mother," she said simply, as though that explained it all. "I am sorry you could not tell me."

"I..." Robyn blinked, her face still slack with astonishment. She covered Sophie's hand with her own, holding it to her cheek. "I'm sorry, *Mamá*. I..." she shrugged helplessly.

Sophie patted her cheek and withdrew her hand. "I know, *cariña*." She glanced over at me and smiled. "I am very fond of your Caidence. She is good for you."

Robyn looked between the two of us in surprise before smiling and saying quietly, "I am very fond of my Caidence as well." Her arm tightened on my waist briefly and I squeezed back.

"I know that too, *cariña*." She smiled at both of us, and then turned her attention back to Trish, who had been watching the scene unfold in stunned silence. "And now, Patricia, you know this, too. And you will treat Caidence as someone your sister cares about deeply. Yes?"

Sophie's hands were back on her hips again and her tone brooked no argument. I had to fight the urge to straighten and say "Yes, ma'am!"

Trish looked down at the desk uncomfortably. "Yes, *Mamá*." She looked up again and her expression held a hint of what could have been genuine apology when her glance touched Robyn.

"Good." Sophie nodded decisively and moved to the door. "Now, Patricia, you must get back to the party—there were many people asking for you, and Julian and Mark, they are fighting again. You know they do not listen to me."

"Yes, *Mamá*," Trish said again obediently, casting a quick glance at Robyn and me. "Robby..."

Robyn held up a hand and shook her head. "Later."

Trish nodded, and after one last look at the two of us, she left the office. Sophie eyed Robyn sternly. "Elora and Will are wondering where you are—they need to leave soon and get home to the little ones. They are out on the patio now. You will bring Caidence there, hmm?"

Robyn flicked a questioning glance at me, and I realized she was asking what I wanted to do. I nodded slightly and she looked back at Sophie. "Yes, *Mamá*."

Sophie's dark eyes watched the interaction with interest and after a moment, she nodded briskly. "I should go see how Patricia is faring with Julian...he is such a big *bebé*, I don't know why she puts up with him."

We both watched the door for several seconds after she left, neither of us speaking.

"Hell of a party, huh?" Robyn said finally and pulled me against her, smiling wryly and dropping a light kiss on my temple. "I'm sorry about all this, Caid. I was planning on telling my family, but that wasn't quite how I'd planned it."

"No worries." I turned fully into her embrace and gave her a quick kiss. "Never a dull moment around you, that's for sure."

She smiled slightly. "I wouldn't want you to get bored with me."

"Not much chance of that." I grinned. "You're more entertaining than a six-pack of Huber and bucket full of Legos."

Her mouth twitched and an eyebrow crept up her forehead. "Am I?"

"Oh, yeah." I gave her another quick kiss. "That's good stuff where I come from, baby."

She smiled fully and shook her head. "Damn, I love you."

We smiled at each other and then she stepped back after a final squeeze. "Come on, sweet thing, let's go meet the family." She snagged my hand, talking over her shoulder as she pulled me toward the door. "Now, don't believe anything they say about me thinking I was Wonder Woman for a summer, sticking peanuts up my nose, or eating mud pies. They're all lies..."

I laughed and followed her out the door.

Chapter
Twenty-Four

I TRAILED LIGHT fingers along naked, still-damp skin, skimming Robyn's back from the sheet bunched at her waist, up between her shoulder blades, and back down, watching the dappled, early morning light play along the smooth expanse. I couldn't remember the last time I felt so happy and content, and let out a long, deep sigh, sated and pleasantly lethargic from our recent activities.

"I do love how you say good morning," I said lazily, shifting a little under her weight.

Robyn, I'd discovered, was very much a morning person, and although I hadn't been one in the past, waking up to her touch could easily become addicting. She was sprawled half across me on her stomach, her leg thrown over my mine and her head resting on my shoulder. I kissed her dark hair softly and continued my caress, receiving a murmur of agreement and a tightening of her arm around my midsection in response.

"I had a good time last night—thank you again for inviting me," I said after we'd been quiet for a few minutes. "I really liked your family."

Despite the altercation with Trish, it had still turned out to be a nice evening, and my introduction to the Ward family a success. As Sophie had promised, most of Robyn's family was gathered in a small, cobblestone courtyard between the restaurant and the neighboring building. After a quiet "ready?" and a smile of encouragement, Robyn had tugged me past potted flowers, small palms, and a scattering of wrought iron café tables to a group gathered around a cluster of tables. The group had greeted Robyn with noisy delight and eyed me curiously, and so had begun my introduction to the Ward clan.

Her father Rich was tall, dark, and quite charismatic, still possessing model good looks, and I gathered from a few stray comments that he had been approached to run for city council in Santa Barbara and was seriously considering it. He had a big laugh and a warm smile, and showed an easy, casual affection for his daughters that caused a brief pang of longing for something I'd never have. Her Aunt Paige was Rich's sister; she and her husband Darrin lived in Thousand Oaks and raised Golden Retrievers for show. They were affable and hilariously goofy, occasionally breaking into song when the mood struck, and managing to sound quite good together. Her sister Lori was very pregnant and she and her husband Will were both very sweet, a quiet, gentle couple who obviously adored each other and talked about little else besides their two children and the one on the way. The final member of the family I met was Robyn's sister Diane. She had an amiable smile, a dry wit, and sharp, dark eyes that watched me knowingly from behind small, rimless glasses.

They were all striking and dark-eyed, friendly and gracious, and each had some feature or mannerism that reminded me of Robyn. Rich's presence, Sophie's smile, Paige's goofy humor, Lori's voice, and Diane's eyes — I liked them all immediately and was pleased that the sentiment seemed to be returned.

"Mmm." She stirred against me and turned her head to kiss my chest. "They loved you, babe." I could feel her smile against my skin. "Paige and Darrin want to adopt you. When you knew the third verse to 'You are my Sunshine,' I thought Paige was going to wet herself."

I smiled. "I'll thank Grandma next time I see her. I also know 'Camptown Ladies' and 'Tiny Bubbles' on the ukulele."

She raised her head to look at me. "Really?"

"Really." I kissed her. "I have all sorts of useless talents. Kazoo, skipping stones, building card houses, hanging a spoon off my nose..."

"You can do that?" she asked curiously, pushing her hair away from her face and tilting her head to the side.

"Yep."

"My, my. I'm even luckier than I'd realized," she said with a smile.

"Uh-huh." I shivered as she leaned down to kiss my neck and her hair brushed along my shoulder. "I'm quite the catch."

"No arguments here," she mumbled against my skin as she kissed along my collarbone and laid her head back on my chest with a sigh.

I resumed stroking her back, and we lay in comfortable silence for several minutes.

"I love this," Robyn said quietly, breaking the silence. "I love going to sleep with you, waking up with you, sharing my morning with you..."

I pressed my lips to the top of her head and tightened my arms around her. "I love it, too, baby."

She rearranged the sheets and rolled onto her back, resting the back of her head on my arm. "Morning has always been my time," she said quietly, staring at the ceiling. "That little sliver of the day that was all mine—sometimes the *only* sliver that was all mine—and I've always been kind of a bitch about sharing it." She turned her head to look at me and reached out to trace the line of my jaw with a long finger. "Now I look forward to spending it with you. Watching you drink your coffee while you read the paper, how you chew on your lip when you concentrate..." She ran her finger over my lower lip, staring at it intently. "Waiting for you to share something you think is interesting, or funny."

I wasn't sure how to respond to that. I felt a little guilty for horning in on her me-time, but she also said she liked our time together. I kissed the finger against my lips and stayed quiet, sensing she wasn't done talking.

She withdrew her finger and turned her head back to stare at the ceiling. She opened her mouth, shut it, looked at me, then back at the ceiling.

I smiled slightly at the atypical display of uncertainty.

"Live with me," she said softly. She turned her head to look at me, her eyes holding both nervousness and hope. "Here, your place, some other place, I don't care. Just..." she reached out again and cupped my cheek gently. "Live with me."

My mouth fell open in shock. "Wha..."

She quieted me with a finger on my lips. "You make me happy, Caid," she said simply. "I'm happier in the last few months than I've ever been in my life, and I've realized that I'm happiest when I'm with you this way, sharing this much. Like in Florida, or at Liz's place, going to bed with you, waking up with you, spending my mornings, my free-time, my evenings with you...*living* with you."

Holy crap.

She'd caught me so off-guard that I was speechless, staring at her in astonishment.

This was it. Everything I wanted, everything I'd hoped for, wished for. Everything.

At my continued silence, she smiled sadly and brushed the back of her hand against my cheek before pulling her hand back. "Well..."

Maybe it was too fast, maybe we were crazy, maybe we weren't thinking this through, but I wasn't going to give up this chance. "Yes," I finally croaked out. I rolled over on top of her and peppered her face, neck and chest with kisses. "Yes, yes, yes, yes, yes, yes, yes..."

She let out a throaty, delighted laugh and threaded her fingers through my hair, tugging my head up. "That's a yes?"

I beamed down at her, my face nearly cracking in two. "That's definitely a yes."

She smiled up at me and I caught my breath.

Whatever happened, however this all played out, whatever the future brought—it would all be worth it, just to see that smile.

FORTHCOMING TITLES
from Yellow Rose Books

Solace: Book V of the Moon Island Series

by Jennifer Fulton

Rebel Monroe is a Californian yachtswoman sailing solo around the world. When her yacht—Solace—capsizes in a perfect storm near the Cook Islands group, she puts to sea in a lifeboat expecting she is not going to make it. Eventually she washes up half-dead on the shores of Moon Island, where she is found by ex-nun Althea Kennedy.

Althea, who entered a Poor Clare order at 20, has recently turned her back on religious life after a traumatic experience in Africa. Questioning both her faith and the church, she is on Moon Island recuperating from malaria and pondering her options.

Rebel, considered a hero by the island's owners, is invited to stay a while and she forms an unlikely friendship with Althea. When this blossoms into something more each woman must rethink her identity, her demons, and her life choices before she can find real happiness.

Coming May 2007

Family Values

by Vicki Stevenson

Devastated by the collapse of her long-term relationship, Alice Cruz decides to begin life anew. She moves to a small town, rents an apartment, and establishes a career in real estate. But when she tries to liquidate some of her investments for a down payment on a house, she discovers that she has been victimized by a con artist.

Local resident Tyler Sorensen has a track record of countless affairs without any emotional involvement. Known for her sexy good looks, easygoing kindness, and unique approach to problems, Tyler is asked by a mutual friend to figure out how Alice can recover her money.

While Tyler's elaborate plan progresses and members of her LGBT family work toward the solution, they discover that the con game involves more people and far higher stakes than they had imagined. As the family encounters unexpected obstacles, Tyler and Alice struggle with a growing emotional connection deeper than either woman has ever experienced.

Coming August 2007

OTHER YELLOW ROSE TITLES

You may also enjoy:

Lavender Secrets

by Sandra Barret

Emma LeVanteur has written off any chance of true love and is focused on her graduate thesis, when Nicole Davis, a beautiful British instructor, turns Emma's world upside down. Emma thinks she can finally break out of a comatose love-life, but when Nicole convinces Emma to help with her upcoming wedding, Emma's brief hope for romance seems lost. But is it?

Nicole Davis is marrying into a socialite family. But Emma's friendship pulls her in another direction, sending her tumbling into a world of undeniable longing. When Nicole can no longer silence her feelings for Emma, will she give up her picture-perfect future to gamble on a love she can barely comprehend, or will she stick with the life she's always known?

Set in New England, "Lavender Secrets" explores the boundaries that define love, lust, and friendship for Emma, Nicole, and the world they live in.

ISBN 978-1-932300-73-4

Butch Girls Can Fix Anything

by Paula Offutt

Kelly Walker can fix anything—except herself. Grace Owens seeks a stable community of friends for herself and her daughter. Lucy Owens wants help with her fourth-grade math. As their stories unfold in the fictional town of High Pond, N.C., each must deal with her own version of trust, risks, and what makes someone strong.

ISBN 978-1-932300-74-1

OTHER YELLOW ROSE PUBLICATIONS

About the Author:

K.E. Lane lives along Colorado's Front Range with her partner and several pets. A software developer when she's not writing, she also enjoys music, reading, and a variety of outdoor activities.

VISIT US ONLINE AT

www.regalcrest.biz

At the Regal Crest Website You'll Find

- The latest news about forthcoming titles and new releases

- Our complete backlist of romance, mystery, thriller and adventure titles

- Information about your favorite authors

- Current bestsellers

Regal Crest titles are available from all progressive booksellers and online at StarCrossed Productions, (www.scp-inc.biz), or at www.amazon.com, www.bamm.com, www.barnesandnoble.com, and many others.

Printed in the United States
102048LV00003B/125/A